HIT

HIT

TARA MOSS

AUSTRALIA'S NO. 1 CRIME WRITER

Published by

MAXCRIME

an imprint of John Blake Publishing Ltd,
3 Bramber Court, 2 Bramber Road,
London W14 9PB, England

www.johnblakepublishing.co.uk

First published in Australia in 2006
Published in 2007 by HarperCollins*Publishers* Australia
This edition published in 2010 by John Blake Publishing

ISBN: 978 1 84454 908 5

British Library Cataloguing-in-Publication Data:
A catalogue record for this book is available from the British Library.

Design by www.envydesign.co.uk

Printed in Great Britain by CPI Bookmarque, Croydon CRO 4TD

1 3 5 7 9 10 8 6 4 2

Papers used by John Blake Publishing are natural, recyclable
products made from wood grown in sustainable forests.
The manufacturing processes conform to the environmental
regulations of the country of origin.

MAXCRIME series commissioning editor: Maxim Jakubowski

OTHER BOOKS BY TARA MOSS

Fetish

Split

Covet

Siren

Tara is the author of four bestselling crime novels published in fifteen countries in ten languages. Writing has been a lifelong passion for her; she began penning gruesome 'Stephen King-inspired' stories for her classmates when she was only ten. Tara enjoyed a successful international career as a fashion model before pursuing professional writing, first earning a Diploma from the Australian College of Journalism. She began writing her debut novel, *Fetish*, when she was just twenty-three. Her crime novels have been nominated for the Davitt and the Ned Kelly awards. She has a star on the Australian Walk of Fame: the first person so inducted for services to literature.

Not a writer to rely solely on imagination, she has toured the FBI Academy at Quantico, spent time in squad cars, morgues, prisons, labs, the Supreme Court and criminology conferences world-wide, taken polygraph tests, shot weapons, conducted surveillance, flown with the RAAF, and acquired her CAMS race driver licence. Tara recently earned her PI licence, and was set on fire by Hollywood stunt company West EFX and choked unconscious by Ultimate Fighter 'Big' John McCarthy for her research.

Born in Victoria, BC, Tara is a proud dual Australian/ Canadian citizen, and divides her time between Sydney, Los Angeles and her hometown in Canada. She is a UNICEF Goodwill Ambassador, as well as an ambassador for the YWCA and the Royal Institute for Deaf and Blind Children.

Visit taramoss.com

to Mum

PROLOGUE

MEAGHAN WALLACE PUSHED a damp lock of pale blonde hair off her face and squinted in the half-light.

What happened to my shoes?

It was just past four on Thursday morning, at the messy end of a private party in a mansion in Sydney's eastern suburbs owned by some high flier Meaghan's boss worked with, and whom she had never met.

Meaghan needed another hit.

At this hour she found herself mysteriously barefoot and unsatisfactorily straight, and she knew that her boss and escort for the evening, Mr Robert Groobelaar, would be of no help in rectifying either problem – he was slumped over a settee in a corner of one of the vast living rooms, sweaty and snoring, head tilted back at an unattractive angle. An eyeful of repulsive white stomach, speckled with grey hair, protruded from under his untucked dress shirt. Groobelaar was oblivious to the other guests, some of whom danced only a foot away. On the opposite end of the very same settee, a couple ran hands over each other's bodies, their mouths locked in drug-fuelled sexual ecstasy, clothes askew to reveal body parts usually exposed only in private. They seemed not to mind their lack of privacy, or Groobelaar's bearlike snores, which were just audible over the din of throbbing dance music.

Grateful to be free of him, Meaghan left her snoring employer and tiptoed as seductively as she could across the carpet towards the open doors of a splendid balcony, making the most of the sway of her sexy black slip dress and purposefully catching the eye of an attractive businessman leaning against a doorframe. She smiled flirtatiously at him, but only briefly, as the movement swiftly reminded her of how much she had indulged. Her head spun and she froze, eyes shut tight, willing the sensation to pass. She licked her dry lips, tasting stale champagne, and felt the numb ache of cocaine that had already lost its edge.

Thirsty.

To add to her discomfort, the Sydney night was humid, and between the dancing and her boss's awkward gropes, she had been perspiring uncomfortably. Her slip dress was slightly damp.

My shoes? Where are they? She couldn't recall where or when she had taken them off.

Oh!

Meaghan patted herself down in a flash of panic. With great relief her fingertips found her small handbag, hanging reliably across her body on its delicate leather strap. Her life was in that thing: her apartment keys; her trusty mobile phone, from which she had already sent at least a dozen SMS messages during the course of the party telling each of her girlfriends which celebrities and corporate types she had spotted together and what they were up to; her lipgloss, and a small, expensive packet of party powder she was hoarding for the right occasion. This was not the right occasion. As she saw it, the most financially challenged, attractive and single young blonde at this kind of monied soiree should not be expected to amuse herself with her own stash.

Meaghan was not rich, powerful or famous. She had scored an invite to this exclusive house party because her boss wanted to get into her pants. At twenty-three, she was already quite familiar with the desires of men, and she had no illusions about Groobelaar's intentions – at least, not now when he and his octopus hands were passed out before her, and sobriety was settling in on her like an unwelcomed cold front.

Maybe that nice man leaning in the doorway has a little something for me?

When she looked back in his direction, though, he was gone.

There was a line-up for the guest bathroom, and Meaghan joined the end of the queue. A small mirror mounted on the wall outside provided her with an opportunity to freshen up while she waited. Since she was little, her mother had told her she had a pretty face. Meaghan's features were even and fine – a slim, pointed nose, wide eyes and a small mouth. She took out her make-up compact and cleaned up the dark liner that had smudged across her eyelids, examining her reflection as she did so. Meaghan was a petite and curvy blonde, with tanned skin that contrasted with her pale yellow hair. Though it was shockingly late for a midweek party and her eyes were red, she felt she still looked pretty; but then, there were a lot of pretty girls there, she noticed – a lot of pretty girls and not enough good-looking men.

A slick of lipgloss and she was looking a bit more fresh. She adjusted her hair, her bob slightly damp in her fingers.

Okay, hurry up already . . .

Meaghan could hear giggling inside the toilet. Whoever was in there was not alone. Suspecting the wait would take longer than she was willing to spare, she left the queue. She didn't have to go that badly. Meaghan also wanted to leave the dance music for a while, not to mention the sight of her boss and his plump white stomach, which was still visible across the vast living room. Perhaps she should make her way through the party and happen across some fabulously wealthy prince who would sweep her off her feet? Groobelaar had said this gathering would be A-list. Her whole life Meaghan had dreamed of being invited into company like this, and she wasn't going to waste what could be a valuable social or romantic opportunity. That was the reason she had agreed to come in the first place – it certainly hadn't been in order to win Groobelaar's attentions.

Meaghan sauntered her way onto the balcony, wondering if the businessman was out there. Instead she found a group of male guests lined up against a railing, sipping cocktails, in various states of undress – shirts open and ties undone, and strangely one man wearing his dress shirt without any pants to speak of, despite the presence of dress shoes and black socks pulled up neatly to his calves. Like spectators watching a titillating bout of female mud wrestling, the men lustily observed a small group of partyers leaping about and splashing in the spectacular pool below.

The blue rectangle of water was illuminated brightly in the dark, showcasing the lithe bodies of its carefree inhabitants: three attractive women stripped down to G-strings and bras, and at least two others swimming in the nude with their skirt suits and dresses crumpled poolside among a scattering of cocktail glasses.

Just beyond the edge of the pool, a trail of polished mosaic tiles led down to a private beach, from where Meaghan heard laughter and more music. To hoots of delight a male guest leaped up the stones two by two, and at the side of the pool stripped down to his boxers, swaying and nearly tripping as he removed his pants. Forgetting his socks, he plunged into the pool to join the women, the voyeurs cheering with gusto from the railing above.

'Go, mate!'

Oh, yes!

Meaghan herself did not cheer, but she was relieved to see her stilettos strewn poolside, where she had carelessly left them so many hours before. The sight brought into hazy recall the hour or so she had spent dipping her feet as the sun went down, the ocean turning indigo and the sky orange while she snorted Charlie and flirted with the attentions of Groobelaar and his colleagues.

So her best shoes were not lost.

Is that . . .? Oh, it is!

Meaghan was distracted by an exciting find in the corner of the balcony to her right. A certain hunky Australian Football League player – a recent *Cleo* Bachelor of the Year – and a famous brunette newsreader could be seen lustily kissing one another on a patio chair, she sitting right in his lap. Trying to act casual, Meaghan opened her purse, removed her ever-present mobile phone and surreptitiously began to film the pair with the phone's video function, as she pretended to be scrolling through a text message and looking at the view of the water. *Wow.* It was dark, but through the screen she could still make out who was making out. The best part about it was that, not only were they both famous, but the newsreader was married – and *not* to the young footy player.

A guest brushed past Meaghan, giving her a fright.

Oops.

Meaghan put her phone away and leaned on the rail for a moment as if nothing had happened. She hoped no one had seen what she was doing. When the guest who had bumped her – an unattractive man and, it turned out, his too-good-looking girlfriend – hung around, Meaghan turned back the way she had come. She moved through the party a little unsteadily, grinning at the scandal she had recorded, passing strangers who danced and swayed, the couple making out on the settee and Groobelaar still snoring in his almost obscene reclined pose.

She slid through a doorway she found on the other side of the room and tiptoed down a beautiful hallway lit by two large candelabras. She stopped to admire paintings in gilded frames and exquisite statues of the type she would normally see only in galleries. At the end of the hallway a timber staircase beckoned, extending upstairs and down, lushly adorned by a strip of Persian carpet in the centre. Meaghan paused on the landing, considering as best she could whether this would be the way to the deck to retrieve her shoes. She couldn't truthfully remember how she had arrived at the living room to begin with.

She shrugged, and began her descent.

Meaghan padded down stair after stair, the music above her fading. Her toes sank into the plush carpet. *One step, two step, three …* Before long she reached the bottom and gripped the railing, smiling mischievously in a shroud of darkness: the stairs had led her to an unlit hallway on the lower floor. Unsure of her surroundings, she looked over her shoulder to see if she was being followed – clearly, this was not an area intended for guests.

Feeling a touch guilty, Meaghan approached the first door of the hall and pressed her ear against it, eavesdropping. She heard the sounds of hushed conversation, and a giggle. So there were guests who wanted privacy, then? Perhaps the brunette newsreader's husband was in there, enjoying some scandalous adultery of his own? How ironic would that be?

Thank goodness I didn't end up in one of those rooms with Groobelaar, she thought with a sneer. He continually tried to push her towards having an affair with him, but she would not. It had always just been work for her. Why did some men find that so difficult to understand?

Tiptoeing further down the hall, Meaghan kept her arms extended in front of her so she would not bump into any unseen obstacles. At the very end of the corridor she could see a door partially ajar, and a faint glow of soft light spilling out onto the hall floor.

This, perhaps, was the way out.

She registered voices inside the room. These could be important guests – perhaps even her handsome businessman from upstairs? Meaghan flicked her hair back and adjusted the straps on her dress in anticipation of the strangers beyond the door. Satisfied that everything was in its place, she licked her lips and raised an arm to push the door open, her fixed smile at the ready. But mere seconds before she moved forwards to enter, she found her eyes focused on a vision through the thin gap of the open door, a sight that made her pause.

Oh!

Meaghan found herself looking at a young man who was immediately familiar to her – not from her own acquaintance, but from the newspapers. He was someone important. Very important. Someone with money. She was aware that she should know who he was, but she couldn't quite place him. She stood and stared through the crack in the door for what could have been ten seconds or ten minutes – she didn't know – and her hand, which had frozen in position halfway to pushing the door open, moved mechanically to her bag and removed her mobile phone. Like an automaton she stepped back and aimed the phone's small video-camera lens through the crack in the door.

My girlfriends won't believe the people I saw tonight.

She realised that the man was arguing with someone. It was odd because his lanky body was unclothed from the waist up, save for a glinting gold watch and some rings, and yet the Asian-looking man he was disagreeing with was fully dressed in a collared shirt and dress pants. Meaghan squinted and cocked her head to one side: something was wrong with what she was seeing. Her heart began pounding in her chest even before her mind fully registered the source of her horror.

The scene through the doorway came into focus slowly, and with awful clarity. Meaghan's breath caught in her throat, her arm suspended motionlessly as she recorded everything on digital video.

Eyes . . . staring . . .

A naked girl lay prone on an unmade bed just inside the doorway. The young face – so close that Meaghan could have reached out and touched it – was turned at an awkward angle in Meaghan's direction, chin buried in a pillow, the dark eyes wide open, staring lifelessly, her mouth gaping in an awful silent scream. A small manicured hand rested inches from where Meaghan stood in the dark hall, the fingers outstretched as if the girl had been reaching for the doorknob in her final breath, a heavy black leather tie dangling from the wrist. A syringe lay on the floor along with fallen bed cushions and an upturned water bottle, near the opening in the doorway. From the bedroom the musty scent of sex mixed with a horrible, sickly sweet odour Meaghan had not encountered before.

Death.

Meaghan's stomach lurched. She brought her hand down, stopping the recording. She could not believe what she was seeing.

Oh my God . . .

The girl on the bed was Asian in appearance and young. *Too young.* Was she twelve? Fourteen? Dark glossy hair fanned out around her head as she lay stomach down, back and buttocks fully exposed, her diminutive body clothed only in a frilly hot-pink garterbelt that contrasted sharply with the grim setting and the bluey-ashen pallor of her skin. A large intricate tattoo that seemed out of place coloured her lower back in a pattern of lines or script that Meaghan could not make out.

She wanted to tell herself that this girl could simply be unconscious, but those staring eyes were too unresponsive. And besides, death was immediately recognisable: no sleep was so grim and terrible on an otherwise fair face; no living state left a person so empty-looking.

The famous man she had been recording stood at the foot of the bed arguing animatedly with the other man, neither of them bothering to attempt to revive the girl or cover her nakedness. The girl's body looked so small and vulnerable in death, her limbs splayed out. And those unseeing eyes. The

11

eyes seemed to look at Meaghan. Above the dead girl, the men were engaged in a hushed but heated argument – Meaghan could tell that they did not wish to be overheard. The implications of what she was witnessing were enormous, and difficult to fathom, particularly in her state.

What is that guy doing there with a girl so young and so . . . dead?

'Hey!'

A man's booming voice yelled at her from the hallway behind. Meaghan jumped with fright at the sound, letting out a shocked yelp. Instinctively she palmed her phone behind her back and whirled around to face the voice. It belonged to a strong, even-featured young man who was barely two metres away and closing fast. Behind her the bedroom door was slammed shut from the inside. She heard a scuffle within as the inhabitants realised they had been spotted. Meaghan wore a bold smile for the stranger in the hallway while her fingers worked the buttons of the mobile keypad behind her back, trying to send a video of the dead girl to the first person listed in her phone book.

Should she tell this stranger what she had seen?

'What do you think you're doing?' he asked accusingly, standing over her aggressively.

She continued pressing buttons, with no time to consider to whom the video might be delivered.

'Hey! I'm talking to you!'

With that he lunged forwards and grabbed Meaghan's wrists from behind her back. The phone slipped from her hands and dropped to the hardwood floor with a loud thwack, the battery separating from the phone and skittering a few feet away.

No!

'Ouch! Wait!' she protested. The man had a painful, vicelike grip; and, to her alarm, he wasn't easing off. His face was mere centimetres from hers as he held her wrists, and she could see that he was very unhappy with her – a little *too* unhappy. With his sun-kissed hair, white teeth and tan, he looked to Meaghan like a handsome male model or a movie star. He certainly didn't fit her idea of a security guard. But his eyes were angry, and Meaghan could not yet register why he would be so cross with her. What had she done to him?

'I *said*, what do you think you're doing?' he bellowed angrily.

She flinched and closed her eyes. 'Oh … I … you don't understand …' she began feebly. Slowly he eased his grip on her, nonetheless keeping her cornered and bearing down on her without a trace of friendliness. She smiled coyly in response, in a way she hoped would be disarming. 'There must be some misunderstanding,' she continued, deciding it was far too risky to admit what she had seen. 'I'm looking for the deck. Is it this way? I didn't take anything if that's what you're thinking. I'm a guest here, with Mr Groobelaar of Trident Realty –'

And then, to her shock, the man deliberately stomped his foot down on her mobile. She heard pieces of the phone crunch and scatter in the hall.

Oh!

Sickening adrenaline rushed through her as the realisation hit.

He is with them. He knows there is a dead girl in the next room.

Meaghan could see by the look in this man's eyes that there was no room for outrage. He knew perfectly well what he was doing, and what was happening behind that closed bedroom door – and he also knew that *she* knew. Meaghan was now very much afraid. She knew the significance of what she had been recording. Though she still couldn't recall the name of the shirtless man in the room, she knew that he was important, that he was famous, and that he was in a room with a dead underaged girl. And she'd seen it. Meaghan had watched enough movies to know that people were killed for knowing less.

The blond man grabbed her forcefully by the shoulders with both hands while Meaghan panicked inside.

'Don't you know it's not polite to spy?'

She was hauled down the corridor away from the bedroom door, with her shattered phone lying in pieces on the hallway floor, the only evidence of what she had seen now destroyed. Shocked by the stranger's aggression and looking for any chance to escape, Meaghan was being half dragged, half carried away down one corridor to the next, before being pushed through a doorway into a cold, dark space.

It was a garage. The lights flickered and came on with a hum. Meaghan's eyes widened. The garage housed several luxury automobiles: a Jag, a BMW four-wheel drive and what she thought was a Ferrari or Lamborghini or something. She didn't know cars well, but she knew an expensive car when she saw it. These people were very, *very* rich.

'Are you going to calm down now?' the man said.

She stood rigid, unsure of what would happen next.

I just saw a dead girl. A dead girl . . .

'No one is going to hurt you,' he said, palms extended as if to offer a truce. Under the present circumstances, though, she wasn't so sure she believed him. 'Now just get in. Please . . .' He opened the passenger-side door of the four-wheel drive and signalled for her to step in.

She stood her ground.

'Relax, babe. I'm only driving you home,' he said, and smiled for the first time, his teeth dazzling.

'But my shoes are at the pool,' she protested and looked down at her feet. 'I took them off earlier. It will take me two seconds to get them.'

He didn't go for it.

'Get in the car,' he said.

Groobelaar was asleep upstairs – too far to run

15

to – and she certainly couldn't cry out and be heard with all that dance music pounding through the house. And this man was blocking the door to the garage. He was much bigger than her, and certainly far stronger. There was no way she would make it past him.

With reluctance, Meaghan did as the stranger said and got in, trying to ignore the sinking feeling in her chest. *I should never have let him get me in the car. This is bad. This is really bad.* She was strapped in and the door closed. A flurry of scenarios buzzed through her mind: *What if I leap out as we leave the drive, and flee into the neighbouring yards? Would he come after me if I did?*

The man adjusted the seat back on his side and leaned over to the glove box to get the keys, brushing briefly against her bare legs.

'Okay, where am I taking you?'

The statement had been so without malice that she wasn't sure what she should say. 'Um, near the Cross,' she managed, as if acting like everything was fine would make it so. She would get him to drop her a few blocks away from her apartment, she decided, and sprint the rest of the way home. She wanted to get as far away from that house and that dead girl as possible, and she would tell Groobelaar all about it tomorrow, and he would see to it that things were taken care of. He had such a mad crush on her that he would do anything she said, she was sure of it.

The man pressed a remote-control unit that

sat in the centre console, and the broad garage door lifted, exposing darkness and a light rain, which must only have just started. It was very early in the morning. Soon the sun would peek over the horizon and this horrible night would be through. She wished it would end soon. She wished she had never accepted Groobelaar's invitation to come as his guest.

In silence, the man drove them out of the garage and into the wet streets while Meaghan fretted, wondering where he would take her and what would become of the poor dead girl. They had driven for perhaps ten minutes before he spoke.

'Are you thirsty?'

Meaghan nodded, puzzled by his unexpected thoughtfulness. Her lips were so dry. She'd drunk too much champagne and it always made her feel like this. She desperately craved a glass of water.

'Have a sip. You look parched,' he said, and passed her a plain bottle of water from beside him. The seal was already broken. 'Go ahead,' he said, urging her to drink. 'See, I'm not going to hurt you. Drink it. You'll feel much better.'

She unscrewed the cap, which opened easily, and took a small swig from the bottle. The water was flat. It tasted a bit salty.

'Go on,' he urged her.

She took another sip.

'Good girl. Now, that's better, isn't it?'

Meaghan did feel a touch better for a moment.

Her parched lips were grateful for the liquid, and at least this stranger was no longer jumping down her throat like he had been in the hallway. She wanted him to stay calm. Maybe he really would let her get home. Maybe.

And then the spike hit.

Oh fuck . . . oh my God . . . oh fuck . . .

A pure, beautiful euphoria overwhelmed Meaghan's senses. She took a deep breath and let her head fall against the seat, chin tilted skywards. She let out a shocked moan, the pleasure taking her by surprise.

'Good girl. Now, where am I taking you?'

She straightened her head and looked at him. *There was something in the water . . . something in the water.* Whatever it was, it had worked fast. Her head was not just in the car but up and up and going, floating, floating everywhere. She felt extremely tipsy, or like she had taken ecstasy, and yet neither: this was something else. Everything felt wonderful: her bare feet on the carpet of the car; the seat under her hands. She fell into a state of profound relaxation. Any alarm or distress she had experienced was so remote now that it no longer mattered. It was okay. He was a new and trustworthy friend. There was nothing to fear.

'Come on, babe – where am I taking you? Where do you live?' her new friend asked, his voice now sounding so much more friendly in her ears.

'Oh, Potts Point,' she explained, giving him

her full address. He responded with a warm smile and she giggled slowly, awash with safety and contentedness. 'I feel so good.'

'Good girl,' he said to her. 'Now, what's your name?'

'Meaghan Wallace. My mum calls me Meg.'

'Good. And who brought you to the party tonight, Meaghan?'

'Uh … my boss, Robert Groobelaar. He's asleep in the living room.'

He touched her knee with one hand. His fingertips felt nice. 'And what do you do for Mr Groobelaar?'

'I'm his PA,' she said, feeling so happy to be able to be there, talking with this handsome man who was so nice.

'Lucky Robert. See, we're all friends here. We can be honest with one another. Now, tell me what you remember.'

She fell silent. There was something she didn't want to talk about, something that was bad, but the roads drifted past in beautiful soft tones, the car was warm and lovely, and she felt good. Meaghan had been drugged and she knew it, but for some reason it didn't bother her. Nothing bothered her.

'Come on now. Just between friends,' he continued. 'What do you think you saw?' He patted her knee again as he kept driving. When she looked over at him he flashed her the most handsome smile. A friendly smile.

'There was a … dead girl back in that room,'

she said, smiling because everything seemed okay now. 'She was like twelve or something, and she was wearing make-up and everything, and I think she was dead.' Meaghan felt no fear or inhibition. It was all right to say it.

He shook his head. 'No, no, no. I don't know where you got that idea. You did not see a dead girl. Don't be crazy. There was just a little accident, that's all, but everyone is fine.'

She nodded. 'Okay.'

'Good girl. You just had a bit too much to drink, so I have to drive you home, that's all.'

She looked out the car window and could see familiar streets. He was driving in the right direction to take her home. They were turning onto her street.

'It's that one,' she blurted.

'Which one?' he asked.

'That one, with the pink paint.'

'Okay.' He pulled up right out the front. 'I'll walk you up to make sure you get home safely,' he said.

Meaghan opened the door before he could get around to her side of the car, and she fell out clumsily onto the pavement, grazing her knee. Strangely it didn't hurt, though she could see that the rough concrete had drawn blood. She stayed on all fours for a while, laughing at her own inability to walk. It seemed terribly amusing.

'Oopsy daisy. Let me help you,' the man said, assisting her to stand.

Meaghan realised that she could not control her body, could not get her limbs to hold her up, but it didn't seem so bad. The nice man picked her up in a fireman's lift and carried her, and she felt calm and relaxed in his arms. Her heartbeat was slowing, things were turning vague. She felt sleep approaching like a cool and welcome blanket of darkness, moving over her from the toes up. Now the blanket of sleep moved higher, slowing her organs as it passed over her torso with its cold quiet. Higher now and covering her face until she couldn't see, and all the sounds around her faded into a quiet buzzing.

'Get some beauty sleep, babe,' a distant voice said, and Meaghan Wallace drifted away.

CHAPTER 1

AT SEVEN O'CLOCK on Thursday evening, Makedde Vanderwall stood in the kitchen of the terrace house she shared with her Australian boyfriend, holding a freshly minted celebrity cookbook in her hand and trying not to feel out of place.

Dammit, I suck at this.

Attempts at domesticity were awkward for the Canadian. Makedde — or Mak, as her friends called her — knew her way around a cookbook and a kitchen like Archbishop George Pell knew his way around the annual Gay and Lesbian Mardi Gras — which is to say, not at all. Her total lack of culinary skills was a source of great amusement for her friends, and buying cookbooks for her had become a running gag: *The Australian Women's Weekly Cookbook*, the *Donna Hay* cookbooks, *Cooking for Idiots*. Mak's friend Detective Karen Mahoney had recently purchased this latest one for her, and Mak was determined to prepare the pasta dish on page 135 to surprise her live-in lover. It was only pasta, after all. How hard could it be?

With something short of confidence, Mak watched the potful of pre-prepared pasta sauce bubble on the stove. The empty jar she'd poured it from sat upturned on the counter nearby, a smear of red sauce oozing out. The penne should be ready by now, she figured. She wrapped her hand loosely in a tea towel and grabbed the handle of the boiling pot on the stove.

'Ouch! Dammit!'

In a flash she had pulled her hand back and licked the pad of her index finger. A burn. She nursed her finger, and gingerly poured the penne into the sieve with her unburned hand, cursing.

'Bloody dangerous things, kitchens ...'

Though domestically handicapped, Mak had skills in other areas of her life. She had finished her forensic psychology PhD back in her native country a mere eighteen months earlier, scoring very well with her thesis on the variables affecting eyewitness testimony. The topic was something she'd ended up having far too much first-hand experience with, by becoming an intimate witness to the sadistic acts of her friend Catherine's deranged murderer. At times Mak thought she might never finish her PhD, but she had refused to let her personal dramas stop her just short of her dream. Sure, most of the other students were nearly a decade younger, but she had finally done it.

Then Mak had bitten the bullet and moved to Sydney to be with her boyfriend, Andy, shortly after. At twenty-nine, it seemed that a more-or-less normal life was finally within her reach. A new country. A new beginning.

Isn't it an unwritten rule that everyone is supposed to have their life in order before they turn thirty?

Mak still had a chance at it — if she worked fast. Maybe then her father would stop giving her those doubtful looks, and her happily married and once again pregnant sister, Theresa, would stop gloating all the time.

Hmmm.

She inspected the pasta in the sieve; it didn't look right. Mak glanced at the picture in the book, and then at her efforts, and screwed up her face with disapproval. *Her* meal looked white and soggy, each piece of penne limply oozing against its neighbour. Had she overcooked it? She didn't know. It was all so much more complicated than instant noodles.

I suck at this.

Mak might never be a chef, but her boss thought she was showing promise at her part-time job. She had stumbled onto a lucrative side-gig working for Marian Wendell, the infamous Sydney private investigator — much to the chagrin of her boyfriend and her father, both of them cops. But Mak needed work. Once she had quit her fifteen-year middle-of-the-road modelling career, she couldn't just sit on her butt and hope for a windfall. After answering an advertisement for a part-time research job, she had hit it off with

Marian and become intrigued by the work of her investigation agency. At Marian's urging, Mak had even successfully completed her Certificate III in Investigative Services, the basic licensing requirement for professional investigators.

The work was helping her save up the money she needed to open her own psychology practice, and, what's more, she was enjoying it. Certainly she found it a lot more engaging than her previous rent-paying job as a fashion model, a career that had taken her on photo shoots around the globe but was ultimately unsatisfying. The jobs Marian put her to were varied: running background checks, checking public records, photographing and conducting basic surveillance, and more. One of her easiest jobs to date had taken place only the evening before, when she had been paid a handsome $500 cheque for a mere ninety minutes of work, to chat up the sleazy husband of one of Marian's clients and see if he would follow her back to a hotel room for sex if she propositioned him. He had come to the room, all right – only Mak hadn't been there when he had. His wife had been waiting at the door. The long-suffering spouse got her money's worth of truth; Mak got paid handsomely to do nothing more than pretend to flirt with a stranger in a bar for an hour and enjoy tax-deductible cocktails; and her employer, Ms Wendell, was impressed once more with the attractive new secret weapon her agency could provide for hire.

Five hundred dollars to chat with some idiot. That even beat some modelling gigs for pay. Why would she want to stand around a boring studio all day, being told what to wear and how to pose, when she could command decent cash and be right in the thick of it, using her brain and her instincts on her own terms? Besides, she had been hit on by many a sleazebag in her life – at least now she was getting paid for it.

Her wallet lined with a fresh pay cheque, and feeling positive, Mak had sped home from Marian's office on her motorbike, stopping by the supermarket for supplies first. She had stripped out of her overheated leathers, showered, and changed into a light, easy summer dress in anticipation of dinner with her boyfriend. Her leathers now lay dishevelled in the entry hall and shopping bags were strewn over the kitchen countertop. With the few extra bucks in her pocket she'd even bought a nice Merlot.

Mak looked at the time. It was nearly seven-thirty. He was late. She wasn't sure what to do with the soggy pasta to keep it warm. Should she microwave it?

★   ★   ★

At eight-fifteen, Mak heard a car pull up outside.
Footsteps.
A key in the front door.
Andy. Finally.

26

She hurriedly zapped the pasta in the microwave, laid out the salad and made her way down the hall, pausing to lean in the hallway, attempting to look cool.

Detective Senior Sergeant Andy Flynn stepped inside the terrace they shared, fussing with his keys, and at first failing to look up and see Mak in her carefully nonchalant stance. Her eyes took him in greedily, nonetheless.

Andy wore his usual plain-clothes uniform of suit and tie. He was older than Mak by a few years, his short-cropped hair still dark and full. He had an unrefined, masculine appeal she had found maddeningly attractive since day one of their tempestuous union – the strong frame, the square jaw, the generous mouth and imperfect features, the scar on his chin – and, of course, that irresistible Aussie accent. It had probably also helped that he always wore a piece and some handcuffs under his jacket – a kind of fetish of Makedde's.

But though she was pleased to see Andy awake and upright, Mak had to admit that he looked tired. His deep green eyes were underlined with dark circles, his jaw darkened with stubble. Perhaps the years of police work and the inevitable overtime were taking their toll. He was dedicated to his work, so it was hardly surprising that this dinner would be the first they had shared in ages. Despite moving to Australia just over a year earlier to become what the Department of Immigration, Multicultural and Indigenous Affairs rather unromantically termed a 'de facto spouse', she and Andy had not seen nearly enough of each other of late. And, to make things worse, he was about to head overseas for a while.

Now the table was set and the candles lit, the Merlot freshly opened and ready to pour. This was not just some penne: this was a peace offering, albeit a soggy one.

He'll be so surprised.

'Andy ...'

She gave him a hug, her body grateful for the contact. At six foot four, he was one of the few whom she could literally look up to – a quality she found intoxicating, for although she was just over six foot tall herself, he towered over her barefoot.

She tilted her face up to his. 'How were things today?' she asked. Mak couldn't wait to show him the dining room. He wouldn't believe it – the candles, the effort.

'Yeah, good, thanks,' he muttered. 'You know ... I'm looking forward to getting stuck into it.' There had always been one hitch or another – a lack of funding, a change of politics, a shift of focus in the Federal Police – but now Andy was finally getting traction with the project he had long pushed for: a top-notch national unit dedicated to solving violent serial crime, Andy's speciality. It would be based in Canberra, the national capital, and aligned with the US Federal Bureau of

Investigation's program at their academy in Quantico, Virginia. He would do a three-month stint at the academy in preparation, starting in a few days. Andy would take on major national violent serial crime cases, help train up new profilers and oversee their work in the field. It was a far more exciting and senior position. It was what he had always dreamed of.

'Well, relax, take your coat off . . .' Mak began.

But Andy frowned. 'There was a shooting at Pyrmont where the old Water Police station used to be,' he stated abruptly, sounding harried. 'Sorry, but I gotta run. Just changing my shirt.'

Mak's smile faltered as her romantic plans came to an abrupt halt. 'Oh.' A little knot formed in her stomach.

Andy grabbed his tie in one hand and loosened it. 'I've got crap all over it,' he said, pulling back his jacket to show brown and red stains along the front of the pale blue shirt. 'This kid has gone and decapitated himself on a fence, running away from Deller. I can't believe it.'

'Oh.' She took leave of his chest as she realised it was most probably the kid's blood that had stained the shirt.

Andy's eyes moved this way and that, recalling something that frustrated him, his mouth caught in a tight frown. 'He was only wanted for questioning.'

Not any more, Mak thought darkly.

Retreating a couple of steps down the hall,

Mak managed to flick the dining room door closed with one foot, blocking the view of the candlelit dinner set up inside. She didn't want him seeing what she had attempted – not like this. Thankfully Andy failed to notice her actions. He was wrestling with his shirt buttons instead.

Beep.

'What was that?' he asked.

It was the sound of the microwave finishing in the kitchen. Mak had reheated the pasta for dinner. She thought she'd nuked it for a minute, but maybe she had hit ten ... It would be like rubber now.

'What was what? I didn't hear anything,' she lied.

He shook his head. 'Well, this bloody kid tried to jump a fence or something and caught his neck on some cable. I have to help them sort everything out. I'm sorry, Mak, I won't be long. Just a couple of more hours.'

There goes dinner.

Mak nodded. 'Oh, that's bad luck,' she said, pretending to arrange her motorcycle jacket and helmet on the hall table. 'Is that still your job now? I mean ... you leave on Saturday ...'

'Jimmy wanted me to help out. I know all the boys and ... you know.'

She did know – too well.

'Do you have time for a bite or anything?' she said, even though she was sure the answer would be no.

Andy paused. 'I'm sorry, Mak. Jimmy's waiting outside. We've gotta go.'

She nodded again, her thoughts a swirl of black clouds.

'Oh ... dammit.' Recognition flitted across his face. 'Oh, Mak, I'm sorry about dinner. I should have called ahead.'

Yes, you should have. 'It's no big deal.'

'Well, I'll be back in a couple of hours at the most. Sorry, Mak.'

'That's fine. No problem. I know it's important,' she said.

Andy moved past her and up the staircase to the bedroom they shared, while she remained planted in the hallway, secretly livid.

Mak had called him earlier in the day to confirm their dinner date at seven. It was just a normal weekday – not a weekend or a holiday, or a full moon when everyone ran out and started killing one another. It was a simple, boring Thursday night, so why would he have not called once he knew he couldn't make it? Why couldn't he have let her know before she made an ass of herself waiting around and trying to play bloody Martha Stewart? He had forgotten completely, and had no doubt also forgotten their discussion about why spending some time together was important at the moment. They only had two days left, and America was a long way away. If she couldn't afford to visit him there, they would not see each other for three whole months.

31

'You're going to force me to have an affair, Andy,' she'd joked. Half joked.

She wasn't about to remind him of their discussion now, not in the state the two of them were in: her angry and him stressed. It would come out all wrong, anyway. He had the scene of a fatality to attend to; who cared if his girlfriend had cooked her first meal in history? What did it matter? It didn't.

Feeling the razor-sharp clarity that always consumed her when she was annoyed, Mak walked towards the front door and stepped out into the darkening evening. A stiff summer breeze tossed her dress around, the clouds above turning purple and gold with the last of the setting sun.

A police cruiser waited at the kerb with Andy's longtime police partner, Detective Senior Constable Jimmy Cassimatis, in the passenger seat. Where Andy was tall, lean and strong, Jimmy was fuzzy and rounded like a man-sized teddy bear or football mascot. He was a man perpetually eating and finding excuses to look at, or talk about, women's anatomy. On this occasion he appeared to be doing both.

Eyes narrow with coiled tension, Mak walked down the path towards him, dress floating, hands on hips.

'Hello, Jimmy,' she said, and came towards the window of the cruiser.

He started, dropping a magazine in his lap and

spilling a bag of salty chips. Flustered, he shoved the publication down by his side and out of view, but not before Mak caught an eyeful of fleshy amateur photographs on the pages. She saw the words HORNBAG NEXT DOOR CONTEST printed above someone's labia and smile. SEND YOUR PHOTO IN AND WIN $50!

Yeah, I'll be sure to do that.

'*Skata*. You shouldn't go sneaking up on me like that,' Jimmy squeaked awkwardly.

'Catching up on world news while you're waiting?'

He nodded, his face turning crimson.

Mak leaned straight into the window, her blonde mane falling forwards, deliberately hovering above him as he sat helplessly strapped into the car seat, sinking ever lower.

'So what *are* the latest presidential polls?' Mak asked, her tone dripping with sarcasm. 'Is Bush in or out?'

Jimmy coughed.

'Out of favour, then? Hmm, yes, it would seem so,' she replied with mock thoughtfulness and placed an arm on the top of the car. 'You boys had a rough one today by the sound of it.'

'Uh-huh,' he said, clearly uncomfortable.

Mak was well aware that she could make Jimmy Cassimatis nervous, and she had years ago decided that it was the best way to deal with him. They'd had a rocky relationship from the start. Four-and-a-half years ago, when Mak had only just met Andy and he was little more than the detective in charge of her friend's murder case, Jimmy had tracked down a photo of 22-year-old Makedde in a bikini – complete with golden tan and heaving breasts – from a back issue of *Sports Illustrated*, and had posted it on a very public evidence board in police headquarters. He had even gone to the effort of circling her private areas in a bright felt-tip pen, as one sometimes did with crime-scene photographs. The entire Homicide Squad had seen it. Years on, not much had changed between them.

A cursory inspection of the car revealed Freddo Frog chocolate wrappers and an empty KFC carton in addition to the toppled bag of salt and vinegar chips. 'Dinner?' she asked.

'Uh, lunch.'

Jimmy had not improved his health habits one iota, despite his doctor's warnings and a near-fatal stroke that had left one side of his face with a slight droop that seemed only to add to his hangdog expression. Perhaps he believed that the blood-thinning Warfarin medication he was taking had been provided merely to support his desired cuisine preferences. There was probably little that his long-suffering wife, Angie, could say to teach her old dog new tricks.

'What do you think of Andy's new job?' Mak asked him.

Jimmy frowned. She could see that he didn't like losing his old police partner to a new position. 'He's a lucky sonofabitch.'

'Yeah, it will be good for his career.'

It was a return visit – he had trained as a pro-filer there as part of their international program.

Mak changed the subject. 'So is Deller under a bit of pressure now?'

'Cos of the runner? I dunno. Don't think so. He didn't tell the kid to bolt off and try to leap over a wire barricade. He told him to stop.' Jimmy shifted in his seat. 'What about you? You still playing PI?' He said the words tauntingly, clearly looking for some subject to give him the upper hand.

'Playing' PI.

Mak smiled mischievously, trying not to show her annoyance with his tone. 'Why? Do you need some help with something?'

He smiled smugly. 'Hey, has Andy told you about Ferris Hetherington, the ex-cop?'

He had. Many times. Mak was aware that her work with Marian was causing some minor friction with Andy, but she loved her new-found freedom far too much to dwell on any negative attitudes he and his colleagues might have towards private investigators and their trade. What she did was legal and professional, and it had a place. People needed the services Marian's agency provided, and those who were coming to her for the wrong reasons – to get some professional help to stalk an ex or to spy on a rival business – were quickly vetted out. Marian was an excellent judge of character, and so long as her clients didn't lie to her – about the things that counted, anyway – and they fell within her basic amoral–moral guidelines, the judging stopped there.

'Ferris,' Jimmy said, 'quit his *real* job to start a private investigation agency. He tried to break into a room at the Westin –'

'Yes, I know,' Mak broke in. 'Ferris tried to pick the lock on the hotel room door with his driver's licence, and it got stuck in the door.' Hard to talk your way out of that.

'You heard the story, then?'

Mak continued the story, verbatim, the way she'd heard it from Andy a dozen times since she started working for Marian. 'He got arrested for breaking and entering, lost his licence and went broke after six months. Fascinating story, Jimmy, but one I've heard before. Oh, Pete says hi, by the way,' she countered.

'Oh, yeah,' he said sheepishly. 'Tell him I say hi.' He shifted in his seat. 'He's a good man, Pete.'

Pete Don was ex-undercover Drug Squad. He had quit the force to start an investigation agency after being outed in a freak intelligence bungle that saw him nearly killed by a major organised crime syndicate. The entire police force had a quiet respect for him, and Mak knew damned well that he had, on occasion, done work for various cops, even though it was not something she discussed with him. Pete was one of Marian's friendly rivals, and he had been a lecturer in Mak's investigator course.

Mak heard footsteps and turned. Andy had changed into a fresh shirt and was walking towards her.

'Sorry about dinner,' he said and kissed her on the mouth. 'I hope you didn't prepare anything.'

She licked her lips when he pulled away. 'Me? Are you kidding? Ha!' She let out an exaggerated laugh as he moved around the car and got in the driver's seat.

Jimmy laughed as well, but more genuinely. 'Fat chance!' He knew Mak wasn't the cooking type. His wife, meanwhile, prepared hearty, home-cooked, three-course meals on a nightly basis.

'We'll go out tomorrow night, I promise,' Andy said. He seemed sincere about it. 'I'll take you somewhere nice.'

So we can celebrate our last night.

She smiled. 'Consider that a deal.'

'I'll be home in a couple of hours.'

'See ya, boys,' Mak replied and stepped back from the cruiser.

They drove off.

'Fuck,' she said to the quiet street.

Mak stood for a moment with her arms crossed, feeling the breeze whip around her. She felt a long way from home, and she had begun to question the wisdom of the choices that had taken her so far away. Looking back, she could see how it had happened, step by inevitable step. The years had mapped out a roller-coaster of emotions and difficult decisions, and now she was here in Sydney, Australia, so far from her birthplace. In her dreams, things had run a lot more smoothly. In her dreams, she and Andy shared normal, simple domestic bliss – although one that didn't involve her doing any cooking. In her dreams she had not abandoned her widowed father in the country of her birth.

'It will work itself out,' she muttered under her breath. 'It always does.'

She loved Andy. Where there was love, there was a way, right?

Mak walked back inside and locked the door behind her. She snatched her backpack off the bench and strode through the open doorway of the dining room, throwing the pack on the table in front of the empty plates. It skidded along the oak and knocked over a candle, spilling a teaspoon of white wax on the surface of the wood.

Wait.

She had closed the dining room door after Andy arrived home, but the door was now open ... So Andy *had* seen the dining table laid out.

Great. That's just great.

With little feeling of occasion, Mak poured a glass of the Merlot and swigged it down like grape juice. Grumbling to herself, she then dished up a couple of ladles' worth of the penne from the microwave. Her cooking had not gained any appeal in the interim, sadly. The little pasta pieces looked suspiciously like tyre tread. She brought one forkful to her lips. She tasted. She lowered her fork. Then she took her bowl back to the kitchen and slid the starchy contents into the bin.

Mak poured herself a bowl of cereal instead, and she ate it by candlelight while she flipped through the real estate listings in the *Wentworth Courier*, in search of affordable office space for her psychology practice. Thus far there was little that was affordable in any suburbs she might conceivably wish to work from. It would come with time, she hoped. She had to try to be patient.

And if you move to Canberra when Andy gets back, you'll have to start looking all over again . . .

She polished off her unsatisfying bowl of cereal – which tasted at odds with the wine – and she called Karen Mahoney to tell her how unsuccessful her attempt at pasta had been.

Karen didn't answer. She, like Mak's boyfriend, was working overtime on this parti-cular Thursday night.

★ ★ ★

What a waste.

Detective Constable Karen Mahoney stood at the feet of a recently deceased young woman, observing the scene of her death, police notepad and pen in hand. It was a Thursday night, and Karen had just been looking forward to going home when the call came in to the Homicide Squad. Now she found herself in this sad one-bedroom apartment, taking in every bit of information she could to piece together what had happened.

About an hour earlier, nearby Kings Cross Police Station had received two complaints from separate neighbours about the sounds of a violent argument. When they sent a couple of connies over, the boys had found much more than the expected domestic disagreement. The tenant, a young woman, had received multiple stab wounds to the chest. The officers said she was already dead when they arrived.

An as-yet-unidentified young man was also in the apartment at the time, seeming to be disoriented, and holding in his hand a blood-drenched knife – the obvious murder weapon. He had not attempted to flee. The young man was now in police custody, being interviewed. He had track marks on his arms: a junkie. It looked like a drug-fuelled burglary gone wrong. Perhaps she had surprised him while he was stealing from her, or perhaps he had made an unsuccessful attempt at rape.

What a horrible way to die.

The victim was clothed in blue jeans and a pale blue top, now marred excessively with blood that a mere sixty minutes before had been coursing through her veins. She wore a pair of white socks but no shoes, suggesting she had been relaxing at home when attacked. Karen noticed blood on the victim's hands, and what might have been defence wounds. Her arms and legs were splayed, platinum-blonde hair swept messily across her forehead. Since the moment of death, the victim's body had been cooling one or two degrees per hour, and her skin had already begun to turn waxy and pale, giving her the appearance of a smooth mannequin.

What a damned waste.

Karen, who had made detective recently, had seen a few crimes like this. Such scenes did not exactly reinforce the idealistic views of human nature she had entertained in her days as a rookie cop, especially as she had learned that the majority of violent crimes were committed by those known intimately to the victims – lovers, family, friends. *So much for the ties that bind.* And she'd seen complete strangers kill one another over something as petty as jewellery or cash, even a pair of running shoes. Or drugs.

Crime-scene investigators moved around the apartment like busy worker bees, going about the painstaking ritual of collecting microscopic forensic evidence. A photographer recorded the body from various angles and then moved on to concentrate on other minute details, his flash illuminating the rooms.

Karen crouched near the victim and peered at her face through a mess of pale, blood-streaked hair. She had been pretty. Karen noticed that the victim wore no wedding band or rings; her only jewellery was a pair of stud earrings with the two distinctive linked letter C's of the company

Chanel. There did not appear to be any lacerations above the neck, the concentration of wounds being to the chest. Her attacker had missed her heart, leaving time for her to suffer. Crimson handprints traced a fatal struggle around the room, leaving blood across the coffee-table legs and top, an area of white-painted wall and the floor. A stack of magazines had slid off the table; picture frames were on their sides. One frame containing a photo of a middle-aged couple – probably her parents – lay on the floor in a spray of broken glass. It appeared that the struggle might have lasted some time before the stab wounds ended the woman's life.

You fought back. You tried.

An officer swathed in protective clothing moved in and Karen stepped back to give him room. He covered the victim's hands with brown paper bags and tied off the bags so they were secure for the trip to the morgue, preserving any damning microscopic DNA evidence of the attacker's flesh under her nails.

Karen had once seen a rookie cop named Finker use plastic bags instead of paper, causing a murder victim's skin to slough off inside the moist bags until there weren't even fingerprints left when the body reached its destination. Karen thanked her lucky stars that she had never done anything quite so damagingly inept in her stage of initiation – not that she was accepted as part of the gang just yet. She was still considered a 'newbie'. Karen may have thrown up at her first dismembered victim, but that was almost a rite of passage. Besides, she'd managed to miss most of the evidence, and that's what counted.

'Fifteen minutes earlier and we might have caught him in time,' someone commented.

Karen looked over her shoulder to see the uniformed officer who had spoken. He appeared shaken, standing with her superior, Detective Senior Sergeant Bradley Hunt, as he was questioned by the older man. She guessed that it was probably the constable's first homicide or, at least, his first stabbing homicide. Karen wondered if the two connies had taken their time in arriving, considering that the complaint from the neighbours would have seemed routine. The young constable might be troubled by guilt if that were the case.

It's too late now.

There was nothing anyone could do that would bring this young woman back to life. Immediate family would soon be informed. Karen only hoped she wouldn't have to be the one to lie to the family that their daughter 'did not suffer'.

At only twenty-three years of age, Meaghan Wallace was dead.

CHAPTER 2

'I'LL JUST BE a sec, babe.'

Simon Aston wore little more than low-rise board shorts and his smooth signature smile. He had been working on his tan and, thanks to the warm weather of late, it was looking good. *He* was looking good and he knew it – and his latest guest at the summery beachfront abode seemed to agree. He left her curled up seductively at one end of the cream sofa in the living room, her denim miniskirt riding up to show a glimpse of the toned curve of her bottom. She was a small dark girl with a full mouth and big brown eyes, and Simon hoped to examine that pert derrière much more closely by night's end. She worked in 'promotions', she'd said.

He was having a good night. Not a bad pull for a Thursday.

Now Simon was in the small kitchen, searching through the cupboards. There was one more bottle in there, he was sure.

Ah, yes. Excellent.

He sauntered back into the living room,

grinning and holding the slightly warm, unopened bottle of Moët et Chandon champagne by the neck. A soft breeze stirred the chimes on the patio; the doors were opened wide to accept the dark, balmy evening.

Simon noticed that his guest had slipped off her cowboy boots and was twirling her dark hair around a manicured finger. Her tan legs glistened invitingly in the humid evening air. They would enjoy a few more drinks, and then he would walk her down to Tamarama Beach across the road and let the sand and the warm summer night do their magic. It worked every time.

Yes, life was good.

'I found us another bottle, babe,' he said. *Jessica? Or just Jess?* He had forgotten. 'It's a bit warm, but I'll take care of that.' He pulled the empty bottle out of the silver champagne bucket on the coffee table, and plunked the fresh one in, the wet ice making a *shloosh* sound, the cubes melting fast in the heat. Simon and his guest had already polished off their first bottle of champagne as if it were tap-water.

'S-i-i-imon …' the promotions girl purred, leaning towards him and throwing an arm around a cushion, her brown eyes large. 'You haven't answered my question yet. Do you already have a date for the big party, or what?'

'Not yet, babe.' He gave her a sly smile to encourage the idea that he would take her. Every young thing in Sydney wanted to score an invite to Damien Cavanagh's lavish thirtieth birthday party next weekend, and as Damien's best friend, Simon was gatekeeper to the coveted invitation. It would be the social event of the year. Simon wasn't about to bring a little promotions girl to it, but she didn't need to know that now. There were plenty more opportunities to get laid in the lead-up to the party.

'Oh,' she said and moved another inch towards him, beaming. She flicked her hair.

His mobile phone rang and his guest seemed instantly bored, the sound of the ring switching off her attentive charm like a lamp. Simon impatiently pulled the phone from the pocket of his shorts and looked at its display. It was a private number.

'Hello,' he answered.

The girl downed the last drops of her champagne, and then gestured to her empty glass with an impatient pout.

'It's me.'

Me?

'Who is *me*?' Simon said, rolling his eyes for Jess's benefit. She perked up and giggled at his display. He threw her another look, cocking an eyebrow suggestively.

She seemed to think him hilarious, and tossed her head back in a tipsy laugh, putting a finger up to her lips. 'Shhhh!' she said, the sound trailing off in a giggle. He definitely needed to keep her going on that champagne.

'It's Warwick,' said the voice on the other end of the line.

Warwick O'Connor.

'Ah ... yes,' Simon replied curtly, now wishing he hadn't answered the call. His throat tightened a little. He was not in a work mood, and this was a particularly unpleasant matter. He'd hoped he wouldn't need to hear about it until morning.

'Hey, man, how's it all coming along?' he said, not waiting for a reply. 'Look, I'm a little busy at the moment. This isn't a good time.' Simon played it cool for the benefit of his guest. 'I'll call you tomorrow and we'll chat ... Okay, talk to you then –'

'It's about the money,' came Warwick's voice, cutting him off.

The money.

Simon might have guessed it would be about the money.

Warwick was little more than a thug, but he wouldn't go away easily, Simon knew. He covered the receiver.

'I'll be back in one sec,' he told Jess. He didn't want the promotions girl overhearing anything too interesting. She pouted and lifted her empty champagne glass as he left her again to stalk out onto the open patio. The breeze was getting stronger, the chimes making their chaotic music with more vigour.

'The money's all good, man. The other half is

right here for you,' Simon assured Warwick. He didn't want any trouble brewing. 'We can meet at the Ravesi bar downstairs tomorrow afternoon. It'll all be there.'

'I left you a message an hour ago. We need to renegotiate. I can make this hard or I can make this easy.'

'You've been watching too many movies, man,' Simon replied irritably. 'You did your job, and now you'll get paid what we agreed. Nuff said.' It was ridiculous for Warwick to think he could renegotiate now. This guy was seriously burning his bridges – Simon had connections with a lot of important people; important people who might one day want the type of services that Warwick could provide.

'There is no renegotiating,' Simon told him firmly. 'You'll be lucky now to get the second half of the payment with all this grief you're causing me.'

A salty breeze whipped around Simon, setting off the chimes again and lifting the sun-bleached hair off his tanned nape. He felt his face getting warm with irritation.

'Don't push me, man,' he added.

'I've been busy doing my homework,' Warwick said. 'Your mate's old man would be more than interested in my offer, I think.'

Simon's heart skipped. '*Don't you . . . don't –*'

'The new price is one mill. Cash.'

Simon reeled. 'What? What the fuck? *A*

million dollars? What are you, on crack? This is *bullshit!*' he yelled at the top of his voice, his words carrying across the rooftops on the wind. 'Forget it. Forget it, man.' He'd agreed to $15 000 to take care of a little problem. Now what was this about one million? Ludicrous. Simon was losing his temper, and his patience.

I should hang up to show him who's boss, he thought. But before he did, Warwick spoke again.

'Your mate is not going to want this made public, and neither is his old man.'

'Come on, man,' Simon said quietly, panicking inside. His stomach had tightened, the champagne taste turning sour in his mouth. What if Warwick really *did* know the connection, and had proof? What if he sold the story to some reporter?

'You tell your mate I want an answer by one o'clock tomorrow,' Warwick continued, 'and if I don't get the answer I want, the price will go up. Take him out for lunch, why don't you? Have a nice chat about it. I am sure he'll agree it's worth it not to make this thing public.'

This was going all wrong now. How could it be going wrong like this? He was supposed to have the upper hand. He'd *hired* this guy, for God's sake. It should have all been fine – taken care of – *nothing*.

'You're bluffing,' Simon said.

'You *know* I'm not,' Warwick said ominously. 'One mill in cash. That's the price.'

'Come on, man,' Simon repeated and

laughed, trying another tactic. His laughter sounded too nervous in his own ears, and his body was on edge, pumping with adrenaline. But he tried to sound relaxed. 'Okay, I'll see you tomorrow at Ravesi. I've got your seven-and-a-half grand waiting for you, all right? And another few grand for your trouble. No worries, mate. We'll make it twenty-five now all up. Okay? No worries. See you then . . .'

'One million dollars. I want an answer by tomorrow at one, or I'll contact the big man myself,' Warwick threatened again.

Simon was about to get in another word when his mobile went quiet, the call ended.

'Fuck!' he shouted to the sky. Warwick had actually hung up on him. This fucking guy had hung up on *Simon Aston*?

Simon stood in shock on the patio in the humid air, looking towards the darkening sky, one hand nervously rubbing his tight, muscled stomach, his fingers circling his bellybutton.

I can't believe he hung up on me. I can't believe it.

He cooled off for a few minutes, having felt so furious that he was unable to speak. When he felt in control again he walked back into the living room where his guest was waiting. She had opened the champagne bottle without him. She looked bored, picking at her French manicure, her glass half empty and her bare feet up on the arm of the couch. His face must have still been red with anger from the phone call, because she could tell that something was wrong.

'What's up?' she asked when she saw him.

'Nothing. Here ...' He pulled the champagne bottle out of the ice bucket, which was filled with water and the remaining shapes of a few melted ice cubes. The bottle itself was not chilled enough, but he didn't care. Silently Simon topped up his guest's glass sloppily and then filled his own. He sat heavily in an easy chair, frowning and holding his drink. Warwick's call had ruined his evening.

Should I say anything to Damien about it? he wondered. *Absolutely not.*

The guy was bluffing, and his friend was better off not being hassled with the details. It would be fine. He's greedy, that's all. He's just trying it on.

But what if he isn't bluffing?

CHAPTER 13

ON FRIDAY MORNING Makedde Vanderwall opened her eyes to the sound of the front door closing.

She shifted in bed and frowned, not needing to check the clock. She knew it would be too early. Outside, she heard a car drive off. Mak vaguely remembered Andy coming to bed. He had crept onto his side and slid under the covers, careful not to disturb her. The thing was, she had *wanted* him to disturb her. Despite her resistance, Mak was becoming familiar with the pent-up sexual frustration of the work-widowed spouse, and she wasn't even married. They'd only been living together for a year. Would it only get worse? Would his three months at Quantico bring them closer together or further apart?

Is there such a thing as a one-year itch?

If Mak thought this state of frequent absences and near-platonic boredom was less than ideal, she wondered how their relationship would be once he had returned and had to be on site at the new Canberra unit a full five days a week. They had not yet discussed it, but the obvious unspoken result of his move was that she would have to consider moving there with him, even though her few friends in Australia were all in Sydney, and so was her work. Would she have to give up her investigation work with Marian, the work she currently thrived on? Trying to find an appropriate space in Sydney for her practice hardly seemed worth it now, with their lives in flux. The thought of moving to a new city with Andy, leaving behind the few tenuous ties she had built in the past year – her friendship with Karen, her time with her dear friend Loulou, her work with Marian – made her sad.

Don't worry about that just yet . . .

It would be months before the unit was running. She would deal with those decisions when the time came.

★ ★ ★

'So how was it last night?'

Detective Andy Flynn looked up quizzically from the table and found his partner Jimmy Cassimatis strolling over to him, having walked into their favourite café twenty minutes late.

'How was *what* last night?' Andy asked. They had been working together on Jimmy's homicide mess until late, so he was not sure what his former partner could have thought he had missed.

'Come on – you slipped her some sausage,

didn't you?' Jimmy quipped, slapping Andy's shoulder and making a phallic-looking fist in the air that he proceeded to shake. 'Make-up sex is the best. Did she handcuff you again? I bet she did.'

'Shut up and sit down,' Andy said darkly, ignoring the comments. He glanced around, but the other diners seemed unperturbed by Jimmy's rude gestures. Sophomoric references to sex spewed forth from Jimmy's lips on a regular basis. Perhaps it was part of his 'charm'. And this particular topic of conversation was not an unusual one for Jimmy, who, even after all the years had passed, still liked to let it be known that he thought his mate was legendary for 'bagging an *SI* model', as he so elegantly put it – a one-time *Sports Illustrated* pin-up with a thing for cops and handcuffs, no less. '*Skata!* You are the stuff of legend, mate!' he'd said on far too many occasions. There was more depth to Jimmy, Andy knew, but he just didn't seem to like showing it.

'*Skata!* She snuck up on me like a vampire while I was waiting in the car, and freaked me out something shocking,' Jimmy persisted, nodding his head as he pulled out the metal chair with a squeak on the linoleum. 'Yup, she was sure pissed off with you. Pissed!' He was never one to know when to stop.

'I picked up on that, thank you,' Andy replied, wishing Jimmy would just shut up about Mak. She *had* been angry, though she rarely said as

54

much in words. She was so different from his late ex-wife, Cassandra, who had been the type to scream, cry and throw things.

Andy sometimes felt out of his depth with Mak. She was quiet when she was angry, as she had been last night. Quiet – but intensely so. He didn't have a reference point for women like that. But surely by now she understood that frequent late nights and absences were part of his job. She *should* understand – she was the daughter of a cop, after all.

Mak's father was the formidable ex-Detective Inspector Les Vanderwall, and though his career had been in Canada, his influence seemed to reach much further. Andy knew that Les didn't approve of his daughter's choice of boyfriend, and that he kept tabs on their life together. By falling for Mak and taking on their living arrangements, Andy had also taken on her strong will, quiet moods and sharp intelligence. He'd also taken on the role that every man involved with a very beautiful woman was used to – every time they went out, other men stared at his girlfriend, and sometimes other women did too. All that, combined with the private prying eyes of her detective father, and Andy had taken on quite a handful with Makedde Vanderwall. And that was *before* she started dabbling in investigation.

'I have to try to get us a table at somewhere tonight. Something fancy. Maybe Icebergs?'

Andy knew it was booked out weeks in advance.

'Deller knows the chef. He owes him a favour,' Jimmy said.

'And Deller owes *me* a favour.' That would help Andy to book a table at short notice. Hopefully. 'How are the little ones?' he asked, wanting to change the subject from Mak.

'Yeah, good,' Jimmy replied. He was a good Greek father of four now, with more on the way soon, Andy felt sure. The waitress arrived. 'I'll have a cup of coffee and your full breakfast – two fried eggs, beans, bacon and sausage.'

'Coffee, and beans on toast,' Andy ordered.

'*Skata*. You look like crap.'

'I know,' Andy agreed.

'They working you hard, huh?'

Andy shrugged.

'So how is all that crap going with Canberra, anyway?'

'Uh, okay.' Andy played with a paper napkin. 'We're doing all this groundwork, and talks, and talks and more talks. I don't think I'm cut out for all this political bullshit. It's like everyone talks and nobody does anything.'

'You're a fuck of a lot more political than me,' Jimmy commented.

That was true. Jimmy would long ago have been promoted to a higher rank if not for his complete and utter lack of social grace and political drive. He was a good cop, and he would give his right arm for Andy, but those on high did not smile upon him. He didn't have what it took for leadership, and he knew it too.

'I think Kelley wants to see you off ... your last day and all.' *Detective Inspector Roderick Kelley*. 'You're his golden boy.'

'I wouldn't say that.'

It was partially true, though. Kelley had protected Andy as best he could when things had got bad. When Andy solved the major Stiletto Murder case, it had vindicated Kelley's position; but Andy had let him down on occasion too. If he was a golden boy, it was tarnished gold.

The coffees arrived and Jimmy dumped three packets of sugar into his cup. 'Sometimes I wish I was going with you. Things are starting to suck around here,' he complained. 'It won't be the same. I can already tell.'

'Good morning,' Detective Inspector Roderick Kelley said, interrupting their banter before Jimmy could continue. They were both caught by surprise, and Andy wondered if Inspector Kelley had overheard Jimmy's comments.

Jimmy stopped his babbling and wiped coffee from the corner of his mouth. 'Hey, sir,' he said clumsily.

'Good morning, Inspector.' Andy stood and shook Kelley's hand.

'Getting my morning coffee,' Kelley said. 'Say, can you drop in to my office this morning?' he asked Andy. 'There're a few things I would like to discuss.'

Andy nodded.

The Detective Inspector was someone Andy admired enormously. He wasn't one of the political paper-pushers who were so often in jobs like his these days. He was old school, the kind of cop who had actually spent his time learning on the street and not in a classroom. There was not one whiff of bullshit or political aspiration about him. And what about Andy? With all Andy's talk about the unit, he was beginning to feel like the men he had always abhorred. He wished he could get back to doing his job instead of talking about it. But he wouldn't have to wait much longer, which was good, because he doubted he had much more patience.

Kelley took his coffee and a muesli bar to go, and returned to headquarters across the street.

'Golden boy,' Jimmy griped.

Andy rolled his eyes.

Jimmy persisted. 'You have been the golden boy since the Stiletto Murder case and you know it.'

The case had been the most high-profile of Andy's career, and a major turning point for him both professionally and personally. The killer had cut a swathe of violence through Sydney, and had become obsessed with Andy, the profiler leading the investigation. Andy's ex-wife had been murdered, and he'd met Makedde, a witness. Everything in his world had changed. And when he had cracked the case and found the killer, a successful career had been assured. Jimmy was right: in some ways he was Kelley's protégé. But Andy had paid a heavy price for his success in that case.

★ ★ ★

Fifteen minutes later, Andy and Jimmy entered HQ together. Kelley approached Andy, and several of the other detectives looked up to watch the interaction, probably wishing their careers were also on Kelley's radar.

'My office,' Kelley said. His invitation did not extend to Jimmy.

'Yes, sir.'

Jimmy took a seat at his measly desk, and pretended to look through some paperwork. He was used to being excluded. Kelley and Andy walked across the floor, passing constables at their desks, many of whom looked up as they went by. Andy could feel their eyes on him.

They reached Kelley's office.

'Shut the door. Take a seat.'

Andy did.

Inspector Kelley remained standing, looking out through his well-earned window to a view of Hyde Park, where fairy lights decorated the trees. After dark, bats would fly out of those trees by the thousands, just some of the creatures that ventured out into the city at night.

'I'm putting Deller on leave for a couple of weeks.'

Andy flexed his jaw. Deller would be disappointed, but he understood Kelley's logic. 'Will there be an investigation?'

'Yes. Routine.'

Andy nodded. Deller would have to take trauma counselling after the incident. Andy had been there himself from time to time; he knew the concept was a good one. Police officers dealt with death and violence all the time and they needed help to relieve the stress of their jobs. But Andy was not always convinced that a psychologist was the best person to assist. Not that he would ever admit this to Mak, of course.

Inspector Kelley kept his back to Andy, his hands folded neatly in the small of his back; Andy waited until he was addressed. The inspector was always economical in both word and action. When he spoke his words had great weight, especially to Andy. Kelley wasn't the type who wanted the air filled with nonsense talk. He wasn't the type for any kind of nonsense at all.

Finally he turned. 'Pleased with your new post?' he asked, those sharp slate-grey eyes unreadable. Was *he* happy about Andy's post? Unhappy? Surely his recommendation had helped Andy get it. Was there something he knew about the project that Andy didn't? The set-up for the unit was experimental in some ways, but Kelley was one of those who had strongly supported the idea.

I'll be more excited about it when I finally get to do something, instead of talk about it.

'Yes,' Andy admitted. 'It's been a long time coming.' He'd spent frustrating years pushing it along with politicians who seemed to change position for or against on the whims of popular opinion.

Kelley took the comment in with a slight smile, as if he knew from experience just how slowly the wheels of progress moved with such projects. He then took a seat in his leather chair, and it creaked under his weight. He was a tall man, and fit for his age – or, indeed, any age. He was less than five years from retirement, but he was still in more formidable shape than half of the department.

'I'll miss it here, though, I think.'

'Well, don't you go missing us just yet. You don't leave till tomorrow. You can still make yourself useful.' Andy opened his mouth to say that he would be delighted to be made useful, but Kelley was already busy explaining what needed doing. 'A girl was found behind a dumpster this morning in Surry Hills. She'd been there a few days. It looks like a sexual homicide. Maybe a serial. I'll have you take a look. Talk the boys through it if you can. They could learn from you while we still have you.'

Consulting on cases was what Andy's future held. He would no longer be part of the same team.

'Thank you, sir. Who found her?'

If the body was a few days old – the smell would be very bad, especially in the high February summer temperatures.

'Go with Cassimatis to check it out. Peterson's there – he'll have the details.'

Kelley slid a piece of paper across to him with an address on it.

'Oh, and try to get some sleep on that plane tomorrow. You look tired.'

Andy nodded. He'd been burning the candle at both ends, and that was hardly about to stop. 'Um, sir, will Deller be all right?' he asked before he left. Deller was not a friend, but he was a colleague, and Andy wanted to see that Deller would not be demoted for a situation that had been beyond his control.

'Don't worry about him,' Kelley said. 'You have your own problems.'

★   ★   ★

Andy and Jimmy pulled up on a side road near the mouth of a lane blocked off with crime-scene tape. Andy killed the engine, and opened the glove box. *Damn bloody headaches.* He popped two tablets of aspirin into his hand and swallowed them dry.

'Okay, let's check this out,' he said and stepped out of their unmarked car.

The filthy back lane where all the activity was smelled terribly, not only of foul garbage, but also of death. Andy was glad he wasn't planning on eating a big lunch. He ducked under blue-and-white chequered crime-scene tape, Jimmy at his heels. Though they'd just eaten breakfast, Jimmy was already chewing on a Mars Bar. He grumbled something about the stench.

Jimmy had worked with Andy for many years, and the two had become nearly inseparable, despite some of Jimmy's less popular qualities. It wasn't Jimmy's colourful way with words – his speech peppered with Greek and the expletives he sometimes called 'French' – that Andy disliked, and it wasn't his sometimes destructive lack of ambition. It was his way with food. Surrounded by filth and the stench of decay, Jimmy continued to eat his Mars Bar unfazed, the chocolate all over his fingers. Andy gave him a look and Jimmy pocketed the bar. He licked his fingers clean.

The centre of activity was a garbage dumpster in the lane. The crime-scene team was already there in Hazmat suits, collecting evidence. Just behind the dumpster, the body of a young woman lay decomposing. A photographer's flash illuminated the victim. Her bare legs were splayed out, dappled with rot and filth. She appeared to be naked except for a hot-pink garter belt around her hips. It looked to Andy like a sexual homicide.

'No ID as yet,' Detective Peterson said. 'I've checked on the garbage runs. Last pick-up was Sunday. She must have been dumped after that.'

'Has anyone touched her?' Andy asked. It

didn't matter how many times they were briefed on crime-scene procedure, there was always a risk of someone – usually a rookie – contaminating something. This victim looked tampered with.

'No one touched her until the team arrived. They've lifted garbage off her, that's it.'

Dammit. Perhaps no one had known he was on his way. Andy would examine the crime-scene photographs; hopefully there was adequate coverage of her original position, as found.

'She's still *in situ*, apart from the garbage,' Peterson continued.

'Who found her?' said Andy.

The girl had been discovered by a homeless man as he scrounged through the heaps of cardboard next to the dumpster to find something worth keeping, perhaps as shelter. The man, who called himself Barney, was occupying a couple of constables with his rambling account of the discovery.

'... my wife, she don't see me no more ...'

'Yes, Barney,' the constable pressed. 'But tell us again about how you found the body.'

Barney's eyes rolled back and popped forwards again. He had a long beard and deeply lined skin. 'I was jus' looking round. I thought I smelled somethin'. I thought it might be rotten fruit. I thought I could find somethin' to eat.'

Andy grimaced. He would let the constables deal with Barney.

'*Skata*,' Jimmy offered. 'She's ripe, all right.'

The autopsy would give a better idea of the time of death, but Andy guessed that the remains were a couple of days old, perhaps accelerated by the weather. He covered his mouth and nose with one hand and moved closer to her. The girl looked Asian, and young, though given the state of the body it was difficult to tell whether she was in her teens or twenties. He noticed lacerations around her wrists. She had been tied up, but there were no binds on her now.

Andy wondered what could have happened for her to end up in a back lane like this, becoming his last gruesome case as part of the team he had worked with for so many years.

CHAPTER 4

SIMON ASTON WALKED across one of the vast living rooms of the Cavanagh house, his sneakers treading on a giant, cream fur rug that stretched metres across the hardwood floor. Through the glass doors that opened out to the harbour, Damien was laid out on a sun lounge, wearing silk shorts as he baked himself on the balcony. An exotic silk robe hung over the lounge at his back and a newspaper lay in sections beside him.

'So, man, how are you?' said Simon.

Despite Damien's relaxed surroundings, he didn't seem settled. The dark circles under his eyes were more pronounced than usual. He looked up when Simon approached, but said nothing.

'Yo,' Simon said, 'I brought you a coffee from your favourite. Double shot.'

Damien snatched it without thanking him. 'This new maid makes shit coffee,' he murmured.

Simon nodded and pulled up a lounge next to his friend. 'So, how are plans for the party coming?'

'I dunno,' Damien said dismissively and looked out at the water. He sipped the coffee from its cardboard cup.

Simon took a furtive glance at his watch; it was approaching eleven. He wanted to call Warwick O'Connor well before one o'clock, just to be on the safe side. It would be best if he knew whether or not he would have any cash to negotiate with before he called. In Simon's experience, cash had a great way of solving problems. In fact, he couldn't think of any problem that money couldn't solve. It just depended on how much you had to throw at it.

'Look, buddy, I hate to bring it up,' he said nervously, now wringing his hands. 'But, uh, I'm going to need a bit more money to wrap this thing up.'

Damien looked over at him. 'Is it that guy Lee?'

'No, Lee is fine.'

'So what is it, then?' he said with audible impatience.

One million dollars. I want an answer by tomorrow at one, or I'll contact the big man myself . . .

Simon couldn't tell Damien about the trouble with Warwick. There was no way he could tell Damien that some lowlife wanted one million dollars of his money and was threatening to blackmail his father. What if it was seen as Simon's fault? He would quickly become persona non grata, not just with the Cavanaghs but the whole of Sydney's A-list.

'Nothing,' Simon lied. 'Everything's fine. It's just a little extra to cover all the bases.'

Surely Warwick was bluffing. Surely he wouldn't really contact Jack Cavanagh himself? He doesn't have the balls, does he?

Damien dropped a hand over the side of the lounge, the cup of coffee dangling. He let go, and it dropped the few inches to the floor and fell on its side. Simon dived in to right it again, but the remaining coffee had spilled.

'Leave it,' Damien said and turned his head. 'Estelle!' He began fumbling through the pockets of the silk robe for his cigarettes. 'Did Lee say anything?' he asked, still searching. 'Estelle!' he yelled again. *'Where the fuck are my cigarettes?'*

Estelle instantaneously appeared with a packet and placed it in Damien's open hand. She was the new maid; lithe, pale and beautiful, with cascading locks of raven hair tied in a loose ponytail at her nape. Her eyes were huge and doelike. Estelle was gorgeous and French. Only the Cavanaghs would have a French maid who was actually French, probably to try to appear more cultured. They went through a maid once or twice a year it seemed. Damien drove the ugly ones away, and messed with the pretty ones. He wondered if Damien had fucked her already or not, or if he'd be okay with him making a try.

Damien put a cigarette in his lips and Estelle lit it. In a flash she had mopped up the coffee and disappeared again.

Simon watched the exchange with fascination. 'Lee's fine. It's nothing,' he continued, getting the conversation back on track. Time was ticking on. 'He doesn't have a problem at all. It's just a bit of extra dough to smooth things out.'

Even if he was foolish enough to ask for it, Simon knew that Damien didn't have access to a million dollars. Not liquid, anyway. His father, Jack, controlled the family fortune, and what Damien himself actually had in his name was a mere drop in the ocean compared to his mighty father's personal wealth, or compared to what Cavanagh Incorporated was worth, with all its various interests. Simon wouldn't dream of getting them to cough up a cool mill for the likes of Warwick O'Connor. That would be outrageous, a rip-off, and probably the end of his friendship with Damien. Anyway, O'Connor was probably bluffing about what he knew.

Simon was sure that if he could meet with him face to face and show him what another twenty grand in cash looked like, he would stop his quibbling and take the money. Warwick was no big-timer; all that cash was bound to look good to him. And then this thing would be over ...

'I want a new personal trainer,' Damien said out of the blue, pinching one of his oiled-up browned biceps.

'You look good, man,' Simon told him, though he didn't really think so. His friend was already starting to look a bit drug ravaged.

Besides, Damien never worked hard enough to get the muscles he wanted. He had a slim build and he was slightly concave chested. There wasn't much to him. He'd gone through four or five trainers in the past year but always ended up dumping them. He'd sacked his last trainer, Dave, two weeks before. Simon wondered why Damien bothered with training at all, when he obviously didn't like being told what to do.

'Who's that guy Will keeps talking about?' *Will Smith*. 'The guy who got him in shape for that film?' Damien asked. 'You know the one?'

'I dunno. I'll ask him.'

Damien dragged on his cigarette and watched the boats. 'How much do you need for this thing to go away?' he said.

'Thirty-five,' Simon found himself saying. He'd planned to ask for twenty, but he'd decided that he needed the extra fifteen for his own spending money. He was broke again after the last party. It could get expensive being a friend of the rich.

Damien nodded. 'I'll organise it.'

'It would be good if I could have it, uh … soon.'

Damien seemed unperturbed by the demand. He dragged on his cigarette. 'I think we've got that in the safe.'

Simon was quietly relieved. If Damien hurried, Simon might still have time to get to Warwick with some tempting cash at one o'clock.

Damien flicked the waistband of his black silk

shorts, making a snapping sound. 'Do you like these?' The waistband announced that they were a Prada design.

'They look good on you, man. Super cool,' Simon told him, nodding.

Damien sighed at Simon's comment, and gave a sneer at them. 'I dunno ...'

And with that, the subject had been changed.

CHAPTER 5

AT TWELVE-THIRTY Makedde Vanderwall's mobile phone rang. She turned *The Monster Show* by David J Skal face down and snatched the phone off the coffee table. She'd spent the morning reading through a psychology journal on advancements in the experimental treatment of violent psychopathic inmates in Canada and had eventually moved on to lighter fare – and different monsters.

'Hello?' she answered.

'Are you still in bed?' The familiar voice was accusing.

'No. It's the afternoon. Do you think I am out every night until six?'

'If I were your age, I would be. And I would enjoy it, too.' The voice belonged to Makedde's sometime employer, Marian Wendell.

Mak chuckled.

Marian was quickly down to business. 'I have something for you if you want it. The client just left my office. Are you available?'

'Yup.' Mak sat up.

'You would be needed all week,' Marian warned.

'Even better.'

A meaty job was just what Mak wanted to sink her teeth into. A lot of jobs could be knocked over in a few days – a full week's work would be her longest assignment to date. Normally it was Marian's more experienced investigators who got the bigger gigs.

'The job starts today. What time can you get here?' Marian asked.

'Give me thirty minutes.'

Mak didn't bother asking what the assignment was. If Marian was throwing a job her way, she would take it without hesitation – particularly if it was a full week's work. She needed the money.

After a lightning-fast shower and basic grooming, Mak was primed and on the road in her motorcycle leathers within fifteen minutes. The quickest way to get anywhere in Sydney was on two wheels, and Mak's horny 1200cc bike was her transportation mode of choice since her move to the city. Thanks to her bike, the astronomical price of car parking was an expense she rarely had to contend with; and with soaring petrol prices, the economy of her bike was even more appealing by the day. On the occasions that she grudgingly borrowed Andy's car for work, she found herself spotting gaps in the traffic and wanting to accelerate through – a physical impossibility on four wheels.

Of course, a scooter might be equally practical for the city, but it had never been an option for Mak. A particularly infantile pleasure of hers was to pull up to scooter-riding men at the traffic lights and smile at them from the vantage point of her big BMW bike.

Vroom.

Now Mak's tall, naked K1200R tore up the roads towards busy Bondi Junction and passed the standard daily traffic jams with an ease possible only on two wheels. With time to spare, she stopped her bike on the kerb outside Marian's office, flicked it into neutral, placed it gently on its kickstand and shut the warm engine off. She grabbed her backpack and made her way inside the building.

Marian Wendell's office was on the second floor of a three-storey block that Mak imagined might have been glamorous when Marian had first bought up in 1975. It had all the hallmarks of an ill-conceived mid-seventies architectural vision that now left it looking like a rundown concrete box. The colour scheme was brown and weak yellow; the token ground-floor lobby had wood veneer panelling where wallpaper would otherwise be; and the fixtures were decidedly tired. But rather than offend Mak's aesthetic sensibilities, she felt the place had atmosphere. Mak used her favourite word of the Australian vernacular when describing the building; it was 'daggy' – dishevelled, uncool, but rich with character. Thanks to the colourful history of Marian Wendell's private investigation agency, a lot of exciting cases had passed through those doors, and Mak thought she could sense it in the walls.

If only the wood veneer could talk.

She made her way up in the slow-moving elevator, ready to take on her new assignment, helmet and backpack in hand. When she stepped out onto the off-green and yellow carpet of the second-floor hallway, she found that she was not alone. A small bespectacled man a few feet down the hall stiffened at her presence and gave her a long unfriendly look before disappearing into the shared bathrooms at the end of the hall.

Well, hello to you, too, she thought, slightly perplexed by his aggressive glare. He looked like one of the stiffs who worked in the accountancy practice across the hall. Mak realised that when she came to and from work on her bike she probably looked more like a motorbike courier – or maybe even a member of a bikie gang – than a young investigator with a PhD to boot. And some people just had issues with motorcyclists. On one amusing occasion Mak had decided to do some banking on the way home, and a man on a bench seated outside the bank had been utterly convinced that she was about to stage a hold-up before leaping onto her bike and speeding off. He'd been so relieved when she had calmly emerged with her helmet in hand and put her bank slip away that he actually told her what he'd thought she was going to do.

Mak had chosen a sporty bike, but she might as well have a long beard and a Harley.

'Boo,' she said under her breath, but the freaked-out accountant couldn't hear her. She left the man to his paranoia and, with a faint rustle of leather on leather, stepped through the door of Marian's office, on which was written:

MARIAN WENDELL AND ASSOCIATES
PROFESSIONAL PRIVATE INVESTIGATIONS

A bell chimed to alert Marian that she had a visitor. A closed-circuit camera would confirm Mak's identity to her boss as she walked in.

'Be with you soon, Mak,' came Marian's booming voice from down the hallway.

'Okay,' Mak called back, and took a seat in the waiting room.

She made herself comfortable, taking her stiff leather jacket off and looking for something to read. She sifted through a couple of newspapers and a selection of out-of-date magazines in a stack on a glass coffee table in the waiting area. *The Australian Women's Weekly*, *New Woman*, *Woman's Day*, *National Geographic*, *Cleo* – the plethora of women's titles was there for Marian's strong female client base, the women who came to her with problems of errant husbands or suspicious work practices and wanted a 'private dick without the dick', as Marian put it. Having read each of the old magazines twice over on previous visits to the office, Mak found a copy of the previous day's *Australian* newspaper and perused it instead, speed reading articles on business and federal politics, the sale of Telstra, troops in the Middle East and handshaking on plans for a bullet train between Sydney and Melbourne.

After a couple of minutes Marian stepped out of her office and waved Mak in.

The infamous Marian Wendell was a woman of perhaps sixty-five years, and birdlike in size compared to Makedde's Amazonian stature. She had big auburn hair that almost seemed to dwarf her features, and a penchant for expensive, glamorous clothing. She had been a very attractive woman in her youth, as evidenced by photos on a filing cabinet, and in her later years she still took great pride in her appearance and presentation. Marian's hair was always meticulously dyed and styled and her make-up flawless; and, though a bit outdated, her wardrobe was flattering and well maintained. Marian had a handsome office – a practical space cluttered with neat files, but also a soothing space, with the distinctly feminine touches of a ceramic aromatherapy oil burner on the wide working desk, along with a crystal vase that was always stocked with yellow roses, and a romantic-looking Art Deco statue of a nymph on a square display table taking pride of place in the room. Behind it, an Aboriginal dot painting of muted earthy tones depicted a giant serpent of the Dreamtime. Another wall was entirely covered by an impressively jumbled floor-to-ceiling bookshelf. From one tall window there was a view of the Sydney cityscape. Not a postcard of the Opera House exactly, but an impressive view nonetheless. It was a far cry from the dark, masculine quarters of a Philip Marlowe or a Mike Hammer.

'This guy in the hallway freaked out when he saw me step out of the elevator. I think he figured you're doing work for bikie gangs now.'

Marian laughed.

Mak was used to being misunderstood. The expression 'looks are deceiving' was not the exception but the rule for her. Marian, at least, thought it helped her protégée to look past the appearances of others to see their true nature. Perhaps that was right.

'You are my secret weapon,' Marian said, clearly pleased with her new agent. 'Mrs Anderson was very happy with the result. Her husband was so embarrassed at being caught out that he's agreed to half of her demands already.'

'I am glad she was pleased,' Mak replied.

When it came to domestic jobs, not all clients were happy with an investigator's results. The truth could hurt – *a lot*. Which was one of the many reasons Marian discouraged marital jobs from male clients. A woman might see evidence of her husband rooting the secretary and respond by getting a good lawyer, while a man might respond to the same situation by getting himself a good baseball bat, and then there were serious domestic violence issues to contend with on top of everything else. It was that ugly side of the business that gave it a bad name, depending on the way the operator handled it.

Even the most respected PIs found themselves on the occasional infidelity case, though many of the big agencies denied it and discouraged such jobs in favour of corporate clients. However, infidelity was the bread-and-butter work. The three full pages of ads for Investigators in the Yellow Pages were a testament to the popularity of marital mistrust:

DO YOU NEED PROOF OF INFIDELITY?
IS YOUR PARTNER CHEATING???
DON'T BE THE LAST TO KNOW.

To her many female clients, some of whom were likely soon to be divorced, Marian represented not only a 'private dick without the dick' but a necessary role model at a time when the clients needed a reminder that successful singledom was possible. Marian had been widowed some twenty years and yet she was happily solo and successful. A photo of her late second husband, Reg, still sat in a frame on the filing cabinet. As Marian had confided in Mak, Reg had been a much older man who was her 'soul mate'. He had respected her independence, her business acumen and her decision to never bear children; she clearly felt no need to replace him. Marian spoke of Reg often. She never talked of her first husband, however, and Mak guessed it had not ended amicably. Perhaps one of those desperate-sounding ads for AAAA CHEATERS Investigation Agency – the 'AAAA' ensuring the first listing in the phone book – was what had given Marian the idea of becoming a private investigator in the first place. Maybe she had taken it upon herself to bust the kind of bastard she had first married?

'Sit down, honey,' Marian said. 'This is a good one. Top rates.'

Top rates for Mak meant $80 an hour for research and $100 an hour for field work. The job paid well, though not as well as some of her modelling gigs had, of course.

Mak's special 'entrapment' rate for luring errant husbands to hotel rooms was much higher because of her close proximity to the target – and her particularly good qualifications for the job. So far she had a 100 per cent success rate in the handful of such jobs she had completed. Had Mrs Anderson's glowing report spurred Marian into giving Mak this new job? Or was it just that none of her more experienced investigators was available?

Mak took a seat. Her black leather pants squeaked faintly as she crossed her legs.

Marian had a couple of notes in front of her but

she didn't look at them. She closed her eyes as she spoke, recalling the meeting with her formidable memory. 'The client is Mr Robert Groobelaar, a real estate agent, originally from South Africa. He has a company called Trident Real Estate. His personal assistant was found murdered in her apartment last night. A young girl. Good-looking.' Marian pushed a glossy photo across the desk. It showed a smiling girl with a pale blonde bob that fell just below her jaw.

Wow. A murder case.

Mak felt a weird mix of sadness and a rush of excitement. This was more than the usual domestic dispute or corporate espionage case. She pulled a large notepad out of her backpack and wrote down the details. *Trident Real Estate. Robert Groobelaar . . .*

'Her name?'

Marian closed her eyes again. 'Meaghan Wallace – he says she was unmarried, no children, twenty-three years of age,' she explained. 'She worked for him for about the past six months. I'll get my contacts to run off a file for you with her stats.'

Mak wrote it all down. 'Okay.'

'The police have a suspect in custody. The client wants to know everything you can get on him.'

'No problem.' A few background checks would not take a lot of time. Marian had great contacts she could rely on to get leads on up-to-date information. A fair number of Marian's investigations were to find missing persons – runaway teenagers, AWOL spouses, deadbeat dads, that sort of thing. Record checks on any vehicles, leases, mortgages or change-of-address applications in their names were invaluable in revealing not only a person's whereabouts but a lot about their lifestyle and habits as well. If this subject was in jail already, though, Mak couldn't see how she would be needed for more than two or three days of work at the most. Given Marian's magical and somewhat mysterious contacts, there would be little for her to do.

'The client wants a complete report on the suspect's background, and what the case is against him.'

Ah. The case against him. Was Mak expected to lean on her police contacts to learn about the case?

'Do you know the kind of outcome he is searching for?' Mak said. 'Perhaps to get the information he feels the police don't have, or aren't telling him?'

Marian looked up. 'I would say so,' she said. 'He wants everything you can get.'

So he feels dissatisfied by the way the police are approaching the investigation . . .

Mak shifted awkwardly in her chair. 'Um, Marian, I didn't get the job because I have police contacts, did I?'

'You got the job because you are turning into a good investigator,' Marian said.

Mak smiled at the compliment.

'Who has good contacts,' she added sharply. 'Nearly all of my investigators have police contacts of some kind, Mak. No one is expecting you to jeopardise your relationships for an investigation. That would be counterproductive.'

Mak nodded. 'Okay,' she said, though she still wondered if those relationships were the main reason she had been chosen. Her ties to the police – to both her lover, Andy, and her friend Detective Mahoney – might give her an advantage in a case like this, but if either of them helped her out with information and was discovered, it could put their careers at serious risk. So far, she had not considered exploiting them for that kind of help.

Marian slid a piece of paper with a name and address on it across the desk. 'The client took his PA to a party on Wednesday night and that was the last he saw of her. Yesterday she left him a message that worried him. That was the last anyone seems to have heard from her. The client thinks she might have gone home with someone who was there called Simon Aston. He wants you to check him out.'

Sounds like a jealous lover to me.

'Where was the party on Wednesday night?' Mak asked, her pen poised.

'He wouldn't say.'

Mak frowned. 'He wouldn't say, or he didn't say?'

'He wouldn't say,' Marian repeated.

'Well, do I get to meet the client? Ask him a few more questions?' Mak asked eagerly. She was new to the business of private investigation, but it seemed to her that she could get a lot more information if she just talked to the client directly.

'No. As far as he is concerned you don't even know his name, so there are to be no mentions of him and no contacting him. He is paranoid about his confidentiality.'

'Oh,' Mak replied, disappointed. She thought for a moment. 'Is he married?' She suspected a guilty affair with the deceased.

'Yes,' Marian answered, but failed to add any juicy personal details. 'Mak, stop analysing the client. That's not your job.'

Mak smiled. *Sorry.*

'There's more.' Marian closed her eyes again as she continued to speak. It was one of her unusual quirks that she spoke this way – eyes closed – when recalling details of a case or a conversation. It was rumoured that she had a photographic memory. Mak sometimes found this mannerism of Marian's unsettling. She never knew where to look. The tops of her boss's lavender-painted eyelids? The desktop? 'The client wants everything you can get on the victim's life in the weeks leading up to her murder – her close contacts, secret lovers – everything, and any relationship she might have been having with this Simon Aston, any contact they had with one another.'

Mak nodded. She was beginning to see why it would take a week. In fact, it would probably take longer with that kind of field work. 'That's a lot to cover.'

'He has you on retainer for a week, all expenses. Get everything you can.'

This was definitely Mak's biggest job to date. With any luck she would be able to tuck another couple of grand into her savings account soon. 'Does he want photographs, a log of the guy's activities, anything like that? Does he want this Simon Aston followed, or does he just want information?'

'Information. He already knows Aston and what he looks like. Follow him if it helps, but the client isn't asking for surveillance.'

He just wants to know if the guy was banging her. And maybe if the suspect was too. I get it.

'No problem. What do we know about the guy in custody?'

'His name is Tobias Murphy,' Marian said.

'Where are they holding him, do we know?'

'He's in juvey.'

Mak was surprised. 'Really? He's underage?' That might blow her theory on the victim having an affair with the murder suspect. Maybe.

'It seems so. The boy has some priors, according to the client. That's what the police told him, anyway.'

Getting records of any convictions on a juvenile was tricky.

'I don't want to ask too many stupid questions here but if the police already have a suspect in custody, why does the client want it all investigated? Did he say?' Mak asked.

Marian's sharp hazel eyes opened. 'It's not our job to wonder why we have been hired. The client is happy to pay your rate for at least a week, possibly more. It's legit work. That's all we need to know. He is particularly paranoid about confidentiality, are you clear? So you didn't get his details from me.'

'Yeah.'

'*Particularly paranoid,*' Marian repeated, as if she had read Mak's thoughts.

'If he didn't want me to know who he was, then why did you tell me?'

Marian smiled slyly. 'Because I knew the first thing you would do was waste his paying time figuring out who hired you.'

Mak laughed. Marian was right.

'So now you know. Go do your job.'

'One last thing . . .'

'Yes?'

'You said the victim left the client "a message that worried him". What was the message?' Makedde asked.

'Yesterday Meaghan called his private line to apologise to him that she wasn't feeling well and couldn't come in to work. She said that someone at the party had drugged her, and she also said she had something important she wanted to tell him.'

Something important . . .

'She never got the chance to tell him. Groobelaar wasn't at work – he missed the day and only heard the message when he got to work this morning, right before learning of her murder.'

Mak narrowed her eyes. *And it didn't take him long to decide to look up a private investigation agency.*

'Okay. I'm on it,' Mak said, her mind brimming with unanswered questions. She needed to find out everything she could about Tobias Murphy and Meaghan Wallace, and her first stop would be the simple, unglamorous basics: the local telephone directory and the wonders of the internet.

CHAPTER 6

MAYBE SHE LIKED the water. She just wanted to touch it.

Tobias Murphy felt boneless and anaemic, his flesh trembling uncontrollably in a way that made his teeth chatter. He could not sleep. He held his arms close to try to stop the shaking, shaking, shaking – but the shaking wouldn't stop.

Why won't it stop?

'Krista!'

Memories leaped forwards into the space where Tobias's thoughts should have been. Instead of the white room he was trapped in, he saw scenes of his childhood in washed-out colours and grainy shapes, like an old colourised movie, scratched and decaying. Fading. The voices sounded tinny. He heard his mother calling out for her two-year-old niece, Krista. '*Krista?*' He saw the linoleum of the kitchen floor, and he saw the cupboard handles that came up to his chest. Crawling, he hid under a kitchen chair and wrapped his arms around the wooden crossbars, his chubby legs sticking out straight. He saw a scab, poking out under a curling sticking plaster on his shin, and he picked at it. His mother came back into the kitchen, still looking, still searching. '*Krista?*' He crawled over and tugged on her long skirt, but she didn't say anything. He clung to the fabric, his small white fingers disappearing into the colourful pattern of flowers.

'Krista, sweetheart? Where are you?' his mother called out. She stood for a moment, and he clung, his face resting on her knee.

'*Krista!*'

Her voice changed when she saw the backyard swimming pool. She flinched, covered her mouth, then tore away from him. Tobias's little fingertips lost their grip on her. In a whirl of linen flowers she was out the back door and running down the path towards the swimming pool. Tobias walked out after his mum in time to see her poised at the edge, her face drained of all colour.

And then she dived in.

Tobias had fought long and hard to keep those recollections away, but he was weak now, the shaking wouldn't stop and he couldn't fight it. Krista was somewhere near the bottom – not moving, not breathing – and that was bad, so very bad. Tobias didn't understand what it meant but it was a bad, bad, bad thing that had happened, and nothing would ever be the same.

Stop!

The cold, wet hands of Krista Garrison were

on his shaking ankles – still two years old, cada-verous and caught in her tiny youth.

Stop!

Tobias opened his stinging eyes in a panic. Of course she wasn't there. He was met instead with a vision of institutional white: starched white sheets, white walls, white floors scrubbed clean with disinfectant, and a white door with a small murky window, lined with cell bars.

Tobias's body was slick with a heavy sweat, fighting against an unseen force, the shaking and perspiring said to be his body's way of flushing the enemy out of his system. But the enemy was still there, omnipresent and omnipotent – in the room, in the walls, filling every sweating pore, inhabiting every tiny cell and playing these tricks on his mind. Making the shaking, shaking, shaking, and making him remember.

What did they know? *WHAT DID THEY KNOW?*

All this was doing was bringing Krista back, and his mother, who wouldn't get out of bed any more, wouldn't feed him in the morning, wouldn't help him dress. His mother who was there but not. Shaking, shaking, shaking. She was gone to him. It was bad, so bad, and things were never the same.

What did they know about what was best for him?

WHAT DID THEY KNOW?

Things were never going to be the same.

CHAPTER 7

AT ONE-FORTY on Friday afternoon Simon Aston stood nervously at the street corner of the Ravesi bar and hotel at Bondi Beach, still hoping that Warwick O'Connor would show up to see him. He'd been waiting around for nearly an hour, growing increasingly tense. Warwick, the small-time thug Simon had falsely believed would be easy to control, was now nowhere to be found; and, worse, he was not answering Simon's calls.

Simon was panicking.

Come on, you prick, pick up your goddamned phone.

In Simon's briefcase was $20 000 and change. All in cash. He'd already stashed away the $15 000 extra. If Warwick showed, that twenty grand would be all his, and hopefully it would sway him from taking any steps towards making Simon further regret having ever hired him.

Simon paced back and forth along the pavement. He dialled Warwick again.

Pick up, pick up.

'Hello.'

'Warwick, you're there,' he said, relieved. 'It's me, Simon.'

'Do you have it?'

Simon smiled, and made his voice as friendly as he could. 'I have a lot of cash right here waiting for you, pal. I'm at the Ravesi, like I said I would be. Come on down and we'll have a chat.'

'You have the full mill?'

Simon hesitated.

'You and I have nothing to chat about if you don't have the money,' Warwick said.

Simon's throat tightened. He licked his lips. 'Man, just come on down. I got a heap of cash for you. We'll work something out.'

There was a pause.

'I know what this is worth. If you can't get what I want, I will have to go to the big man …'

'No, don't, don't,' Simon pleaded, becoming desperate.

Oh fuck … he wouldn't really, would he?

'No, man, don't do that. Just come on down and we'll chat –'

The phone went dead.

CHAPTER 8

MAKEDDE STRODE UP the moving escalator of the massive, upscale Bondi Junction shopping centre, her backpack and leather jacket slung over one shoulder and a folder of information in her hand. At least here in the mall the looks she got in her motorbike gear were more of curiosity or admiration than suspicion. One teenage boy with studs through his face gave her a nod of approval. Like her, he was wearing leather trousers. She winked at him playfully as she moved past him on the escalator, nudging his ribcage with her helmet.

Mak was a couple of minutes early for her customary late lunch with Loulou. The food court that she and her girlfriend frequented was on the top floor of the complex. It did not offer the usual subterranean, greasy fast-food stuff that Mak could only tolerate if she was hungover. Instead this was a stylish new space, with an open plan, lots of windows, mountains of fresh food and a good sushi bar – something like the healthy places that she used to frequent near her university in Vancouver, the ones with organic tags all over everything. On the flip side, there was the drawcard of a certain warm chocolate fountain they were both addicted to. Like something out of *Charlie and the Chocolate Factory*, the fountain was made of pure melted chocolate, flowing luxuriously in wait for the next chocoholic to take a cupful. Mak resisted the pull to the chocolate fountain until her friend arrived. She found a spot at one of the sleek tables, where she could pore over the info she was compiling for her investigation. Mak had trolled the directory databases and tracked down the addresses and telephone numbers for Noelene and Ralph Wallace – the parents of the victim, the deceased Meaghan Wallace – and the very alive Simon Aston. There had been no listings for the suspect, Tobias Murphy, probably because he was far too young to have anything listed in his own name. Mak had not yet had time to do a full internet or newspaper archive search on any of them – she would get to that after her lunch break with Loulou.

While Mak had been running checks through the directory, finding things that any Jo Blo could look up if they really wanted to and knew how, Marian had pulled valuable statistical info for her with awe-inspiring ease, thanks to informants in various government departments whom she had nurtured relationships with over her many years of investigations. And in what must have been two or three phone calls she'd got a pretty good run-down on the suspect's criminal record as well, even though he was a juvenile – all without Mak needing to lean on any of her precious police contacts. Mak felt slightly embarrassed about her little outburst earlier. She had a lot to learn, and she knew it.

Mak opened the file, and began with the young murder suspect: *Tobias Alexander Murphy*.

Tobias was only sixteen years old. Born in Sydney. His mother was recently deceased, his father long since remarried. Mak dared not ask how Marian had found the next bit of information, which was protected for those under-eighteens who'd had a brush or two with the law, so that their earlier mistakes didn't hinder their entire adult lives. The police had been straight with Mak's client, Mr Groobelaar, about the suspect. The young Tobias had a list of priors, all right: minor thefts, drug possession and even loitering. She noticed he didn't have any violent offence charges to his name until now, though.

Murder is a big step up from loitering.

On paper, Tobias was the very embodiment of a lost teen. Not exactly a classic murder suspect, but he certainly qualified as a sufficiently unpredictable troubled youth. He'd been kicked out of a number of schools for disruptive behaviour, and been unsuccessfully enrolled in several youth programs. His recent history was tainted by apparent homelessness, which further explained why there was no listing for him in the phone book. Mak suspected that he must have committed many more thefts than the handful he had been busted for over the years. How else could he possibly have survived on the streets, if that was indeed where he was living?

However, his history of lawlessness was not the only thing Mak thought her client might find of interest. Tobias had been put in his first foster home at only four years of age, and between the ages of four and fourteen he had stayed in not one but nine different foster homes. *Nine.* That was about one a year. Both of his biological parents had been alive until his mother's death two years ago. Why had no family members stepped in to take care of him? Why was Tobias shuffled around so relentlessly, or what was it that he hated so much about his carers that he was constantly running away?

Then, incredibly, for nearly two years there was nothing on him at all. No contact with the law. No contact with support services, teachers, foster carers. No record of address. No contact with his living father. Had he slipped through the cracks at the tender age of fourteen? How could that have happened? How could someone that young just disappear in a developed country like Australia?

Where did you go? How did you survive for that long, Tobias?

And now that he had been found again, it was as a suspect for murder.

Mak didn't get much more of a chance to

ponder the facts in greater depth before a flash of colour diverted her attention away from her reading. A young woman with bleached blonde mohawk-like hair – every strand gelled to a cockatoo peak in the centre – was bounding towards the food court wearing a tartan miniskirt, chunky purple fishnets and a cropped jacket with enormous bell sleeves. She was a veritable moving lecture in Björk dressing.

Loulou.

Mak was still relatively new to Sydney, and as anyone who has relocated abroad knows, finding trustworthy friends in a new city is not a quick task. Thankfully, Mak had met Loulou years before when she was modelling, and bit by bit Loulou had turned into a great girlfriend. When Loulou wasn't painting the faces of the beautiful or the famous for photo shoots or rock videos, she was waiting for her artists' agency to call her for her next booking – and there had been a lot of waiting by the phone lately, from what Mak could tell. That was a predicament they both had in common for the moment. Work for Loulou was usually dead slow in January and February each year, so she had developed the habit of taking the bus into Bondi Junction to peruse the shops at the sprawling shopping centre, passing the time by looking at style magazines in the shops or staring lustfully at the designer displays for Bettina Liano, Morrissey and Versace, unable to afford the clothes – a kind of retail therapy without the actual retail transaction. And the shopping centre was just a few blocks from Marian's office, so Mak and Loulou's lunch dates at the food court were long and frequent, as was the ritualistic cup dip into that deliciously naughty chocolate fountain. A few more weeks of this and Mak was convinced that she wouldn't be able to fit into her leathers any more.

'Over here, Loulou,' Mak said, waving her arms.

'Sweetie!' Loulou cried out, and then embraced Makedde enthusiastically, her mohawk vibrating. They might have appeared like long-lost, albeit slightly mismatched, sisters reunited after decades apart. No one would have guessed that they had seen each other in the same food court barely a week earlier.

'How are you?' Mak asked, extracting herself from Loulou's paws.

'I am *fabulous!*' The mohawk shook again.

I'll have whatever she's having, Mak thought. *How can she always be so full of energy?*

Loulou was a wild young woman with a heart as big as the Australian sky, and she was someone Mak had grown close to during some fairly recent trying times. Anyone who would stay up until four in the morning to hold Mak's hair back, as she vomited from an excess of cocktails and nerves the night before she was to be a witness in the Stiletto Murder trial, was a true friend. In fact, that was probably the turning point for them. Loulou had graduated from crazy friend to confidante and saviour that night.

'Fabulous?' Mak said. 'That sounds pretty good. Where do you get a dose of fabulous these days?' A bit of that Loulou enthusiasm would be good for the spirit.

'Awww, are you worried about Andy leaving tomorrow?'

'Nah, it's fine,' Mak said, not entirely truthfully.

'I have great news!' Loulou exclaimed. She was simply bursting, as was so often the case. Mak hoped the news was in relation to a great new job, or a sudden windfall that would help cover Loulou's rent. When it came to financial difficulties, Mak's concerns about opening her practice paled in comparison to Loulou's woes. Loulou had a credit card debt of over forty grand, and she hadn't paid off her humble 'dag-mobile' car either. She could use every bit of good luck she could find.

Loulou gripped Mak's hands across the tabletop. 'I met someone!' she cried, practically before her bottom had hit the chair.

Mak took her seat. 'Oh, well that's good,' she responded cautiously. She'd heard this before, too many times to count. Sadly, previous exclamations of this kind from Loulou had always ended in tears.

'He's the frontman in a band called 'Electric Possum'. He's soooo cute,' Loulou gushed enthusiastically. Her idea of cute was usually a greasy young man covered in tattoos, holding a microphone and smoking a joint.

'What's his name?' Mak dared to ask.

'Drayson,' Loulou purred.

'Jason. That's nice.'

'No, Drayson,' Loulou corrected her.

'His first name?' Mak asked.

'Is Drayson, yeah. We're moving in together.'

'What!'

Where did this guy suddenly come from?

Mak had seen Loulou last week and there was no cute singer in the picture then.

'He's really nice,' her friend continued, apparently unaware that she had slipped into lust-induced romantic insanity. Mak wondered fleetingly if this guy was even aware that they were moving in together.

'Hang on, hang on. Walk me through this. When did you meet this guy?' Mak pressed, trying to put the brakes on just a bit, in her friend's best interests.

'At that 16DD gig at the Annandale Hotel.' The Annandale was one of Loulou's usual rock hangouts. 'It went off!'

'Wasn't that gig on last weekend?' Mak asked, confused.

'Yeah.'

Right. 'So … you're talking about moving in with a guy you met a few days ago?' she said, just to clarify.

'A week ago, yeah,' Loulou corrected her.

'Six days,' Mak corrected in return.

'He needs a room-mate and I do, too,' Loulou said, as if the logic was obvious.

Mak nodded slowly. 'Okay. A room-mate would be great, but how about you put an ad up somewhere? You're close to the university. I'm sure lots of students would respond. You'd have a roomie in a week. Or one of your friends might need a place. Have you asked around?'

'Drayson *is* a friend.'

'How about someone who is *just* a friend?'

Loulou just went on smiling and ignored Mak's logical suggestion.

'Do you want me to step in here?' Mak persisted, starting to feel like a stick-in-the-mud. 'I don't mean to dampen your mood, but didn't you tell me that you were going to ban yourself from musicians for a while? Wasn't that your New Year's resolution?'

'Oh yeah.'

'I think you said something like, "Just stop me if I start showing interest in another muso …"'

It was February and it seemed like a lot of resolutions had already been forgotten – like Mak's vow to stop analysing her friend and her relationships. So much for that.

'Yeah. I think I did make that resolution,' Loulou admitted.

Good. Mak was not imagining the conversation. 'We had that chat not all that long ago,' she pointed out. 'Two months ago, maybe.'

'But Drayson is not just "some musician". He's special. Trust me.'

Mak did trust Loulou – she trusted her with her life, in fact. But she didn't trust Loulou with her *own* life.

'Okay, tell me all about Mr Special while we grab some sushi,' Mak said, relenting. 'I'm starving.'

Loulou threw her coat over the chair and got up. Her shirt was emblazoned with the words YES, BUT NOT WITH YOU. The two of them made a beeline for the sushi bar and loaded up on California rolls and sashimi.

Their miso soups were being prepared when Loulou said, 'Apparently he has this *fabulous* pad in Melbourne that he shares with an artist friend. So I'll move down and –'

'*Melbourne!* Did you say he lives in *Melbourne?*'

Loulou nodded.

Melbourne was about a thousand kilometres from Sydney, but it could have been 100 000 kilometres given the way most Sydneysiders talked about it. Mak had been reliably informed that it was a place where people wore black and clutched umbrellas in the heaving rain, trapped in a bleak and eternal winter with no nightlife and no respite.

Mak decided to deal with the situation logically. She leaned against the counter with her tray, and spoke slowly. 'But, Loulou, you live in *Sydney*. Why would you want to move to a whole different state six days after meeting a man who happens to be a musician, which happens to be exactly the kind of guy you vowed to give up not two months ago? You haven't seen the place. You don't even know this guy. He could be some kind of psycho.'

'I know, I know,' Loulou said, grabbing her miso soup and toddling back to the table. 'But he *is* really cute.'

There was no way to fight Loulou Logic.

Mak took some solace in the fact that this boy could quite possibly be forgotten by nightfall, and Mak would never hear about him – or her much-needed best friend moving to Melbourne – ever again. She couldn't lose Andy to Quantico *and* Loulou to Melbourne. That would be a disaster.

They took their seats and started sipping at their soups. Loulou fished around in hers for a mouthful of seaweed and tofu. 'I'm going down tomorrow.'

'You're going tomorrow! Great.'

'I won't have time to pack all my stuff so I will just spend the weekend down there. We can't stand to be apart.'

'Well, you seemed to survive apart just fine before six days ago,' Mak muttered. *Thank God she hasn't given notice on her apartment right away*, she thought.

'I gave notice at my apartment, but I have to pay the lease until the fifteenth,' Loulou

103

continued. 'Why don't you come down with me? We'll have fun!'

Mak put down her chopsticks and stared at her friend. She didn't know what to say.

Please tell me this will last two weeks. Or one week. Please.

'Come down this weekend and meet him. We would have a blast tearing it up in Mel-boring!'

'Sorry, Loulou,' Mak said. 'I have to work.'

'Awww, please? You have to meet him!'

'What's the rush? If you two are going to move in together, I'll have plenty of time to meet him. Maybe I'll meet him at your wedding next month ...'

Loulou squealed with laughter.

Truthfully, Mak didn't want to think about the possibility of her friend moving interstate; she could literally count her true friends in Sydney on her thumbs. It was depressing. She changed the subject. 'I'm seeing your friend Brenda again this afternoon.'

Loulou had asked – no, pleaded – for Mak to see Brenda Bale, a woman who had a few psychological issues she wanted to work through. They had a session for an hour every Friday in Mak's living room. Loulou had seen Mak at her worst and stood by her as a true friend, and so when Loulou had begged her to talk to this woman as a 'huge favour', Mak had caved in, agreeing to a session or two.

So far it had been every Friday for *nine weeks*.

'Oh! I can't thank you enough,' Loulou squealed again. 'Brenda says it is sooooo helpful. Really. It's helping her big-time.'

'I feel like a bit of a fraud, you know. She would probably benefit a lot more from seeing a real therapist.'

'But you are a shrink,' Loulou said, confused.

'Yes, but I don't specialise in the right field. She needs a ... *different* kind of psychologist. Trust me.'

'It's helping her so much, though. She's really grateful.'

Mak wasn't charging Brenda for the weekly sessions, although truthfully she could use every cent she could scrape together.

The friends downed a few pieces of California roll and fought over the last piece of inari.

'I got a new assignment today. An investigation,' Mak said with a slight smile. It was exciting – an assignment just big enough to feel like a real job.

Loulou sat forward, extra-attentive. 'So what is it? What are you working on?' She gestured to the file. 'T-o-b-i-a-s M-u-r-p-h-y' she read upside down off the folder.

'I just got it today, so I only have the most basic details. It's confidential, of course, so I can't say much.' Mak pulled the folder away from Loulou's prying eyes.

Loulou worked away on another California roll and her can of soft drink. 'Come on. I would love to go on one of your stakeouts. *Pleeease?* I'm sure I could help!'

'Loulou.'

'Please? I think it is so cool that I have a friend who's a PI.'

Mak rolled her eyes.

'Well! What is it? Another bastard cheating on his wife? Are you gonna nail him?'

Mak smiled. 'Actually, it's not a marital case this time at all. It's a bit more interesting ...'

CHAPTER 9

THE PHONE CALL came to Jack Cavanagh's city office just after two.

Joy Fregon, Jack Cavanagh's loyal secretary, put the call through. 'Mr Cavanagh, there is a man on line one who wants to speak to you. He won't give his name and he says that he doesn't want an appointment.' She sounded a touch anxious, which was out of character for her.

Jack shook his head. 'Well, tell him to go away,' he said impatiently.

'Um, Mr Cavanagh, he says he wants to speak to you *about Damien*.' She paused. 'I wonder what you would like me to do?'

Jack sat forwards in his leather chair, brow furrowed. *What in God's name has my son done now?* A jet drifted through the blue sky outside his window, the city bustling on the streets far below. He shifted, contemplating what to do.

'That's okay, Joy,' he finally replied. 'Put him through.'

'Yes, Mr Cavanagh,' she said.

Jack braced himself for some unpleasantness.

He picked up the receiver and pressed the flashing line button. 'This is Jack Cavanagh.'

'We have some business to discuss,' came a muffled voice down the line.

'To whom am I speaking?'

'I'm the man who is doing a favour for your son,' came the response.

'Is that so?'

'The favour is that I am coming to you first. I am giving you a chance to make me happy before I go to the press.'

Jack tensed and sat up in his chair. *Go to the press with what?*

'Your son has some rather unsavoury private activities. I think you will want these activities of his to *remain* private.'

Blackmail. This arsehole thinks he's going to blackmail me.

Jack's eyes narrowed. It wasn't the first time he had been threatened. Men like this made him furious – men who wanted something for nothing because they were too damned lazy to do the work for themselves.

'And what activities should I be discussing with a man too cowardly to even tell me his name?' Jack demanded angrily. Though he was listening carefully, he did not recognise the man's voice. However, he thought he detected a very slight Irish accent mixed with his typical Australian sounds.

There was no response.

Jack waited through a few seconds of silence. 'I am hanging up the phone now –'

'I don't think you should do that, *Jack*,' came the voice on the line.

Jack didn't much care for the tone, or the address. Apart from family, very few people called Cavanagh senior 'Jack'. In fact, every single person who worked for him called him 'Mr Cavanagh'. Even Joy, who had worked for him for thirty-one years, did not presume to call him by his first name.

'I'm waiting,' Jack said.

'I'll cut to the chase. I have an incriminating video of your son with an underaged girl who is now in the morgue. You won't want anyone else seeing this footage. All it will take is two million dollars to make me happy and I will forget all about it. Me and this problem will go away,' the stranger said. 'Two million dollars is cheap as chips for a man of your means.'

Jack took in the information with a mixture of scepticism and concern. His son was a disappointment, but this might be beneath even Damien's capabilities.

'Why should I believe you?' Jack asked the man coolly.

'Ask your son if he has anything to hide,' was the ominous response. 'I'll give you until this time tomorrow to think about it. If you don't meet the price, I know I will get plenty from the media for it. They will like this story, I think.'

'That's enough,' said the older man. 'How will I contact you?'

'You won't.'

He hung up in Jack Cavanagh's ear.

Jack held the phone out from his head, then placed it slowly back in its cradle. He pulled open the top drawer of his desk and extracted a rolled Cuban cigar from a small box, cut the tip and lit it. The cigar had been intended for celebrating the transportation contract, but now he needed it to think. For ten minutes Jack sat in his leather chair with his arms crossed, intermittently puffing on the Cuban and watching the clouds outside his high window. When he was done collecting his thoughts, he pulled his private phone over and dialled.

'Hello, Bob? It's Jack. I was wondering if you might swing by my office ...'

CHAPTER 10

'IT'S THE ONLY time I feel *alive* ...'

At four forty-nine on Friday afternoon, Makedde Vanderwall sat in her living room across from Loulou's friend Brenda Bale, listening to the complicated, flame-haired woman wrestle with psychological self-examination. Mak shifted on the sofa, wearing the plain black pantsuit she used on such occasions – a kind of psychologist's uniform, she thought. Her thoughts drifted a little: Andy's trip; his new job; her dad's new life in Canada with his girlfriend, Ann; Loulou's crazy infatuation with yet another muso.

The terrace house Mak and Andy shared was old – built in the early 1900s – and it sometimes had a faint musty smell that Mak couldn't escape. She watched the sunlight that came through the old bay window. The sun's rays moved subtly, striking objects and casting shadows; everything changing, the world in flux.

'... like I wouldn't even exist without it.'

Mak nodded and waited for Brenda to continue.

This was their ninth session, but Mak was not at all confident that their hours together had been effective. The main problem was that Mak was a forensic psychologist – and not even a practising one – and she did not specialise in this sort of work. The kind of therapy-based sessions that Brenda required were more suited to a clinical psychologist like her father's girlfriend, Dr Ann Morgan, or perhaps even the famed sex therapist Dr Ruth.

'You exist right now, Brenda. You are here. You are alive,' Mak responded, stating the all-important obvious.

'I know, I know. You're right,' Brenda said. She bit her lip, giving her canines a vampire-like look as she stained them with bright red lipstick.

'You feel empowered in the role-play scenario,' Mak said.

'Yes,' Brenda conceded.

That was no surprise. Brenda Bale, as it had turned out, worked several evenings a week as a highly paid bondage mistress. She arrived at Mak's house each Friday afternoon smartly dressed: suit, heels and matching handbag, hair slicked back in a ponytail, the very picture of corporate style. The only hint as to Brenda's clandestine work activities was her unnaturally bright red dyed hair and scarlet lips – hence the name she used for work, Mistress Scarlet. It had taken Mak until their second session to clue into this pertinent information, which appeared to be quite relevant to Brenda's concerns. Loulou had not informed Mak of this, but, knowing her mohawked friend, Mak was hardly surprised that Brenda Bale had an unconventional career. Everyone Loulou knew seemed to be unconventional.

'But there are other ways you can feel empowered outside of your work. We have spoken before about this,' Mak reminded her.

Brenda Bale was a youthful and sexual forty-two, intelligent and successful in her trade. She had previously worked in a well-known bondage–dominance house called The Tower, but now operated from home, where she had the necessary accoutrements and a dedicated 'slave' named Julio who guarded her safety. But Brenda had grown increasingly concerned that she was becoming 'less Brenda and more Mistress Scarlet' with each passing day. Makedde now suggested that taking her work home might have caused this psychological shift, blurring the lines between Brenda Bale and Mistress Scarlet until the more dominant of the two was taking over.

Brenda shook her head at Mak's comment, seemingly frustrated with herself, her bright red ponytail flipping back and forth. 'I tried joining one of those rock-climbing classes you suggested and I just felt so out of place,' she said, exasperated.

'That's okay. It may take a while for you to find activities that connect with you outside of the role you play in your work life. The more dedication you give to developing activities and friendships in your personal life, the more fulfilling your personal life is likely to become. It's like anything else: the more you put in, the more you get back.'

'I know ... you're right ...'

'Give some more thought to what we've discussed,' Mak said, wrapping up.

'Oh yes, thank you. I will,' the red lips responded.

It was now ten to five and the fifty-minute hour of the psychologist was up.

'I hope you have found our sessions helpful. You know, this is not my area of expertise. I still suggest that if this issue remains unresolved, you would really benefit from speaking to a specialist in the area. I would be able to get the name of someone for you.'

'I know, I know,' Brenda responded. 'I really do appreciate our talks, though.' Brenda stood and straightened her suit. She looked to Mak, and the arched eyebrows lifted in a sincere expression. 'You've helped me so much. You're really good.' She leaned in to give a hearty handshake.

I am?

'I won't impose on you much longer, I promise. But I really feel we are getting somewhere. I feel I'm close to a breakthrough,' Brenda continued, bringing her smooth pale hands to her sides and making determined fists.

Mak hoped she was right. She couldn't afford to keep doing this for free for ever.

'If there is ever anything I can do for you, let me know,' Brenda continued. 'And I mean *anything*. I have all kinds of friends who owe me favours,' she said.

Mak didn't venture to think what kind of favours might be returned.

She saw Brenda out, bade her farewell for another week and closed the door behind her. She locked it.

Mak walked back and looked around the living room. It was furnished with a plush sofa-and-chair set she didn't particularly like, and a handsome oak table she had covered in photo frames and books. She had ushered out a bouquet of dead flowers just prior to Brenda's arrival and now she noticed that a stem of pollen had fallen on the carpet, making a small bright yellow stain.

'Oops.'

Makedde hurried to the kitchen and returned with a damp soapy cloth to try to fix the carpet. She got on her knees and scrubbed away at the stubborn mark. Slowly, the pollen's colour faded. Hunched down like that, Mak's eyes were level to the low table, and her focus rested on a small framed photo she liked of her widowed father, Les, and his girlfriend, backdropped by the familiar doorstep of the Canadian west coast home of her youth. At the sight of it her mouth curved upwards in the sad, sentimental smile of those who have strayed far from home.

Dad.

She blinked.

She frowned.

This wasn't how she had imagined things would be when she left Canada. It had been eighteen months since Mak had finished her PhD and postgraduate studies, one of only a handful of PhD grads that year who were already in their late twenties. A slew of personal and family crises had at one point made her feel like she would never get there. However, despite all the obstacles put in her way, she'd made it this far. But this wasn't a practice: this was chatting with an identity-conflicted bondage mistress for an hour a week.

So Mak's existence in Sydney wasn't quite what she had planned – and her being with a cop was not what her father had wanted.

You warned me he'd never be home.

The yellow pollen stain was now more faint, but it wouldn't come out completely. Mak didn't know what else she could do. These little household spills and stains were the kind of things mums automatically knew how to fix, but Mak was clueless in these areas, and she didn't have a mum to call.

Mak wisely sensed that her thoughts were spiralling into unproductive territory. As she often did in such circumstances, she abandoned them in favour of work activity.

Meaghan Wallace.

She made for her laptop, which was plugged in and ready for her on the dining-room table, a spot she often used as an impromptu office. Mak sat down and unbuttoned her suit jacket. She threw it over the chair, unsnapped her bra with one hand and pulled it off from underneath her black singlet. Now comfortable, she got to work.

One of the first things Mak had learned about investigation work was that a valuable part of the inquiry into a person's background could be done online. Some good cyber-sleuthing often saved a lot of field work down the track.

She had three names to check up on: Meaghan Wallace, Simon Aston and Tobias Murphy. And while she was at it, she might just spend a minute or two finding out a few things about her secretive client, Robert Groobelaar, and his company. It wasn't part of her job, but it couldn't hurt to get a better idea of where he was coming from.

These days the vast majority of people under fifty – university students, board members, people in every imaginable type of interest group, bloggers, photo-mad personal website posters and anyone with a passing moment in the public eye – left their mark on the internet. A simple Google search could bring up all kinds of gems.

Mak began with the murder victim, Meaghan.

MEAGHAN WALLACE. SEARCH.

Mak frowned. Google showed remarkably little on 'Meaghan Wallace'.

MEAGAN WALLACE. SEARCH.

The change of spelling showed many entries on various Meagan Wallaces that were sadly nothing near Meaghan's match.

Damn.

She tried again.

MEG WALLACE. SEARCH.

There were a lot of hits. Millions. And most of them looked useless. Mak checked the option for Australian pages only, and that narrowed down the listings, but there were still too many. Mak tried the image search instead. It came up with brunettes, redheads, the wrong blondes, some men, and even a labrador retriever.

On the third page of Meg Wallace image results, the search brought up a single photo of the same Meg Mak was after. She felt a small rush of excitement when her eyes fixed on the familiar face.

Bingo.

The image source was a website for a Sydney nightclub called The Rocking Horse. Mak clicked on it.

The caption read: JAG LESLIE, MEG WALLACE AND AMY CAMILLERI ENJOY THE ROCKING HORSE NYE CELEBRATIONS.

It was definitely Meaghan. She and her friends were sexily dressed in the photo, wearing lycra crop tops and mini-dresses. Meg's tiny shirt had the word 'TRINITY' printed across the chest. It was a photo clearly taken after dark – all three of them had red-eye from the flash. The club was near black behind them, but the camera had picked up a glinting disco ball, some reflecting lights and the backs of various clubbers dancing away, oblivious to the camera.

Jag Leslie and Amy Camilleri. They could be close friends of Meaghan's. Mak would track them down. She had a thought about the T-shirt, too. Maybe it was a company or a club Meaghan had worked for?

TRINITY. SEARCH.

Mak's computer came up with millions of Holy Trinity biblical sites and fan sites for Carrie-Anne Moss's character in the *Matrix* series.

It's probably nothing.

Mak didn't have access to Marian's professional directories or contacts from home, so she went to her simple dog-eared phone book and looked up Jag Leslie first. Surely there couldn't be that many Jags out there who weren't automobiles. If Jag had been a good friend of Meaghan's, she might know something about who the girl had been seeing and what she had been up to before her murder. Perhaps even more than Meaghan's parents would know, if and when Mak could get them to talk to her.

L . . . Leslie . . . Leslie, J . . .

It was amazing how many people overlooked the simple, uncomplicated effectiveness of the common phone directory when looking for someone. In fact, a startling number of investigation cases that came into Marian's office were solved by a simple flick through the phone book and a knock on the door. Employers wanted to hunt down rogue employees, mothers wanted to hunt down exes who failed to pay child support, and much of it could be done simply by the phone book and its old slogan, 'let your fingers do the walking'. True to form, in only a few minutes Mak had come up with a number of Leslies: a slew of Jane Leslies and John Leslies, and the ones that looked like her best bet, J Leslies.

Mak phoned the first J Leslie listing, dialling #1 first to ensure that the number she was calling from was safely blocked. She dialled a J Leslie of Rose Bay, whose phone rang out until an answering machine picked up. Disappointed, Mak didn't leave a message. She couldn't leave a return number for this ring-around. She moved on to J Leslie number two.

The phone rang three times.

'Hello?'

'May I speak to Jag Leslie please?' Mak asked politely.

'Jade?'

'Sorry – I'm looking for Jag. Perhaps I have the wrong number?'

There was a dial tone.

Thank you for hanging up. That's very nice.

Mak had been hung up on many times in her work, so she wasn't offended by it – she just wished they'd warn her first. Sometimes a phone slamming down hurt her ears. Undeterred, she lifted the receiver again and called the number of J Leslie of Newtown, New South Wales. If this wasn't her, she would check through the database Marian had access to.

Someone picked up. 'Yeah?' came the answer.

'Hello, is this Jag Leslie?' Makedde asked.

'Speaking.'

Mak smiled. 'I'm calling from The Rocking Horse Nightclub. You've just been nominated for a Gold VIP pass.'

'Really? I haven't been there in like ... months.' The woman sounded genuinely surprised, and not as excited as Mak had hoped.

'Well, you must have an admirer. Your nomination has been accepted.' Mak concocted the details as she went along, trying to make the deal sound as exciting as humanly possible. She'd heard enough telephone sales lines to slip into the jargon. 'Your *exclusive* Gold VIP pass allows you free entry and two free drinks for the next twelve months, including free entry to our next New Year's Eve party.'

'But it's February.'

Come on, a little more enthusiasm, please. I'm trying here ...

'Yes. You will get to use the pass all year,' Mak replied patiently. 'Right through to January first. We need to send the pass out to you. What is the best mailing address for you?'

Jag paused. 'Um, this isn't going to cost anything, is it?'

'No,' Mak assured her. *It will only cost you a free visit from me.* 'This is an exclusive Gold VIP pass. It can't be bought.'

That statement finally seemed to work.

'Okay. Cool. My address is post office box –'

Crap.

Mak couldn't work with a post office box. 'I'm sorry,' Makedde interjected, 'we can't accept PO boxes on our database. Do you have a business or residential address I can type in?'

There was another pause.

'Okay.' Finally Jag gave out an address – hopefully her home address – and Mak gave her a spiel about how exclusive and fabulous the VIP pass was.

Mak wrote down the address, which was different to the one listed in the phone book – the phone book was never as up to date as Marian's full database system. Someone young and unattached like Jag might move every six months.

Mak would attempt to make contact on Saturday. With any luck, Jag knew Meaghan well, and would have a thing or two to say about her friend's murder.

CHAPTER 11

DAMIEN CAVANAGH DROVE his new black Diablo into the bowels of a private underground car park in Sydney's CBD, ignoring the attendant who uttered some moronic, smiling welcome from the booth as Damien coasted past with the windows up and the stereo on. Engine purring, he reverse-parked into a spot reserved for him alone – a spot that had been vacant for the three weeks since his last visit.

God, I hate coming here.

He cut the engine and stepped out wearing expensive ripped jeans, and Gucci sneakers and cap. He knew he would be the only one in the building not wearing the uniform of business, and the idea pleased him. The vehicle bleeped twice as he clicked the transponder button over his shoulder to lock it.

Damien hated driving here to the 'Cavanagh building', where his father, despite being past retirement age at sixty-seven, still insisted on working. He hated walking through the building, most often at his father's side, suffering all those sycophantic fools who actually thought Damien cared who they were and that he gave a damn about their jobs – or even his own coveted position as a company director. His father liked meeting him here to make him feel guilty about his lack of interest in the family company. He kept that parking spot reserved for Damien even though he didn't want it. He insisted that his son make appearances.

Damien hit the button for the elevator. It soon collected him. At ground level the doors opened again to take another passenger.

'Good afternoon, Mr Cavanagh.'

'Hi, Julie,' Damien said. This was the only perk he saw in his visits. He eyed the young woman with appreciation as she entered the lift and pressed her floor. She worked in marketing or something, and, more importantly to Damien, she looked tidy in a trim grey skirt suit and heels. His friend Simon had said she was looking good lately, and she was. She was part of the local scene; she'd been to the house to party a few times.

'Have you been working out?' he commented with an intentionally salacious grin. He watched her for a reaction.

Julie shifted uncomfortably under his gaze. 'Oh, not really, but thank you.' She stood in awkward silence as the elevator ascended, her left hand scrunched up as she absentmindedly touched the band of her engagement ring with her thumb.

An engagement meant nothing. Damien should know – he had been engaged for the past six months to Carolyn, a pretty but boring young woman of whom his parents approved. The engagement had not even slightly dampened his nocturnal activities; if anything, he pursued his extracurricular games with more relish, the illicit thrill heightened.

'I'm getting out here,' Julie said on the ninth floor. 'It's good to see you, Damien. Take care.'

Damien let his eyes linger over her form as she left. She'd been quite raunchy at one time, he reflected. He wondered fleetingly whether he could get her to sleep with him again.

You are Damien Cavanagh. Of course you can.

The party she'd attended at the house a couple of years earlier had involved a lot of cocaine and a hot tub full of people enjoying one another. He distinctly remembered that Julie was one of the girls he and Simon had had a threesome with. She'd liked it at the time, and from her awkward behaviour in the elevator, she remembered it too.

Soon the doors slid back to the fourteenth floor. Damien Cavanagh frowned.

Grimacing at the disdainful familiarity of his father's office reception, he shoved his hands in his jeans pockets and stepped out.

'Good afternoon, Mr Cavanagh,' came a greeting from one of the inconsequential staff.

'Good to see you, Mr Cavanagh.'

'G'day, Mr Cavanagh. Can I get you anything?'

Oh shut up, he wanted to say. *Sycophants, all of you.*

Damien sauntered darkly past the reception area and the staff who sang out their greetings to him like their scripted phone greetings.

Cavanagh Incorporated, how may I help you?

He'd hoped some of them would have left work already, but alas, they were still there, slaving away on a Friday afternoon and offering their pathetic greetings. He made his way down a hallway bedecked with sporting memorabilia: a cricket bat signed by fast bowler Brett Lee; a Sydney Swans football jersey signed by the first Grand Final-winning team in seventy-two years. He walked past his father's receptionist Joy, who stood graciously to say hello, and without knocking entered through the open door of his father's spacious office. Hands still in his pockets, he crossed the room without a word and sat in the chair opposite the vast mahogany working desk of his father, *the* Jack Cavanagh, anticipating his usual lecture about being more productive, more responsible, more befitting the mantle his father was so eager to bestow upon him. As soon as his bottom hit the chair he slid his weight to the edge, slouching casually, his legs stretched out and crossed at the ankle. He played with the frayed edge of one of the rips in his jeans.

His dad was on a phone call.

'I have to go. My son is here,' Jack told

whoever was on the line. 'Yeah, I will. Say hello to Helen and the kids for me … Yes, we had a lovely time … Yes, we'll do that. Okay, mate, speak to you soon.' Jack hung up.

'Hello, Father,' Damien said to him, not bothering to make eye contact. He looked out the window, already bored in anticipation of their discussion. These mundane 'talks' always began with some cliché like 'With privilege comes responsibility, son', and the retelling of the now-famous story of Jack Cavanagh: how he had built the Cavanagh family empire from the ground up, the son of a mere janitor; how he had bought the very building where Grandfather Cavanagh had toiled away his years to scrape together enough money to send his only son, Jack, to a good school; and how Jack had always done his best to not let his father down, to not ever take for granted how hard he had worked, how hard it was to get to the top, and what a responsibility it was to be there. And then he would tell Damien to get his act together, be more responsible, take more interest in the family company. *You are a director of this company, must I remind you? Stop being seen with a different girl every week. Stop having those outrageous parties, and be more cautious for the benefit of the Cavanagh family public image. Be kinder to your mother.*

Don't you know how much we care for you?

Damien had studied at Wharton. He'd proposed to his fiancée, Carolyn, just as his parents had wanted. What more could they possibly want of him?

Jack was looking at Damien hard, staring into the side of his head, and Damien could feel it. When he finally spoke to Damien, he was more grave than usual, and impatient. He did not start with any of the usual clichés, or the *It's time for us to have a father–son chat* bullshit.

'Damien,' Jack said, then paused. 'We need to talk about something serious. We have to be very open here. This is for you and I to discuss *openly* right now.' He got up from behind his desk and walked across the room to close his office door. When he returned to his desk, he sat in his creaking leather chair and leaned forwards. His voice was lower than usual. 'Son, a man threatened me today. I need to know what is going on,' he said tersely.

Damien looked back from the window, genuinely surprised. This was not the usual discussion. 'What ... what do you mean?'

'A man contacted me today and told me that he has a videotape of you caught in the act of doing something I would be very unhappy about, something with serious consequences for you, for us, for the company. Can you think of what that might be?'

Damien felt the blood drain from his face. So this was why his father had insisted so strongly that he come to see him immediately.

The girl from the party. Oh no ...

He withdrew his hands from his pockets and sat on them, feeling suddenly like a small boy. He tried not to appear panicked as his mind raced over the possible proof that may exist of his activities, how things might look. There was a lot that he kept from his father.

But Simon would have told me if there was a serious problem, he thought. *Simon would know. Simon had said it would be taken care of. He said he'd make it go away.*

He wanted to call Simon right away to find out what was going on.

'Dad,' Damien said, motioning to get up. 'I need to make a quick phone call –'

'*No* you don't.' The tone in his father's booming voice made Damien sit right back down in the chair.

'I just need to call Simon,' he said weakly.

'You are *not* calling that man. Now level with me, son. What happened? What is this all about?'

Damien felt anxious and claustrophobic. He wanted so badly to call Simon, but his father motioned him to put the BlackBerry down. He turned it off and put it in his pocket, feeling lost without it, and lost without the counsel of his friend.

'It wasn't a bluff, was it,' his father stated more than asked. Damien could see that he was angry and very concerned. 'What have you done? What is this video?'

'No, Dad. Well, I ...'

What if he knows? What if it's a real threat?
What if . . .?

Damien crumpled. The hollow confidence he
wore like armour leaked out of him at the first
sign of his father's outrage, leaving him
vulnerable and afraid. He wished Simon was
there; Simon always seemed to know what to
do. Damien balled himself up in the chair,
picking at his hands nervously. It was as if he was
twelve again and he had crashed Dad's Mercedes
into the gate down the drive. He'd messed up.
He thought of that girl thrashing around on the
bed, and growing still and cold, and his stomach
began twisting in knots. It had been a horrible
sight. He had never seen anyone die before, not
even Grandpa when he went. It had been awful.
He hadn't liked it at all.

But Simon told me it would be okay. He told me he
would have everything under control. He said it would
be fine!

'Whatever you do, don't lie to me, son,' Jack
said. 'Just tell me exactly what happened. I need
to know the truth. I need to know what we are
up against.'

Damien felt flustered, his careful cool
shattered. He unsuccessfully urged himself to stay
calm. It was humiliating for his father to see him
like this. He would have to think hard about
what to say. If he said the wrong thing it would
only make things worse.

'Dad, I just want you to know that it isn't

130

what you think ...' he started, not even sure what his father thought 'it' was. 'It's just ...'

Jack sat in place, patient but uncharacteristically grim, leaning forwards on his massive mahogany desk on both elbows, waiting for Damien to explain.

Damien's mouth only opened and closed with the beginnings of possible responses. Nothing complete came out. He didn't know which lie he should tell.

'Have you been doing drugs, son?'

'Well, yeah, but ...' Damien admitted, ashamed.

But what? But that isn't the worst of it?

Jack shook his head. 'I knew it. We spoke about that. You have to be careful, son. You are not like everyone else. You have to be above them. You have more to lose.' He paused. 'Tell me the rest.'

He seemed to know more. How much did he know?

Jack took a deep, disappointed breath. 'You know, son, we are close to sealing this tender for the transport contract. It will be one of the biggest deals made in this country. This is important. I am out there trying to make history for us while you piss away everything I've made over a lifetime of work with your ... your parties ... your fun? I can't let you do that. A scandal now could ruin all we've done. We have to have higher standards, son. We have to keep our noses clean. Always.'

Damien thought about the drugs that had been lying around at the party. Could anyone actually prove that they had been his or that he knew they were there? But of course that wouldn't be the worst of it. If there really was a video with his recognisable face ... There was the girl ... the stupid girl. Lee had been a witness, too.

'Well, speak to me!' Jack's fist slammed on the desk, rattling his son. He didn't often raise his voice to Damien, but now he was positively exploding. 'Speak to me now!'

'At the party there was some stuff,' Damien blurted. He opened his mouth to continue but stopped. Grim recognition spread across his father's face, as if he had already feared that his son's parties had got out of control. The Cavanagh household was a huge sprawling home, a show house. Damien's parents went to their more modest Palm Beach house on the weekends, and sometimes during the week – as they had done on Wednesday – and it was then that there were the parties. Jack knew very little about what happened in the family home when he was away, and that was how Damien had hoped it would stay.

'A few things were happening ... just a bit of fun. Simon caught some girl taping stuff, that's all, but he said he would take care of it.'

Damien worried that things had been screwed up. Was this the same video taken by the girl Simon had told him about? What about that girl? What had Simon done to shut her up? He didn't know. Simon had said it would all be fine, it would all be taken care of. But what if this was the video? What if it wasn't a bluff? He wasn't even sure what was on it. How much was on tape?

Jack picked up the phone and dialled. In a few moments he said into the phone, 'Yes, I will need you ... Five more minutes? ... Good.' He hung up.

'Who was that?' Damien asked, bewildered.

'That was Bob.'

'Bob? *The American*?' Damien asked. He swallowed nervously.

Everyone in the family and in the inner sanctum of the company knew about 'The American', though few had exchanged words with him or even laid eyes on him. Damien had met him on two occasions and still knew little about the man except that he had at one point been the head of FBI headquarters in California, and since retiring had started his own small security services company in the private sector. Six years previously, when Cavanagh Incorporated had been threatened by the kidnapping of a top-level executive in the Middle East, Jack had brought The American on board, and he had been a distant but constant presence since. No one except Jack seemed to know exactly what The American did, but there had been no serious security problems since his tenure had begun.

'Hey,' Jack said to his son to get his attention – Damien had been staring out the window. 'Simon said he would "take care of it"? Tell me what specifically, and how exactly did Simon take care of it? Tell me, son,' he urged.

But Damien wasn't sure how to answer. He knew very little about the specifics, and he hadn't wanted to know, either. Simon had said it was best that way – best that he didn't know. He'd said he needed $15 000 to make the problem go away. He'd needed more than that after, another thirty-five, but that should have been it. He said it wouldn't be a problem. Simon had said that everything would be fine.

'Why now?' Jack was clearly upset. 'Why now, son? Do you recognise the importance of the transport contract? Do you? And you choose now – just as we are on the verge of winning the tender, just months before you are due to be married – to take part in something so ... something so *sordid*?'

'Father, I know, but ...'

'No. I don't think you do know.' Jack shook his head with disappointment. 'An underaged girl? Why?'

Damien was stunned. How did his dad know about his proclivity for young girls?

'This man who threatened me is someone your friend Simon Aston got involved, isn't he?'

Damien shrugged sheepishly. 'I don't know. It sounds like it. I mean, he could be.' He wanted to sink right into the chair and disappear, like he had never even existed. Oh, how he would have loved to be somewhere else – anywhere but in his father's office.

'Right. Simon is involved, then. He will be the one to deliver the money to Mr Hand personally.'

'What? Who is Mr Hand?'

But his father was no longer listening to him. He was staring gravely at the embossed writing tray on his desk. 'I will not allow this family to be blackmailed by a lowlife scumbag. Do you hear me?' he said. 'I will not let your life be ruined. This has to be taken care of properly, professionally. If this video is embarrassing or incriminating and it gets out, your life as you know it will be over and our family's reputation will be ruined. I won't let that happen to you, son. I won't let that happen to *us*.'

Damien swallowed nervously.

There was a knock on the door, and he jumped.

'Ah, Bob has arrived. Let him in, son.'

The American. Damien felt weak. His thoughts were jumbled up into an incoherent mess. He couldn't talk his way out of this one, he realised. This was serious. This was real. Damien moved across the room in stunned silence. He opened the door to find The

American waiting patiently outside, hands held behind his back like a general. *Bob White.* The American walked in, unassuming as ever, closed the door behind him and waited for Damien to be seated before asking gently if he could sit beside the younger Cavanagh.

Damien nodded a nervous yes.

The American sat with erect posture, one leg crossed over the other. He was a fit man with grey hair worn short around the ears and collar. He was of average build and appearance, only neater, more precise. The funny thing about The American was that, no matter how many times you met him, you still didn't know anything about him that was not on his business card. And the only thing distinguishing about him was his American accent – hence his nickname. Of course, he was also distinguished by reputation and rumour, mysterious though it was, but the stories could never be verified.

The American spoke to Damien. 'I understand we have a situation.'

'Well, I uh ... I don't know if –' Damien began, his face feeling so hot he thought it must be swollen to twice its size.

Jack stopped him with a raised hand.

'Bob, thanks for joining us here. It looks as if Simon Aston ... You remember Damien's friend Simon Aston?'

The American nodded.

'Well, it would seem that Damien has got

himself into some trouble, and his friend Simon Aston hired someone to sort it out for him, and managed to make the situation worse. I am fairly certain this is the same man who has threatened to blackmail us.'

Sickening. Sickening.

Sick.

Damien felt desperately ill, being in the presence of The American, and in the presence of his own father talking of blackmail and problems that needed to be fixed. What about Simon? Where was his trusted friend Simon in all this?

'The wheels are already in motion,' The American told Jack. 'With your confirmation, Mr Hand will be on a plane tomorrow. He comes highly recommended.'

Who is this Mr Hand?

Jack took a deep, contemplative breath. 'Son, I will organise to dock your personal account by one million dollars.'

'One million!' Damien protested. 'But ...'

But Simon had only needed an extra $35 000 to tie up the loose ends. What would they need one million dollars for?

Jack leaned forwards again, getting Damien's undivided attention. 'The price to clean up your mess is two-and-a-half million dollars, son. I am taking one million from your account because you need to learn that money is not free. I will have to cover the rest. We cannot afford any mistakes. Not now. And I don't want to hear a word from you about it – ever. Not to your mother and not to anyone else.

'I want your friend Simon here in one hour,' Jack continued. 'No excuses. You can call him now to tell him to come here, and that is all you will say to him.'

Jack stood up.

'Now you and Bob will have a chat about a few things. Answer all of his questions, son – everything,' he said with a pointed finger. 'I don't need to know the details. I don't want to know. I'll be back in fifteen minutes. After you have told Bob *everything* you know, you will not think about all this again, and you certainly will not discuss it with anyone, *ever*. Not even your friend Simon. He will have his own problems.'

Jack shut the door behind him, leaving Damien alone with The American.

CHAPTER 12

IT WAS FIVE-THIRTY on Friday afternoon, and Mak was just thinking about finishing up at her computer and making her first house visit for Groobelaar's investigation.

The home phone rang, and she sprang up to grab it, hoping it was Andy calling with their dinner arrangements.

He'll be gone tomorrow. Gone for three months.

'Hello?'

'Hello, Mak.' It was her father, Les.

'Dad! How are you? I've been thinking about you a lot today. I miss you.'

There were very few people who rang the house line except Andy and her dad. Mak savoured her father's voice. She smiled, cradling the phone between her shoulder and ear. Her laptop was glowing beyond the doorway in the dining room, where she had spent half an hour searching online newspaper archives and other websites for the subjects of her investigation.

'It's great to hear from you. It must be late?'

From her position in the hall Mak looked back towards her father's photo on the living room table.

'Mak, there is an opportunity I want you to know about. It's something I really think you should consider.'

'Um, okay.' Mak knew that her father kept tabs on her life in Australia, even though she asked him repeatedly not to snoop around in it. He had local contacts, as it turned out, and he seemed to get the inside scoop on everything Andy was doing before Mak even knew a thing about it. 'What is it? What kind of opportunity?'

'The Justice Department here has an opening for a forensic psychologist. They've seen your application and they are very interested.'

'My *application*?' Mak was furious. How could her father apply for a job on her behalf without even asking her – a job *on the other side of the world* for goodness' sake?

'I'm sure the job will be yours,' he said. 'It would be great for you.'

Mak closed her eyes. 'But, Dad, I can't work in Canada. I am living in Australia. This is where I live,' she said, exasperated.

'You can't stay there for ever.'

Mak put her hand to her forehead. 'Yes I can, Dad.'

Or can I?

He paused.

'Mak, you aren't working. You need a job.'

'I *am* working,' she explained. 'I am just about to head out the door to interview someone for an investigation. Soon I will have saved up enough money and then I will be able to get my practice started.'

He didn't respond to her explanations.

Les Vanderwall had been one of Vancouver Island's longest-serving detective inspectors; as his eldest daughter, Makedde had seen a lot of crime in her twenty-nine years. That was why she had chosen the field of forensic psychology in the first place, and it was also, perhaps, where her knack for investigation had come from. From the very first time aged twelve she had seen a murder victim in the local morgue during a father-daughter bonding field trip, Mak had wanted to understand crime – particularly violent crime. She longed to comprehend why people did the things they did to one another, and exactly what made a criminal recidivist tick. She didn't have the answers yet, but she was sure she would. Some day. Les, who had dealt with criminals his whole life, had once said – with some sarcasm – that Mak should give him a call when she figured out what made criminals commit crimes. She'd said he would be the first person she'd call.

'How is Ann? Is she good?' Mak asked.

Makedde had lost her mother, Jane, five years earlier. She could hardly believe it had been that long; it had been a tough stretch of time.

Thankfully, Les was no longer alone. He had found Ann, a psychologist. Mak liked Ann a lot – though of course she would never replace her mum.

'She's good,' he said. 'I think you should consider the Justice Department job, Mak. Come back.'

'Dad, no. Not now. I am setting my life up here at the moment. Well, trying to …' But she still felt bad for abandoning him. 'I have to go now, Dad.' She had planned on making her house call after work hours, but just before dinner, so she would have to hurry up. 'And you should go to bed. I love you, Dad. I'll call you tomorrow, okay?' Mak hung up and frowned. She'd forgotten to ask about her pregnant sister, Theresa. Mak doubted *she* ever met with such disapproval.

★ ★ ★

Mak pulled up at a modest single-level house in Parramatta, in Sydney's west, and tossed the Sydways map into the back seat with a thunk.

This is it.

She parked Andy's red Honda on the street directly in front of the house, and made her way up a paved path towards the door, her heart beating fast with nerves. It was a small fifties-style home with an unkempt garden, and windows full of pot plants and white lace curtains. It looked bleak within the small windows – a still place where no light entered.

Mak felt awkward about visiting Meaghan Wallace's parents. She knew it was part of her job, part of the chores her client was paying for her to do, but she found herself feeling sad for the Wallaces, and sorry that she was going to bother them in their grief. She had not done this sort of thing before.

Taking a deep breath, Mak knocked on the door.

Shuffling footsteps moved towards the door. It opened to reveal a weathered woman who looked at Mak with fragile, red-rimmed eyes. 'Hello, young lady,' the woman said. 'May I help you?'

Mak was not sure how she would be received. Either very well, or very badly ...

'My name is Makedde Vanderwall. May I speak with you for a moment, Mrs Wallace?' she asked, assuming this was Meaghan's bereaved mother, Noelene.

Meaghan's mother seemed surprised. 'Oh yes, please come in.' The woman stepped aside for Mak to enter. 'Would you like some tea?' Mrs Wallace asked.

Now it was Mak's turn to be surprised. 'Tea? Um, certainly. Yes. Thank you,' she replied clumsily.

Makedde was already inside the front door, which was a better result than she had expected in so short a time. She was inexperienced about what to expect of bereaved strangers. Andy had performed many death knocks as a constable, and said that nothing surprised him any more: tears, screams, laughter, fidgeting or numb silence. With all that in mind, tea seemed a very civilised option coming from the bereaved Mrs Wallace.

The woman shuffled away towards her kitchen, and Mak trailed her several feet behind, unsure if it was okay to follow or if she should wait in the hall. She stopped just on the edge of the kitchen linoleum.

'You're with the police?' the woman said.

Here was the moment of truth. Mak could tell any number of fibs, but one thing that was too legally risky was to lie about being a police officer. She wouldn't do that.

'Mrs Wallace,' she began from the safety of the orange hall carpet, 'I'm not with the police. I am a private investigator looking into your daughter's death. I am going to do my best to find the whole truth of what happened.' She opened her wallet and passed the older woman a business card. 'I am so very sorry to disturb you. I know this must be a difficult time, but if it is all right, I would like to talk to you about Meaghan.'

The woman kept her back to Makedde as she prepared the tea. Mak thought there was a fifty-fifty chance she would be immediately kicked out.

Mrs Wallace hesitated for a few seconds before saying, 'Do you take milk and sugar?'

'Yes, please.'

Noelene Wallace put the kettle on and laid out cups and saucers. She led Mak into a dark living room, where her husband, Ralph, was watching television. The curtains were already closed, although the sun was still up. Ralph Wallace didn't get out of his chair, and Mak couldn't help but imagine that he had sat down in that spot when he heard of his daughter's murder and not moved since.

Mrs Wallace laid out the tray of tea and biscuits, and gestured for Mak to take a seat on the lounge.

'Thank you,' Mak began. 'I appreciate your time. I am very sorry for your loss. Your daughter was very lovely.'

Ralph Wallace eyed Mak suspiciously, but nodded to acknowledge her words. He raised the remote control in his hand and turned the television to mute. He had been watching the soap opera *Neighbours* with the sound low.

'You're a cop?' he asked, without taking his eyes from the screen.

'No, sir, I'm not. I am a private investigator looking into the circumstances of what happened to your daughter.'

She leaned over to pass him a card, and when he did not offer his hand to take it, she placed the card on the TV table beside him.

'Who you workin' for?' he asked.

'I work for Marian Wendell Private Investigations. A friend of Meaghan's has hired me to look into Meaghan's, um, death ...' She hesitated to use the word 'murder'.

'She was murdered. You can call it what it is,' Mr Wallace said bluntly. 'Stabbed. She deserved better than that.'

Mak nodded. 'You are right.' She had thought the very same thing herself when her friend Catherine Gerber had been murdered five years earlier. People had spoken of 'loss' and 'passing', but Catherine too had been taken violently. It was not just a death – it was *murder*.

'Who would do that? Who would pay for all that?' Mr Wallace asked Mak.

'Someone who cared very much for your daughter,' Mak said, hoping that was true. 'I understand this must be hard for both of you. Can you tell me if you saw any changes in your daughter leading up to her death? Anything unusual? New habits? Friends? Behaviour?'

'Meg was a good girl,' Mrs Wallace said. 'She was a mystery to me ...' She shook her head. 'So independent. I don't know how much help we might be with your questions.'

Mak was relieved to no longer be justifying herself to them. 'Anything would be of help –'

Mrs Wallace paused and looked into Mak's face with a strange familiarity. 'You look like a model.'

Mak was thrown by the comment, considering the setting. 'Um, I used to model.'

'Oh, how wonderful. Meg was very pretty,

like you. She did some modelling. She was always such a pretty little girl.'

'Did she do a lot of modelling?' Mak asked.

'She did some photo shoots but they kept telling her she was too short.'

'I see.'

Mrs Wallace got up and wandered away, leaving Mak with her husband. He was staring at the television screen as if Mak wasn't there. Thankfully, Mrs Wallace returned a few minutes later. She had a small album of photos in her hands.

'See how pretty she was?'

Mak took in the photographs slowly. They showed Meaghan posing in a glamour studio in a gold bikini, heavily made up. Mak understood now why Meaghan's mother had made the comment about Mak's appearance, and perhaps why Mak had been so easily received. Noelene had been proud of her daughter's appearance. Her daughter had once dreamed of being a rich and famous model. It was a common dream, and one that was rarely realised.

'She looks very pretty. Those are very nice photos,' Mak said, feeling strange to be making such comments. 'Did she do any modelling recently? In the past few weeks?'

Mrs Wallace shook her head.

'Did Meg visit you often, Mrs Wallace?'

'Occasionally she'd find time to visit us boring folks,' Mr Wallace blurted from his lounge chair, then clenched his jaw and continued staring in the direction of the mute television. *He might as well have kept the sound on*, Mak thought.

'She used to visit once a month or so,' Mrs Wallace said.

Once a month didn't seem like much, especially as Meaghan had only lived thirty minutes' drive away, but every family was different and there could have been all kinds of dynamics happening within the Wallace family. Mak was so often far from home that the idea of seeing her dad at least once a month seemed like heaven. Even with all his meddling, she missed him terribly.

'What sort of things did you talk about when she visited?' Mak asked Mrs Wallace.

'Oh, this and that. She told us how good things were going with that real estate company, and she'd show me her new clothes. She always dressed well, kept herself nice. I wished she'd find someone, but she never seemed excited about anyone special. We'd hoped she would have settled down ...'

Her words trailed off, the unspoken hanging in the air: *Now she never will find someone.* Meaghan was an only child; there would be no grandchildren now. No new Wallaces for Ralph and Noelene.

'Do you recall the name Simon Aston? Did she ever mention him?'

'Simon Aston?' Noelene said. 'Well, no. Were they *together*?'

'I'm not sure that they were together,' Mak replied cautiously. 'But they knew each other, I believe.' She had cut out a photo of Simon from a printed image off the internet, and she showed it to Mrs Wallace. 'Do you recognise him?'

'No. What did he do? Was he involved?'

'No, no. I was just wondering if your daughter ever brought him up in conversation.' *Damn.* She'd been hoping for some recognition. 'Did Meaghan ever mention a girl named Jag? Or Amy?'

'Um, Amy ... yes. Meg did have a friend named Amy, but she moved interstate, I think. I met her a few times. She was a pretty girl, too, but a bit ... wild.'

'I see,' Mak said. 'Do you remember where Amy moved to?'

'Melbourne, I think.'

'And who were Meaghan's best friends – the friends she spent the most time with?' Mak asked, but Mrs Wallace was no longer really listening. She seemed to be lost in her own thoughts.

'She was a good girl, Meg,' Mrs Wallace rambled, looking as if she may be on the verge of tears. 'Meg, she ...'

In that moment Mak felt horrible about being there, probing into the details of their life with their murdered daughter, taken too soon from them at the age of twenty-three. *Is this what I am destined to do? Probe into the grief of other people like this, for a simple assignment? For no reason but to report some information back to a client?*

'Would you like a tour of the house?' Noelene Wallace said suddenly.

Mak took a moment to respond. She had not been expecting the offer.

'Certainly.'

CHAPTER 1/3

SIMON ASTON ENTERED the reception area of Jack Cavanagh's office on the fourteenth floor of the famous Cavanagh building on George Street, his nerves ruffled by Damien's call. The sun was going down and the area of the CBD outside the building was like a ghost town. Apart from small groups of businesspeople milling around the after-work bars, it was terribly quiet.

The Cavanagh building felt empty. Fluorescent lighting buzzed.

'Someone tried to blackmail my dad, Simon! I thought you said it would be okay? I thought you said it would be taken care of? I gave you that money. You said it would be okay . . .

'My dad wants to see you in one hour. And he's said if you don't show up, he will forbid you from ever showing your face around the family again.'

Things were spiralling out of control. Fast.

Simon had been the best friend of Sydney's richest young heir for years, and in all that time he had never been invited to Cavanagh senior's office. Considering the situation, the building felt oppressive, the weight of all that power and influence pushing down on him.

All that money.

All that power.

Simon was so close to it, and yet so far away. He was not Damien Cavanagh. He was not protected by the wealth and influence of Jack Cavanagh.

Even before Damien's panicked phone call an hour earlier, Simon could see that things had gone bad. Warwick's phone call had put him on edge, but still, Simon had not really believed he would follow through. After all, how could any video actually exist? He'd crushed the phone of that meddling Meaghan woman. Wasn't that enough? Had that not destroyed it?

If a video exists, there's going to be serious trouble.

With that in mind, Simon straightened his tie and mentally prepared himself to be his most convivial. He would have to handle this situation very cautiously, and with charm. He had worn his only suit specially for the occasion, to try to impress on Mr Cavanagh that he was a concerned, upstanding and loyal friend of Damien's.

The offices were dead quiet – everyone had gone home. The vast windows were not curtained, and he could see straight into the modern office buildings next door, where the lights inside were already off, and his own eerie reflection moved across the glass. The hallway from the elevator was still lit, and he walked down it towards the desk of Mr Cavanagh's personal receptionist with a thinly veiled dread.

'Hello, I'm Simon Aston.'

The receptionist wore a tight, impenetrable smile. Amongst various cards, framed family photos and trays of neatly kept paperwork on her desk, he noticed a small name plate which simply said 'Joy', but even before he could open his mouth to address her by name, she said, 'Mr Cavanagh is expecting you. Please come this way.'

Joy stood gracefully and led him towards Mr Cavanagh's office. She opened the door for him. Simon was terrified at what he might find inside.

'Mr Aston is here to see you, Mr Cavanagh.'

'Thank you, Joy.'

With that Joy disappeared and Simon remained in the doorway, temporarily unable to move forwards. Jack Cavanagh sat in a chair behind a massive office desk. His office was the size of some people's entire homes. He was not alone, Simon noticed – there was a man in the office who Simon did not recognise. A man who looked serious.

'You wanted to see me, sir?' Simon said from his position across the room.

'Come in. Sit down, Simon,' Mr Cavanagh said in a way that was neither openly angry or welcoming.

Simon's mouth felt dry. His hands were wet.

He entered timorously, remembering to smile. *Confidence.* If he seemed relaxed about it, they would be more relaxed about it. Confidence was the key. Confidence and attitude, he reminded himself.

Mr Cavanagh's guest did not seem to be leaving. Damien had mentioned a man he called 'The American', and Simon guessed that this must be him. But the man was introduced as Mr White.

'Hello, Mr White,' Simon said and offered a hand that Mr White did not shake.

'Mr White will need to be privy to all the information. He needs to know everything,' Mr Cavanagh said ominously.

Everything.

Simon took a chair, the three of them in a semicircle with Mr Cavanagh sitting behind his imposing desk. Joy shut the office door.

It was odd for Simon to see Jack Cavanagh this way. He had seen Damien's father in the flesh as often as he had seen him in newspapers or on the cover of business magazines. In the flesh he could often be found smiling. He was not smiling now. Mr Cavanagh and Mr White were both looking at Simon and waiting for him to speak, but Simon didn't know what he should say.

'Sir, may I speak frankly?' Simon began in his most disarming tone. He crossed his legs and gestured with one hand. 'I —'

'You had better,' Mr Cavanagh snapped back. 'Or you won't be speaking to my son again. Ever.'

That gave Simon pause. Was that a real threat? Would Jack really cut Damien off from him?

'Yes, sir,' Simon began again. 'Um – can I just say firstly what an honour it is to be invited here to speak with you. I only wish the circumstances were better.'

Mr Cavanagh narrowed his eyes. 'Cut the bullshit,' he said. 'Tell us about this man who tried to blackmail me today.'

Simon had to collect himself. This was all moving too quickly. Warwick had hung up on him and hadn't called him back or answered his phone. Damien was freaking out about his dad.

'*Who is he?*' Mr Cavanagh demanded.

Simon hesitated. 'I honestly don't know who contacted you, sir. I am not sure why you think I would be involved with something like that, but I am confident we will get to the bottom of it all.'

Jack leaned towards him. He was a man who liked to remain casual and personal, despite his great success and formidable influence. He was known to value professionalism, but honesty and mateship even more. He took his employees out on a boat once a year. He gave bonuses. He asked about people's families and took an interest in their health and wellbeing. But now he was not being low-key or disarming. Simon was getting a taste of the more formidable side of Jack Cavanagh. It was a darker side that journalists sometimes hinted at – a more ruthless side. Mr Jack Cavanagh clearly did not take threats to him or his family lightly.

'Don't fuck with me, Simon,' he said, swearing for the first time Simon had ever heard, and making the small blond hairs on the back of his neck stand up. 'I can make your life very different, very quickly.'

Simon believed him. If Jack Cavanagh cut him off from Damien, everyone in Sydney would know about it in a matter of days. Simon's connections would instantly fizzle. It would be a disaster – social suicide. Financial suicide.

'I mean no disrespect, sir,' Simon responded, trying to regain some ground. 'I just am not sure ... I didn't mean ... I found out about him through a friend ...' he babbled. He took a breath and tried to slow down. 'Look, I came across this thing happening. I was, you know, *shocked*. And this woman was there filming it. I wanted to protect my friend. I know people, and I knew they could make this problem go away for Damien. I was only trying to protect him.'

The American, who up until now had not entered into the conversation, pulled his chair forwards and opened a notepad. He took a pen from inside his jacket pocket and, when he had it ready, his eyes met Simon's with a cool gaze. He said, 'What was the name of the woman who was doing the filming?'

'Um ... she was nobody. Just a guest.'

'Name please,' Mr White said simply.

If he finds out the name, he will find out what's happened to her.

The American waited. Simon was too fearful of him to deny him an answer. 'Her name was, uh, Meaghan Wallace. She worked as a PA for Robert Groobelaar at Trident Realty. Robert's a colleague of yours, I think.'

Jack nodded thoughtfully. 'Robert has worked with me on some minor real estate.'

The American took note, but he was not finished with Simon's last statement. 'You ordered that something be done to silence this Meaghan Wallace?' he pressed. He must have noticed that Simon had spoken of the woman in the past tense.

Simon nodded sheepishly in reply to The American's brutally direct question, his eyes to the floor. The words sounded horrible: *You ordered that something be done to silence this Meaghan Wallace?* Had he done that? Yes, he supposed he had. But he had not wanted to – he'd had no choice. He'd had to have her taken care of.

'Okay. We'll get back to her in a moment,' The American said. 'You said you found this man through a friend of yours. I need to know the name of this friend.'

He waited for an answer.

Simon was panicking inside. He had not found Warwick through a friend, but how would it sound to Mr Cavanagh if he admitted he was the sort of person who knew people like that personally? Still, he was afraid to lie to The

157

American. Warwick had done odd jobs for Simon before. If Simon gave them a false name, he felt sure he would be found out. Simon knew that just by looking at him.

For the first time in Simon's life, truth seemed like the best policy, and his only option.

'Um, I approached the man directly, sir,' he admitted.

The American wrote something on his small notepad. Jack Cavanagh was grim-faced throughout, but said nothing.

'The man's full name?'

'Warwick O'Connor.'

When Warwick had run a few errands for Simon in the past, they had mostly been for buddies in need. His price was $15 000 to take care of someone like this girl they had been having trouble with. It was a good price: competitive – cheap, to be exact. Warwick had been paid half in advance. Simon wondered if Jack already knew that his son had actually paid Simon an accumulated $50 000 to take care of the problem, no questions asked. Simon thought of the extra as a kind of administration fee, but Jack might see it differently, especially given how things were turning out. He wondered if he should give back the latest $35 000. He didn't really want to do that.

Simon would tell only what he had to.

'You dealt directly with Warwick O'Connor,' said The American.

Simon nodded.

'And Damien?'

'Damien has never met him.'

'Good,' Jack Cavanagh interjected. 'There are no other loose ends to tie up with regard to the hiring of this lowlife? Just you and this man, Warwick – no one else?'

Simon felt uneasy about the way he'd said 'loose ends' but he nodded his head.

The American stepped in again. 'What was the recording device used by the woman?'

Simon looked shocked. 'I have never seen a video. I didn't think there was one. But, uh, she was using her mobile phone at the party and I caught her recording. That could be it.'

'Good. Let's hope that any recording is of low quality. Do you remember the make and model of the phone?' The American asked.

'Uh … no.' Simon did not take note of things like that. At least, not in those circumstances.

'We will need to find the phone. Do you know where it is now?' The American asked.

Simon bit his lip. 'I broke it. When I saw her recording I took the phone off her and stepped on it.'

The American kept taking his notes. 'And then what happened to the phone?'

'It was broken so I threw it out,' Simon explained.

The American looked at him like he was a moron. 'So you saw this woman making a recording at the party and you "stepped on" her phone. Did you check to see if there was anything damaging on it before you threw it out? Did you check to see if there was any recorded material on it, or if anything sensitive had been sent to anyone?'

Simon felt the blood drain from his face. 'No, sir. It was broken. I just got rid of it.'

'Where did you dispose of it?'

'In the wastebasket at the house.'

Jack Cavanagh slammed a fist down on the desk, making Simon jump with fright in his chair. His heart began pounding even harder. He felt like a man staring at a noose that was made for his neck alone.

'Has the rubbish been collected since the party?' The American asked Jack.

'Yes. Estelle, the maid, cleans the rubbish out daily. It would be long gone,' Mr Cavanagh said, sounding very displeased.

'Is there any chance she, or another of your staff, might have seen something?'

'No, no,' Simon tried to reassure them. 'The phone was in pieces, I swear. No one could have used it.'

'We need to find out what was on it,' The American said. 'And if anything sensitive on it was sent to anyone else.'

'But I don't know how,' Simon pleaded. 'The phone was wrecked. I just didn't think −'

'No, you didn't,' Jack Cavanagh hissed.

'Let me take care of that,' The American said.

Mr Cavanagh was clearly livid now. He sat behind his desk, seething. Then he pointed a finger at Simon. If it were a gun he would have pulled the trigger, Simon felt sure.

'Because you failed to come to me when there was an issue concerning the protection of my family, you will now have the responsibility of seeing that things are made right,' Mr Cavanagh said darkly. 'This is an opportunity to regain my faith, Simon.

'There will be a man arriving this weekend from Mumbai. He will have the relevant details of the situation and he will contact you. Bob here will make sure you are ready for him when he does. Everything – and I mean *everything* – you know about this Warwick O'Connor who has come to blackmail this family, you are to tell Bob. Everything. Everything you know about this video, the people in it, how they came to be in it and how the video came to be in someone's possession, you will tell him. You will tell Bob everything about these people, and everything about what my son has been getting into.'

The American sat quietly with his notepad.

'I do not want or need to know the details. You tell Bob everything, and you listen to what he says.'

'Um, yes, sir,' Simon replied nervously.

'I will arrange for money and instructions to be made available, and you will deliver them to him personally. Bob will oversee the transaction to

make sure there are no mistakes. Is that all clear?'
Simon did not answer. 'I said, is that clear?'

'Um, yes, sir, it is clear. But ... what does he look like? How will I know –'

'I want no questions from you – just answers. You give Bob all the information he asks for. I do not need to know any more of the sordid details of this mess you and my son have made. I will leave you two to discuss this further.'

Jack Cavanagh stood up from behind his massive mahogany desk.

'I am very disappointed, Simon. *Very* disappointed. I don't want this situation spoken about to anyone, *ever*. Not even to me, unless I ask you directly about it. Is that clear?'

Simon nodded. 'Yes, sir, it is.'

'If I discover that you have not been truthful with me or with Mr White here, or that you mentioned this conversation to anyone at all ... Well, I know my son will be very sad to lose his friend.'

Simon accepted his orders, and Jack Cavanagh left him with The American, his notepad, and the certainty that this was indeed serious. Simon would have to tell it all. No amount of charm would get him out of this one.

CHAPTER 14

AT EIGHT O'CLOCK, Mak was still sitting in the childhood bedroom of the deceased young Meaghan Wallace, talking with her bereaved mother and being shown album after album of family photographs. She found herself being sucked into the woman's raw grief. Seeing all these photographs of Meaghan when she was a baby and a toddler, and going to school for the first time – it was not helpful. Things had gone completely off track, but Mak found it difficult to break away. This woman seemed to need her there. She just wanted someone to listen to her stories about her daughter. She wanted someone to see the albums and the memories, and see Meg as she did.

Mak looked over at a bedside clock and saw the time.

Damn.

She and Andy had an eight o'clock dinner date at Icebergs restaurant. She would be at least thirty minutes late now, and she still didn't have what she needed. She had to wrap it up.

'Um, Mrs Wallace,' Mak started.

'Call me Noelene.'

'Noelene, may I use your bathroom?'

'Oh yes. Yes, of course.' Noelene closed the album she was showing Mak and put it lovingly back into its place in the stack on the bedroom dresser. She pointed the way and Mak walked out of Meaghan Wallace's bedroom and down the hall to the toilet, feeling relief in having escaped the room.

Oh God, poor woman. Poor woman.

Makedde flicked the light on. The bathroom was wallpapered with teal flowers; the towels were all in the same shade. Mak closed the bathroom door behind her and snatched her phone out of her pocket. It had a number of voicemail messages and missed calls. She had switched it to silent so as not to disturb the Wallaces.

Mak didn't bother to check her voicemail messages. Instead, she called Andy right away. He was probably waiting angrily in the living room for her to return, or worse – he might be at the restaurant sipping a drink by himself while she stood in a sea of teal in a bereaved stranger's bathroom.

'Flynn,' he answered.

'I will be there in twenty minutes. I'm so sorry,' Makedde said in an apologetic whisper.

'Why are you whispering?' he asked.

'I can't explain right now. I'm in someone's bathroom, but I'll be there as soon as I can.' She cupped her hand around the phone to further muffle her talking.

'Bathroom? I'm not at the restaurant yet. The reservation isn't till nine. I couldn't get us in until then. I'll meet you at the house at quarter to – I'm still with Jimmy,' Andy said.

He's still at work? Suddenly Mak didn't feel so bad.

'I'll be home in half an hour, tops,' she told him. 'I love you.'

Mak hung up and tucked her mobile phone away. Before she stepped out, she caught a glimpse of herself in the bathroom mirror. Her eyes were red, and there was an unmistakable sadness in them. Mak noticed some vague similarity between herself and the photos she had seen of Meaghan. It was far from a strong resemblance: Meaghan had been shorter, younger and more of a yellowy blonde, but perhaps Noelene was opening up to Mak in part because she was a young woman a bit like her daughter.

What would it be like to lose a daughter? She knew what it was like to lose a mother.

Mak shut the light off and stepped back into the hall just as Noelene was closing the door of her daughter's room. Mak had spent over an hour and a half with her and had well and truly let things get off track. Now, before she left, it was time to broach the difficult subject of Tobias Murphy.

'Mrs Wallace, how do you feel about the police case? The suspect they have, Tobias Murphy –'

'Oh,' Noelene said, and shook her head back and forth. Mak could see that the name had struck a chord. How would it be to have someone mention the name of the person accused of killing your own child? Noelene took a few steps down the hall and paused, and Mak became worried that she'd lost her. Mak had waited as long as she could, and been as gentle as she could. Perhaps she had asked the wrong way? She probably should have taken a seat somewhere and had more tea first.

'My sister ... she was the black sheep of the family ... after what happened,' Noelene said, and touched the doorknob of her dead daughter's bedroom thoughtfully. She seemed reluctant to move from that room, and those memories.

Mak was confused. 'Your sister?'

'Tobias always seemed like a nice enough kid,' Noelene offered graciously. She looked down the hall to Ralph, who still sat in place in the living room, his arms crossed, the television volume up.

'Are you saying that you *know* Tobias?'

'Of course,' she said. 'He's our nephew.'

Mak reeled at the news. Tobias Murphy was Meaghan's cousin?

He killed his own cousin?

'You know, that poor kid had a rough time from the start. I loved my sister. I will always love her, but she let Tobias and Georgina down. She just wasn't strong enough for what happened. She never forgave herself.'

166

Mak waited, her eyes wide.

'Barbara finally killed herself two years ago.' Noelene crossed herself and shook her head. 'She'd tried so many times before.'

'Oh. Oh, I am so sorry to hear that.'

'She had been depressed for a long time. She never really got over what happened to … Krista. Or to Georgina.'

The names squeaked out unwillingly. Mak didn't understand – who were Krista and Georgina? She took mental notes as she listened, but did not interfere as Noelene spoke. She obviously had a lot more homework to do if she had let such an important piece of information slip past.

'She didn't take proper care of them after that,' Mrs Wallace continued. 'She couldn't even take care of herself. None of us was surprised when Kev left.'

Kevin Murphy. Tobias's father.

Mak nodded solemnly, pretending she had already figured it all out. 'And then Kev …?' she prompted.

'Remarried. He got married a number of years ago. He has kids with his new wife now.'

Mak nodded.

So Kevin Murphy had moved on and started a new life for himself. Mak wondered how open he and his new wife had been to young Tobias, the one remaining tie to Kevin's first marriage – and she wondered how open Tobias had been to them? Mak had seen the name 'Kevin Murphy' in the Tobias Murphy file, along with the name of a woman whom she had initially assumed was Tobias's biological mother. A lot of women didn't change their names after marriage any more, so it was foolish to assume anything.

Mak looked at her notepad. 'You mentioned a Georgina?'

'Barb's daughter.'

'And where is Georgina now?'

'She suicided when she was fifteen. It was an overdose.'

Mak nodded solemnly. *Fifteen.* 'I am so sorry to hear that. She was Tobias's older sister?'

Noelene nodded.

One suicide at fifteen, and a runaway at fourteen who is now charged with murder. Mak could see how lucky she had been in her own life. Up until her mother had passed away from cancer, her family life on the west coast of Canada had been idyllic. The Vanderwalls had been a strong family, and seemingly one of the few families at Mak's school which had not been fragmented by divorce or death. Mak's schoolfriends had always wanted to come over to her place because her parents were so normal. No evil step-parent or drunken brothers – just a normal and safe family home, with the added bonus of the mystique of having a powerful police officer for a father. They'd always wanted to sneak into her father's office to see his trophies and awards, his handcuffs – and his gun. He must have known, too, because he never left it out.

'Did Meaghan and Tobias know each other well?'

'When they were very little they were inseparable.' Noelene looked towards her feet. 'Barbara was sick a lot. Tobias often stayed with us when she wasn't well. Meg and Toby played and played. Meg liked to take care of him. In those days Kev couldn't care for Toby on his own, so we saw a lot of him. They didn't have stay-at-home dads back then.'

She said this last sentence pointedly, as if she held some bitter feeling that Makedde's generation had it easier.

'Meg used to take care of him all the time … like she enjoyed playing mother to him. When she was twelve she used to put him in the pram and push him around the yard …'

This memory seemed to be too much for Noelene – she finally broke down. Her face crumpled, tears springing from her eyes.

Mak felt responsible for Noelene's rehashing of painful memories, for her tears. 'I'm so sorry for your loss,' she said feebly, and placed a hand gently on the woman's arm as she shook and wept.

'Did he really murder my girl? Did he?' Noelene cried.

Who on earth – let alone Meaghan's mother – would want to believe that Meaghan's own cousin could have stabbed her for nothing but a hit and a bit of cash?

'Did he really do it?' Noelene repeated, sobbing. 'Do you think someone else might have done it?'

Back in the living room Mr Wallace seemed tense at the sound of his wife's tears. His response was to turn up the volume on the television while Noelene wrung her hands, wrinkling her dress. Tears continued to roll down her face.

'I'm very sorry,' Mak said, feeling helpless. She stood in the hallway next to the woman, touching her arm, and wishing there was something more she could do.

'Toby could not have done this,' Noelene said, this time with certainty. 'If we had the money, we would hire someone like you to find the real killer.' She spoke with such clarity that it took Mak by surprise.

'You think they have the wrong person?' Mak asked in response, and immediately regretted her choice of words. It wasn't fair of her to confuse this woman at a time when she was so vulnerable. Making a baseless suggestion that the police might have the wrong suspect was irresponsible and wrong. She felt like she was getting everything wrong.

'Meg was ... She was doing things that ... that she wasn't telling us about,' Noelene said between sobs. 'I knew it. I knew something was going on.'

Mak could see that the older woman had thought this through, probably obsessing over everything her daughter had said to her in the months before her death.

'Miss Vanderwall ... as you can probably tell, my husband and I aren't rich. We get by, but we aren't rich people. Meg used to give us stuff all the time. There wasn't a single visit she made in the past two years where she didn't bring something for us. Like that TV that Ralph is watching.' Mak had noticed it was a large flat-screen model – pretty flash. 'She was always bringing things for us, and she insisted we take them.' Noelene took a deep breath. 'I started wondering where she was getting it all. Where was she getting the money from? That television was way too expensive for our blood. How could she afford all that?'

Mak didn't know what to say, but Noelene was right to think that her daughter's salary would not support such lavish gifts.

'She was into something,' Noelene said, more calmly now. 'Someone else did this to her. Someone ...'

CHAPTER 15

THE AMERICAN, BOB White, sat in the office of his client Jack Cavanagh, considering what he knew of the situation at hand. It was getting late on Friday evening, and they were the last souls remaining on the office floor. Jack had even sent home his secretary, Joy.

Simon Aston, the party-boy friend of Damien Cavanagh, had gone home with his tail between his legs after telling Bob every last detail of his foolish dealings. And his dealings had indeed been foolish. Simon had not impressed Bob: he'd seen recklessly self-serving and arrogant young men like Simon before. Simon was a leech on Damien and the Cavanagh fortune, and now he had jeopardised their security.

'How bad is it?' Jack Cavanagh asked The American. He had not been present for Damien's and Simon's full confessions – a precaution to keep him innocent of any incriminating details. The less he knew, the better it was for him. He would stay as clean as possible during the events that were about to unfold.

Bob delivered the news. 'In my professional estimation, we do need Mr Hand's expertise on this. I recommend we make the confirmation immediately.'

Jack nodded. 'Okay. Make it happen.' He had already known.

Mr Hand's involvement meant that the situation was bad. You didn't bring a man like him in without things being very, *very* serious.

'And this Mr Hand … he is highly recommended?' Jack asked.

'Very,' Bob assured him. 'And he is an expatriate Australian, so he knows Sydney well. I recommend that you not know more than that. Forget you ever heard his name.'

The American's contact, known only as Madame Q, had nominated her man Luther Hand for the job. He was said to be methodical, fast-working and virtually anonymous, and he had no restrictions on the profile or number of targets he would accept. Black or white; man, woman or child – given the orders, Madame Q's man Mr Hand would eliminate them all. That was a characteristic not shared by everyone in his profession.

'I think it is best to keep yourself and your son as distant from this clean-up as possible,' The American continued.

Jack agreed.

Bob considered his response for a while before he spoke again. 'The activities your son engaged in could give him a sentence of perhaps five to ten years. More, if convicted of manslaughter.'

Jack sat upright in his chair, startled, but said nothing.

'We do need to take that threat seriously. I will have to use some of your contacts within the police.'

Jack nodded. 'I have some favours I can call on. There is one man – a Detective Hunt, I think. He would be close to it, and should prove helpful.'

Bob wrote the name down.

'I will handle it with discretion. You need not become involved. If anyone tries to contact you directly, deny any knowledge. This Warwick O'Connor may be bluffing about having an actual video. He may have learned something about the recording from another source – even Simon himself – without actually being in possession of it. But it still seems likely that such a video does exist, and we must take every precaution in relation to containing it. There may already be copies.'

Jack nodded solemnly.

'It may not seem so right now, but all this may in fact be a blessing in disguise,' Bob told him. 'We now know about your son's activities and we may be able to contain the damage. Left much longer, it would have become more dangerous. If a recording of these activities exists, we need to find out exactly what was recorded and who might have seen it. That is my top priority.'

Jack knew The American well enough not to ask how he would get his information and how he would handle those who might have seen something dangerous. He had worked with him many years, through many crises ... though perhaps none had been as close to home as this, and Jack trusted the man's judgment implicitly.

'With your permission, I will get my men to search your home for all mobile phones or phone fragments. I would like to find that phone.'

'Okay. Do it, but do it quietly,' Jack said. 'I don't want my wife catching wind of any of this.'

'Understood. I will need a list of Beverley's movements, and I will need you to excuse your house staff for the day.'

'Okay.'

'I need your permission to take whatever steps are necessary and reasonable to remove the threat of the video evidence of your son's activities. It could come at considerable expense.'

'Do it,' Jack replied without hesitation.

The American had reliable and discreet contacts who could help him track down any transmission sent from that phone, including the video recording, if it existed. He had to get rid of evidence, and witnesses. There were ways to minimise or eliminate those threats, but Jack had to be clear about what that might mean.

'Do what you need to, Bob,' Jack said once

more. 'Any means you deem necessary. You know how important this is right now.'

The American understood. 'I will set the wheels in motion immediately. Things will happen very quickly.'

Jack nodded his head sadly. 'Just, um ...' he began, uncharacteristically caught on his words. His throat sounded tight. 'I don't want anyone suffering unnecessarily ...'

'Understood,' The American reassured him. 'Don't give it any further thought.'

At this point, however, suffering was unavoidable.

CHAPTER 16

DETECTIVE ANDY FLYNN looked up to see Makedde crossing the restaurant towards him, returning from the ladies room. She looked damned gorgeous, and the sight of her gave him a tingle in his stomach that was something like pain. He would miss her, and worry.

Mak ...

She wore a simple black dress that followed her curves, her stride unselfconscious, her fair hair falling naturally around her face and down to her chest. Her movement was part youthful bounce and part sophisticated saunter from her days on the catwalk. But that wasn't all she'd retained from the catwalk: Mak still had the long slim legs and head-turning hourglass figure of a model, and several patrons in the restaurant looked up as she made her way to the table. She seemed blissfully unaware of the effect she had on other people; he'd always liked that about her. She'd never been what he deemed a typical model. In fact, there had never been anything typical about her.

The outright stares in Mak's direction did not make Andy jealous. He was used to them by now, having been with her on and off for nearly five years, during which time she seemed only to grow more frustratingly striking, not less. Whether in jeans and sneakers or in a gown, she had a quality that turned heads. But Andy could never quite give in enough to his feelings to fall fully in love with her again, the way he had before she refused his hand in marriage. Perhaps it was fear of rejection. Sure, she was loving and attentive, but also unpredictable and independent and exciting, even more independent than his ex-wife, Cassandra, had been.

Cassandra had divorced him. It had stung.

Now Andy was with Mak, but he could never quite have her completely, he sensed. Still, something in him wished he could. That desire to possess her was a beast Mak awoke in many men – not just Andy, and some of them less than desirable. There was a quality about her that made men want to tame her. Perhaps it was that fierce independence and strength; her kamikaze dedication to life. She was unique.

I'll miss her.

Would absence make her heart grow fonder? Perhaps then she would reconsider his offer.

★ ★ ★

Makedde took her seat across the intimate table

setting of their candlelit dinner at Bondi Icebergs. Andy watched her as she took her seat and she gave him a champagne grin.

She liked the way he was looking at her. He looked delicious in a dark suit and open shirt, and she leaned in to him, her full mouth closed in a pleasant, pouting grin, urging him to cover the remaining distance to kiss her. He did.

Mmmm ...

She'd had a couple of glasses of champagne since they'd arrived at the restaurant and her cheeks felt warm. There were two fresh glasses of bubbly on the table, and a candle flickering in the centre of the white tablecloth. Oysters had come and gone.

This had been a good idea. This restaurant was booked out weeks in advance for a Friday night; he'd done well to get them in. She was pleased that he'd made the effort.

'I love this,' she said and smiled. She didn't want to talk about his flight to Virginia, or his impending three-month absence. For now she just wanted to bask in the champagne glow and relax in his presence. It felt like it had been ages since they'd dined together – or made love.

How long have we been together?

Five years.

It had been just over five years since they'd first met on the beach at La Perouse. It had hardly been an ideal encounter, considering that she was at the time the traumatised witness to the body of her murdered best friend, Cat, and the site of her brief initial meeting with Andy was a bloody crime scene. But somehow, in the ensuing weeks, and despite the horror of that beginning, an attraction had blossomed. It had been a rocky five years, but despite their on-again, off-again start, they had managed to spend the past year living together.

'It's great to be here, just you and me,' she said. 'The bubbly is nice, too.'

Mak waited for him to respond as she smiled and sipped from her glass of champagne. He returned her playful look, which she found encouraging.

'You look great tonight. It makes me wish I wasn't leaving,' he said.

That's the idea.

Mak crossed her legs and leaned back into the chair. 'You scrub up okay yourself, detective. I have to grudgingly admit that I'll probably miss the sight of you ... a little.' She laughed and he looked at her with one of his sexy, lopsided grins.

'Andy, I'm really sorry I was so late tonight. I didn't expect my meeting to go that long,' she apologised again.

'Don't worry about it. It worked out perfectly. Stop thinking about it.'

'Okay,' she agreed. 'We haven't been to this place since ...' She paused. '*Years ago,*' she said, avoiding a discussion of the circumstances of that last dinner here.

'I pulled a few strings to get us in,' Andy admitted. 'Someone owed me a favour.'

It had been more than two years since they had dined here. And that had been at the end of the first triumphant day of the Stiletto Murder trial. That night everyone had been delighted, not least her and Andy. They had broken up for several months and had dated other people – or at least *he* had – but they found themselves coming together that night over more than a few champagnes, the stress of the trial lifted. Mak vividly recalled their erotic reacquaintance, how they had found themselves entwined in a rocky overhang by the nearby cliffs, eagerly making up for their time apart. He'd had to go to work the next day with rock rash on his palms and elbows, from fucking her over and over at the cliff's edge. She wondered if she could lure him back to that rocky outcrop once more, on this eve of his Quantico trip.

Mak craned her neck in the direction of the crashing waves outside the large windows, and said, 'It really is beautiful out there.' The spectacular view – which they could see but not fully enjoy from their table – overlooked famous Bondi Beach, which was lit up in a speckle of lights at night, the fine white sand and crested waves moonlit.

'What was your meeting tonight? You said you were in someone's bathroom.'

Mak smiled. 'Yes. Meaghan Wallace's parents. I've been hired to look into her murder. I'm really excited about it, actually,' Mak finished the

181

last of her champagne. 'The case is complicated, and interesting.'

Andy frowned. 'Hunt told me about it. A junkie kid stabbed someone for cash for his next fix. It happens all the time.'

Mak pulled back a touch from the table. He had a way of subtly belittling her work that sometimes irritated her.

'It's not that simple, Andy,' she retorted.

'Isn't it that simple? Sweetheart, really ...' He took her hand. 'Try telling that to that girl's parents.'

'I did. Only a couple of hours ago,' she shot back and pulled her hand away. 'That's why I was late. It's interesting, but the victim's mother doesn't think the suspect the police have is the right one.'

He didn't have a response to that. At least a minute passed with Andy looking awkwardly at the table, and Mak looking off at the distant window and the view, obstructed by the other diners, her jaw held tight.

Fuck. The mood could change just like that.

'Let's talk about something else,' she suggested.

'Tell me about what's happening with you, really,' said Andy. His tone was apologetic. 'I want to listen.'

'Well, Loulou has a new boyfriend,' she told him. And she'll be in Melbourne with him. *In Melbourne, where Meaghan Wallace's friend Amy lives.* 'I think I'll make the effort to meet him this weekend,' she found herself saying. 'Apparently he lives in Melbourne. Loulou will be there with him, so I'll visit.

'I think I'll leave tomorrow,' Mak said with more conviction. 'I don't want to be in that empty house this weekend, knowing you won't be back for so long.'

'Oh, Mak, I'm sorry.'

'Don't be. It's great for your career. It's the right thing to do. You have to. I just wish I had the money to visit you a few times. Three months is ... a long time.'

'It will go past before we know it.'

Mak offered him a smile.

I hope so.

CHAPTER 17

LUTHER HAND SAT in the window seat of the business-class cabin of a 747 headed for Sydney, Australia. The breadth of his shoulders allowed him just enough space to turn on a slight angle and watch the ground fall out from beneath him, the palm trees and masses of scattered buildings of the Mumbai Chattrapathi Shivaji international airport shrinking to dots behind him. The view from the air always pleased him, giving him a glimpse of the gods, he felt, and Luther always took the window position to enjoy that special vantage point.

The flight was busy. Every single seat in the entire aircraft was taken, save for the one beside him. It was equipped with a headset, blanket and toiletries kit, and yet it sat empty. He was happy for his privacy but, truthfully, Luther seldom had to worry about sitting next to nosy passengers. He was a big man; imposing, some said. Passengers usually found ways to avoid sitting next to him, and so Luther always had space to stretch out in and to think. He would be well rested for his work in Sydney.

Luther had a new assignment.

Madame Q, one of the contacts through which he was given new assignments, had confirmed his urgent job in Australia only hours before. Luther had been born and raised in Sydney – not that he bore much resemblance to the boy he'd been. His reputation and his familiarity with the city made him a good choice for this assignment. And, although Luther had spent much of his life in Sydney, he was still a safely anonymous figure there, as he had not returned in nearly five years. His presence would be unexpected, and his knowledge of the suburbs and culture would be an asset. Interestingly, though, this was the first job of this kind for him in the country of his birth since he had moved overseas, most likely because he was now priced well outside the range affordable to the majority of Australian clients.

Luther had found success since leaving his homeland and he had built a formidable reputation for his trade among the right international circles. The spoils of his success had afforded him a stunning, modern high-rise apartment in the district of Colaba in Mumbai – not that any amount of money would clear away the beggars or the stench of the betel juice that was spat on the sidewalks. But, as a foreigner, he was not bothered there. He could go about his business as he chose. Apart from his apartment, his freedom and his work, Luther did not have anything; men like him rarely did.

Still, his freedom was more than many in his occupation had.

Luther, 'the hands of Lucifer' – or 'Mr Hand', as he was called professionally – was what was referred to as 'a cleaner' in some circles, but naturally he did not specialise in windows, or bathrooms, or hotel rooms.

Luther was an exterminator.

He removed problems. He cleaned.

This new assignment paid a top-dollar retainer. It was open-ended, but would contractually require not less than two hits. A few more jobs like this and Luther could retire ... though he did not know what he had to retire to.

He had a pleasant enough feeling about the impending job, despite the potential for a number of last-minute variables. For instance: the client had not been able to specify precisely how many marks he would require Luther to take care of. The deposit, however, had been confirmed in his Swiss bank account before his departure, despite the short notice of the booking, and the amount comfortably covered a number of targets. The price agreed upon had been high, and had the potential of rising, which gave Luther sufficient reason to feel satisfied.

Luther was an adaptable contractor, and experienced. And, as it turned out, the world was a very big place, filled with a lot of people who needed a lot of cleaning.

Unlike a Mafia hit man, Luther had no family

ties, no affiliations and no favours owing. He was a free agent, and he could work anywhere and for anyone. He could go in, do the job and get out with no established connection to the crime, or to the client. And Luther did not cling to any idealistic codes. He would clean anyone, regardless of age or sex, and he could handle multiples, or the kind of uncertainties that his job in Sydney held. As a cleaner, he was adaptable and unattached – all considered great assets in his trade.

Luther now had a thriving international practice. He had contact with good agents who got him frequent bookings, and he was even able to select jobs and in many cases name his own price, as he had on this occasion.

All this – the money, the clothes, the apartment, the jet-set life beset with carefully planned acts of termination – was a long way from his humble beginnings in Redfern in inner Sydney. Luther had grown up with his mother, Cathy, in a two-room flat on a street where no taxi would dare to stop. His childhood stomping ground was an area of housing-commission flats and back-alley deals for drugs and sex, where the 'blackfellas' liked to stage the occasional riot to express their discontent. It had been a law-enforcement black hole during the years of his youth; a poor suburb invisible to the authorities, deemed either too unimportant or too troublesome to deal with. The streets governed themselves.

That hard youth had set Luther up just fine.

He had been in a lot of scraps as a young boy, many of which left noticeable scars to his face and hands, and by the time he was a young man he was working as muscle, and he looked the part. His appearance had caused his mother sorrow, but certainly had not bothered Luther.

Until he had become interested in girls.

Luther had witnessed his repellent effect on women many times. In his teenage years it had been hard for him, but despite this extreme side effect, his appearance became a clear asset in his fledgling career.

Luther had started out enforcing for small-timers and slowly worked his way up the food chain to bigger players. Luther was ugly. He was big. He was strong. People gave him money to be imposing. It was as if he had been designed for his profession. But the real money was in killing, as he discovered. He found it ironic that clients still put such a lofty price on life. Why be paid less to rough a guy up and leave him alive to identify you when you could kill him instead, get away clean and be paid more for the pleasure? As a cleaner, he earned more than he could have possibly imagined back in Redfern.

Berlin. Paris. Rome. Moscow. Dubai. Johannesburg. Bangkok. Hong Kong.

Luther had a stake in a number of markets. Anywhere there were already plenty of thugs and killers, it seemed that certain clients with enough financial backing periodically needed a cleaner to simplify their employee structure. Luther was perfect for the job.

Coming to Sydney, however, brought up another issue he had not thought about for some time.

Cathy Davis.

Should he try to see her?

Perhaps not. How could a man like Luther explain his long absence, his appearance, his changed name, his fine clothes, to his own mother? He had changed a lot in the five years since he'd last been home to Australia. He had been small-time then. Luther drove a good car and wore good clothes now, and looked different as well – almost unrecognisably so. He'd used some of his money for surgery in Asia to try to fix the damage done to his face from earlier jobs; damage inflicted with fists, and iron knuckles and crowbars.

No one touched his face now.

No one ever got that close.

CHAPTER 18

JACK CAVANAGH LAY restless in the master bedroom of his huge waterfront mansion, next to the warm sleeping body of his wife, Beverley. While she slumbered soundly, his eyes were wide and staring into black shadows.

Why, Damien? How did I fail you?

Jack was deeply troubled by what his son had done, and he was troubled too by what he had just consented to. There were things that The American would make happen, terrible things that would be done in the pursuit of damage control. And though the true seriousness of Mr Hand's work was never uttered, the word '*murder*' not actually stated, that knowledge was implicit.

Jack would never pull a trigger, but neither was he innocent. He knew full well that his consent to Mr Hand's activities would mean death for some human being, or beings, out there. Mr Hand meant to murder those who would topple the hard-earned Cavanagh empire, and Jack would pay him handsomely for it.

Jack's throat tightened. His eyes grew sore, fighting tears he would not allow.

He felt ashamed.

Jack Cavanagh felt the weight of his own father's judgment on him. What would he have done in Jack's place? Would he have given consent to what was about to take place – those unmentioned, terrible things he 'did not need to know about'?

Why, Damien? Why?

How did I fail you?

Such musings were pointless.

It was done. The wheels were in motion.

★ ★ ★

While Jack Cavanagh stared at the dark ceiling of his luxurious bedroom, lying next to his wife, his highly paid security consultant was hard at work. No idealistic concerns entered the mind of The American; he was trained for such eventualities, and familiar with making the hard choices necessary to ensure the security of his clients.

Bob had a lot of work to do.

In the interests of his billionaire client, it was of paramount importance that he track down all communications that the girl at the party, Meaghan Wallace, had made in the time leading up to her death; specifically, any SMS and video messages from her mobile phone that might contain evidence of Damien Cavanagh's involvment in criminal activities. He had to establish the level of threat and the seriousness of the leak, and he needed to stay under the radar of the Australian authorities and the public as he went about his work.

Having spent over a decade of his career as the head of the Federal Bureau of Investigation's headquarters in California, The American was well connected and well respected, even now as an independent contractor. He had people he could call on in instances such as these.

George would be an asset in what he had to accomplish, albeit an expensive one.

The American dialled using his personal Iridium satellite phone – the signals from which were non-geostationary and too fast-moving to be effectively tapped – and reached his contact at his home in Maryland around six in the morning.

'George, it's Bob calling from Australia. I am sorry to wake you.'

'Bob? I don't believe it.' George gave out a good-natured laugh, his American accent sounding more prominent than Bob had remembered. With the years he had grown used to the Australian twang. 'Nah, I wasn't sleeping. At my age you don't need much sleep. Tell me, how are things down unda?'

'Very well, George. Very well.' After some friendly chitchat he got to the task at hand. 'George, I have another favour to ask ... on similar terms ...'

George was high in the command at the US National Security Agency. And the NSA, along with Britain's GCHQ, ran an intelligence program codenamed 'Echelon' which was of particular value in solving Bob's problem for his client. Australia was one of the five countries cooperating in the signals intelligence (SigInt) program. The secretive, decades-old UK–USA alliance bound together signals intelligence agencies in the United Kingdom, Canada, New Zealand and Australia with the NSA to scan every single phone call, fax, email and SMS message in Australia – and the world – for the interests of security. Thus the communications of Meaghan Wallace had already been intercepted by the electronic ears at the Geraldton facility in Western Australia and automatically sent on to the US, where the men at the NSA could now retrieve them. Strictly speaking, the system was used for spying on communications in the interests of national security: communications relating to North Korean military plans, Pakistani nuclear development and, since 9/11, terrorist activity. Every single communication in the world went through the sophisticated program called 'The Dictionary', which flagged topics of interest based on relevant keywords, names and phone numbers. The giant global spy system had other commercial and political uses, too. When she was in office, British Prime Minister Margaret Thatcher famously ordered a tap on two of her Cabinet members, and also used the Canadian arm of Echelon to bug the mobile phone of Margaret Trudeau, wife of the then Prime Minister Pierre Trudeau. Bob himself had personally ordered the surveillance of certain multinational companies through Echelon's vast capabilities in the lead-up to one of Jack Cavanagh's biggest international commercial deals, and it had given them a great edge over the competition.

Bob's latest request would go against SigInt's new rules, but it could be done.

For a price.

To see that his client's multimillion-dollar transportation deal went through smoothly, there was little Bob White would not, or could not, do. Within twenty-four hours he should have traced the call received by Jack Cavanagh, tracked down the potential blackmailer, Warwick O'Connor, and traced all of Meaghan Wallace's recent communications. By then, Madame Q's man Mr Hand would be on the ground and ready to move on the list of targets.

CHAPTER 19

OH GOD . . .

Makedde ran as fast as her legs could transport her, muscles aching with the effort. There was no time. She needed to get there FAST, and if she didn't get there fast enough, he would take another life – her mother's life. Without Jane all would be lost. How could the world keep turning without her? The sun would stop shining. All life would come to a terrible end, leaving only a desolate world devoid of meaning. *I must get there in time. I have to save her.* With adrenaline pumping loud in her ears, Mak kicked through the door and into the room.

Almost too late. Almost too late. Almost . . .

'Stop!' she called out, trying to raise her weapon. 'Put it down! Don't do it!'

There it was.

She saw IT – that dark, malevolent thing lingering like a dense shadow in the room, a shadow made up of tiny fragments of hate, the very embodiment of utter evil. IT was holding her mother down on a bed – *Makedde's own mother.*

IT had a blade in its hand. A scalpel.

Makedde tried to lift her gun to shoot but her father's police uniform held her arm down, the sleeves too heavy to bear, too tough to lift. The gun turned to pure lead – heavy, so heavy – and it too could not be lifted. Her arm stayed at her side, useless, pointless, the gun too much for her. Helplessly, she watched the blade of the scalpel come down in a swift arc, the faceless demon laughing at her feeble efforts to prevent the death of her mother.

Makedde's feet were glued in place, the floor sticky with red fluid. She tried to leap forward to stop the blade as it swung down, but it was no use. She could only watch.

'*Noooo!*'

She was too late. Again.

The scalpel continued its arc, the room turning crimson, everything now deep red – everyone; the shadow was red, her mother was red, and the stench of death was overpowering. The shadow laughed at her, revelling in her horror, revelling in the crimson – crimson everywhere, covering everything, covering her eyes. Beneath the red she saw tall grasses swaying in the wind. She smelled salty sea air. There was death in the air and on the wind. The grasses began to turn and as they did, blade by blade, they turned the red colour of freshly spilled blood.

Mak cried out.

'Are you okay?' a voice said.

The shadowy creature was laughing, the sound filling her heart with horrible heaviness. She felt like she was dying ...

'Mak!'

A voice broke through the fragments of her murky thoughts. Someone was drawing her out of that horrible scene, her failed attempt to save her mother, the terrifyingly sadistic torture and abduction, Catherine's torn body; Mak's heart filling with darkness; the shadowy demon, faceless and terrible, laughing at her failure; the overwhelming blood and death.

'Mak – wake up! Wake up! You're having a nightmare.'

Andy was shaking her gently by the shoulders, and Makedde found that she was already sitting up in bed.

Oh God. I've had another bad dream.

'Mak, are you okay? What was it about, the nightmare?' he asked.

'I was dreaming, wasn't I?' she said, disoriented, but already knowing it was a dream, and a familiar one.

Makedde was in their dark bedroom. Moonlight crept in through the half-open blinds, casting faint light in odd shapes across the bed covers. As her eyes adjusted she could make out Andy's face; she reached out to him and stroked it with one hand. Her fingertips felt stubble.

'You're here ...'

'What was your nightmare about?' he asked.

He had both hands on her shoulders, gripping her softly.

'I can't quite remember,' she mumbled, searching for the dream that was slipping away on waking.

'Look at you,' he said. In the faint light she could see that he was shaking his head.

Mak put her hands to her face and neck and realised that her skin was glistening with sweat. Her pillow felt damp. It had been a very vivid dream; they always were.

'Are you okay? You seemed pretty scared. Was it that same dream?'

She squinted and rubbed her forehead. 'Yes. But ... it was a little different this time. I should get my dream diary. Where did I put it?'

Mak had suffered nightmares and insomnia on and off for the five years, since her abduction by a sadistic criminal who had tied her to a bed in a cabin out in the woods – before this man who now lay beside her, Detective Andy Flynn, had intervened, saving her life. Her father's girlfriend, Dr Ann Morgan, had recommended that Mak start a dream diary to record her sleeping habits and the details of her dreams. She had not made an entry for some time. She had, in fact, thought her sleeping was back to normal – but now, in her dreams at least, it felt like some terrible thing had returned to her life. The dark thing that had haunted her was back.

'You can do that in the morning,' Andy said

of her dream diary. 'Don't think about it any more, okay? Come here.' He pulled her into his arms, and she pressed her face against his soft chest hair.

Mak was glad of his presence, and glad it had just been a dream. She liked the feeling of him against her, and she liked when he was tender like this.

Her death was not your fault. It wasn't anyone's.

Jane Vanderwall had died of cancer, not at the hands of some demonic creature Mak failed to save her from. Cancer was a horrible disease that had taken not only her mother, but so many other people as well. She was not alone in having lost a parent. It had been five-and-a-half years since her mother, bald and painfully swollen from chemotherapy, had finally lost her brave battle.

And the world had continued to turn after she was gone. You didn't think it would.

During the months when her mother was in hospital suffering through a bone marrow transplant, and the prognosis was bad, Makedde had really wondered if her own heart could keep on beating without the woman who had brought her into the world.

But it had.

Jane Vanderwall fell, and the brutal momentum of life just continued.

'You haven't had nightmares for a while,' Andy said bluntly, concern in his voice. He was right: she hadn't. It had seemed like it was a good year or two since it had been a major problem for her. For a time she had felt quite freed of the death that had shadowed her life for too long, but now there was this dream, and these feelings again. She hoped it was not a bad omen. Perhaps it had to do with Andy's leaving.

'Everything gets so mixed up in my dreams,' Mak said.

There was her mother on the bed under that horrible blade – rather than Makedde herself, as it had really been. Mak was always wearing her father's police uniform in her nightmare, and it never fitted her. It stopped her from moving forwards. And, of course, that nightmare always featured Death, and the cutting scalpel of her attacker. The only thing that really made sense upon waking was her feeling of horror and loss. That feeling was real, even if all the elements were mixed up.

She looked at the clock. It was 2 a.m.

Makedde tried to shut off her brain. Thoughts were slippery and unbalanced in half-waking. It was not a good time to try to solve the world's problems: there was nothing she could do at two in the morning that would make things more clear. Andy would leave, and she would go to Melbourne to visit Loulou and track down Meaghan's friend Amy. She needed to keep herself busy.

'I'm going to take a shower,' Makedde said

abruptly and threw back the sheet on her side of the bed. 'I feel all ... *icky*.'

For fifteen minutes Mak stood under the hot pulsing jets of their cramped en-suite shower, the slippery spiral of thoughts and nightmarish images seeming to fall off her with the water, swirling down the drain at her feet and disappearing – for the moment, at least.

She shut off the tap and took a deep breath. Her naked body felt refreshed and clean. Beads of water trickled down her skin.

Mak walked back into the bedroom with a towel wrapped around her. When she returned, Andy was halfway between sleep and waking. Moonlight and shadow played across the light bedsheets, the summer evening warm and the window open.

'Andy,' she whispered, but then decided she didn't want to use words.

Mak knelt on the edge of the bed and let her towel drop. Slowly, she pushed the sheet back. In the low light she could see Andy's naked masculine form in its entirety. He lay on his back on the bed, his tall frame stretched from pillow to foot, arms above his head. She ran her warm hands across his naked body, and followed her fingertips with gentle kisses, first on his chest, one nipple and then the other, then down his stomach along the thin line of dark hair that trailed to his groin. Andy lay still while her hands found him, caressed him, urged him to attention.

Before long she had crawled on top of him, straddling his hips and pressing her mouth to his. They kissed passionately, as those who have been starved of sexual love do. Tongues darted in and out. He grabbed the back of her head, his fingers in her wet hair, pulling her closer.

Mak pulled away. 'I'll miss this,' she whispered in his ear, and pushed her hips down on him. It was so good to feel him enter her. They fitted together tightly like puzzle pieces, and began to move in unison. Andy was hard and eager, and his hands were caressing her flesh, moving from one soft place to another, reaching up for her neck, her shoulders, her nipples, her firm breasts, as his pelvis moved and rocked. Her breasts swayed slightly as she leaned over him, her nipples brushing against his chest. She threw her wet hair back, sending a small shower of droplets over them, and he gripped her waist while she rode him, water dripping slowly down her torso.

CHAPTER 20

ON SATURDAY MORNING, Mak found herself stretched across the bed with one hand tightly gripping the bedhead. It took her a while to focus. Her eyelids felt heavy.

'Andy?'

He often got up early. Even while he was in town, he could not be found waking with her. But if he had already gone, it would mean she'd missed him.

She felt a flash of panic.

Wait.

A noise.

Mak sat up and covered her breasts with the sheet. 'Hello?'

'Hey.'

Andy sauntered into the bedroom, half-dressed. His white dress shirt was open to show a lean and tan chest. He had a line of hair trailing down into his boxer shorts. She remembered kissing that hair inch by inch. It made her smile.

'Come here,' she said provocatively.

'I have to go.'

Her heart sank, though she had known it was coming.

'Come here anyway,' she dared him.

'When's your flight to Melbourne?' he asked, standing his ground near the dresser as he did up his buttons.

'I'll go in the early afternoon.' She had to call Marian and check with her first. If the client really wanted such a thorough check done, Mak felt justified in tracking Amy down. Hopefully Amy would be forthcoming, and would know something about Simon Aston.

'Oh,' Andy said. 'I thought you were leaving earlier. I agreed to go along with Jimmy to this autopsy from the dumpster case. He'll drive me straight to the airport.'

'Well, take it easy on breakfast then,' she quipped, trying to make light of their last minutes together.

It's a Saturday. He is going to the morgue on a Saturday before his flight.

'You know, you are going to have to stop holding Jimmy's hand eventually.'

Andy's expression turned dark.

'Sorry,' she back-pedalled. 'You know what I mean. But it's cool. I have something to do before I head out anyway, so I'd better get going myself.' She was pretending that she hadn't wanted him to just leap back into bed and make love to her again before he left. 'Do you need a lift or anything?' she asked.

'No.'

'Okay.' She watched him as he slipped his pants on and his shoes. 'I love you,' she said as he tied his laces.

'Ditto.'

'Ditto' had never quite seemed an adequate reply to Mak, but it was one she was accustomed to hearing.

Laces tied and ready to go, Andy moved towards her and bent to kiss her gently on the mouth.

'Have a good trip. Kick butt,' she said, and he smiled.

She watched him leave, then listened to his footsteps as he went down the stairs and out the front door. When she heard the door slam she pulled the sheet over her head.

Fuck!

★ ★ ★

By 8.59 a.m. Detective Andrew Flynn was sitting in the viewing theatre of the NSW Forensic Institute, packed and ready for his flight, his bags in Jimmy's car, reviewing the paperwork on the Surry Hills 'dumpster girl' case. He'd wanted to crawl back into bed with Makedde, but yet another death called him. And when death called, he always answered. Understanding murder was Andy's life.

The seats in the small gallery were elevated, as if overlooking an intimate theatrical performance.

He and Detective Jimmy Cassimatis had taken a seat at the back of the six rows.

The fact that the as-yet-unidentified body of the girl had been found *behind* a dumpster gave Andy reason to suspect that this was not a murder committed by someone with a great deal of planning or experience. Perhaps the perpetrator had intended to dispose of the body within the deep dumpster itself, but had been unable to lift it high enough on his own, and had had to settle for leaving it behind the dumpster amongst the garbage bags? Andy guessed that the suspect was inexperienced and not very strong.

The gruesome work of maggots – nature's natural cleaning helpers – and the presence of certain insects in the victim's eyes, nose and mouth, as well as gas blisters and early swelling, had led to an estimated time of death as about three days prior. Upon completion of a full medico-legal autopsy, the results would be narrowed down to a more exact time frame, although not nearly as exact as the popular forensic television shows would have the public believe. There were too many variables affecting decomposition to be able to say with any certainty that 'the victim died at 8.32'. Nonetheless, the life cycles of the insects that aid decomposition are so exact that the forensic entomologists would have a date and a time of day narrowed to perhaps one hour. The days had been warm, so the weather would have accelerated the decomposition process.

If the girl had been left inside the dumpster she would probably not have been discovered until the Sunday night garbage rounds. Andy could only guess that her body had been placed there well after the previous garbage pick-up, but mere hours after her actual death. By the time she'd reached that alley, her struggle for life had been well and truly over.

There was a noise, and they looked up.

The doors of the autopsy gallery opened and an attendant entered in his scrub suit and shoe covers, pushing a gurney. The small body of the victim lay under a white sheet. Within minutes he had transferred the deceased to the autopsy table and pulled a clear plastic shield down over his face. The pathologist entered, and removed the white sheet.

Andy was taken aback by her youth. The girl appeared to be no older than thirteen, perhaps younger. Her body was swelling from the gases of decomposition. There was little dignity in nature's death process.

So young.

'*Skata*, she's just a kid.'

'Yeah.'

The Dumpster Girl was of Thai descent. She had no identification on her, so they were in the process of running dental records, fingerprints – anything they could – to try to figure out who the young woman had been. Thus far, the only possible clue to her identity was a very large, intricate tattoo across her lower back. That, at least, was one identifying marker that might help the investigation. Although tattoos were commonplace, they were highly unusual on someone her age; most parlours in Australia would not perform work on a minor. The style and age of the tattoo might just lead them to a list of possible tattoo parlours where the work had been done – assuming that she had been born in Australia. Andy was no expert on tattoos; in fact, he was revolted by them, thanks to the large number of criminals who bore them. But the presence of such brandings often aided in identifying both criminals and victims in a variety of cases.

As with all homicides, the girl's hands had been covered in paper bags to retain any important evidence, and Andy noticed that the bags had already been removed. The examiners had no doubt worked tirelessly to find any skin under her fingernails, or any substances that might be traced. In many ways it was a saving grace that she had been discovered just behind the dumpster rather than in the thing itself, as the garbage would have contaminated any evidence infinitely more.

Now the internal examination would begin.

The head pathologist began with the traditional Y incision extending from shoulder to shoulder, meeting at the breastbone, and finally extending all the way to the pubic bone. Andy was grateful for the panes of glass separating them from the autopsy. He had seen enough autopsies to be used to them, but the smell was something that no one ever fully adapted to. The word *autopsy* comes from the Greek *autopsia*, meaning 'seeing for oneself'. Andy was content to see for himself and leave the smell on the other side of the glass.

His mobile phone was on vibrate, and it buzzed twice. Andy surreptiously checked the text message.

I LOVE YOU, SEXY. HAVE A GREAT TRIP.

It was Mak.

She'd been so responsive, so eager. The sight of her body laid out on the bed, nude and welcoming, was a vivid memory. Her breasts were soft and full, her waist the perfect size to fit his arm around while they made love. He hadn't wanted to leave.

Andy read the message furtively and hid it from Jimmy. He tucked his phone away and looked up just in time to see the young girl's chest being opened with the surgical equivalent of a large wrench. For a moment the mental image of Makedde's nakedness and the Dumpster Girl mixed in his head, and he felt sick.

'Sooooo, was that yer girlfriend?' Jimmy teased, seemingly oblivious to their location. 'Was it hot make-up sex? Did she spank you or anything?'

'Not now,' Andy snapped, not wanting to play Jimmy's little game while he was viewing some poor girl's organs being taken in one connected block and placed on a stainless steel tray. Andy never understood how Jimmy could talk about things like that while an autopsy was going on in full view a few metres away.

'Come on, mate, don't be like that. You know I gotta live vicariously through you.' Jimmy knew Andy wouldn't answer him, so he got onto business. 'Okay, I've got the guys doing the rounds of the tattoo parlours checking on that ink, like you suggested. They were able to make up a pretty clear shot of it for us.' He passed an enlarged photo to Andy. It was a good image, certainly clear enough for someone to identify.

'Let's hope she's local and that she had the work done here,' Andy commented, inspecting the photograph.

'Who here would work on a girl under eighteen?'

'I hope to find out.'

They had not got a match on her prints. If they couldn't get any clues to her identity she might end up as just another Jane Doe, stored away indefinitely in the freezers of the morgue, both her murder and her identity a mystery.

There was a sound from outside the viewing theatre and Jimmy and Andy both looked towards it. The door opened and Detective Sergeant Hunt entered.

'Hunt?' Andy said softly.

'Yeah, he's taken over now,' Jimmy whispered with little enthusiasm. He had not worked with Hunt before.

'I'm sure you two will be like best mates in no time,' Andy answered under his breath.

'*Skata*.'

Hunt was in his late thirties, with a good suit, a light blond brush cut and an exaggerated chin like a hero in a Marvel comic. He was ambitious, political and slick – everything Jimmy was not. Hunt had worked under Andy at one point, and had soon risen through the ranks with unprecedented speed. Now he outranked Jimmy, who had been in the coppers for nearly ten years longer.

The detective sergeant approached.

'Hunt,' Flynn addressed him.

'Flynn.'

Hunt took a seat one row ahead of them, in the centre, inadvertently giving Jimmy an opportunity to make faces at his back. Jimmy cupped his hand and jerked it around near his groin, mouthing the word 'wanker'.

'I haven't missed anything, have I?' Hunt said stupidly, leaning back with his arms extended like he was watching TV in his lounge room.

Andy looked down on the sad, bloated corpse through the glass. 'No, they're just getting started.'

It seemed to Andy that Hunt had probably avoided as many autopsy viewings as possible in the past.

'Aren't you leaving today?'

'Yes,' Andy replied distractedly, his eyes drawn to the girl's heart as it was separated from the other organs and weighed.

CHAPTER 21

MAKEDDE CHECKED THE contents of her overnight bag: change of clothes, make-up, wallet, notepad, monocular, camera. She zipped up the bag and slung it over her shoulder. Marian had booked her a cheap flight for one o'clock and organised a hotel at the other end. The client was happy for Mak to seek information from Meaghan's interstate friend – so long as it didn't cost him too much, so Mak imagined the hotel wouldn't be too flash.

She had a couple of hours up her sleeve before the flight, so she figured she had time to make one stop before boarding her flight for Melbourne.

Jag.

It was best not to turn up in leathers if she wanted to gain the girl's trust, so Mak made her way downstairs and scrounged around in the miscellaneous drawer in the kitchen to find the spare set of keys to Andy's little red Honda among a bunch of elastic bands, paperclips and unused suitcase locks. The airport parking for two days was more than it would cost her for a cab, so she would return with the car in time to take a taxi.

Mak left her packed overnight bag by the front door and set off.

Meaghan's friend Jag lived in a crumbly terrace in the suburb of Newtown, a groovy 'alternative' area of Sydney, with cafés, CD and book shops, and fetish stores. Mak took a deep breath and walked up to Jag's front door.

Okay, here goes.

Thankfully she found that she felt nowhere near as awkward as she had walking up to the Wallace household the day before. Perhaps she was getting used to knocking on strangers' doors.

Makedde rang the doorbell. There were footsteps, and then a young man with spiky blond Billy Idol hair opened the door.

'Hey, is Jag around?' Mak asked casually.

'Ah, no, she's gone to the Angelo,' he said, as if that should make sense to her.

'Oh, the Angelo. Yeah. Where is that again?' Mak asked.

'Just on the corner,' he said. 'It's, like, two blocks that way.' He pointed west.

'Cool, yeah. Thanks,' Mak replied, and trundled off in the direction in which he had pointed. He watched her go, perhaps wondering who she was.

Mak had no idea what the Angelo was, but she hoped she would spot it easily enough, and she also hoped that Jag would look like her picture.

The Michelangelo Café was indeed two blocks from Jag's place. It was a run–down and dusty little place with wooden tables and a badly executed mural of Michelangelo's 'David' painted across the walls and ceiling. There were few patrons, but they included a girl who fitted Jag's description seated near the back of the place, hunched over a plate. Mak had the distinct impression that the young woman was hungover. She had a plate of fried eggs and bacon in front of her, largely untouched.

Mak sidled up beside her.

'Hey, Jag, how are you?' she said casually.

Jag looked up, startled. Her reactions seemed a bit slow.

'How's it going? Big night, huh?'

Jag nodded.

'Can I sit down?' Mak asked, and pulled out a chair for herself before the young woman could answer.

'Do I know you?' Jag said, looking at her suspiciously.

'Well,' Mak told her, 'this is about your friend Meaghan Wallace.'

Jag stopped her feeble attempts at eating. 'Megs?'

'Yeah,' Mak said. 'Megs.'

The girl nodded. 'It's awful what happened to her.'

'It is,' Mak agreed. She could see that Jag was sharp, even when hungover. Pulling the wool over her eyes seemed unnecessary. 'Jag, I am trying to figure out what happened to her. I'm working on behalf of someone who really cares about her, and wants to know the truth about her murder.'

'You're a . . .'

'Private investigator, yes.'

Jag folded her arms. 'Well, that's great but I don't know anything.'

'Maybe,' Mak replied, giving her verbal room to move, 'but I just thought I'd chat to you, because she considered you a friend. Sometimes we can know something helpful without realising it.'

'Who are you working for, exactly?'

'That's confidential, I'm afraid. But I'm not working for the cops, or the Feds, I can tell you that much.' She slipped a card across the table and Jag looked it over.

'Her parents hired you, didn't they?' she said.

Mak didn't answer. If she wanted to believe it was Meaghan's parents who had hired her, that might be a good thing.

'Do you know Noelene and Ralph well?' Mak asked.

Jag shook her head. 'Nah. Megs mentioned them, though. Look, I don't know why you think I'd be helpful, but I don't know anything. I didn't really know her that well.'

'You were friends, though,' Mak pressed.

'We partied together a few times, that's all.

215

Her parents should be sending you to someone like Amy, not me. Amy was her best friend. She knew her a lot better than I did.'

'That's fine.' Mak paused. 'When was the last time you saw Meaghan?'

'Are you sure you're not a cop?' Jag asked, suspicious again.

'Yes I'm sure. And I'd have to tell you if I was a cop, you know,' Mak said, fibbing a little. 'That's the law.' Undercover cops could say what they wanted, and they did.

'Okay. I haven't seen her since New Year's, I think. Like I said, we weren't that close.'

'How about Simon Aston? You know him well?' Mak had a photo ready in case she needed it. But she didn't.

'Simon? Ha! I wish. All the girls wished they knew Simon.'

'Why is that?'

'He was the big tipper, you know. Him and his rich mate, Damien Cavanagh. They used to visit the club a lot.'

'The Rocking Horse?'

'The strip clubs, babe. You know – where Meaghan and I worked?'

Meaghan Wallace had been a stripper – that was where she was getting the money her mother was so confused about. She would never have told her mum. Not a mum like Noelene.

'Amy worked there, too, didn't she?' Mak said with false confidence. That might explain the sexy outfits all three were wearing in the photo. They worked together, they danced together and sometimes partied together.

'Yeah, Amy,' Jag confirmed. 'She works at the Thunderball Club now. I don't know how she makes ends meet. The cash is better up here.'

'Yeah, I heard that,' Mak lied. 'So you hadn't seen Megs since the New Year?'

Jag nodded. 'She had a straight job and she didn't come out much any more.'

Mak understood.

So when she got her straight job, did she stop with the gifts for her folks? Or was she still dabbling on the side?

'Tell the Wallaces I am really sorry about Megs.'

'I'll tell them,' Mak said. 'Thanks for your time. You call me if you think of anything else, okay?'

She nodded, and Mak left the girl with her greasy hangover breakfast.

CHAPTER 22

THE FLIGHT LASTED barely an hour, but Makedde noticed the drop in temperature as soon as she stepped off the plane in Melbourne. Not exactly a snowstorm – as some Sydneysiders had her believing – but it was about 10 degrees cooler. Considering the recent humidity in Sydney, the change was a relief.

'How far is it to ...?' She read the address off her notes to the taxidriver at the airport. 'To St Kilda?'

'Is no problem. Twenty minutes this time of day. Tops.'

Makedde smiled as the taxi passed a bright yellow rod, like a giant French fry, jutting 50 metres into the sky – someone's idea of art. They drove through a space-age tunnel and across an overpass that afforded Mak her first view of the city.

It was already two-thirty in the afternoon. Mak would check in to her hotel, freshen up quickly and make it out to Amy Camilleri's Richmond residential address by perhaps three-thirty; Marian had hunted down the address, so hopefully it was current. Mak would take note of the surrounding area and, if necessary, gently interrogate some of Amy's neighbours to see if she could make any further ground. If Amy was as good a friend of Meaghan's as Jag had suggested, then she should potentially be a great source of information. She could have been privy to a lot of details about Meaghan's personal life; certainly, more than poor Mrs Wallace seemed to know about her daughter, and more than Jag knew or was willing to divulge. Perhaps Amy even knew something about Meaghan's involvement with Simon Aston, if there had been any.

'All the girls wished they knew Simon.'

It worried Mak a little that Amy was not answering the home number she had for her. Mak had tried her a couple of times to use the same Rocking Horse Club ruse to confirm her address, but Amy never answered and, even stranger, she had no answering machine or voicemail. What young woman these days didn't have voicemail? Hopefully the address was up to date, and she would find her at home. And with any luck, Mak hoped, Amy would open up to her.

Marian had organised for Mak to stay at a small St Kilda hotel called the Tolarno. As the taxi pulled up, Mak was surprised to see that the building was a quaint three levels high, and that the front sported a Heineken sign and windows handpainted with swirls of kitsch leaves and a smiling sun. The name 'Tolarno' was painted right across it, so the cabbie was clearly not mistaken. This had to be the right place.

Mak tipped the driver and asked him to wait for her. She didn't know how much time it might take to catch another taxi, and she always liked to have transportation ready when in unfamiliar territory. It was another of her many paranoid habits.

What, exactly, is this place?

Shoulders back and head high, she strode to the bright red front door, overnight bag in hand, turning the heads of a couple of beer-swilling patrons sitting at picnic benches on the Fitzroy Street sidewalk outside. Stepping inside, she had the feeling that she had been mistakenly dropped off at the entrance to a restaurant by the same name. There were signs for 'Le Bar' and 'Le Bistro' and a life-sized modern bronze statue of a couple holding hands. No lobby. No porters.

Right.

There were menus propped up on a wooden easel, and signs for the toilets. Mak stood in the entry for a few seconds feeling disoriented before making her way down a meandering hallway, past walls lined with quirky artworks. The passage eventually opened up into a small lobby and sitting room.

This is more like it.

Mak plonked her bag on the desk and checked in. This was her first interstate job for Marian, and for some reason she had envisaged being booked into a depressing three-star corporate number with bland name-tagged staff, bland halls that smelled vaguely of detergent and cigarettes, and the same bland copied painting of a bouquet in each room. This was an offbeat, retro sort of place, closer to the kind of boutique hotels she had stayed in when she was modelling in Europe. It might have been Australian, but it seemed Euro to Mak, right down to the oversized key, rambling staircase and lack of elevator. Mak found room 222 on the second floor at the end of a big hallway and down an odd set of stairs. Inside was a striking crimson wall and a giant abstract painting of a woman. No flower painting. The room had a good position overlooking the street, the view clear through open wooden slats over the windows. The balcony was exposed; Mak wouldn't use it.

She closed the slats and peeked out through them secretively. She could clearly see the activity on the street. Her taxi was dutifully waiting for her at the kerb.

Mak brushed her teeth, changed her top, slicked deodorant under her arms, packed her long-lens digital camera, pocket-sized monocular, notepad and mini flashlight into her purse, and dashed out the door again. She had been less than ten minutes.

Soon Mak was in the suburb of Richmond. She found Amy's home address a few doors past an old television studio in a large brick building branded with an ancient-looking TVN 9 sign on one side. With few exceptions, the houses in the area looked like wartime shacks: all single-level, with small windows and no yards – far from the sprawling lawns of even the most modest houses on Vancouver Island. Mak let the taxi drive past until she was a block away from Amy's residence. She paid him, got out and walked back slowly along the street, looking perhaps as if she were on her way to the studio. As she walked she took in the neighbourhood, the movement on the street, and any shrub cover or fences she could use to hide behind if she decided to watch the activity at Amy's house for a while.

Amy Camilleri did not live terribly well.

The house she rented appeared to be little more than a one-level weatherboard granny flat extended off another modest single-storey residence. Together the two might just make one small house, by most standards. The house did not seem to be very well kept – the white paint of the front had turned grey and patchy – and it looked like it would be very cramped inside. There was a small tangle of weeds where a garden might have been. It had a single window at the front with curtains drawn, and no driveway or garage. Amy had a fifteen-year-old Peugeot registered to her name, but Mak couldn't see it parked in the surrounding area. At least the lack of garage was good for Mak's spying purposes, as was the clear view of the front door.

The curtains were drawn and motionless. The house looked to be unoccupied, which was terribly disappointing for Mak. She took a chance and knocked quietly on Amy's door. There was no answer. Discreetly, she peered into the mailbox next to the door. It was positively stuffed full of mail, junk mail, advertising flyers and letters. An unopened telephone bill was visible.

She walked around to the side of the house. There was barely a foot between the house and the next one, and nothing in between them but more weeds and a rusted hubcap. She could not comfortably walk between the buildings.

Shit.

Mak circled the block once by foot, noticing that the houses were backed by a narrow laneway of parked cars and rubbish bins. She strolled down it until she came to the back of Amy's house. It had one back door and no other windows.

The place really is a dump.

She approached Amy's garbage bin. She was not above lifting the lid on it, and she did so slowly, with her nose turned up in distaste. She had been taught in her PI course that trash could reveal a lot about a person. Empty champagne bottles and shopping bags said very different things about a person's lifestyle than a bin full of diapers and bulk potato-chip packets. It was creepy, but still totally legal to search through anyone's garbage bins. Sadly, though, Amy's trash had been collected recently. Mak found herself staring for a moment into a smelly, empty bin and wondering how she got from catwalking in the Milan shows to checking out other people's garbage in only a couple of years.

Ah well. Half those outfits were garbage anyway . . .

And when she finally saved enough to open her forensic psychology practice, the only garbage she would have to check through would be in people's heads, she assured herself.

So Amy Camilleri had lots of mail and no garbage. That was not what Mak had come to Melbourne to find out. She guessed that Amy had not been home for at least a week, so the trip might be a bust. She'd have to come back with some kind of result, otherwise it would look like she had simply gone to Melbourne as a holiday to visit Loulou on the client's budget. Which was something that had crossed her mind . . .

Mak wondered again if the client would cover a rental car. If she had needed to stake out Amy's place, it would be much easier and more comfortable in a parked car; but, now that it seemed that Amy had not been home for a while, such plans were pointless. Amy could be away for some time.

Disappointed but not discouraged, Makedde Vanderwall returned to her hotel to get ready for her dinner date with Loulou and her new musician boyfriend. She was not worried just yet. She had at least one more trick up her sleeve.

But the next stage of her investigation could not begin until the sun went down.

CHAPTER 23

SIMON ASTON HELD himself stiffly as he stepped out the front door of his Tamarama abode, gripping the handle of a heavy briefcase that was not his own. He nervously scanned the beach paths and glanced up the street in both directions before locking the front door behind him and approaching his vehicle. The sun was beginning to set, the air cooling. Locals in board shorts and bikinis could be seen gathering their blankets and packing up for the walk home, bodies tanned and sprinkled with salt and sand.

Wasting no time, Simon strode to his prized nocturnal 'party van', placed the briefcase carefully on the passenger seat and set off for the city. A young man normally unhindered by schedules and commitments, Simon was, for once, mindful of the time. The American had instructed him earlier that afternoon that at six o'clock sharp he was to meet with Mr Hand to give him cash and instructions. It was five-forty now, which allowed him just enough time to get to this important appointment. Some cash was in the briefcase, and a set of instructions was in a sealed envelope in his jacket pocket. When The American had entrusted him with the envelope it was already sealed and the case locked. Simon didn't dare open either, and he dared not be late delivering them.

Truthfully, he had been severely shaken by the shocking turn of events.

Since the tense meeting in Jack Cavanagh's office, Simon had not spoken to anyone except The American – not even his mates – and he had not slept. Rather than attending an all-night party with Damien or bedding the latest hot model, visiting socialite or ambitious promotions girl, Simon had spent this last sleepless night at home alone, intensely uneasy about his future. Fear and uncertainty were not feelings he was accustomed to, and the vibe didn't sit well with him. Lying in bed and staring at the ceiling, all kinds of ideas had run through Simon's head – everything from fear of jail to ideas of blackmail and escape. He'd thought about using what evidence he had to dob in Jack and his pushy sidekick to the cops, or teaming up with Warwick to try to bring the Cavanagh empire to its knees through blackmail or scandal. Both the media and the authorities would have a field day with a story like this one, and Simon could deliver the whole sordid tale personally. After The American had met with him that afternoon, he had even briefly imagined breaking open the case, taking all that money and leaving town with it. Hundreds of thousands of dollars could get him somewhere – maybe to a comfortable new life in Bali …

But no.

Simon was no model citizen. He had not so much a skeleton in his closet as a whole crypt, so he was hardly going to speak to any police or reporters. And he knew he had nowhere to run to. Even the money in the case would not sustain him.

He had no choice but to try to salvage the situation, even if it meant being pushed around by Damien's father. Simon needed Damien and his Cavanagh connections for everything he did in his life.

Unlike most of his friends, Simon didn't have a title or an impressive career. He was little more than a part-time procurer who dealt in the occasional weed or cocaine, hookers or heroin – whatever people were into. As he saw it, he was not exactly a drug-dealer; he was just a guy who got stuff for Damien and their friends when they wanted it. And, while not a full-time job by any description, the money he made from those casual transactions was all the income he had. He had his looks, the designer clothes on his back and his Cavanagh connections, and those three things were literally his only assets. Even his van was on lease.

Without wealthy friends who wanted to party, Simon could kiss his little money-making ventures goodbye. And without Damien he could kiss his living arrangements goodbye, too. The Tamarama house he stayed in belonged to the Cavanagh family. It was one of the standard late-seventies buildings of the area with a great view and bad plumbing, and the family was going to knock it down, rebuild and resell it. Damien had talked his father into letting Simon live there in the meantime. So far, Simon had stayed blissfully rent-free for the past two-and-a-half years.

Being cut off would mean disaster for him on every level. It would mean social and financial suicide, and he knew it.

It is your responsibility to make it right, Jack had said.

Responsibility had nothing to do with it, however; Simon would do what he needed to retain his lifestyle.

★ ★ ★

At one minute past six, Simon Aston arrived at the Inter-Continental Hotel on Macquarie Street in the city, leaving his van with the valet and telling him he wouldn't be long. He *hoped* he wouldn't be long. He didn't fully know what this meeting would entail, but he wanted to get it over with as soon as possible.

Simon entered the sliding glass doors with his head down.

'Simon? Is that you?' came a voice.

He whirled around, his heart pounding. It was Julie from the Cavanagh offices.

'Um, hi, Julie,' he said, completely unprepared to run into anyone he knew.

'Are you feeling okay?' she asked, looking at him oddly.

'Sure,' he said. A trickle of sweat ran down from his temple.

'Is Damien around?' she asked, casting a glance around the lobby.

'No! No, he's not here. I'm just, um, meeting a client,' he stuttered.

'Oh. Why don't you guys meet us up in the club lounge for a drink, then?'

'Okay. Um, I gotta go,' he said vaguely. She seemed puzzled as he walked away through the lobby towards the elevators.

Minutes later, it was with great apprehension that Simon knocked on the door of room 2908. 'Excuse me,' he said through the door, feeling hugely uncomfortable. 'I'm here for Mr Hand.'

He waited only a few seconds before a deep voice replied from the other side of the door: 'The time.'

Simon looked at his watch out of instinct.

'Eleven eleven,' he said. He'd been told it was a code.

Then the door was unlocked and opened only enough to set it slightly ajar, so that it wouldn't slide back and lock itself. After a quick pause, Simon pushed it open and stepped inside. The door shut behind him and he was alone, holding the briefcase and the small envelope containing the unknown instructions for Mr Hand. His heart was in his throat.

From what he could see, room 2908 looked to be an average five-star hotel room, complete with double bed, television and small sitting area. The room was dark, except for a floor lamp in the far corner. Simon guessed it would have a nice aspect of Sydney Harbour, but an opaque blind was obscuring the view. Light seeped through the heavy blinds in blurred patches of colour.

A large man in a dark suit sat in a chair in the corner of the sitting area, with his back to the wall. *Mr Hand*, Simon thought. The floor lamp seemed to cast dim light across everything except the man's face, and Simon could not yet make out his features. After the overlit hotel corridor, it was taking a while for Simon's eyes to adjust, and it made him feel even more disadvantaged in this awkward situation.

Great. I can't see him properly, I don't know the plan and I don't know what the fuck I am doing here...

'You must be Mr Hand,' Simon said stupidly to the dark figure in the corner.

The man simply said, 'Simon Ricards Aston.' Again his voice was low and in a monotone, as it had been through the door.

'Um, yes.' Simon didn't think a lot of people knew his middle name. Where had Mr Hand learned it?

'Sit. You have something for me?'

'Um, yeah. Instructions, and money.' Simon crossed the floor with reluctance, not wanting to be close to the man. He bent at the edge of the coffee table and placed the unopened briefcase carefully on it, and slid the envelope across the glass top towards him. Despite the offer to sit, he continued standing awkwardly for a minute before doing so. He kept trying to think of a line or a gesture he could use to make the best of the situation, but could come up with none.

'Open it,' Mr Hand said, gesturing to the briefcase.

Open it? 'But I was not given the combination number,' Simon protested, panicking.

Mr Hand fixed him with an imperturbable gaze that Simon felt more than saw. Finally Mr Hand leaned forwards to get the envelope and his face came into the light for a moment, illuminating disharmonious features.

Holy shit . . .

Mr Hand was a very ugly man. Most obvious was the scarring across his face that left it uneven and pulpy-looking. His face didn't *look right*, and Simon also noticed that one of his ears was an odd shape, like the top part of it was missing.

Alarmingly, Mr Hand pulled a small glinting blade out of his breast pocket to slit the top of the envelope open. Normally such a diminutive knife would not be cause for concern, but the sight of it in this man's hand sent a shiver through Simon. He wanted to get away from the room as soon as possible.

Fuck, fuck, fuck! You are in over your head.

'You noticed my ear,' said the man, shrouded again in darkness.

'Um … what?' Simon said, busted. He swallowed hard. 'What do you mean?'

It's not polite to stare, dear …

'A man cut part of it off. The doctors can't fix it right.'

'Oh … Oh, really? I hadn't noticed,' Simon lied, trying not to shake.

Mr Hand ignored him. He pulled the sheets of paper out of the envelope and held the instructions under the light to read them. The combination to the briefcase lock must have been there, because he pulled the case over, set the combination and opened it. Simon stared out of the corner of his eye at the incredible stack of cash. This was supposedly only a small slice of the deal – playmoney in local currency. The advance had been paid into a bank account before Mr Hand had even left for Sydney, and the rest of it was to be paid upon completion. This man would be paid millions for whatever he was to do.

Mr Hand closed and relocked the case and went back to reading the instructions. Simon took the opportunity to familiarise himself with the room and try to covertly study this man whose odd features were now becoming more clear as Simon's eyes adjusted to the dim light. Who was this guy? Where and how had they found him? And what would happen next? What exactly did The American mean when he said this man was going to 'take care of the situation'? And what precisely would Mr Hand do for his hefty fee?

Simon noticed there was another briefcase directly next to the man on the floor beside his chair. He wondered what was in it.

After yesterday's crisis meeting, Simon had thought Jack Cavanagh and his military-like security adviser formidable, but Mr Hand looked to be an altogether more overt menace. Where The American was quiet and precise, Mr Hand had a discomfiting, brute physicality that Simon did not see in his own privileged social circles. Even seated, it was clear that Mr Hand was built like a gladiator, with wide shoulders and a muscular neck visible atop his business shirt and slick dark suit, and those battle scars across his face and hands would give anyone pause. If someone could give *him* those scars, Simon shuddered to think what grief they had been dealt by Mr Hand in return. And, even apart from the scars, Simon suspected that there really was something else wrong with Mr Hand's face. He'd spent a lot of time around those for whom plastic surgery was a form of maintenance, like getting a manicure or doing sit-ups, and he thought he recognised in Mr Hand a botched face job of some kind. Perhaps he had gone under the knife to correct a broken nose or jaw; it was hard to tell, but whatever it was, the end result was not pretty. His face was meaty and shapeless, his eyes small.

Simon found himself frightened to be sitting in the same room with Mr Hand. He even found himself wishing that The American was there to walk him through it.

Oh . . . get this over with and get out of here . . .

Mr Hand finished with the instructions and slid all but one of the pages back into the envelope, folded the envelope twice and lit the corner with a shiny silver lighter, watching the paper dispassionately as it smouldered in the coffee table ashtray. Simon still didn't know what the instructions had said.

Mr Hand addressed him now. 'Tell me everything you know about Warwick O'Connor.'

Simon shifted uncomfortably. 'Um … He hasn't called me back. He's done some work for me before. Never like this, of course –'

Mr Hand cut him off. 'Alias. Address. Photographs.'

'Oh, of course.' Simon thought about his answers. 'I don't think he has an alias. I only know him as Warwick, actually. I don't have any photographs either.' He felt pathetic.

Mr Hand passed the remaining piece of paper across. 'Is this him?'

Simon was surprised to see that it was a

photocopy of Warwick's driver's licence. 'Um, yeah. That's him.' It had his address on it too. There was another driver's licence copied below it, this time for Lee Lin Tan. 'And that is the guy I get Damien's girls through,' Simon said, pointing at the second photo. 'He was there when the chick freaked out and died. He was probably on the video.'

Lee was a pimp for Asian sex workers. Simon frequently contacted him to bring girls over for Damien's special parties, and he always had a fresh batch of pretty faces. Damien liked Lee's Asian girls because they were petite and pretty, and they didn't speak English or question anything. There was none of the 'I'll do this, but I don't do that' or the 'You can touch me here, but not there' that they would get with the Australian girls. They never complained, even when Damien left them with burns, bruises or whip marks. And Lee could get them young.

Simon had called Lee straight over and complained when there had been a problem with the girl at the party.

Now that Simon had confirmed the identities of the two men on the photocopy, Mr Hand tucked the piece of paper away.

Simon swallowed hard. In the presence of this man, and in light of the recent turn of events with Warwick, he was finding it difficult to maintain his composure. It was clear that in the situation he found himself in, he was the bottom of the food chain and should be grateful that he wasn't just being eaten alive.

'If you don't need me for anything else …' Simon began, eager to make his exit.

'Get a towel from the bathroom and bring it here.'

Simon froze. *What?*

'Do it.'

Mechanically Simon rose, walked to the bathroom and took one of the fresh white towels off the rack. He returned and held it out to Mr Hand.

'Now kneel.'

'What?' Simon's veins stood out, panic coursing through him. He flinched to one side, but Mr Hand had already pounced. He pinned Simon to the floor, head against the soft white hotel towel. Mr Hand's crushing body weight bore down, and in his panic Simon peed himself. He lost control, his jeans feeling wet and warm. He felt humiliated and scared, but that was not the worst of it. In one quick motion Mr Hand pushed Simon's head down and whipped his small razor-sharp blade against Simon's neck, cutting a painful but superficial wound down the length of it and right across his chin.

'*Ahhhhhh!*'

Simon cried out with the white-hot pain, and balled himself up, crying.

Body in a foetal position, utterly humiliated

and agonised, Simon felt Mr Hand move to get something. It was a bottle from the minibar. He opened it and poured something straight onto the wound, the alcohol splashing and dripping down his face and neck. The pain was agony, the like of which Simon had never before experienced.

Mr Hand had disfigured that pretty face.

He came right up to Simon's ear and whispered words to him that Simon would never forget, and when he finished uttering his chilling warnings he pulled away, Simon's face dripping with bourbon and blood.

Even once Simon was relieved of his crushing weight, he did not move a muscle. He was too shocked.

'Go.'

CHAPTER 24

MAK LOOKED UP through the taxi window at a five-storey Gothic building. The evening sun washed the old stone in an orange glow, illuminating the arched windows. Menacing gargoyles perched on its corners, facing east and west, to fend off evil spirits. Across the front was carved the numerals '1902'. Even from within the taxi, the lively din of music and conversation floated down from the top floor of the building, where a glow of light illuminated a small balcony.

Mak looked down again at the note she had scribbled with Loulou's garbled instructions.

This is it.

'I'll get out here,' Mak said. 'Thank you.' She paid the driver and got out. The street was cold. She buttoned her coat and scanned the area.

The address Loulou had directed her to was one of the taller buildings in Elwood, a beachside suburb of Melbourne just beyond the area of St Kilda, where Mak was staying. Here the buildings were huddled together, each seeming to lean on the next. Few were modern. There were a number of sixties- and seventies-style apartment blocks and some terrace homes. The shops in the area looked to be eclectic, much like the locals: a number of cafés, a corner store and a laundromat, a couple of bottle shops, a comic book shop, designer boutique and a cobbler. Mak was surprised to see geriatrics with walkers and punks with mohawks occupying the same footpaths in the evening.

Mak stepped up to the building. She pressed the bottom buzzer, MCGILL, and after a few seconds was met with a booming static which she assumed was the doorbell being answered. She responded to the static with 'Hi, it's Mak'.

There was a loud squeal on the other end, which she also heard from above. It couldn't be anyone but Loulou – it seemed Mak had the right place. She was buzzed in, and made her way inside to discover that there was no elevator, just like her hotel. Step by step she hauled herself up five floors of creaky stairs, grimacing as the muscles in her quads and calves burned. When she'd been working in Manhattan as a fashion model she had lived in a five-floor walk-up like this, but she had obviously been younger and fitter then, because this felt like harder work than she had remembered.

By the third flight of stairs light moisture beaded her brow. She would have to sign up for some more kickboxing classes, she decided. And since she'd started working strange hours for Marian, she had not stuck to her usual routine of running 50 kilometres a week, either. She would need to retain her fitness for her odd jobs as an investigator. Who knew when she might need to outrun someone? She'd heard plenty of war stories about investigators being confronted and even chased by tipped-off – and ticked-off – subjects.

After what seemed like twice as many flights of stairs as there actually were, Mak reached the top landing. Loulou burst out of the apartment door in a whirl of red-and-black stripes. Mak braced herself for the impact. The ensuing hug was fierce and heartfelt.

'Oh, darling! It's so good to see you!'

Loulou was, as always, a sight to behold. She was clothed in a striped top and fingerless glove ensemble, with black zippered jeans and what looked like Doc Martens. Ever the make-up artist, her visage was striking, though anything but natural. Dark extended eyelashes curled upwards to caress her eyebrows with their length, and multicoloured eyeshadow swept with a theatrical flair towards her temples. And since the last time Mak had seen her – although only yesterday – Loulou had dyed her mullet-cum-swept-up mohawk hairdo a raven black with dramatic red tips at the ends.

Where did she find the time, Mak wondered.

Everything about Loulou was dramatic. Always. They embraced and Loulou dragged her inside excitedly.

'You're here! You're here! Sweetie, this is so great! You *so* have to meet everyone!'

The apartment had walls covered in sketches hung with thumbtacks, and bright abstract paintings, save for one side of the room that was painted from floor to ceiling in a striking cherry red which Loulou seemed to have subconsciously colour-coordinated herself with. There was a drop cloth and easel in one corner of the living room, the canvas half painted in burgundy and black brushstrokes, awaiting further inspiration. Someone here was an artist.

In the centre of the room, a large wooden dining table was set for six people and covered in dripping red candles. Two young men with greasy hair and acres of tattoos greeted her, as did a young woman with hair as wildly coloured as Loulou's. Mak recognised the shade of red: they had both matched themselves, obviously sharing the same dye kit. Who thought to do that?

Loulou introduced her boyfriend first. 'Mak, this is Drayson McGill,' she said with proud affection, squeezing the arm of one of the two young men. He was just a touch taller than Loulou, with dark generous features and sleepy bedroom eyes. He seemed in need of a wash, and perhaps a wake-up.

So this is the singer she's fallen for?

Loulou licked Drayson's ear enthusiastically and giggled. They looked happy, at least, although Mak couldn't help but recall Loulou's

242

earlier pledge to avoid musicians exactly like him. She had her 'type' down to a science: always the greasy, unkempt hair; always the overload of ink; always the laconic attitude. In Mak's eyes he looked nearly identical to Loulou's four previous conquests.

'Nice to meet you,' Mak said, extending a hand towards Drayson's unoccupied arm.

Drayson nodded slowly and pleasantly in her direction, and shook her hand softly, like a man half-asleep but content with whatever dreams he was caught in. He was either an extremely relaxed character, or stoned. Mak resisted the urge to wave her hands in front of his face to see if he flinched.

'This is Donkey.' Loulou gestured to a buffed young man with a long face and sleeves of green and red Japanese-style tattoos on his sculpted arms. He seemed not to have a single ounce of body fat on him. 'He's the drummer,' Loulou explained. Donkey was big, strong and wired, quite the opposite to Drayson's sleepy demeanour. He seemed ready to take off at any minute.

'And this is Maroon,' Loulou said, continuing the introductions. Maroon was petite, swathed in black, with shoulder-length hair that matched her name, and Loulou. Did she change names with hair colour, Mak wondered. 'She's the painter.'

Mak looked around at the work adorning the living room. 'I like your stuff,' she said. The comment wasn't empty flattery. The paintings on the walls were raw, perhaps, but there was genuine talent in the expression, composition and colour. And she seemed prolific, if this was a recent sampling of her work. Perhaps she had a bright future as an artist ahead of her?

'Oh, and this is Bogey. He's the one who can cook ...'

Bogey was just emerging from the kitchen as he was introduced. Mak got a little shock when she saw him, unaware that there was a fourth person to be introduced to. He walked forwards with a tea towel draped over his shoulder and extended his hand, a gentle smile on his lips. His jet-black hair was spiked up, his attentive green eyes framed in black-rimmed glasses. He was perhaps six foot tall, just eye to eye with Mak, and he wore slim black jeans with a chain hanging from his belt, a fitted black T-shirt and lace-up Doc Marten boots. His hairstyle was loosely reminiscent of a late-fifties Elvis, and with that and the black specs, he brought to mind a lead in a David Lynch film, or a kind of Elvis man living in a time warp. An Elvis who could cook.

There was a lot of black going on. *Come to think of it, half the people in Melbourne seem to wear a lot of black. Are they all mourning something?*

'Hi, Bogey,' Mak said and reached out to shake his hand.

Mak and Bogey continued to clasp hands for a fraction too long, their eyes locked for a strange

244

moment. Mak wondered if anyone else had noticed. For a second she thought they might have met before, but she knew they had not.

'It's nice to meet you all,' she said, disengaging from him and addressing the group a bit more formally than she'd intended. 'I'm Makedde.' She wished she could say she had heard lots about them, but she hadn't. The Loulou–Drayson romance was far too much of a whirlwind for Mak to keep up. She knew very little about these people.

'Ma-what?' It was Donkey who spoke. Or grunted.

'Sorry?'

'Your name is Ma-what? Malady?' he said.

'Um, Makedde. It's M-A-K-E-D-D-E,' she corrected him.

There was nothing new about confusion surrounding the pronunciation of her name. She was quite accustomed to repeating it a few times in new company.

Donkey screwed his face up, raising his lip on one side. 'That's a *weeeeeird* name,' he said bluntly, and walked back towards the dining table.

Maroon. Drayson. Bogey. Donkey. I'm the one with the weird name in this room?

The group gathered at the dining table, and the Elvis man went to finish up in the kitchen, insisting that he did not need help. Mak took a seat, admiring the wonderfully uneven knots and scrapes in the wooden table while Loulou ran

245

around the apartment to shut off the remaining lights, leaving the candles to glow.

· Maroon poured some red wine into each of the glasses. 'You would like some?'

Mak nodded.

'So how do you say it?' Maroon asked, taking her seat.

Mak couldn't help but respond with her usual spiel, having been asked that very question at least once a week since she was in primary school. 'It's pronounced "Ma–Kay–Dee". I don't know what my parents were thinking.'

'I like it,' the painter decided.

'You can call me Mak, though. My friends call me Mak. It's easier.'

'What's in a name?' Drayson recited laconically from the head of the table, waving his arms around like his hands might be butterflies. 'That which we call a rose by any other name would smell as sweet.'

Loulou threw herself at her boyfriend in response, pulling at one of his ear piercings with her red lips, leaving a lipstick print on the titanium barbell, while Mak gaped at him with puzzlement.

Yup, definitely stoned.

'*Romeo and Juliet*,' Mak noted, not sure how else to respond to the display except to recognise the origin of his little speech. 'Don't you two lovebirds end up like them, now.'

What are you saying, you idiot?

Loulou cackled at her comment, so Mak left it

246

at that, vowing to stop saying every stupid thing that came into her head just because she was in new company and didn't know what else to say.

★　★　★

Throughout dinner Mak kept to herself, as she often did at parties where she didn't know most of the people present. She preferred instead to hang back and observe the new faces; a typical shrink, she supposed. She quickly deduced that Donkey's nickname originated not from his long face but as a reference to his intellect. Drayson, on the other hand, was no fool, coming out with the occasional insightful comment that took Mak by surprise. Maroon could keep up with the boys just fine, bantering with Donkey and giving him a hard time at every opportunity; Mak wondered if she secretly had a crush on the brute. Bogey, the Elvis man, was the quiet one of the bunch. Mak didn't have him figured out yet, but if she had to guess, she had him as owning a restored Cadillac and an Elvis pinball machine, and having a girlfriend who was a struggling songwriter. Part poet, part rock'n'roller? He had barely said a word to Mak all evening since their introduction, even though he was seated right next to her. Was he always so shy?

Mak quietly enjoyed her time in this different setting, and with people who certainly in no way resembled cops. It kept her mind from the fact that when she returned home – if that terrace could be called home – it would be empty.

But she couldn't enjoy herself too much in this new company. She had work to do in a few hours.

CHAPTER 25

THE INFORMATION Mr Hand had received from his client was accurate and exhaustive, right down to driver's licences, registered addresses, known contacts, photographs and other background on the chosen targets.

The instructions were extremely specific.

Madame Q had told him that his client was well organised and well connected, and Luther had not been disappointed. As usual, he had not been told the details of the client, but he had quickly guessed that the job was something to do with the wealthy Cavanagh family. Having grown up in Sydney, he was well aware of their influence. Only a handful of others in Australia would be able to afford his price. The Cavanaghs were one of the top three richest families in the country, boasting an empire built in only two generations.

Now that Luther had his tools, local currency and exact instructions, and had provided his lesson to Simon Aston – a warning sealed with his own brand of physical reminder – he was ready for work.

Before midnight, one of the targets on his client's list would be dead.

CHAPTER 26

WHERE IS AMY Camilleri? On holiday? At her mother's?

For the past thirty minutes Makedde had been having an internal dialogue of her own, quite apart from the company she was in. She wondered what she could do to draw Amy out, and what pretext she could use to talk with her if and when she finally found her. What was the best approach? She would have to figure out pretty quickly whether Amy was just absent, or purposely hiding – the answer would make a vast difference to how Mak was received, and how she should proceed with her. But how long should she waste on trying to find her? She didn't have much experience with these things. Admittedly, Mak's trip to Melbourne had been half motivated by the opportunity to visit Loulou. But how much of her client's money should she spend trying to track the girl down? And if she was still unable to find her by noon the next day, should she return to Sydney empty-handed?

'Get you another glass, sweetie?'

Mak looked up, startled.

Loulou had asked the question, having momentarily detached herself from her boyfriend's ear to offer Mak a freshly opened bottle of pinot noir. She held the bottle at a precarious angle in one hand; the wine was nearly spilling from the top.

'Sure,' Mak answered.

Loulou passed the bottle down the table, and when it reached the shy Elvis man he took it and gallantly poured a glass for her. Mak wondered if the real men of the fifties had been so polite, or had known how to cook such delicious curried fish and vegetables. She suspected not.

Bogey passed the bottle back around and ran a hand through his Brylcreamed hair before taking a sip from his own glass.

'Cheers,' Mak said, raising her glass.

'Cheers. Next time you visit you should stay with us,' Drayson said, smiling sleepily. His comment prompted Loulou to kiss him on the cheek. Come to think of it, everything he did seemed to prompt her to kiss him.

The group paused their various conversations momentarily to clink glasses over their empty plates. The white cloth napkins scattered around the table were now stained with curry, the plates and some of the wooden table underneath decorated with leftover rice and the occasional near-translucent fishbone. The meal had been excellent, and the banter at the table was energising, if erratic. Mak wondered if she was finding the company of these lively strangers particularly refreshing after the claustrophobic feelings she was beginning to suffer because of her routine with Andy. Perhaps the three-month break would not be such a bad thing.

Mak checked her watch. It was ten o'clock.

It's too early.

Although she was obviously not going to get much quality time with Loulou, she still had an hour or so to kill before she could get back to work.

Makedde took a sip from her glass and looked to the end of the table, at her friend draped around her man of the moment, laughing. They looked cute together. Mak hoped for Loulou's sake that it lasted more than the weekend. The only problem was that it would mean that her closest friend would be spending all her time interstate. Apart from Andy and Karen Mahoney, with whom she was becoming good friends, Loulou was her closest companion. Mak had been living in Australia for one year. Perhaps she should have more friends by now?

You do not trust the way everyone else does.

Her friend Catherine had been murdered, her mother had died, and her father and sister were thousands of miles away, so one could hardly blame her for being a little less open than the average girl. But Mak was lonely at times, especially with Andy's long work hours. She envied people who lived their lives enveloped by a comforting circle of close and trusted long-term friends. It just hadn't worked out that way for her. She wanted Loulou to find happiness, but she would be sad to lose her to Melbourne.

Just try to be social.

Mak turned to the Elvis man. Someone had to start the talk flowing between them, so it might as well be her. 'So, um, were you born in Melbourne?' she asked.

He looked up from his glass with a ready smile. 'No. I moved here a few years ago. I was born near Darwin. You're from Canada, right?'

Mak nodded. 'Gee, you're good. I can't tell you how many Australians think I sound American.'

'You're married to an Australian, then?' Bogey asked.

Mak felt her throat tighten. 'Well, no …' She raised her left hand. 'See, no rings. I am in a relationship, but not married. Or engaged.' *Next subject, please.* 'You're from Darwin? I've never been.'

The Elvis man nodded casually. 'It's beautiful, but isolated. How long have you been in Oz?'

'A year or so. So, are you in the band with Drayson?' she asked, wanting to keep the subject off herself and her relationship with Andy.

'I used to be in Possum,' Bogey said. 'But not any more. I make furniture now. I have a little shop down in St Kilda.'

Mak watched him speak, struck by the fact

that Bogey was actually very attractive, in an artistic sort of a way. Beneath those big, black-rimmed glasses he had long, dark lashes and sympathetic brows. He had roughed up his even features with the light stubble along his jaw and the spiked-up hair, Mak noticed, but it didn't change the fact that he was classically handsome. His mouth had a pleasing shape, with a plump cupid's bow in the centre that she tried not to stare at.

Slow down on the wine, girl. You are going to need to be sharp later . . .

'How nice,' Mak said. 'What kind of stuff do you make?'

'Custom furniture,' Bogey answered. 'Cabinets, chairs, tables – that sort of thing. I work with a variety of materials.'

'Ha!' Donkey blurted from across the table quite unexpectedly, intruding on their conversation. 'He also works with *pine*.'

'I'm sorry. Please ignore him,' Bogey said softly, not meeting the other man's eyes. 'You're in Melbourne for work?' he asked, attentively directing his focus to Mak.

Mak was about to answer him when Drayson piped up from the end of the table. 'Go ahead, tell her your trade.' He leaned forwards and grinned with a tannin-stained mouth while Loulou clung lovingly to him. She'd abandoned her chair to perch in her lover's lap.

Mak waited for Bogey to respond but he tried

255

to deflect the interest in himself by raising the bottle of pinot noir and asking if anyone wanted another top-up.

'Come on, Booooogey Man!' Donkey called obnoxiously. He was obviously stirring the pot about something, and it seemed to be a little annoying to Bogey, who heard the nickname and rolled his eyes.

'I make *furniture*,' he repeated, looking down at his plate. He doesn't seem to like talking about himself, Mak noticed.

'Come on. Your *trade*,' Drayson said, not letting up.

This is beginning to sound like a good story, Mak thought, intrigued when the teasing wouldn't stop. What was it about his trade?

Bogey took a breath. 'Technically,' he said softly, 'my trade is coffin maker.'

Mak's jaw fell open. Now he had her complete, undivided attention. 'A coffin-maker? I haven't met a coffin-maker before. How interesting.'

'I haven't done it for a while,' he said dismissively into his glass. 'I don't know why they want to bring it up.'

Here he had been shy all evening and he was quite possibly the most interesting person at the table. She wished she'd got him talking earlier. She wanted to hear more. 'How long did you do that for?'

Bogey shifted in his chair. 'I worked full-time

as a coffin-maker for about five years before starting with furniture. The work was fine, but I prefer to make furniture for the living.'

Coffins. Furniture for the dead. Mak had never thought of it that way.

'He's the Booooogey Man!' Donkey yelled with glee, clearly thinking himself very clever. Mak was starting to see that the man was, quite literally, rather asinine. Perhaps he had done too many steroids to get that physique, or snorted one too many protein powders? She wondered if he was one of the reasons Bogey was no longer with the band.

'Come on, Bogey, tell us more!' Loulou said enthusiastically. 'Her dad's a cop and she loves the gruesome stuff!'

Oh right, I love the gruesome stuff. Thanks, Loulou.

'Your father's a cop?' Bogey asked, catching her eye.

Mak nodded. *And my boyfriend, but I don't want to think about him right now . . .*

'Well, it was before I moved to Melbourne from a town near Darwin,' Bogey explained. He did not seem entirely comfortable in the role of resident curiosity, but he continued nonetheless. 'I was a teenager. I studied as a coffin-maker and worked for the local funeral parlour. It was no big deal. I lived in a small town, so everyone had to multi-task. I would pick up the bodies in my van, bring them back to the freezer, measure them up, build a coffin and then drive them out to the funerals. For a while there the funeral van had P-plates on it.'

Probationary driver's plates on a hearse – that would have been a sight to behold.

'He had to do everything,' Loulou said, chin in hand and long-lashed eyes so wide that the tips curled right over her arched pencilled eyebrows. 'Imagine ...' She was clearly mesmerised by her own maudlin thoughts. She blinked her eyelids and they looked to Mak like two black butterflies taking flight.

'Did you do any embalming?' Makedde asked him matter-of-factly. If he had to multi-task, it was a good possibility.

'No,' Bogey said, 'I didn't learn embalming. I don't think it would have been my thing. I don't know that I could ...' He trailed off thoughtfully.

'I once met an ex-model who was a part-time make-up artist, part-time embalmer,' Mak offered. The model had been a stunning young woman, and unique thanks to her unusual trade. Like Bogey, she had needed some encouragement to talk about it, and most of the clients she worked with in the fashion industry had no idea of her day job. 'She did the faces of both the living and the departed,' Mak said. 'She was a very interesting girl. Very level-headed. Someone has to do it, after all.'

Bogey nodded. 'Not me, though. I still remember some of those people as it is.' His eyes stared into space as he recalled something of his former career. 'The toughest one … the one who always gets me was this Aboriginal guy. He'd hanged himself in one of the overnight cells and the police called me to pick him up. When I came in he was still hanging there. I didn't like that. It wasn't my job – I just picked them up. I didn't … you know, take them down or prepare them. I could see this guy's face as he hung there from a noose he had made of his clothing, and it really disturbed me. The anguish on his face was terrible. He had not died peacefully. The pain in that cell was … palpable.' Bogey swallowed and took a breath. 'I did what I had to do, but that image really stuck with me. The next day – *and I swear this is true* – I was in the line-up for the welfare cheque for my mum, and this guy at the front of the queue starts screaming his head off. I looked up to see what was happening and it was *him*. It was the same guy I had taken down from his home-made noose and put in the freezer. I freaked out completely. I ran up to him and embraced him, and said, "Oh my God, you're alive! How can you be alive?"'

Mak was stunned. She was stuck on Bogey's every word, right along with the entire table, although presumably they had heard the story before.

But …?

'The man in the queue was the identical twin brother of the man who had hanged himself in

259

the cell,' Bogey explained. '*Identical*. He needed his cheque early so he could afford to get to the funeral. But they refused him.'

Mak didn't know what to say. 'That's very sad,' she managed. She could see it was not just some spooky party tale to him. To Bogey, that memory hit a real chord.

After a brief, eerie silence, Donkey, with all the sensitivity of a sledgehammer, broke into another of his hecklings. 'Tell her about the bikie gang! Go on, tell her! This is a *great* story. You'll love this.' He chuckled to himself in anticipation of the story.

Bogey now appeared a little less awkward about telling the tales of his past, but it didn't stop his hesitations. 'I am sure Mak is bored with all this. It was such a long time ago.'

'No. I find it interesting ... if you don't mind telling me?' she said.

'Sure.' He took a sip of his wine before continuing. 'Well, I got to be known for making good coffins – remember, this was a small town, so there wasn't much competition. There is a gang in Australia called the Coffin Cheaters. You may have heard of them, I'm not sure. The Coffin Cheaters are a big bikie gang, and they swung through our little town and asked me to make some coffins for their clubhouse – you know, Eskies, tables, that sort of thing.'

Everyone else at the table had clearly heard the punchline of this story before, and they were grinning while they watched Mak for her response. She simply nodded for him to go on.

'I did it for them,' Bogey said, 'and in exchange for furnishing their clubhouse with coffins, they tattooed me and gave me more drugs in that week than I have seen in my life since.' Bogey looked to the table. 'That's all. That's the story. Okay, someone else tell a story now ... come on, guys.'

Mak was mesmerised. She wondered about the tattoos he might have. What would a gang like that brand someone with? A great big coffin, maybe? A skull and crossbones? Was Bogey a 'MUM' tattoo kind of a guy with a nice, big fat heart inked onto his bicep under those black T-shirt sleeves?

'How long ago did all that happen?' Mak asked him.

'Oh, about ten years ago. Ages.' Mak began the mental calculation and Bogey confirmed her guess. 'I was about eighteen at the time,' he said.

So Bogey was twenty-eight, only a year younger than her. For some reason he looked younger to Mak – perhaps compared to Andy's hardened gaze. Drayson and Donkey were probably in their mid-twenties, and Maroon was the youngest at the table, Mak guessed. It was always impossible to guess Loulou's age. She had the energy of a child, and her skin was always hidden under layers of carefully applied make-up. But Mak knew she was older than she let on

– Loulou had even rubbed out the birth date on her passport.

'So Bogey's eighteen,' Loulou said with glee, the wine making her yet more animated than usual, 'and he's driving a van full of bodies and a hearse, working for the Munsters' bloody funeral home and getting tattooed by a bikie gang. *Awesome*,' she said. 'Makes *Six Feet Under* look like the *Brady Bunch*.'

Bogey gave a tight-lipped smile. 'The family I worked for was a little strange, I have to admit. Some of those things stay with me,' he said.

'Yeah, like those tatts,' Donkey quipped, laughing.

'Yeah, like those.'

Mak had the feeling that Bogey had meant the dead people he had seen, not the bikie tattoos he'd been branded with. As Mak herself knew, seeing a dead body – *any* body – was an experience that stayed with you, but especially when you see someone who has had their life ended violently. Images like that stick with a person for life. They had driven Andy to drink, and Mak to insomnia at one point in her life. Everyone handles the trauma of being introduced to violent death differently. But Mak felt that the peacefully departed had a different impact to offer. She felt that it was healthy for a young person to see a dead body in the morgue or in a hospital as part of their learning about life. That was how it had happened to her: she had seen her first dead body with her detective inspector father at the age of twelve. The impression she'd had, that the person lying on the slab was an empty shell and that some mysterious life force had very obviously moved on, had given her a belief in a spiritual realm that religion alone had not fully explained to her since. She'd seen that there was something there – something real and yet otherworldly. *Something*.

There is no way to adequately describe death to someone who has never seen it.

'Learning about death can teach us more about life,' Mak whispered quietly for Bogey alone.

He turned to her and nodded. Their eyes connected again. It could be that they shared a common bond in death; maybe it was that which she had noticed in him earlier.

'Anyway, I am a furniture-maker now,' Bogey said, for the moment wrapping up his tales of life as a teenage taxidriver for the departed.

'Yeah, he's boring now,' Donkey said, and downed his glass of wine.

Mak didn't think he was boring at all, though. She found her eyes drifting down to his lips again, to that plump cupid's bow, before she pulled herself back.

No, Mak. You don't want to start looking at him like that.

CHAPTER 27

WARWICK O'CONNOR.

Luther recognised the name. When he'd last heard of him, Warwick was pushing drugs to kids at the preppy schools on Sydney's north shore. It seemed his career had not evolved all that far since then. Luther found the house Warwick shared with his wife, exactly where his instructions indicated. According to his information, Warwick had no children and no known pets. That meant no barking dogs.

Good.

Luther Hand sat outside the house of Warwick O'Connor, watching and making plans. It was late, and Warwick's wife, Madeline, was home. He saw her in her pink bathrobe as she pulled down the curtains and settled in for the evening, cigarette dangling from her lips. Warwick wouldn't be going out; they were packing it in for the night.

The woman would die only if absolutely necessary.

Luther could pick the lock on the front door,

make his way up the stairs and be in the bedroom in minutes. The main target would then be eliminated. But he resisted. He would adhere to the plan. If he went in now he would need to kill them both, rough up the house to make it look like a botched robbery and get out again. The police would take somewhat more interest in a husband-and-wife dual homicide. There were better ways to eliminate someone like Warwick, and Luther guessed that that was why his client wanted him to wait until Warwick was outside his home. A person like Warwick had crossed so many people that the list of suspects with sufficient motive would be endless. As long as it looked messy, it would be assumed that a rival thug committed his murder.

Your days are numbered, my colleague.

Luther packed up his things and prepared to make his way to Surry Hills.

It was nearly time to execute his first hit.

CHAPTER 28

BY ELEVEN MAK was preparing to make her exit from the party at Drayson and Maroon's Elwood apartment. She stood and began collecting the plates to take to the kitchen.

'Thanks for dinner. It was lovely.'

'You're a guest here. You don't have to do that,' Maroon said of Mak's plate collecting.

Mak waved the comment away and kept stacking dishes. She moved around to the other side of the table, and when she took Donkey's dirty plate she swore he looked straight down her top. 'So you model, right?' he said, sounding like he had downed one too many. After dinner he had moved onto a steady diet of beer. 'You were a supermodel, right?' he stated more than asked.

'Supermodel? Noooo, I wouldn't say that,' Mak responded. 'I modelled for a number of years. It paid me through uni, that's all. I don't really do it any more, though.'

Mak took the stack of plates into the kitchen, happy to disengage.

'You look like you could still model,' Donkey

called after her as she went. She could feel his eyes wander over her backside. *Nice.*

When she returned he had not dropped the subject. 'You could still model,' he repeated, slurring his words slightly.

'Thanks, but I'm much happier in my new career.' *Not that I'm practising yet, exactly.* 'Besides,' she said, 'the fashion industry seems rather partial to the sixteen-year-old couture-waif look this particular decade. I'll be thirty soon. That is ancient in modelling years, you see. It works a bit like dog years.'

There were a couple of laughs at the table.

Bogey stood and collected the napkins. When he passed her he said, 'You are a beautiful woman and you will always look precisely the right age for who you are.' He said the words in a low voice, meant only for her.

Mak grinned, but she didn't know how to respond. Was he trying to flatter her? Because if he was, it was working. She felt a slight blush coming on.

'Wow! You are 250 in dog years!' Donkey blurted insensitively, breaking Mak's train of thought.

She smiled despite him. 'You mean 210, if I catch your drift,' she retorted. 'But no. I think that if I was to put it in numbers, models are actually closer to one-and-a-half years for every human year, not seven. Yes. I think that's probably it,' she decided. 'A fifteen-year-old model presents like a twenty-two-year-old. A twenty-year-old is a bit like a thirty-year-old, and so on.'

Maroon frowned. 'That's a scary theory.'

'Not quite scientific,' Mak said, 'but I think it might have merit.'

'That's it. I hate fashion magazines,' Maroon said bitterly. 'They are a man's conspiracy to keep women preoccupied with their appearance so that they can't do anything more significant that might upset the status quo.'

'That's a good theory to a point, but everything I've seen tells me that women fuel fashion magazines, not men,' Mak challenged. 'Most men would rather look at any sexy woman than the androgenous teens modelling expensive couture in *Vogue*. They like pin-up curves or toned athleticism, neither of which particularly feature in fashion mags. It's not about men. If it were, the models in men's and women's magazines would be the same shape. In my experience, most guys hardly care what a woman is dressed in or if she wears her hair in the latest style, so long as she is somewhat sexually attractive and, on a subconscious level, fertile-looking to them. Women tend to be much harder on other women than men are. There is a whole language of body shape, clothing styles and attitude for women.'

'That totally sucks. We should be able to be ourselves.'

'And no one is stopping us. When I see a

fourteen-year-old in a skin-care ad I find it farcical, not threatening. But I do wish sometimes that those magazines would allow their models to age. Look at Christie Brinkley – she's gorgeous. And there must be lesser-known women out there who could be modelling into their forties, fifties and onwards, too.'

'A lot of women have more character with age,' Bogey said, putting in his two cents' worth as he returned to the table to pick up the last of the cutlery.

What would Andy's response be in a similar situation? He would probably stay out of it, knowing that emotions ran high among women when it came to body image. But Mak smiled at Bogey's well-chosen comment, feeling she had found a co-conspirator at the table in this Elvis man who seemed far too sensitive to be a friend of a guy named Donkey.

Maroon still had some anger to vent. 'Yeah, how come men are allowed to grow old and have "character", when a woman just gets "wrinkles"?'

Donkey looked bored. 'Just as long as they're hot, go naked,' he said.

Mak was no longer in the spirit of their little debate. She had other things on her mind.

Speaking of body images . . .

'Hey, guys, sorry to change the subject, but does anyone know where Lonsdale Street is?'

'Lonsdale Street? Sure,' Maroon answered. 'That's where all the barristers and strip clubs are.

It's about fifteen minutes by car. Is that where your hotel is?'

Strip clubs and barristers . . . an interesting mix.

'No, it's just a work thing.'

'Mak's a private eye,' Loulou said proudly, making Mak sound like she should be wearing a fedora and smoking a cigarette. 'Are you on trial?'

Mak smiled and shook her head. 'Nah. I'm not on trial.' *Not this time.*

She had been briefed in her investigators course on how to handle giving evidence in the witness box if the situation came up. Mak could probably have used some of those pointers when she'd taken the witness box in the Stiletto Murder trial. Perhaps that would have kept the tears from rolling down her cheeks while she was asked to recall every last gruesome detail of her abduction and attack. Most likely she wouldn't need to get back in a witness box again until she was practising in psychology. That was, unless she got herself mixed up in something really messy with her investigation work.

'I'm sorry to eat and run, but I do have to get going.' Mak stood up. 'It was really nice to meet you all. Thanks for dinner.'

'Oh, sweetie! Stay for another drink!' Loulou cried, clearly not wanting to let her friend go.

'I have to go, really. It's a school night for me. I have a big day ahead tomorrow.'

'You have to stay over here next time, though, okay? Promise me?' Loulou urged. 'We have a guest bedroom and it would be all yours. *Pleeeease?*

Mak was amazed at how quickly Drayson and Loulou had shacked up together, and how quickly her friend was using the word 'we' – '*We* have a guest bedroom'. Loulou's kamikaze relationship style was probably not the most successful, but still, Mak had to admire her openness. It took Mak much longer to trust anyone. Maybe it took her too long.

'Okay,' Mak agreed with some reluctance. 'Next time I promise I'll stay. But now I have to go.'

'I have to head home, too,' came a voice. It was Bogey. He had put on his leather jacket, having already cleaned up the kitchen while Loulou, Drayson and Maroon were busy drinking. He didn't even live there and he cooked and cleaned the place. *Wow.* 'I have a project that needs delivering in two days,' he explained, grabbing a big set of keys off the hall table. 'I haven't even begun the staining yet.'

'Ohhh, now everyone is leaving!' Loulou cried, obviously upset that the evening was coming to an end so soon.

'I'm staying,' Donkey muttered. 'You've got more beer, right?'

★ ★ ★

Bogey and Mak descended the five flights of stairs in uncomfortable silence.

'Would you like a lift?' he asked as they reached street-level.

Oh boy.

Mak thought it might be safer, temptation-wise, to say no, but she didn't have a car – and, in truth, she wanted to find out more about him.

'Yeah. That would be great,' she answered, not looking in his direction. 'Is Lonsdale Street too far out of your way?'

'No problem at all.'

If she had been single she would not have been able to resist asking him for a drink somewhere before she went off to work. But she was not single: she was what the Australian Immigration Department referred to as a 'de facto spouse'. A spouse of any description was someone who was far from unattached and, furthermore, she was attached to a high-ranking homicide detective. Her live-in boyfriend had barely left the country.

A ride made sense, though.

When they reached the open street she saw that Bogey drove an immaculately restored late-sixties blue convertible Mustang. Not quite the enormous Cadillac she'd imagined, but close enough. And it was awfully close in body shape and appearance to Zhora, her beloved turquoise 1967 Dodge Dart Swinger, which she had reluctantly sold when she'd moved from Canada to Australia. With the Australian roads geared to driving on the opposite side, it would have been an unnecessarily expensive and complicated proposition to ship it down and mutilate it for local driving. *Ah, Zhora*. Mak missed her. She had named her car after the ill-fated snake-carrying replicant in *Blade Runner*. She named all her vehicles. Her bike was *Theroux*.

'I'm sorry for boring you with those stories,' Bogey said. 'I don't know why they made me tell you all that stuff.'

'I found it interesting. Really. I've never met a coffin maker before.'

'And I've never met a PI.'

Mak smiled as he opened the passenger-side door for her. She got in and buckled up, the seat making a soft hiss under her weight. The seats were leather – and beautifully kept – not like her Zhora, whose vinyl bucket seats had been in terrible shape from the day she bought her. Mak had never got around to fixing her up properly. But this man clearly loved his car, and was happy to sink time and money into restoring it.

'Where to on Lonsdale Street?' he asked as he started the engine. The car purred.

Mak told him the address and he looked puzzled.

'I didn't know there was a hotel around there,' he said.

'There isn't.'

CHAPTER 29

IT TOOK LUTHER Hand little time to track down the house in the inner-city suburb of Surry Hills.

He arrived wearing black from glove to boot, blending into the shadows as he moved. He was more than ready to get the assignment under way, and he had in his kill kit one additional item specific to the job.

A hatchet.

Luther did not ring the doorbell. He picked the lock and slipped inside, and within seconds he had sped up the stairs and entered the hallway. Everything was as his instructions had said: the number of steps, the layout of the building. The office of Lee Lin Tan was two doors to the left at the top of the stairs, but even before he reached it, a man appeared in the doorway before him. He had been heard.

Luther recognised the man from his driver's licence photo. 'Lee Lin Tan,' Luther said.

There was recognition.

'Are you Lee Lin Tan?' Luther demanded again. He wanted an answer.

There was a weak nod.

Luther gripped the hatchet and swung, not quite taking Lee's head straight off in the first blow. A spray of blood spread out across the doorway behind him, pooling and beginning to run along the paint. Lee gripped his neck as he went down, blood spilling through his fingers. It had been an effective first blow.

Good.

Luther stood over Lee Lin Tan as the man crawled pathetically along the hallway carpet, perhaps trying for the stairs and the front door, choking and gurgling on his own blood. Incredibly, he managed to lift himself up to a half-standing position against the wall, shaking with shock.

Luther swung again, this time precisely.

He took off the man's left arm at the shoulder joint, and the dismembered arm fell to the carpet with a sickly thump. Lee's eyes lost focus and he fell back against the corridor wall, leaving a bloody handprint and a downward streak across the wall. His head fell forwards and his last breath was expelled from his body with one final gurgle.

There was a scream.

Luther spun around in the direction of the noise, ready. He had been warned that Mrs Tan might be present.

A woman burst into the hallway. She had a

shotgun in her hands and raised it unsteadily, her awkward grip on the trigger revealing her lack of experience with the weapon. Her dark eyes drifted to the sight of her husband in bloody pieces in the hallway, and she let out an even more high-pitched scream, dropping the gun to her side, the butt slipping and hitting the carpet. Luther moved towards her and she retreated in a panicked run to the office, a ramshackle room with a desk and shelves, and a threadbare couch that looked like it had been doubling as someone's bed. She tried to close the door before he reached it, and failed, so she backed herself into a corner by an open drawer, whimpering and crying hysterically.

She tried to hide her face under the overhang of the heavy open wooden drawer.

Luther strode forwards, pulled the drawer straight out of the cabinet and tossed it behind him with a crash, then grabbed the woman by the hair in one hand and raised her to her feet. He swung the hatchet. It took her head clean off, and her body dropped to the floor underneath it, leaving the head dangling in his hand, her tangled hair like Medusa and her serpents.

Luther dropped the head next to her body and looked around.

He squinted. The drawer he had flung across the room had been full of passports – Filipino, Thai, Chinese, Vietnamese, Cambodian. The passports and documents were spread all around the room.

Voices.

More witnesses.

Luther left the office and made his way down the hall with the crimson-soaked hatchet in his hand, ready for a methodical search for witnesses if necessary. There were voices beyond one of the doors.

He flung it open.

Inside were women – at least a dozen of them, some wearing silk slips, some in jeans and bra tops. They huddled in fear at the sight of him filling their doorway holding the dripping hatchet. A few of the women mumbled in unfamiliar languages through hot tears, but not one of them screamed. They were too terrified.

Witnesses. A dozen of them.

He noticed there were bars on the window. The beds were few, but it was clear they had all been living together in that wretched room.

Luther stepped back into the hallway and closed the door again. As soon as he did, the voices began again, the low and quivering tones of frightened women who did not know what was going on. Still, no one screamed.

He considered his options.

These women were no threat to his client. They would not talk. And even if they did have anything to say about a man in black with a balaclava and a hatchet, they would be deported before they testified.

Luther walked back along the corridor to the

office, picked up several of the passports and returned to the door. He opened the bedroom door and left the passports in a pile.

He stepped over the body of Lee Lin Tan on the way out, and left the Surry Hills house with the front door wide open.

CHAPTER 30

'I NEVER DID ask ... what's your instrument?'

The city centre was only about fifteen minutes from the Elwood apartment, and the trip seemed to go by too quickly for Mak, who was enjoying the former coffin-maker's intriguing company. They had driven most of the way caught up in small talk about Bogey's experiences in Drayson's band.

'Guitar,' Bogey replied, his eyes on the road.

My God, he is Elvis, Mak thought. She smiled mischievously, and he turned in her direction in time to catch her expression.

'What?' he asked.

'Oh, nothing.'

The streets were quiet as they cruised through the central business district of Melbourne, a concrete jungle of metal and glass where the buildings were tall and modern, and the streets were nearly empty at this late hour. The suits that crowded the footpaths during the weekdays had dispersed to their various suburbs to rest in closets for the weekend, starched and pressed for their Monday meetings.

'No, really,' Bogey said. 'What is it? What's that look? Mak couldn't help it. She kept grinning. 'I hope you don't take this the wrong way,' she ventured, 'but when I first saw you I figured you as an Elvis man. I should have guessed that you played guitar. I can just picture you on stage with a guitar strap around your neck, swivelling your pelvis.'

Bogey huffed a little laugh. Thankfully he didn't seem offended by the comparison. 'You take me as an Elvis man, do you?'

She nodded. 'Well, they do say Elvis is king.'

'Elvis *is* king,' he agreed. 'Do you imagine me in one of those white satin jumpsuits with the big collar?'

'Oh, no, no.' She shook her head. 'I'm thinking of his black-suit-and-skinny-tie phase. Young Elvis,' she assured him.

'But I can't sing. I listen more to the Sex Pistols, Spiderbait or The White Stripes.'

'If Elvis were alive I'm sure he would be listening to The White Stripes, too,' Mak said.

He pulled up at a red light. 'You're in Melbourne for a job?' he asked, and turned to her while he waited for the light to change. He had that pleasing face, but she could see his punk influence too. He might be more Sex Pistols than 'Blue Suede Shoes', but she still thought he looked like an Elvis man. Maybe a punk Elvis?

She looked away. 'Um ... yeah, I'm working,

but visiting Loulou mostly,' she answered, wanting to evade the details of her work. 'We're good friends. Pretty inseparable most of the time. I moved to Australia only a year or so ago and I still don't know that many people,' she admitted. She hoped her comment didn't make her sound lonely. 'Still, I've been here longer than in most cities I've lived in.'

Bogey nodded in response, then turned right down a main street and drove a few blocks. They passed the Supreme Court and the Magistrates' Courts. 'It sounds like you've travelled a lot.'

'Yeah,' Mak agreed. 'I've become so used to it over the years that I don't even notice any more. The other day I realised that since I have been an adult I had never actually lived in any country for longer than twelve months. This has literally been my longest stay anywhere.' Mak realised she was telling him her life history for some reason, and thought she really should switch the subject. 'So how did you get a name like Bogey? Is that Bogey as in an evil or mischievous spirit, or the number of strokes a player is likely to need to finish a golf hole?'

He glanced at her with a raised a eyebrow, and Mak recalled, too late, that not everyone liked to read the dictionary for kicks.

'It's no golf reference. It's because my name is Humphrey. Humphrey Mortimer.' He said the name quietly, and rather quickly, she thought.

'Ah, Humphrey. Actually, Humphrey Mortimer

281

is not such a bad name,' she said, trying to reassure him. 'It couldn't be any worse than mine, surely — "Makedde Vanderwall" is a mouthful! Humphrey suited Mr Bogart just fine. You know, my *opa* looked exactly like Humphrey Bogart. In all my old black-and-white photos of him, he's the spitting image . . .'

'Yeah?'

They had reached Lonsdale Street.

Well, that's it.

Mak looked out the window at the grand neon signage of Thunderball Gentlemen's Club. The entrance to the club opened brazenly and incongruously onto a street almost entirely inhabited by barristers' chambers, just as Maroon had said. Both the Magistrates' and Supreme courts were a stone's throw up the road. It seemed an odd location for a club of its kind. She could guess that more than a couple of the Melbourne legal fraternity would be on a first-name basis with the staff inside. Perhaps that had come in handy from time to time for the owner.

'Well, um . . . I'll get out here. Thanks for the lift,' she said, regretting the end of their little journey together.

Bogey pulled the car into one of the available spots on the street and shut off the engine. Mak opened her door, panicking inside. *Why is the engine off? What is he doing?*

'You're going into the club, right?' he asked her.

Mak nodded, not looking in his direction. She gathered her purse as casually as she could and turned to say goodbye. When she looked at him their eyes locked again like they had in Drayson's apartment, only this time she could see that he was concerned.

He broke their gaze and looked down at the steering wheel. 'It worries me a bit that you are going in there alone.'

Mak felt a rush of relief that his turning off the car had to do with her getting a lecture on safety, and not a pressured sexual proposition of any kind – not that this guy seemed the type. She laughed. Any hormonally influenced thoughts had no doubt been entirely in *her* head.

'I've been a lot of places,' Mak said. 'A strip joint doesn't worry me, honestly.'

A stranger like this could not guess what she had gone through in her life. Walking into a men's club would surely be the least of her horrors.

'I am an investigator. This sort of thing is what I do, and I do it alone.'

Well, that was embellishing it a bit – she was only a fledgling PI and she had never actually been into a proper strip club before, let alone on her own. But he didn't need to know that. His being worried was silly, regardless.

'All the same,' he said, 'I think I'd like to wait outside with the car in case you have some trouble.'

Mak didn't have a response ready: she had not

seen this coming. 'You want to wait outside until I'm done?' she asked incredulously. 'You would do that?'

'I'll be parked right here,' Bogey insisted.

'No, no ... that's crazy. I'll be a while, and you have your project to start on tomorrow – the staining you haven't started yet, remember?'

'I know.' But he seemed to be immovable in his desire to see that she was safe. 'I'm just not comfortable leaving you in this area when you are alone and you have no car.'

Mak sat glued to the passenger seat, the door open and one foot on the kerb, considering his words. She was at an impasse. She hadn't planned on letting anyone but Marian Wendell in on her little mission. And she certainly didn't need a babysitter, day or night, café or strip bar. If she didn't like Bogey, she would have blown him off already, but he seemed sincere. And perhaps he could be helpful? A young woman in a gentlemen's club alone might become a target for the other patrons, or even a threat to some of the girls working there. Having a man with her might help her to blend in.

'Well,' she said, somewhat reluctantly. 'I don't need a babysitter. I want you to know that. But, if you're going to insist on waiting here anyway, you might as well come in for a drink.'

She ignored the voice in her head that told her she might also be asking him inside for the wrong reasons.

★ ★ ★

Despite living much of her life near Vancouver, a city with one of the most thriving strip scenes in North America, Makedde Vanderwall had little experience with gentlemen's clubs. She'd partied in some gay clubs in New York and been subjected to the usual buffed-up male strippers in requisite construction-worker costume, swinging their hammers, so to speak, and she'd seen half-naked burlesque performers at some extravagant parties. But despite the passing fad of going to strip joints en masse with the girls, a proper gentlemen's club was something Mak had only seen in movies. She certainly would not have imagined that the first time she found herself purposefully walking into a 'girlie bar', she would be doing it in Australia, as a private investigator, flanked by a coffin-maker she'd only met that night, and there to try to solve a complete stranger's murder.

Life is strange . . .

Mak approached the front door of Thunderball with her punk Elvis next to her, his hands in his pockets. An entirely expressionless security guard in a dark suit stood at the front door of the club and watched their approach. 'Good evening,' he mumbled. He must have been satisfied with the look of them, because without another word he pushed aside a heavy wooden door so they could enter.

The lighting was low inside, and Mak could hear pulsing music from upstairs. Just inside the door was a coat-check area with a cashier.

'Forty dollars each,' the woman at the register said with an insincere smile.

Bogey automatically dug into his jeans to get his wallet, but Mak stopped him with a firm hand. She paid up with a couple of fifties, waited for a receipt, and soon they ascended a staircase together into the club, where the music grew louder, and the light grew dimmer.

'This is on my client's tab,' Mak told him in a loud whisper so she could be heard over the music.

'Oh, okay,' he said.

At the top of the stairs the club opened up into a sprawling space of several bars and performance areas in different sections. Directly in front of them was a billiard table where a group of men were playing a game with scantily clad girls draped over them, giggling and posing as if they were trapped in the foreplay scenes of a bad porn film – 'Ooooh, can I help you with your stick?' Beyond the divider of some gold-painted Roman pillars there was a larger room with a number of round bar tables and a big stage with the expected pole, presently unoccupied. To the right the club opened up even further, with a cocktail bar and several smaller stages where girls in bikinis, frilly underwear and skin-tight lycra micro-dresses swayed and arched for the enjoyment of watching men. A girl performing in hotpants bent straight over and flashed a good part of a fully waxed crotch.

Mak blinked.

It's like something in the movies, Mak thought, only none of the dancers were fully nude. For the moment, anyway. She had expected to see an orgy of naked flesh sliding up and down greased poles, vaginas unleashed in all directions as men bayed and howled like dogs. She was mildly relieved at the reality.

'Let's get a drink,' she suggested to Bogey, and led him to the right. They sidled up to one of the main bars and took position on a couple of stools. Mak swivelled around to face him. 'What do you want?' she offered.

'What are you having?'

It didn't look like the sort of place that would do a satisfying mojito.

'Vodka, lime and soda,' she said.

Bogey flagged down some service while Mak observed the establishment from her barstool vantage point. There were women everywhere, almost outnumbering the men, but Mak was quite possibly the only female there who wasn't working at the place. A few patrons looked in Mak's direction and appraised her openly before refocusing their attention on the undulating performers. Already she was starting to think that having Bogey with her was of some genuine value. He was helping her to blend in, and was quite possibly preventing her from being propositioned as well. She was certain that she could manage fine without him, but clearly his presence was going to make her job easier.

An impossibly large-breasted, bleached blonde bartender appeared, drawing Mak's eyes to the bar once again. She wore an over-strained gingham tie top that could have been made from a cocktail napkin, and looked to be a few days out of high school.

'What can I getcha?' the bartender asked, smiling brightly with a full set of braces.

Oh dear.

Bogey smoothly gave the scantily clad young woman Mak's order of vodka, lime and soda, and asked for a bottle of the Japanese beer Asahi for himself. They didn't have it. 'Heineken?' They didn't have that one either. 'A bottle of Crown?' he asked. She plonked one on the bar and popped the top. Bogey didn't touch it, evidently waiting for Mak to get her drink before he started his beer. If he had ogled the girl's breasts while he ordered, Mak somehow hadn't noticed it. And she *had* been watching.

Impressive.

Mak had to admit that Bogey wasn't really eyeballing the visions of fake-tanned flesh surrounding them, much less howling for them to 'take it all off'. And the women really *were* surrounding them – on the many performance stages, walking past slowly in lingerie, leaning wantonly on pillars in mesh slips and pouring beers wearing improbable tops. It was a visual feast of toned flesh and Worst Dressed List–worthy outfits such as Mak had never seen. Bogey was probably being polite for Mak's sake. His discipline might change after a few beers, she guessed.

Bending over the bar and with breasts jiggling, the bartender presented Mak's drink and Bogey paid for it before Mak could stop him.

'You remember what I said about the client?' Mak reminded him.

'Your tab covers drinks?'

'Everything,' she replied, and took a sip through her straw.

It wasn't the best drink she'd ever tasted. They had some good vodkas displayed along the bar, but she was guessing that none of those had been used to make her drink.

'It must be nice that you can drink on the job and get paid for it,' Bogey commented.

'That's one of the perks of being a *private* detective and not a public one,' Mak explained. 'The cops have so much regulation. Rank. Superiors. Inspectors watching their every move. Every step they make has to be taken thinking that it might be investigated in court and ripped to pieces by a defence barrister. Whereas with me ... well, so long as I don't break the law too badly, I can do just about anything to get the job done. And there's no law against drinking on the job, either. In fact, there's a rather illustrious history of partnership between investigators and their booze.'

Bogey smirked, seeing that she was at least half joking. 'I'll keep that in mind.' He shook his head and did another of his little huff-laughs. 'You sure are surprising,' he said, and lifted the beer to his lips.

Concentrate, Mak. Stop trying to impress this guy and just do your job.

Mak leaned one elbow on the bar and worked on her drink, watching the room for anyone who resembled Amy Camilleri's picture. There were a disproportionate number of blondes, as one might expect, but still no sign of anyone with Amy's face. Mak noticed, to her surprise, that a number of the male customers were actually on their own, or in sedate groupings of two or three. It wasn't the screaming buck's night crowd she'd expected to see.

She also observed with interest the various interactions: lots of looking but no touching, unless it was the girls touching the men. Some ladies working the floor actually leaned against customers as they chatted, seemingly relaxed in their underclothes despite the layers of suits or jeans the men wore. And she noticed that there were a lot of surveillance cameras but, apart from the guard at the front door, Mak had not yet spotted any of the stereotypical frowning no-neck bouncers. They would be there somewhere, she was sure, but they were subtle. Security was probably briefed to keep a low profile so the customers could relax.

Check out their faces . . .

On one of the nearby stages a Latina with huge hoop earrings, a neon-yellow string bikini and clear platform stilettos wiggled and tapped her brown buttocks to the delight of a growing audience. The men seemed mesmerised but helpless, like diabetics in a candy store. They could look but not touch, and there was not much room for conversation with all that staring, so for the most part they just sat and stared mutely. A slim Japanese girl in a schoolgirl uniform shared the other half of the same stage, not working with the Latina dancer, but keeping her back to her and trying to win her own fans. She wore a white tie top and a micro-mini version of the tartan schoolgirl skirt, her white socks pulled up to her knees. An older man leaned forwards, staring at her with his mouth slack. When she kneeled down in front of him and caressed her small breasts through her top, he took a folded bill and slid it into a garter on her thigh.

The goal was cash, and it was every woman for herself.

'Is there anything you want me to do?' Bogey asked after they had sat quietly for a while.

'Nothing for the moment,' Mak responded. 'I just need to check things out for a bit. Is there anyone you want to look at?' She gestured to the girls performing.

'This kind of place isn't my thing,' he said

dismissively. 'I'm just happy wherever you need me to be.'

'It's nice of you to help out like this,' she said, trying to figure out just exactly why he was being so generous with his time, particularly if he had a work project to start on first thing in the morning. 'I know you have to work early.'

Bogey gave her a slow smile. 'Don't say it like I'm a saint or anything. Accompanying someone like you to a place full of naked women is no chore for any man, and don't let them tell you otherwise. I'm not complaining.'

Someone like me?

'About what you said before,' Bogey went on. 'I know you don't need a babysitter. That's not why I wanted to stay. I can tell that you can take care of yourself.'

She waited for him to finish.

'I just didn't feel good about leaving you here on your own. It's not a great part of town to be alone in at night.'

'It's all right, I think it's a nice gesture,' Mak assured him. 'I didn't take it the wrong way.' With a different guy, with a different attitude, though, she might have. 'If I wanted you to leave me alone, I'd have just told you.'

'I believe you would too. Now, if you need me out of your hair so you can work, that's no problem. But I'd really rather not leave you on your own here. I can wait outside until you're done.'

Mak laughed. 'It's too late now, mister. You *can't* leave. You're part of my cover. We are a couple who have come to Thunderball to spice up our sex life with a little titillating entertainment. If you leave me now it will look too obvious.' She cast her eye towards some of the nearby male patrons. 'And I think someone here might take too much notice.'

He nodded, signalling that he understood.

'I'm glad you're here,' she told him. 'This is fun. Cheers,' she said, and clinked his bottle with her glass.

'Cheers.'

'Now check out some babes, will you? Otherwise people will wonder why we're here.' Mak swivelled her chair around and watched a group of patrons in chairs circling a platform where a girl was perched in her underwear. 'Check her out, for instance,' Mak said. 'She's on a train to Boresville.'

A ring of beer-swilling men watched a stunning blonde in black briefs, bra top and classic stripper heels as she lay on her back on a small, circular stage and swirled her legs around occasionally, plainly bored. Her mouth was stuck in an unattractive line, the look in her eyes distant; she was clearly imagining some place she would rather be. She wasn't even trying to appear as though she was into it. Mak caught her yawning and looking at her watch.

Who could find that sexy?

'Did you see that? She's just waiting for her shift to end, poor girl. That can't be good for business,' Mak said.

'It's not,' Bogey said. 'Look ...' A handful of men wandered away from the platform, leaving the seats around her empty. Bogey finished his beer. 'I'll be back in a minute,' he said. 'Do you know which way the men's would be?'

'I saw a sign to the left at the top of the staircase,' Mak told him. She noticed pretty much everything when she was working.

She concentrated on the room again, and her eyes were drawn to the bored blonde once more as she swivelled her legs, circling her ankles in one direction and then the other. Zoned out and distant, she was nothing more than a sensual automaton, unaware or indifferent to the fact that her audience had moved on. She looked every bit as pretty as a lot of the models Mak had worked with, and Mak could not help but wonder why a girl with that face was on a stripper's podium instead of a catwalk somewhere. Did it pay that much better? She sure didn't seem to be there because she loved dancing.

Bogey had been gone for perhaps sixty seconds before Makedde felt a hand on her shoulder.

Oh no.

CHAPTER 31

'THE JOB IS complete.'

Luther Hand sat in the safety of his vehicle, blocks away from the crowded Surry Hills house and dismembered bodies of Mr and Mrs Tan. The first hit had gone smoothly, despite him needing to make a decision about the women trapped in that room.

'How many?' the man with the American accent asked.

'Two. Man and wife,' Luther informed his contact.

There was a pause. 'Fine,' The American replied.

There would be no specifics discussed over the phone.

'And the other?'

Warwick O'Connor.

'Tomorrow. There was his wife,' Luther explained.

'Okay. Take care of that tomorrow as you wish. Your contact will visit you at the hotel on Monday with information about your next assignment. Unless there are any changes before then, you will not hear from me. Tomorrow, leave me a message to let me know it is done.'

'Okay.'

Luther hung up the phone.

Sleep.

He drove off, not towards the city but to the airport, to spend the night in the hotel he had chosen there. The Formule 1 hotel was an inexpensive automated accommodation with no check-in staff. It only required a credit card, of which Luther had many in a number of identities. He would return to his room at the Inter-Continental Hotel on Monday to get the information for his next assignment, but until then he would not be found there.

While his client believed he was relaxing in the five-star Inter-Continental, Luther would be sleeping in the closet of the airport hotel, the bed plumped up with sofa cushions.

It was one of many precautions Mr Hand had learned to take.

CHAPTER 32

'HEY, PRETTY LADY, can I buy you a dance?'

Makedde Vanderwall turned around to find a man in his mid-forties grinning moronically at her, puffed up to the human equivalent of a proud peacock. He was holding a glass of beer in one hand and her shoulder in the other. A trio of his less tipsy friends looked on from a metre further down the bar, watching him make his big move.

'No, thank you,' Mak replied, forcibly removing his hand and turning away on her barstool to further make her point. She put her purse on Bogey's seat so no one would take the spot while he was gone.

Did he say 'can I buy you a dance?' or 'can I buy a dance?'

Now Mak wasn't sure which question he had asked. A flash of uncharacteristic self-conscious-ness caused her to do a rocket-fast self-appraisal: boots, black pants, suit jacket, cleavage carefully covered up. No, there was no mistaking her for one of the ladies working here. It was just the influence of the boys' club atmosphere that had made her question herself. He had been out of line.

Mak stayed sitting with her back to the Peacock Man, putting the minor disturbance literally behind her.

The hand was back.

'Come on, whoever you want. My shout.'

Regrettably Peacock Man was speaking loudly enough that a couple of dancers, eager for the cash, had begun hovering around him at the bar, smiling seductively and touching his shoulder with an intimacy usually reserved for lovers. One was a naturally voluptuous blonde with milky skin wearing white lace lingerie and long fake pearls, hair flowing to her waist. She didn't look anything like Amy's photo, sadly. The other dancer was a slightly more demure and slim-line brunette in a tiny black lycra minidress, and diamanté earrings, bracelet and heels. She had the petite build of a ballerina. The blonde was the bold one of the two, and she leaned on the peacock's shoulder, intentionally brushing one large breast against him. She whispered something into his ear.

Oh, come on. Don't encourage him.

His mates remained uninvolved, except to eye off the two girls and raise a glass to their seemingly clever-as-a-fox mate.

'Anyone you want,' he repeated and gestured to the blonde and the brunette, much as someone might offer dark chocolate or light. Before Mak could contain the situation, a third dancer had joined them. She was a hard dark brunette in a plunging red one-piece satin teddy, and by the look in her eye Mak thought she might have been working there a long time. She stood over the petite girl with her hands on her carved hips and her impressive chest pushed out, pouting. She was as tall as Mak, and she looked as tough as a Texas warden.

'Which one do you want?' the man persisted, now grinning his moronic smile while presenting all three with a sweep of his hand, like a game-show model presents a row of dishwashers.

Short brunette fast rinse, blonde full wash or long, hard spin cycle? What's your preference?

Mak had to say something. 'They are all stunning women, but honestly, no thanks. If I want a dance from one of these beautiful ladies, I will ask for one myself. I have my own money.'

At her comment, the hard one shifted her focus to Mak, perhaps hoping to appeal to her as one tall woman to another.

'Oh,' the Peacock Man huffed loudly, evidently taking Mak's comment as some sort of assault on his manliness – worst of all here, in this club, one of the last bastions of male freedom. In retaliation for this perceived assault, he dragged some crinkled fifties out of his wallet and waved them around proudly, much to Mak's embarrassment.

Fuck. So much for blending in and observing.

It wasn't long before the flash of cash attracted more girls. Two more arrived to see what was going on. Now there were five scantily clad women pouting and preening around him. This guy was a bloody genius.

'I have money too,' he boasted. A couple of the girls giggled like seasoned actors, pretending he was the clever Casanova of their dreams. He leaned in towards Mak with ill-advised confidence. She could smell the booze on his breath. 'Babe, it would be a crime not to see you naked.'

Oh, that's it. Fuck you.

Mak pictured the sharp heel of her boot digging into the top of his foot so hard that he crumpled and let out a yelp. But putting a hole in the man's foot was not going to help her get what she needed. She was there for a reason, after all, and it wasn't to meet guys like him.

Makedde pulled him close and whispered in his ear, 'No, it would be a crime if I took my glass and smashed your face with it. Back off.'

'Huh?' he blurted, pulling back like he was burned.

Mak smiled sweetly at the man, who now looked completely confused, still holding his money and staring. She ignored him and tried a new tactic, turning to the girl in the black dress and sparkly jewellery. 'Oh, hi. You know my friend Amy, don't you? You're … um … Brit …'

'Charlotte,' the girl told her, looking a little confused herself.

'Oh *Charlotte*, that's right. How are you? Hey, is Amy working tonight?' Mak pretended to look around for a moment, as if searching for the familiar sight of her good friend Amy.

There was a flicker of recognition in the brunette's face. 'Um, yeah, Amy?' she said awkwardly.

But the Texas warden piped up straightaway, cutting the girl off. 'Does an Amy work here, hon? I'm not so sure.'

'Yes, she does,' Mak said with certainty. 'I'm *sure* you know Amy.'

'I haven't seen you in here before.' She looked Mak up and down with new suspicion.

'Oh, she works here,' Mak retorted, standing her ground. 'Amy Camilleri. Very pretty. Light blonde hair, about this long?' She showed the length with her hand.

'I can't recall an *Amy* ...' the tall woman went on, lying so obviously that Mak doubted she was even trying to conceal it. She was being evasive about Amy, but why? Would she rather use the stage name – was that it? 'Do you girls know her?' the Texas warden asked, looking around at the others. But she didn't give them an opportunity to answer, and by the looks of things they weren't going to try to, either. 'Nah ... an Amy doesn't come to mind right now.'

'Right now'. Hmmm. What was going on? A

sense of competition? Sisterly protection? A reaction to some kind of threat?

Through all this, the overzealous patron still held his money up, watching the two towering women with a look of tipsy puzzlement as the strange conversation unfolded. He just couldn't keep up. Mak resisted the urge to close his gaping mouth with one hand. His mates were huddled around their end of the bar, watching with a mix of apprehension and amusement.

'Hi.'

Mak turned.

Bogey was back. He moved quietly to Mak's side and leaned against the bar. She was sure he would be a little surprised to find her surrounded by five dancers and a frustrated-looking man holding a wad of cash, after leaving her by herself only a few minutes earlier. But he didn't interfere.

'Hi. How are you tonight?' the milky blonde asked Bogey, moving to his side. 'Are you having a good time?' She was very curvy and very attractive. Her white lingerie was just see-through enough to make out the shape and the colour of her pink nipples, which Mak jealously witnessed her rub against Bogey's chest in one subtle, rehearsed movement. Mak imagined that most guys would find such a play irresistibly arousing. What would Bogey do? Flirt back?

She watched for his response with more interest than she wished.

'I'm good, thank you,' he replied, and sat down with his back to both the girl and the growing crowd. He was smooth – Mak had to give him that.

'Would you and your boyfriend like a dance?' the blonde asked Mak. She gestured to Bogey.

My boyfriend.

'Maybe later,' Mak said. The comment gave her an idea. 'It's a shame you girls don't remember Amy. I'd love to say hi to her.'

The girls nodded quietly – and guiltily, Mak thought – but the hard woman in red narrowed her eyes at the repeated mention of Amy. She was hostile about something.

Once the girls realised that their chances of being picked for a lap dance were slim, they dispersed like leaves in the wind. All except for the bold blonde, who turned to the cashed-up Peacock Man and dragged him off in the direction of his friends, all of whom appeared to be very happy for her company. She was onto a winner with that group, Mak figured. Now that the milky blonde was distracting him, that jerk would finally leave Mak alone. It was win–win.

Mak turned away from the group and ordered herself another drink.

'Everything okay?' Bogey asked quietly.

'Yup,' she said, a little embarrassed. She didn't want to admit that his presence was a saving grace for her in the club. But she really didn't have to say it: it was obvious. He'd only stepped away for five minutes and there had already been a bizarre exchange with one of the patrons.

On TV screens above the bar, the club rotated a series of promotions and photographs of different dancers pictured in soft focus: bending over the bar in stilettos and G-string; lying on a fur rug by a roaring fire; cinched in by a leather corset in a stark studio. Mak watched the screens scroll from one shot to the next as she waited for her drink.

A sexy photograph of the demure dancer appeared on the many screens positioned around the club. Pictured in reclining pose, leaning on one arm and wearing only a pair of brief briefs, the black-and-white shot looked like an imitation of a Calvin Klein ad. The title underneath said:

CHARLOTTE
PRIVATE DANCES START AT $20

Hello, Charlotte.

Charlotte had seemed a little shy, but in her very few words Mak had registered that she knew something about Amy Camilleri. Mak looked around for where the ballerina-bodied girl had gone and it didn't take long to find her. Charlotte had made her way to one of the small stages, where she was in the middle of performing for a small audience. There were still a few free chairs circling her podium.

The instant Mak's drink arrived, she grabbed it. She put a twenty on the bar and stood up.

'Come on. Let's go see our girl Charlotte,' Mak said, and dragged her punk Elvis man into the crowd.

They weaved through the spectators and took a seat at the small stage, where six different men already sat around Charlotte's table, watching her every move in a state of mute lust. A couple of them broke their mesmerised gaze to look Mak over as she joined them.

If everyone was so cagey about Amy for some reason – especially with that taskmaster of a dancer standing over them – then perhaps the best way to get someone talking would be to get them alone to a place where no one could overhear them.

There's only one spot in a place like this to get one of the girls alone.

Mak and Bogey made themselves comfortable for a couple of minutes, watching Charlotte's routine, then Mak reached over and placed a hand on Bogey's knee. He flinched noticeably.

'Hey, sweetie,' she said, a little louder than she needed to, and taking a leaf out of Loulou's vernacular. 'You like her too, don't you?' Mak gestured towards Charlotte as she wriggled and teasingly pulled down the straps of her dress in a slow, seductive dance. Charlotte's rejoinder to their conversation was made only with flirtatious looks and inviting body language. She communicated skilfully in that way with each member of her audience, making occasional eye contact.

'Do you think we should have a private

dance?' Mak asked Bogey in a stage whisper, and nodded for him to say yes.

His eyes nearly fell out of his head at Mak's suggestion. 'Um, okay,' he said. Bogey had been nothing but cool all evening, but now, even in the low light, Mak thought she could detect a slight blush on his cheeks. A lap dance was probably taking the evening much further than he had expected it to go.

Charlotte had overheard their exchange, as Mak had hoped, and she responded by playing up to Mak's desires, getting on her knees right in front of her and slowly pulling her dress down over her torso, revealing small, well-formed breasts constrained only by a black satin bra. Mak wasn't sure where to look at first; the attention was confronting. She chose to run her eyes up and down the woman's body, mimicking what she had seen the male patrons do. Charlotte danced for her, her body at times only centimetres from Mak's face. She made burning eye contact with Mak before tilting her head back in silent, erotic pleasure, rubbing her hands over herself.

Mak shifted in her chair and swallowed. Was it getting warm in the place, or was it just her?

'We both think you're beautiful. Can we have a private dance?' Makedde managed to ask the tiny dancer, careful to use the terminology from the club's screens. Mak pressed a fifty into the woman's garter while Charlotte kneeled on the stage and arched her back.

Charlotte locked eyes with one of the girls off stage, who quickly took her place. In the wink of an eye she had pulled her black lycra dress up again and had nimbly taken the bills in the garter on her thigh and wrapped them into a tight bundle, storing them in a doubled-over garter on her wrist. Mak had never realised garters were so handy.

The men seated around the platform seemed not to care or barely notice the change of guard. They stared mutely at the next girl, their eyes brimming with the same sexual desire.

'Come with me,' Charlotte said in a low whisper, like she was sharing a secret.

Mak nodded, and turned to Bogey. 'Come on, baby ...'

Mak wanted to laugh, calling Bogey 'Baby'. It was funny. The whole situation seemed funny to her, even if it was about to get a whole lot more intimate than it surely should have been. She'd only just met him and he was about to share her first lap dance experience with her. But screw it – if he hadn't wanted to wait for her so badly, he wouldn't be in there.

This was the price he'd pay – or the reward he'd get – for being a nice guy.

I think I'm about to see a whole lot more of Charlotte than I'd bargained for ...

Without another word the exotic dancer led Makedde Vanderwall with one cool, soft-skinned hand towards the 'private' rooms of the Thunderball Club. These rooms were simply areas sectioned off with opaque glass that offered something only partially resembling privacy. Mak allowed herself to be led, ignoring the outright stares of several men in the club, who turned away from their scantily clad drinking companions and gyrating podium dancers to watch the tall blonde patron being led away for a lap dance.

The ex-coffin-maker, Bogey, trailed along behind the two women, head down and beer in hand, his leather jacket scrunched under one arm.

What must he be thinking?

Makedde watched as Charlotte checked for an empty space in a private room, glancing from one opaque glass-partitioned square to another, all the while holding Mak's hand. She eventually found a room she seemed satisfied with, and led the two of them inside. When she stepped inside the room, Mak was surprised to find a woman getting a lap dance in one corner. It was the only other female patron Mak had seen at the club. The young woman, dressed in pants and a white blouse, seemed to be quietly enjoying having another woman wriggling above her lap as she sipped a martini. There was plenty of space inside the private room, despite the other dancer and her customer, and Mak soon saw that it was dark enough for the other couple to fade to sensual shapes in the background. The room certainly felt more private than it had looked from the outside. There was a low lounge on one side with plush cushions, and Mak and Bogey sat down next to one another, side by side, but purposely not touching.

Mak's heart pounded.

Without any small talk Charlotte began to strip, first swaying to the music and running those cool hands across her slim figure, then teasing with the straps of her dress, as she had on the stage. When she pulled her black dress right down and stepped out of it, she was wearing a matching set of expensive satin underwear. She bent over to delicately place her dress on the arm of the lounge, and Mak flicked her eyes up around the walls of the room.

Ah, there you are.

Security cameras. There were few things in this place that would not be viewed by security, or the club's owner himself, even in the private rooms. They were definitely being watched.

Charlotte came to Mak, bent in front of her and took both of Mak's hands gently in her own. It felt incredibly intimate for Mak to have this near-naked woman hold her hands. Behind Charlotte's petite frame, the vague, sensual shape of the other dancer gyrating naked in the woman's lap caught Mak's eye. Charlotte asked Mak to hold her arms straight out in front of her, and she complied. Charlotte then ran her fingers up and down Mak's bare arms and plunged between them, giving Mak a start. The dancer rested her body weight on Mak's thighs, and let

309

her tiny body slide between Mak's legs, gyrating up and down.

Damn.

It was a strange experience for Makedde: sexual, intimate and yet impersonal. She'd not thought she was harbouring Sapphic desires, but Mak found this woman's erotic ballet arousing. The atmosphere of the club was not erotic – not like this. This was a shock to her system. Mak took a long sip of her drink, nearly finishing it. She felt the alcohol rush to her brain. She glanced over at Bogey, who appeared to be having as much difficulty as she was in determining where to look.

Before long, Charlotte had slipped out of her bra and then her panties. Only those handy garters and her diamanté shoes and jewellery stayed on. She turned her back to them and bent over to touch the floor, her fanny in Makedde's face. She was breathtakingly flexible, hands around her ankles and her face at the floor looking back at Mak. There was not one single mark or flaw on her tanned skin; Mak was amazed. Then Charlotte, with her pert breasts and seamless, toned body, grabbed Bogey's leather jacket and put it on. She posed with it, smiling cheekily, lifting the collar to her face, and rubbing the leather over her torso.

Bogey seemed suddenly to have a dry mouth. He swallowed a couple of times in quick succession, and adjusted the neck of his T-shirt. One Doc Marten boot began tapping.

'Charlotte?' Mak began.

'Yes,' she responded, caressing Bogey's jacket, and posing her small, firm buttocks in his direction.

'You dance beautifully.'

'Thank you.'

'I want you to keep dancing while I ask you a question.'

'Oh?' Charlotte said, bending backwards and displaying her neatly waxed groin again, leaving Mak temporarily without words.

She slid another fifty into the woman's garter. 'You know Amy Camilleri, don't you?'

Charlotte faltered. 'Um, I don't know. Sorry…'

'Yes, you do. She works here,' Mak insisted.

The sexy pout vanished. 'Umm, she doesn't work here right now.'

'But she does work here *normally*, and you do know her.'

Charlotte stopped dancing.

'Please keep dancing,' Mak urged, thinking of the cameras. She pressed another fifty into the garter and Charlotte continued, this time more hesitantly. She ran her hands over her bare skin and swayed in one place, Bogey's jacket still on her. 'Just keep on dancing,' Mak said. 'I like the way you dance.'

Charlotte seemed reassured by this. She went for another dive in between Makedde's legs, sliding up close to her body. When she was close to Mak's ear, she said. 'Who are you?' Her breath was scented with peppermint.

'I am an investigator,' Mak replied, 'helping one of Amy's friends. Amy is not in any trouble, and I don't want you or the other girls here to have any trouble either, so that is why I'm here like this, as a customer just having a little chat. I know you don't want your employer to see you being questioned by police or anyone official. So just tell me about Amy. Where is she staying? I know she hasn't been home in a while.'

Charlotte stopped again.

'Keep dancing, keep dancing … Has she been in to work this week?'

The dancer shook her head.

Amy hasn't been in to work. And she hasn't been home. Why?

Had something terrible happened to Meaghan's friend as well?

'I knew you hadn't been in here before,' Charlotte said. 'I would have remembered you.'

Mak smiled. 'Tell me about Amy, Charlotte.' She slipped another fifty into her garter. 'And dance for me.'

'Something's going on with her,' she said, head upside down between her ankles. Mak kept her eyes on Charlotte's face, and she wasn't sure where Bogey was looking. He was shifting in his seat. He crossed his legs and sat back with his head against the glass wall. 'She hasn't been around since Thursday,' Charlotte said. 'She seemed paranoid.'

Thursday. When Meaghan was killed.

'Paranoid? In what way?' Mak asked.

'Like, you know, paranoid, that's all. She kept asking if anyone had come to the club looking for her. She was scared. I thought she was maybe just doing drugs again and getting all loopy.'

Mak nodded. 'She recently lost a friend. Did she mention anything about that?'

Charlotte shook her head. 'No. That's awful. I don't know her that well – she's just one of the girls here, you know?'

'Meaghan Wallace worked here a bit, too. Did you know her?'

'Meaghan? I don't think so,' she said.

'A blonde with a bob. She went back to Sydney.' It had been a few years.

Charlotte shook her head, and Mak believed her. 'Where can I find Amy at the moment? It's important that I talk to her.'

Charlotte was hesitant.

'Is she staying at a friend's? Her mum's?' Mak pressed.

'I'm really not supposed to tell you. We aren't supposed to talk about it.'

We.

So the other girls all knew something as well. The Texas warden was keeping them in line.

'You have to tell me, Charlotte. It's very important. I know you don't want any trouble.'

As a private investigator, Mak had no more rights or powers than the girl who was dancing for her, but Charlotte didn't need to know that. Implied power was enough.

313

Charlotte seemed unnerved by Mak's inquisition. She clung to Bogey's jacket like a security blanket, the sensuality gone from her movements. Mak could see she wasn't going to do any more dancing. Their time was almost up.

'How do I know you are who you say you are?' she squeaked.

'I'm giving you my business card.' Mak wrapped her card in one last fifty-dollar bill and put it into the woman's garter. Two hundred and fifty dollars was all the money of her client's that she could rationalise spending to try to find Amy's address through her work colleagues. If this didn't work she might have to start thinking of another avenue, or she'd have to discover another friend of Meaghan's who was easier to reach. 'I need tospeak to her and I need you to trust me. This is important.'

'I wouldn't trust you if you weren't a woman.'

Charlotte's customers would not like to hear that.

'You can trust me.'

'I really am not supposed to be telling you this, but Amy is um ... staying with the owner, Larry. Everyone at the club kinda knows, but we're not allowed to talk about it with anyone. Thursday she just stopped coming to work, and word is she shacked up with him.'

'I see,' Mak said, relieved.

She contained her smile.

So that's why she wasn't at her place. She'd shacked up with the owner. That was all?

Mak had been expecting something much worse.

'You mean the owner, Larry Moon, right?' Mak had done her homework on the club.

Charlotte nodded, swinging her hips and doing the occasional half-hearted shimmy.

'You promise not to tell anyone that I told you?' Charlotte said in a nervous voice.

'I promise,' Mak said. 'No more questions now. I liked your dance. Thank you.'

Charlotte lit up, finally off the hook. She seemed very relieved. In one smooth action she took the bills in her garter and again slid them into the other garter she had bunched up on her wrist. She had quite a collection now.

'Wait until I am dressed and we will leave together. That is the way it's done.'

'Okay. Of course,' Mak replied.

When Charlotte was dressed, Mak said, 'I just have one more question to ask – don't worry, it's not related. Does your job pay well? You're a good dancer. What do you pull in, if you don't mind my asking?'

Charlotte looked flattered instead of offended, which was good. 'I do pretty well ... You're not with the Tax Department, are you?'

'No,' Mak said, laughing.

'Well, I don't mind telling you that last night I did four private dances and made over fifteen hundred, cash. My husband and I are saving for a house. Maybe we'll have it by the end of the year.'

'Good luck with that,' Mak said.

Charlotte led Mak out, hand in hand again, with Bogey trailing behind. Charlotte still looked a little nervous about their earlier conversation, but Mak thought she would slide back into character soon, and she did. She left them at the bar and sidled through the crowds of men again to go looking for her next lucrative dance.

Bogey appeared a little awestruck. He had been quiet throughout the dance, perhaps unsure of where to look, or of what could be said, especially in Mak's presence.

'Thanks for that,' Mak told him. 'You were very helpful. I think I got what I needed – my work is done here. Do you want to leave now?'

He nodded. 'Your wish is my command.'

After the crowded and somewhat surreal atmosphere inside the Thunderball Club, walking out into the fresh air on Lonsdale Street was a relief. Mak took a deep breath and tilted her head up to the stars. The air was clear, things were quiet, and there weren't any crowds of men. This was better.

She looked at her watch; it was nearly two in the morning. They had been inside for over two hours.

Suddenly, the tiredness hit her.

Bogey opened the passenger-side door and she

got into his Mustang. He shut the door for her and went around to his side.

'Which hotel are you at?' he asked.

'Tolarno, St Kilda, thanks.'

He started up the car and negotiated the dark streets while Mak ruminated over what had happened. She couldn't believe that all that evasive action by the warden girl was due simply to an in-house rule of not talking about the boss's private life. It had seemed a bit over the top. Mak supposed the girls might be protective of one another, though. Any swearing to secrecy of personal information in that club would be a good thing, she supposed. But she would have to get all the info she could on Larry Moon.

'What did you think of all that?' Mak finally asked Bogey.

He was concentrating on the road. 'What did I think of my beer, or what did I think of you shouting me an expensive lap dance?'

Mak laughed. 'That must have seemed a little weird.'

'No, it's fine. I understand. You needed information from her and you figured that was the best way to get her to talk.'

'Yes.'

Despite the light banter, she sensed that they both felt awkward after the experience. Maybe it hadn't been the best idea to bring him inside. Or, at the very least, it might not have been the best idea to bring him in to that lap dance.

'Do you feel comfortable in places like that?' she asked him.

'Comfortable? Well, I like looking at women,' he said. *An honest answer.* 'Every man does. But places like that aren't as sexy as they are supposed to be. It doesn't offend me or anything, I just don't go for it, that's all.'

'Fair enough,' Mak said.

'Besides, a lot of those girls are far too young.'

'Like the bartender?' Mak offered. She had looked like she belonged on a high-school cheerleading team.

'Yeah. I felt a bit creepy.'

'You did? But you didn't do anything wrong. Most of those girls would have been, what, nineteen, twenty ... or in their mid-twenties? You're in your twenties. They hardly seem too young for someone your age. Did you see all the old farts in there, letching on girls a third of their age?'

He nodded. 'No, it's just not my thing. In an environment like that, everything is forced. And the girls are young, just going through the motions. Most young girls are a blank slate. You can impose your own fantasies on them but they rarely have fantasies of their own. When they get older, women know what they want. They have more character.'

'More baggage,' Mak added, thinking of herself. Not yet thirty, and she'd already had enough break-ups, brushes with death and run-ins with stalkers to qualify, even if she hoped she wasn't as neurotic as the tag implied.

'Baggage *is* character. Anyone without baggage comes into a relationship with nothing,' Bogey said.

Mak thought about that. He was right, of course – by one type of thinking, anyway.

'My baggage comes in being a good coffin-maker and a failed rock star,' he said. 'Yours comes in psycho killers and being a smart woman who has been treated like an idiot for half your life. And someone else's is different.'

Mak's throat tightened. His comments were so close to the mark, they cut. 'I think you know too much about me already,' she said stiffly.

'I'm sorry. I didn't offend you, did I?'

'No,' she said. But his comment had rubbed her the wrong way. It brought to mind all kinds of things she didn't want to think about. Maybe it was the late hour, or the forced intimacy they had shared in the club, but she found his frank insight confronting. She wanted to get home, and get to bed.

'You seem older than you are, Makedde,' Bogey told her.

As Bogey pulled the car into an available spot outside the Tolarno, there was an uncomfortable silence. Neither seemed to know what to do or say to one another.

'I enjoyed spending time with you, Mak.'

'Um, thanks again,' she said, a touch distant,

and walked inside. She resisted the urge to look back, but sensed that he was waiting in his car, watching her go and making sure she got inside safely.

CHAPTER 33

MARIAN WENDELL ARRIVED at her office at nine o'clock sharp, seven days a week. The first hour of her workday was taken up with paperwork and chasing the progress of her active sub-agents so she could keep track of them, and keep her clients informed. Makedde's phone rang at four minutes past nine – first cab off the rank. The phone rang only once before Mak picked up. She had been expecting the call.

'Good morning, Marian,' she said, tired but smiling. 'I can't believe you come in at nine on Sundays, too.'

'Investigations don't stop for the weekend.'

'No, they don't,' Mak agreed.

She lay on top of her hotel sheets in her underwear, slowly stretching and trying to wake herself up. She'd taken her suit out of the closet and draped it over the chair, and then fallen back onto the bed. The previous evening's adventures at the Thunderball Club had gone late, but she felt that it had been a successful night's work.

'What's the update?'

'It's going well so far, I think,' Mak said. 'I'm confident I will find Amy Camilleri later today, and she should know something of Meaghan's private life. She is shacked up with the owner of the strip club she works in. I'm going to pay a visit, but I need a car. Can I get a rental? Can we budget that in?'

Marian paused. 'I'll organise for it to be sent to your hotel in the next hour or two. You need it urgently?'

'No. An hour or two is fine. I have some things I need to do first.'

Like get some more sleep.

'What are the expenses so far?' Marian asked.

Mak reached for her investigations notebook, which she had open on the bedside table. She listed the exact hours she had worked and the price of the taxi fares, the club entry fee, and then the cost of the private dance that had brought her the latest information. Marian liked to keep her clients updated as to the precise amount each day of investigation was costing them, so that there were no surprises when it came to billing. Most jobs could be resolved in under a week, but some investigations stretched on for a month or so and could rack up quite a bill. Mak hadn't been on one of those jobs yet, but she dreamed of it. Being paid handsomely for a long assignment might help her save enough to lease a nice office and some furniture for her practice.

'Did you say you spent 250 dollars in ... private dancing?' Marian asked.

'Yes.' Mak paused. 'Well, it was only one private dance, but it was a good one. The dancer is the one who told me where Amy is holed up. I think Jag was right about Amy and Meaghan being very good friends, because Amy hasn't been coming to work since Meaghan's murder. The girl last night said that Amy sounded upset.'

'You have receipts for everything?'

'I don't know if you have ever tried to get a receipt for a lap dance,' Mak said, 'but it tends not to work that way.'

'Of course, of course – but you have receipts for everything else?'

'Yes.'

'Good girl,' Marian said. It was a turn of phrase she tended to use a lot and, coming from a woman like her, Mak didn't mind it. It was as if she viewed her sub-agents as her own children. 'Don't spend too much more of this guy's money down there. It took a little to convince him that you needed to go interstate.'

'Well, Meaghan's parents, bless them, didn't know that much about their daughter's comings and goings. Amy should, though. I'm planning to be back by late this afternoon.'

'Okay, give me an update again this afternoon and let me know when to book the flight,' Marian told her. 'Your client will be happy to know how long he will have to pay hotel bills for.'

'No problem.'

Mak hung up the phone and rolled over, burying her head in the stiff white hotel sheets. Her body sank gratefully into the mattress. She slept like that for another forty-five minutes.

★　★　★

At 11 a.m., just as she had returned to her room from a delicious full breakfast and a mountain of lattes, Mak received a call from the front desk to tell her that her rental car had arrived. It was sitting out the front of the hotel. She walked back down to take a look.

To her dismay, the rental car was bright orange.

Nice. That won't make me stand out at all.

Mak may not have approved of the colour of her allotted rental vehicle, but at least she had something to get her from A to B. The car was a small Hyundai automatic and easy to drive, a good, suburban-looking model. But orange? Mak could not imagine a more conspicuous colour. She did not want to stand out more than she had to. What if she had to watch the house for hours or tail someone? A non-flashy suburban car was perfect for the work, but not an orange one. As it was, she was likely to be driving the ugliest car on the block. Who could fail to notice that?

She changed into a lightweight suit and wore a low-cut black singlet underneath with one of her reliably impressive push-up bras, which she felt might come in handy.

Mak grabbed her supplies and headed out. She cringed as she approached the car, and started it up.

I hope I don't run into anyone I know . . .

Larry Moon, the owner of Thunderball, had a residence in the suburb of Essendon. It took Mak only thirty minutes to find it using the street directory. She drove past casually at first – or as casually as an orange car could – and then parked a block away from the address. The houses in the area were mostly stucco or faux Tudor, she noticed, but Larry's was a fetching brick veneer with fancy stained-glass windows across the front. Though it was on the same size block of land as the rest, the house was huge, looking as if it might spill onto the neighbouring properties at any moment. Without fear of competition, Larry had the most grand and ostentatious home on the block. Through the slim view provided by the front gate, Mak could see that he also had a jacuzzi built onto one side of the house. She imagined him hosting bikini parties with the girls from the club. Mr Moon was making a lot more money than his employee Amy was, that much was certain.

There was movement in the yard, but Mak couldn't make out who it was through the fence. At least someone was home. Mak approached the house and walked up the tiled driveway to a closed front gate taller than she was, flanked by two artlessly carved stone lions. The gate was electronic, and there was an intercom video system to one side with a small round lens. A high, near-impenetrable fence encompassed the property on all sides. This guy liked his security.

Mak thought about her approach. There was some possibility that Amy would answer, but more likely it would be the club owner, Larry. With that in mind, she took off her suit jacket, slung it over one shoulder, adjusted her top and let her hair out of the ponytail.

She pressed the intercom button.

Okay, Amy. Let's hope you're in there . . .

After about a minute, during which time she heard movement in the yard, the intercom was answered. 'Yeah,' came a gruff voice. It certainly didn't sound like Amy.

Mak smiled and leaned towards the round intercom video lens, which she suspected would capture her from the waist up. 'Hi, I'm looking for Larry.' She put her hands on her waist and flicked her hair when she spoke.

'That's me,' came the voice, a lot friendlier.

'I was hoping we could, uh, chat for a moment . . .' she said, with a hint of seduction.

'Come right in,' the voice said almost immediately, and the gate swung open.

Yes!

Mak walked through swinging her hips. She

wasn't intending to be dishonest exactly, but she was happy for this guy to think she was there for other reasons. If it helped her get through the gate, that was just fine. She'd figured out long ago that some people were going to see her as a sex object whether she liked it or not, so she might as well use it when it came in handy. It might not seem possible now, but who knew – maybe when she was sagging and grey she might even miss the approaches of sleazy men she had endured over the years? She thought it doubtful.

Makedde walked along the driveway and stopped in her tracks beside a low, silver Maserati, dripping alluringly from a recent wash. *Nice.* She forced herself to keep moving, taking in everything she could. She noticed that the garden was brimming and well kept, with stone carvings of female nudes set into water features against the fence. The house itself looked even more surreal up close. The stained-glass detail pictured nude women variously reclining over one another or dancing through green fields with flowers in their hands and their pendulous breasts free to the wind.

She arrived at the front door.

Behind her, the gate shut again. She felt a slight ripple of panic.

The brass doorknob turned and the front door opened. An oversized figure loomed in the doorway. It must be Larry.

Larry Moon, owner of one of Melbourne's

most successful gentlemen's clubs, answered his front door wearing a partially soaked white T-shirt stained with dirt, a pair of green gumboots and red Speedos. Mak saw the square bulge of a packet of cigarettes tucked into his rolled-up T-shirt sleeve, in the style of a young Marlon Brando. But Larry was no young Brando. He was vastly overweight, and Mak thought he looked a bit like *Hustler*'s creator Larry Flynt, only without the wheelchair.

Oh, my eyes. I think I might be scarred for life. Ugh!

Mak could not imagine any occasion for which Speedos and gumboots would be required, especially on a build like his. But she wrenched her attention away from his damp protruding stomach and the clear line of his cave-like bellybutton to look into his face, only to find that he was appraising her body right back.

'Hi, beautiful,' Larry said, continuing to undress her with his eyes. 'I was just in the garden. I wasn't expecting you.'

Ah, the garden.

'I'm Makedde Vanderwall. May I come in for a moment?'

His eyebrows went up and he stepped back with an extravagant wave of his arm to allow her entry. 'Certainly.' He closed the door behind them and led her through an entry hall lit in a strange kaleidoscope of colour from the sun streaming through stained glass. When they reached the base of a spiral staircase under a crystal chandelier, he asked, 'How may I help such a lovely lady?'

Mak smiled with a mix of professionalism and seduction. Now that she was through the gate, there would be no more hair flicking and cleavage revealing. 'Is Amy around?' she asked point-blank.

Larry's smile closed up and he narrowed his eyes.

'Who are you?' he demanded.

'Larry, I'm a private investigator. I'm not a cop. I'm not with the state, or the Feds. I'm not with any collection agency,' she reassured him. 'I am just a private investigator trying to figure out why Amy's friend Meaghan Wallace was murdered last week. I was hoping I could have a quick word with Amy to help my investigation. She's not in any trouble, or wanted for any reason.'

He paused, eyes still narrowed. 'What's in it for you?'

'It's a job,' she said simply. 'But I have a feeling there is more to Meaghan's death than the cops think.'

Mak wasn't really sure what she thought, but her client clearly believed there was more to it, and she figured it sounded good to say.

Larry leaned on the banister contemplatively and reached for the packet of cigarettes tucked in his sleeve. He offered her one, and after she declined he lit one and took a puff. Mak noticed that he had security cameras everywhere in the house, much like he did in the club. This guy was obsessed with both surveillance cameras and security, by the looks of that massive electronic front gate. Maybe he got a bulk deal on the stuff. And he was also obsessed with nudes – not particularly well-executed ones, either. There was a big bronze sculpture of a nude on a hall table next to the stairs. Instead of one of the classic poses, the female figure was on all fours, swinging a mane of hair back, face tilted up, eyes closed and mouth open, frozen in bronzed rapture. A stripper sculpture.

Classy.

More interesting to Mak, there were two pairs of women's shoes scattered in the entrance hall: stilettos and some pink rubber thongs.

'She got killed by some junkie last week, didn't she?' Larry said, smoke floating around his lips.

So Amy has mentioned it to him.

'It looks like that might be the case. Maybe…' Mak allowed room for doubt in her tone. 'Do you remember Meaghan at all? She worked for you for a while.'

'Vaguely.'

'It was a few years ago, I believe,' Mak said, hoping to refresh his memory.

'Yeah. She was cute. Blonde, right? Petite. Tight body. She went up to Queensland to dance at Trinity for a while, then back to Sydney. We didn't have her for long.'

Mak remembered the T-shirt. *Trinity is a club.*

She nodded. Standing there in his Speedos, puffing on a cigarette, Mak could see that Larry was not a man who was intimidated by women. Of course, that didn't mean he wouldn't allow himself to be manipulated by them. Mak guessed that he had been influenced to do a lot of things by a lot of different beautiful girls in his life, but when their use-by date was up, it was up. From the way he was looking at her, Mak hadn't reached his perceived use-by date quite yet.

'She was a lovely person, by all accounts,' Mak said, turning up the charm a notch. 'You didn't keep in touch with Meaghan after she left?'

'Me? Nah. Lots of girls come and work for me,' he said offhandedly. She believed him. 'What do you want with Amy?' he asked protectively, with the tiniest level of concern in his voice.

Although Larry seemingly found Mak's presence unthreatening, it was noteworthy to Mak that he still hadn't invited her to sit down. They were stuck there at the base of his staircase, chatting in short, guarded sentences. There had to be a reason. Mak's best guess was that Amy was home, and she explicitly did not want any visitors. Larry was protecting her.

'I think Amy might be able to help shed some light on things. They were close friends. I just want to talk with her a bit. I want to learn the truth about Meaghan. Meaghan's mother didn't know much about her life or the people in it.'

Mak heard a creak at the top of the staircase and she looked up. A shadow flitted across the wall.

Hello, Amy.

'I'm not here trying to force anyone into anything,' Mak continued. 'I'm no cop. I just want to find out the truth. I want to find out whether there is more to this murder than meets the eye, and I suspect there might be. I think Amy could have something very valuable to add.' Mak deliberately spoke the words a touch louder, hoping to appeal to eavesdropping Amy.

'What the hell is a girl like you doing working as a private dick?' Larry asked with a tone of incredulity, changing the subject completely.

'I'm no dick,' Mak retorted, frustrated that he'd closed off the conversation.

He chuckled at her response. *'I'm no dick* ... I like that.' He took a puff. 'You seem like a smart girl. Why waste your time sniffing around like a dog in other people's affairs, when you could make some good cash using the body God gave you? Why don't you come work for me? You've got the goods.'

'You've got the goods.' Did that line usually work for him?

'Thanks,' she said, and smiled. She wanted to leave it at that.

'No, really,' he pressed. 'Guys really go for your type. Tall, blonde, busty. Long legs. You'd clean up.'

'Thanks, really, I appreciate the compliment,

but right now I'm more interested in having a chat with Amy. Would that be okay?'

'She's not here,' he said, looking away. He was lying.

Mak nodded. 'I see. That's fine. Why don't I leave you my card, and when you see Amy next, you just let her know I dropped by.' She took out a card and scribbled her mobile number on the back before passing it to Larry. 'This is my *private* number.' She said the words loudly, so Amy could hear.

Larry, of course, took it the wrong way.

'Marian Wendell Investigations,' he read off the card. 'How much they pay you?'

'Not enough,' Mak answered.

'My girls can make five hundred … fifteen hundred in a night. Cash. Just dancing. Nothing else. You should think about it. You'd have a good future.'

Just dancing, huh? So why is Amy here in your house then?

'That's an interesting proposition, Mr Moon,' she told him, smiling. 'I'll know who to call if I run out of investigations.'

Larry took a few steps towards the front door and leaned on a fake Roman pillar, putting himself between her and the door. He took another puff.

'So Amy's not around, then?' Mak asked again, knowing that the girl was there somewhere, listening.

333

'Nope,' he lied again.

Bullshit.

'Okay,' Mak said, giving in for the moment. 'There's no pressure. But if you remember anything about Meaghan Wallace, you'll give me a call? It would be really helpful.'

'Oh, I'll call you.'

Mak smirked.

Larry opened the door again and she walked out past the Maserati and the garden nudes. The gate opened magically, and she felt some relief at being outside his lair.

Mak's mobile phone rang as she started the car up. It gave her a fright. Could Amy be calling her so quickly? That would be a lucky break, and just what she needed to get back to Sydney on time with something helpful to go on.

'Hello?'

'Mak, sweetheart!'

'Hi, Loulou. How are you?' *Damn.* It wasn't Amy at all. 'Thanks for having me over for dinner last night. It was good to meet Drayson. He is ...' Mak searched for an honest but kind description of Drayson. *'He has good taste in some of his friends'?*

'Why didn't you let me come with you?' Loulou blurted.

'What?'

'You partied with Bogey at Thunderball last night. Why didn't you let me come along?' she said.

'No, no, Loulou, you have the wrong idea. We weren't partying. It was work. I had a job to do, some investigation stuff. Bogey just got mixed up in it because I was going to be hassled too much by the men in there if I didn't come in with a boyfriend.'

'Boyfriend?'

'You know what I mean.'

'*Awwww*,' Loulou whined. 'I want you to use *me* in one of your investigations. I want to be on the job with a private eye. I could be your bodyguard!'

Mak rolled her eyes. 'It's not like that. It was just an unusual circumstance that came up. Why, what did Bogey tell you?'

'Oh, he didn't tell me anything. He told Drayson that you wanted to be dropped off at Thunderball, and that he came in for a drink to make sure you were all right.'

Good man.

'That's all he said?' Mak asked, impressed.

'Yeah, why? Is there more?'

'No, it's just that I got my first lap dance while trying to get information out of one of the girls.'

'Oh my God!'

Mak started laughing. 'It was pretty funny, actually.'

'So can you come over? I wanna hear all about last night! You can't keep anything from me. Fess up!'

Makedde smiled.

'I'll see what I can do, time-wise. Maybe a quick lunch.'

CHAPTER 34

'THERE IS NO sign of the mobile phone,' The American reported with regret.

Jack Cavanagh had not wanted to meet with his security adviser at home, for fear that his wife would clue in immediately that something was wrong, so they had met at his offices instead. Jack stood by his office window late on Sunday morning with his face just centimetres from the glass, watching the quiet streets below; streets that would be bustling by Monday. He wondered how much time he had before something like this leaked to the papers, and he hoped to God that Bob could prevent that happening.

'I have organised a back-up plan to find out every communication the girl made. It is costly, but very accurate. We should have the contents of any video transmission by the end of the day. If you wish it.'

Jack nodded sombrely. 'Money is no object.'

'My men tell me that Mr Hand is doing his work well.'

Jack did not want to hear about it. He knew

blood would be shed because of his son's foolishness, and it shamed him. Jack wondered where he had gone wrong. He'd sent Damien to the best schools; he had been there for him. He'd tried to give him the most normal life possible, and to teach him the social responsibilities that came with privilege. But look at what had become of Damien – their only son, their only child. It broke poor Bev's heart, and she didn't even know the extent of their son's debauched lifestyle.

'There has been an interesting report about a young woman, a private investigator who paid a visit to the family of the Wallace girl. At first my men ran the licence plate and thought it was a police detective, but it turns out she is the girlfriend of a detective and was driving his car.'

Jack waited for him to finish.

'I doubt we will have any trouble with her, but it does look like she might have been there on business,' The American warned him.

'On business?' Jack didn't want a private investigator poking around.

'It should be fine, but I am getting my men to check her out anyway.'

'What about the man Lee? The one Simon said was bringing those girls? Does he have any evidence? Would he testify against Damien?'

The American shook his head quietly. 'Rest assured, he is not a problem.'

Rest. Jack would not be getting any of that for some time, he felt sure.

CHAPTER 35

'SO, HAS ANDY asked again yet?'

Mak looked up. 'Huh?'

Mak and Loulou had found a fabulous little bakery café called Il Fornaio near Mak's hotel, and had launched into their lunches. Mak had already told her tales of Charlotte's sexy moves, the ridiculous spectacle the Peacock patron had made of himself and Larry Moon's unusual take on daywear.

The pair would have to enjoy their quick catch-up, because Mak planned to head back to Sydney that afternoon, relatively empty-handed. She had a lead with Amy, but no valuable information apart from a confirmation that Meaghan Wallace had worked for a time at Thunderball as a dancer. But Mak couldn't rationalise taking any more time getting to Amy on her client's tab, so Marian had booked her a three o'clock flight.

Should I go back to Noelene Wallace to extract more information from her ... see if there are any address books, diaries? If the police don't already have it all.

'*You* know ...' Loulou continued.

'What?' Mak was still wrapped up in thoughts of the investigation.

'Has he popped the question again?'

Andy. Mak gripped her butter knife. This was an awkward subject. 'Oh ... no. No, we aren't really planning on getting married.'

There had been a time, nearly three years earlier, when Mak and Andy had talked about getting hitched. But it had been too soon. Cautious Makedde had not been ready. Had she been right to hesitate about making that huge commitment?

'It's been a couple of years now, hasn't it?' Loulou said.

'Since he proposed? Yeah, something like that. You have a good memory, don't you? I'd forgotten,' Mak lied.

'Sure you have.' Loulou wasn't fooled.

Mak found herself rattled by Loulou's questioning, especially in light of Andy's absence.

'Are you okay, sweetie?'

'Peachy, thanks.' Mak cleared her throat. 'Not everyone has to get married these days.'

Loulou raised an incredulous eyebrow, and seemed to contemplate her response for a moment while she continued to eat. She was excitable and her lifestyle was a little crazy by most standards, but Loulou wasn't dumb. She knew her friend well. For all Mak's independence and strong will, she still harboured some of that fantasy of finding 'the one', foolish as it was. Mak wanted what her mum and dad had shared for twenty-five years before Jane's death.

'Don't you want the white dress, the church, the whole kit and caboodle one day?' Loulou asked.

'Mmm ... no thanks,' Mak said.

'Well, *I* do!' Loulou offered. 'I want the big meringue dress, the ten bridesmaids and the cake with little people on top!'

Mak smiled. Not only was the unconventional Loulou perpetually single but also, to the best of Mak's knowledge, she had not dated anyone for longer than about ten minutes. Okay, to be fair, she had dated this Melbourne muso for a week now. That was quite possibly a record run already.

'You want to be a meringuatang?' said Mak teasingly. 'Okay. Maybe they can make you those little people for the top of the cake, but with mohawks ...'

Loulou laughed bits of croissant onto her plate.

'Did you just hear my phone?' Mak asked. She thought she'd heard the faint but distinctive ring of her mobile. She reached under the table and grabbed her purse. Deep inside, her mobile had indeed been ringing. There were a number of missed calls and one voicemail message.

'Dammit. How did I miss that? Hang on a sec,' she said, and played the voicemail message back, covering her ear to listen.

'Um, Macaylay Vanderwall?' a woman's voice said. 'I think you have been looking for me? Um

341

... I will be at Leo's Spaghetti Bar at three today, in the back room. If you come, come alone. Please. Um ...' Click.

Oh my God. It's her.

Heart bounding, Mak replayed the message.

'... Leo's Spaghetti Bar at three ...' the message repeated as she played it back.

Where was Leo's Spaghetti Bar? Mak had not heard of it. But whatever and wherever it was, Mak was going to have to be there in less than an hour, and she wouldn't want to rush when she got there.

Mak called Marian immediately.

'Hi, it's Mak. I've decided to stay another night in Melbourne,' she said.

'What do I tell Groobelaar? Are you getting a result?'

'Almost. I'm almost there,' Mak said. 'Simon didn't ring a bell with Meaghan's parents, but if this girl is as good a friend as I am hoping, she will know whether or not Simon was on the scene.'

'Okay.'

'And tell him it will only cost him for hours. He doesn't have to worry about paying accom – I'm staying with a friend tonight.'

'Really? Oh, that's good,' Marian said. Clients always liked saving money. 'When will you be back?'

'I'll be in tomorrow, but I'll check in with you later this afternoon to confirm.'

'Good girl.'

When Mak hung up Loulou practically jumped out of her chair to hug her. 'You are staying over! *Yahooo!* This is going to be sooooo fun!'

Mak smiled. 'I gotta get moving.'

CHAPTER 36

LEO'S SPAGHETTI BAR was impossible to miss, with its huge red neon signage and tableclothed settings of chairs and tables spilling onto Fitzroy Street at St Kilda. As Loulou had promised, it was barely a block from Mak's hotel, so she was there in plenty of time. Loulou had helped Mak to pack up and had taken her overnight bag back to Drayson's place.

Now Mak was alone, just as Amy had requested.

Mak paused near the door and took note of the patrons dining outside. There was a pale couple with British accents wearing bumbags and sneakers; a skinny woman with bleached blonde hair bent over a coffee mug; and two men with leather vests and sleeves of tattoos. At the kerb was a black Mercedes, a beat-up Kombi van and a row of yummy motorcycles, none of them occupied. This inventory-taking was a subconscious and automatic response for Mak, something she had picked up from her father and his police colleagues.

No one at the outside tables seemed interested

in returning her gaze, so Mak entered Leo's through a set of glass doors, hoping that this whole chase was not simply a waste of time. Amy had sounded a little paranoid in her message.

Who or what is Amy so paranoid about? Mak wondered, moving through the restaurant area inside.

Leo's had a busy bar area and dining tables that stretched deep into the back. The message had mentioned the back room at Leo's, so Mak made her way past the seated patrons towards the rear wall, quietly surveying the patrons and the layout of the restaurant as she did so. About a third of the tables were already filled, although it was barely three. As on the street, the clientele were a colourful and eclectic bunch – a man with a matted beard and a pierced nose sat alone at one table, and at the next a beautiful woman in a short dress was being fussed over by an attentive Italian waiter. A group of men in overalls were on a coffee break, their construction hats perched on the table. One long table featured a curious mix of intellectuals, debating animatedly over some obscure topic, fuelled by afternoon chardonnay.

Mak felt eyes on her and paused.

'May I help you?' It was a waiter.

'I am just looking for someone. Thanks,' Mak replied and moved on. She saw signs for the toilets, but no signs for a back room. She climbed a set of stairs and continued, again with the feeling that she was being watched. With a quick glance over her shoulder Mak saw that the woman with bleached hair had moved inside and was in a line by the bar. She didn't look up and catch Mak's eye, so Mak moved on to a hallway where she passed the toilets and found a door for a back room. She pulled on the handle.

It was locked. Stuck in the hallway outside the toilets, Mak detected the faint smell of disinfectant. It made her big toe tingle.

'Hey.'

She took a deep breath and turned around. It was the skinny blonde who had been pushing around a coffee mug.

'Are you looking for someone?' Mak asked.

The young woman nodded. 'Macaylay Vanderwall?' she said with hesitation, screwing up the pronunciation again.

Mak guessed that it had to be Amy. Now that she could see her face, the girl looked a bit like she had in the picture with Meaghan, although her hair was longer and stringier, and she had deep circles under her eyes. 'You can call me Mak if you like.'

'Amy.' The name came out in a tiny, bird-like voice; a quick, frightened chirp.

'It's nice to finally meet you, Amy. Thanks for contacting me.'

Mak looked up to find that they weren't alone. Larry Moon came around the corner, filling the hallway with his girth. He nodded. 'Hello again.'

'Hello to you, too.'

'Don't mind me,' he said and pulled out a packet of cigarettes. 'I'll be out front if you need me, okay?' he told Amy protectively.

Amy nodded, quivering like a nervous animal.

The narrow hallway by the toilets was not quite an ideal meeting place. Mak was pleased to follow Amy to a table near the back of the restaurant, where Amy sat with her shoulders snug against the wall, positioned to overlook the rest of the establishment. It was the 'Clint Chair'. The Clint Chair was the position Mak normally took in any given room. She had spent so much time with cops that she felt on edge in any other position. Eating a meal with her back to the middle of a room was unbearable. She needed a spot where she could see as much as possible: the cash register, and all entrances and exits in case of any number of possible emergencies. The spot Clint Eastwood's Dirty Harry would have chosen. So was this young woman who called herself Amy sitting there out of habit, like Mak, or was she expecting an emergency?

'I thought that it was you, but I had to be sure you came alone,' the blonde said. 'You did come alone, didn't you?'

'Yes,' Mak assured her.

Amy seemed only slightly reassured. She nodded nervously and looked towards the glass doors at the front, obviously petrified of something – or someone. She was small and held herself even smaller, arms folded tightly across her chest. She looked to be no older than twenty, with shiny bare skin and large brown eyes.

'I heard you when you dropped by,' Amy said, keeping her eyes averted. 'Larry has been such a sweetheart, taking care of me. I told him I didn't want anyone to know I was there, you know. That's why he had to say I wasn't home. He did it for me.' When she looked to Mak again she gave her a quizzical look. 'He's right – you do look like a model. You're really a private eye?'

Mak nodded. 'Technically I am a forensic psychologist, but I also work as a licensed private investigator. Here is my card.' She produced a business card from her wallet. 'If you ever need to contact me about anything, you can call me day or night.'

Amy read the card before putting it in her purse. She looked Mak over. 'You never thought about dancing?'

'No, not me,' Mak replied, discomfited by the statement. It seemed an odd thing to say to a near stranger. As a dancer, perhaps it seemed normal to Amy to comment on other women's bodies.

Meaghan had been sucked into that world. Likely this was the reason for the unexplained gifts to her family – wanting to show her mum she was doing all right but still not able to tell her what she was doing to earn it. All the while poor Noelene knew there was something her daughter wasn't telling her, but she didn't know what. Mak wondered if Noelene would want to know, and if she herself should tell her at some point, so that she was no longer in the dark about her daughter's career, or whether it was kindest to leave the grieving mother with her photographs and her memories.

'Thank you for meeting with me,' Mak said. 'Can I get you something to drink? Another coffee?'

Amy looked alarmed.

'I noticed that you had been sitting with a coffee mug before, that's all. But I didn't know it was you.'

Amy shook her head. 'No, thanks. I've had enough coffee … starting to get the jitters.' She did indeed look like she had the jitters. Badly. Mak had got Amy this far, but she could see that the rest wasn't going to be a cakewalk. Amy was a very jumpy young woman.

'What can I get you?' Mak offered again.

She shook her head. 'Nothing.'

'I'll get us some water, okay?'

Mak got up and went to the bar to ask for water, giving the young woman a minute or two to relax.

After she returned with two glasses of water they sat in uncomfortable silence for several seconds. At every noise Amy's red-rimmed eyes darted nervously around the room, with Mak unsure of how to move forwards without further spooking her.

'You haven't been in to work much since all this started?' Mak said to start the conversation.

Amy had acrylic nails, and one was broken. Long nails like those were usually an obsession for dancers, and kept well. Her hair was also unkempt, the dark roots starting to show. She guessed that this girl had not only been absent from work recently, but quite possibly had not left the house since her friend's death.

Amy nodded. 'I wasn't in last night. One of the girls told me you had been looking around.'

Mak nodded. 'Are you getting by all right?'

'Larry's a nice guy,' she said. 'He's just been taking such good care of me and everything. I didn't want to leave the house alone, so he came with me.' Mak could see Larry reading a paper and enjoying a coffee at one of the tables outside. 'Plus I have some savings,' Amy said with a flicker of pride, then looked down quickly.

'That's good,' Mak said.

Like young models, Mak supposed that only a few strippers were good at building solid savings before their lucrative years were up. The temptation of an expensive lifestyle was too alluring for many, and by the time the work began to dry up, it was too late. The ones who were smart with their money could own their own real estate by the time they were twenty, and set themselves up nicely. But Amy hardly seemed like one of those girls. She didn't look secure and pampered. She was pretty, but her eyes were tired and unstable – she was clearly a girl with a lot of late nights up her sleeve, and a lot of worries to keep her from being content.

'So tell me about Meaghan,' Mak said.

Amy looked around nervously.

'You worked with her at Thunderball?'

'Well, sort of. Megs only worked there a few times. She lived in Sydney but, like a lot of the girls, she came over for the Grand Prix weekend a few years ago. It's huge. There are about sixty or seventy girls who come to the club just for that weekend. Big bucks.'

'And you two became friends?' Mak prompted.

'Yeah. I moved to Sydney not long after that and we hung out a lot and worked in a few of the clubs together – Dancers, Legs, MG. But Meaghan wasn't really cut out for it.'

Amy began fidgeting with her hands in her lap, perhaps uncomfortable with what she had revealed. She needn't have worried: Mak, of all people, was not going judge her on her experiments in unconventional career paths.

'So you and Meaghan worked together and became friends.'

Amy nodded.

Okay, here goes . . .

'Amy, do you know a guy named Simon Aston? Was he a friend of Meaghan's?'

Amy's mouth formed a tight line. She didn't answer, but Mak could see that she knew the name.

Come on . . . speak to me.

Mak nodded to indicate that it was okay for Amy to go on. Then she tried a different tack. 'You must be upset over Meaghan. It's terrible, what happened to her.'

Amy nodded, eyes wide and mouth distinctly shut.

'If you have some information that could help bring justice for your friend,' Mak began as cautiously as she could, 'then you need to tell me. It is very important.'

Amy responded by frowning and crossing her arms again.

'It can be hard to be caught up in something like this. I know how you feel. I really do,' Mak said, imploring her to tell all.

'Ha! Like you would know how it feels!' Amy blurted, her words catching in her throat.

Mak gave her a moment to calm her anger before speaking. 'I'll let you know something personal about me. Five years ago my best girlfriend was murdered. She was an orphan. I was the closest person to her; I felt like her big sister. When she was killed I believed I had to take care of things. I took it upon myself to make sure her killer was caught.'

Amy's mouth hung open, and her brown eyes fixed on Mak, listening carefully.

'It was a great responsibility. But I had to do it. I loved her as a friend and I needed to know the truth.' Amy's eyes were widening, her brows turning up at the centre. She was finally connecting with Mak. 'I know how wrong it is when something like this happens. People should not assume the right to kill one another. Your friend's murder is an injustice, and the person who did it should pay.'

Amy's lower lip quivered, those big brown eyes glassing over before she looked away and began madly searching her pockets for something – perhaps her packet of cigarettes, which Mak could see were right in front of her on the table. The search of her pockets became desperate, and tears sprang from her eyes. Mak pushed the cigarettes towards her silently, and when the girl noticed them she opened her mouth to speak but said nothing. She picked up the packet, shaking, but before she could bring the smoke to her lips, she broke down again. She sobbed quietly for a few minutes, holding her face in her hands, mascara-stained tears streaming out from beneath her fingers.

'You can tell me, Amy.'

'No-no ... Simon ... wasn't a friend of Megs. But I know who he is. Everyone knows who he is. His friend ... it's his friend ...'

'What friend? What do you think happened? Do you think the police –'

'Toby didn't do it,' she blurted. 'I know it wasn't him.'

There it was again: that certainty that Tobias was not the one, just as Mrs Wallace had.

'Why do you think that?' Mak asked.

Amy didn't answer. Her face was lined with streaks of wet mascara. She began puffing on her cigarette eagerly.

'Tell me, Amy.'

But Mak could see she had clammed up again.

'Do you know Tobias?' Amy had called him Toby, with a familiar tone. She had to have known him.

'A little,' Amy admitted. 'I met him a couple of times. Megs used to talk about him a bit. He was, like … I dunno, her pet project or something. She wanted to help him. He wouldn't … he wouldn't hurt her. That would make no sense.'

'How do you mean, "pet project"?' Mak asked.

Amy leaned her head to one side, her stringy hair falling with it. 'Well, he was living on the streets. Did you know that? Megs felt sorry for him because he was her cousin. She had a soft spot for him, I guess.'

Mak took mental notes. She didn't want to write anything down in case it made this nervous young woman stop talking. Mak had learned that the hard way in the past, and had developed the skill of sharp memory recall to help her with her work.

'What sort of things did she used to do to help him?' she asked Amy.

'Aww, well she used to give him some money all the time. They had this kind of routine where she would give him cash when she got paid each fortnight.'

Mak began to tingle – this was something. She was actually getting somewhere.

'Do you happen to know which day of the week she got paid?' Mak asked.

Amy frowned. 'Um, Thursdays I think. Doesn't everyone get paid on Thursdays? I dunno. Something like that. Yeah, Thursdays.'

'So he came over every second Thursday,' Mak confirmed.

'Right.'

Meaghan had been killed on a Thursday night, and Tobias had been there. Had one of their usual meetings gone horribly, violently wrong for some reason? Or did someone who had known he would be there set him up?

'How about any other times? Do you know if she saw much of him?'

'I don't think so. It was like he only ever came for the money and she knew it, but didn't care. I think she believed he would change,' Amy said.

The thought made Mak sad. Here was this young woman who had a soft spot for a cousin she used to play with as a kid. Enough of a soft spot to let him into her house every fortnight and give him money out of her own pay cheque. If Tobias really had killed her, it made the act even more heartless and terrible.

If? Mak herself had obviously grown sceptical about his guilt.

'Why do you believe Tobias didn't kill her?'

Amy's demeanour changed. She sat upright

and squinted into the distance, thinking hard. She was struggling with something internally, some decision. Mak thought that the girl seemed so unstable that she was afraid to say anything further to her, in case it set her off. So she just waited until Amy eventually pulled a crinkled piece of newspaper out of her leather purse. It was the front page of the Melbourne *Herald Sun*. She unfolded it.

'Him,' Amy said, pointing to a young man in the newsprint photo, posing in a suit with several other business-suited men. 'He's the guy.' She wiped under one eye, only succeeding in smudging her make-up even more.

Mak examined the piece of newspaper with curiosity. The headline read DEALMAKERS SHAKE ON BULLET TRAIN PLANS.

A group of men in business suits was pictured shaking hands. Mak squinted at the face of the man Amy was pointing at. He was young, perhaps in his early thirties. She didn't recognise him.

'He's *what* guy?' Mak asked.

'He is the reason Megs is dead,' Amy said, her emotions finally giving way to fresh tears that rolled down her cheeks silently. She bowed her head and stared down at her glass of water, hiding her face. She wiped her cheeks.

Mak was trying to come to grips with her statement. What could the connection possibly be between the death of the young woman in Sydney and this Melbourne news article about a group of businessmen and politicians? She looked to the names in the caption: New South Wales Premier John Grant, Victorian Premier Michael Yep and businessmen Jack Cavanagh and Damien Cavanagh. Apart from the Victorian and New South Wales premiers, none of the names rang any bells to Mak. She supposed her Canadian heritage did not always serve her well in matters of Australian current affairs.

'Amy, why do you think this man has something to do with Meaghan's death? What do you know about him?'

Amy raised her head and pushed her hair back. Her mascara was smudged into dark circles and her bare skin was flushed.

'All the girls had heard about him. When I was working the clubs in Sydney he was practically all they talked about.'

'About Damien Cavanagh?' Mak asked, reading the name off the caption to be clear about who Amy was referring to.

Amy winced a little at the sound of his name. 'Yes,' she whispered and looked around. 'I can't be heard mentioning his name. You shouldn't either. Trust me.' She folded the newspaper over to hide the article and continued in a low voice. Mak was concerned that perhaps this young woman's theory was less than real.

'Everyone knows he's one of the richest heirs in Australia,' Amy said. 'He would buy girls the best champagne there was, and he gave the most amazing tips, especially to the little Asian girls. Everyone knew he loved Asian. He used to have these wild parties and invite some of the girls over. I was always hoping to meet him and go to one of his parties, but I never did. Probably wasn't his type. He was the one we always hoped would come in, though. He was free with the tips ... lots of tips for everyone.'

Mak imagined the fuss a group of exotic dancers would make over a rich man like that in a strip joint. He'd make the Peacock Man with his crinkly fifty-dollar notes pale by comparison. Around Damien Cavanagh it would be a free-for-all battle of toned flesh and murmured compliments.

Mak waited to hear more.

'Then, after a few months, he stopped coming to the club. Just like that. We heard that he started getting into those other girls – the Asians who get brought in ... you know, illegal.'

Mak paused. 'Illegal? Do you mean trafficked women?'

'You know, the girls brought from Asia to be hookers. They're everywhere in Sydney these days. Word was that he had an inside track on the new arrivals and was breaking them in.'

Breaking them in.

Mak felt sick to her stomach. She knew that the Government had introduced legislation against trafficking into sexual servitude in 1999, but that the first arrests hadn't taken place until 2003, at which time there had been a couple of small news articles on the first cases going to court. At the time, Mak had read reports that there were up to 1000 trafficked women in Australia, most from poverty-stricken villages in Thailand or the Philippines. Because they were in the country illegally, many of the women were put straight into immigration detention when discovered, and then deported before they got around to testifying against those who had entrapped them. Mak didn't know much about the cases or how the women found themselves working in Australian brothels, but it seemed to be a horrible fate. Whether they were trafficked sex slaves or the more sanitised-sounding 'migrant sex workers', as some described them, it seemed cruel and unjust to force anyone to have to service over 500 men before being free of the debt contracts that had brought them into the country.

Why would a rich boy want to be one of those 500 clients?

'Where did you hear about this?' Mak asked breathlessly.

Amy averted her eyes. 'You know ... word was going around,' she said, avoiding a straight answer. Amy still did not meet Mak's gaze, and Mak became sure that she was keeping something important from her.

But what does all this have to do with Meaghan?

Amy placed her fingers against her forehead as if plugging the hole in a dam of information that wanted to spill out. For a while she didn't respond, still clearly assembling the rest of her response.

'I know Tobias,' Amy finally said. 'He's a junkie but he's no killer. He could never kill someone, let alone Megs. She was the only one who believed in him. She supported him and she was probably the only one in the world who loved him and never gave up on him.'

Mak waited. She could sense that Amy was still not telling her everything.

'Amy, what does this man –' she pointed to the newspaper article – 'have to do with what happened to Meaghan?'

'I saw it. I know why she was killed. Megs was killed because she saw too much. She sent it to me and she got killed.'

'Saw what? What did you see? Tell me, please. Tobias might be in jail for the rest of his life if you don't come forward.'

'I can't. You don't understand.' The crying started again, this time heavier tears and loud sobs.

'You have to. Come on, talk to me,' Mak pressed. 'I can get you police protection. I know a lot of officers. They will take care of you. You will be okay.'

Amy was shaking her head. She looked increasingly distressed. In a flash she darted up from the table and started for the door. Mak grabbed her arm.

'You know you can trust me. This is important – Tobias may be sentenced to life.'

But Amy pulled her arm away violently. 'Sorry ... I'm so sorry ... I can't ...' she mumbled through tears, and fled the restaurant. Mak's heart sank as she watched the girl go. She didn't know what she could do. She couldn't keep her there, and following her out would only upset her more.

Outside the glass doors, Larry Moon sat bolt upright as Amy took him by the arm. She dragged him off, pulling him up the street away from Mak.

Fuck!

For thirty minutes Mak sat bewildered and not much better informed, looking at the crinkled newspaper article Amy had left behind and hoping that she would come back.

She didn't.

Shit, Mak thought. *I was so close. I blew it.*

CHAPTER 37

'WE GOT A match on the print that doesn't fit,' Detective Karen Mahoney declared triumphantly to Detective Cassimatis, her red Irish curls springing. The young detective had rushed up the elevator after hearing the news.

'On ya, girl,' Jimmy said tenderly. He seemed a little down, and more unhealthy than ever.

Mahoney knew that Detective Jimmy Cassimatis had a soft spot for her, mostly because she was good at cursing. She also knew that like her friend Mak, Jimmy would be missing Andy already. Nor did he particularly like working with her boss, Sergeant Hunt.

'The Wallace case?' he asked.

She nodded enthusiastically. A print that had been found at Meaghan Wallace's apartment matched that of a convicted criminal. This was a breakthrough.

Wasting no time, Mahoney strode through the office and made her way to Hunt's desk, declaring the news, but Hunt looked up from his paperwork with mere impatience. 'I was told.' He looked down again, ignoring her.

'Well ...' she said excitedly, waiting for her superior to spring into action, but he didn't move a muscle.

'Well, it's Sunday, and I have more important things to deal with right now. We'll get to it.'

She frowned. *More important than murder?*

Like what, Karen wanted to say, but she had only just made detective not so long ago. She had worked so hard for it, and she feared it could be taken away from her.

'He has a record. I think it's worth checking out. Can I ...?'

'Can you what?'

'Can Matt and I go and ask him some questions?'

Hunt frowned. Karen couldn't imagine why he would be frowning. 'Now?' he asked, as if she was a nuisance. 'You do realise that we've already made an arrest?'

She nodded again. 'Yup.'

'And he was caught red-handed with his prints on the murder weapon?'

She nodded once more. 'Sir, I think we should just rule out all other possibilities.'

Hunt raised his eyebrows and looked at her sternly, clearly unhappy about the prospect of any of his team giving him more work.

'I didn't mean ... it's just that it will maybe make the case more solid ...' she stuttered.

'Okay, go.' He said it flippantly. 'But no bring-ing anyone in for questioning, and no arrests.'

A least that was better than a no.

'Questions only,' she assured him.

Mahoney was used to being treated as second-rate by her superior; it was something that she just assumed came with the role of being the rookie detective. But she was surprised at the new level of disdain he was showing her. She wasn't sure what she was doing so wrong.

'I don't need you making things complicated when we have a perfectly good arrest.'

Complicating things?

Puzzled, she left him and in minutes she had rounded up Detective Matt Parker and headed back to the elevator.

'See ya, Jimmy,' she called out. 'Have fun at those tattoo parlours.' He'd spent much of his day quizzing tattoo artists on a particular design found on the dumpster victim's back.

'Yeah,' he fake-sneered. 'Go get 'em.'

Mahoney wanted to ask Warwick O'Connor how he knew Meaghan Wallace, and exactly why his fingerprint was found in her apartment.

★ ★ ★

'Just shut up, woman!' Warwick O'Connor cried. 'I'm trying to think.'

Warwick was on edge. He was at a crossroads: either about to get the biggest windfall of his life,

or about to find his way back into the slammer ...
for a long time this time around.

His wife, Madeline, paced around the kitchen
in her well-worn pink bathrobe, cigarette dangling
from her lip. She was a chain-smoker, and the
kitchen table was adorned with a heart-shaped tin
ashtray with VEGAS written on it, a souvenir from
their one and only trip overseas, their honeymoon.
The ashtray was overflowing with butts.

Madeline paced, face puckered and grim, her
eyes wild. She was used to such verbal abuse
from her husband, and she was deft at handing it
out as well.

'Oh, you're trying to think, heh? Well, I
won't hold my breath for anything to happen!'
she retorted.

'I'll give you one, woman, I will!' Warwick
said, standing up from the kitchen table and
raising his hand.

'You wouldn't dare,' she replied coolly, and
puffed on her cigarette.

Warwick and Madeline had been married for
seven years. As he saw it, she was a pain in the
arse, but she was still a good egg. She'd stuck by
him when he'd had to do two at Long Bay
Correctional Centre for assault, and that couldn't
be overlooked.

'Mads, I'm tellin' ya, I'm tryin' to think here,'
he said more gently.

'What did he say when you called him?' she
persisted, and dragged on her cigarette again.

She meant Jack Cavanagh.

Warwick had given Jack twenty-four hours to think about the deal, and when he'd called back, Jack had hung up. He'd actually hung up. Since Saturday afternoon Warwick had been thinking hard about what to do. What threat could he make? Could he still get a few quid off Simon Aston and then call it at that?

'Well ...' she said, giving him that hard gaze he despised.

'He ... hung up,' Warwick admitted.

'Well, he's not taking you seriously, hon. Nail 'em. Just –'

'I told you, I'M TRYING TO THINK.'

'Well why don't you take –'

'Shut up!'

She ignored him and went on. 'Why don't you take the video and –'

'I don't have it,' he said in a low voice, staring at the checked tablecloth.

'What? You said –'

'I DON'T HAVE IT,' he said, exasperated. 'I was bluffing.'

Mads stopped. 'Oh.'

Warwick took a deep breath. He'd thought he could fool Jack Cavanagh. But things weren't going as planned. And now he didn't know what to do next.

There was a noise – a car pulling up.

Madeline and Warwick both sensed it at the same time. They froze for only a moment.

Madeline nodded, having looked out the window. Cops. Warwick leaped to his feet and, without saying a word, scrambled to the staircase and ran upstairs.

A few seconds later the doorbell rang. Madeline O'Connor answered the door in her robe, cool as ever.

'Detective Mahoney,' the young redhead said, flashing her badge. 'This is Detective Parker. We have a few questions for your husband, Warwick.'

'Is something wrong?' Madeline asked innocently and took a puff.

'Just routine. We have a few routine questions.'

'He ain't here,' she told them.

There was a noise overhead.

'What was that?' the young detective with the red curls asked.

★ ★ ★

Fuck, fuck, fuck!

That was close.

I knew I was getting myself in too deep.

Warwick crawled out the bedroom window on the top floor, banging his knee on the windowsill as he made his clumsy exit. He crept across the rooftops, keeping down to avoid being seen. The sun was low in the sky but there was enough light for him to be spotted. He had an escape route planned and a stash of $30 000 in cash hidden away in a large toolbox in his friend's shed. He could live on that for a while. And he'd have to. He might have to lie low for longer than usual. Now that he'd been dobbed into the cops there would be heat for a while. Who knew how long? He would have to be careful. He didn't want to end up back inside. He would have to be cautious about contacting Madeline.

Fuck, fuck, fuck . . .

Simon Aston had called the damned cops on him. *That bastard!* Warwick never thought he'd do it. Simon had as much to hide as anyone, so why had he squealed? Jack Cavanagh must have leaned him on. Maybe that was it?

Dammit!

Warwick shinned down the drainpipe of his neighbour's, as he had done many times before. He moved quickly, heart racing. His car was parked in the alley behind the row of houses. He kept a spare key under the wheel rim for emergencies.

There it is.

His car was waiting for him just as he'd left it. He ran to it, felt around for the key, unlocked it and jumped in. He detected the faint smell of petrol. A leak? He put the key in the ignition and started the engine.

Warwick O'Connor was already a block away before he realised he wasn't alone.

There was a man in the back seat.

Someone had been waiting for him.

CHAPTER 38

'IT'S GOOD TO have you with us again.'

Drayson opened the door with a sleepy grin.

'I really appreciate you letting me stay,' Mak said, still catching her breath after the five flights of stairs. 'Especially at such short notice.'

Mak evidently wasn't the only one who appreciated it: Loulou gave Drayson a huge kiss on his cheek and hugged his neck with manic enthusiasm, clearly delighted about her new boyfriend's hospitality. He was definitely scoring some points by letting Mak stay there.

'Come on in,' Drayson managed, Loulou hanging from his neck. He still had the same sleepy bedroom look.

Mak looked around. 'Oh, I see the whole gang is here.'

Bogey was over by the couch in the living room. He stood politely to bid her welcome, the sight of him giving Mak a guilty jolt of excitement. Donkey drifted past with a grunted 'hey'. Only the purple-haired painter was missing.

'Maroon's not here?' Mak said casually, averting her eyes from Bogey.

'Nope. Some people have their *own* lives,' Drayson said with sarcasm, making a deliberate dig at Bogey and Donkey. 'She'll be home late, I think. How long are you in town?' he asked.

'Until tomorrow. I have work back in Sydney.'

'Cool,' he responded.

'Mak is trying to find someone named Amy Camilleri,' Loulou blurted.

Mak shot a look at Loulou – she didn't need anyone else knowing her business arrangements.

'They might be able to help!' Loulou responded defensively. 'Between Drayson and Bogey, I think they know everyone this side of Melbourne.'

'It's true,' Donkey said. 'I know everyone.'

Mak laughed. 'Ah. That's okay. I think I have it sorted now. But thanks.'

I found her, I just wasn't good enough at my job to get her to open up.

She'd replayed the meeting in her mind hundreds of times since that afternoon. She wasn't sure what else she could have done to get Amy to relax and tell all.

Drayson and Loulou disappeared into the kitchen and Mak took a seat on the opposite end of the lounge from Bogey, at an awkward distance. Mak wondered why it seemed so strange. It was the kind of distance people put between each other when they felt funny about getting along so well – or because they had shared a buck-naked lap dance …

'Thanks again for your help last night,' she said to him softly.

'It was my pleasure.' Behind his black-rimmed glasses, he smiled at her with his eyes.

'I guess you have been missing your friend,' he ventured. 'It must be nice to be able to spend time together.'

Mak was relieved that he wasn't intent on recounting their adventures of the night before.

'Yeah,' Mak admitted. 'I am so glad to see Loulou happy. But, to tell you the truth, I am a little concerned that I might lose her to Melbourne.'

'Melbourne isn't so far. And it's getting closer all the time.'

'The flight is pretty quick,' she agreed.

'And soon it looks like there will be that bullet train, too. It will be nothing to get here and visit her.'

Mak must have lost the colour in her face at the mention of the train, because Loulou walked in from the kitchen with two beers and rushed straight over to her. 'What happened?' She played it overdramatically as always. 'What did you say to her, Bogey Man?'

'Nothing!' he protested.

'He didn't say anything. I am pretty stressed with work, that's all,' Mak said.

Bogey gave her a look of concern, perhaps

371

afraid he had inadvertently done something wrong.

'You know, Bogey gives the most amazing massages,' Loulou offered. 'They are really relaxing. It's the best thing for stress.'

'Oh, I'm dying for a massage,' Mak said under her breath. She'd wrenched her back in the economy seat on the short flight south, and dragging her overnight bag around had not helped either.

Loulou jumped straight in. 'You heard the lady – she's dying for a massage, Bogey. Come on, give her one.'

Mak bit her lip. *Oh no, this is ridiculous.*

'It's no problem ... if you want a massage. I would be happy to,' Bogey said – as always, not pressuring her.

'Are you serious? I thought Loulou was just kidding. I don't need a massage, really,' she back-pedalled.

But you want one.

Of course a massage would be great. Who could turn down a decent massage? But it was Bogey and she hardly knew him, except as the shy, charming face seated next to her while a young lady with a stage name of Charlotte displayed her flexibility, unhindered by clothing. It wasn't like a massage would mean she was cheating on Andy or anything. But ...

'No, no, I didn't mean it, really,' Mak

continued. 'I just haven't had one in ages. That's all I meant. I didn't mean to sound like –'

'Like you are a woman who will die if she doesn't have a massage. That's what you said,' Loulou pressed.

'I am not going to die. Stop it. I just meant that ... well, everyone likes massages, don't they? Why is everyone staring at me?'

Drayson and Loulou were both watching her. Bogey was looking determinedly at the coffee table.

'Oh, now you have to!' Loulou urged Bogey, who appeared to be blushing slightly, as he had when Mak had squeezed his knee at the strip club. To make it worse, Loulou elbowed him hard.

If he had been embarrassed at all though, Bogey seemed to recover quickly. 'I could give you a little relaxation massage after dinner if you would like, Mak. It would be no trouble,' he said.

'He's a trained masseur. He's really good.'

Really? A coffin maker rock-'n'-roll-poet masseur?

Mak smiled and finally stopped protesting. It's not that she didn't want to say yes – she just wished she could say no.

So she said nothing.

CHAPTER 39

'NOW STOP THE car,' the deep, monotonous voice said.

Warwick O'Connor put the brakes on slowly, and his car came to rest in a massive parking lot, deserted on a Sunday evening. It was near a construction site, from what Warwick could tell. And it was dark. He and his mysterious companion were alone. Warwick had not yet seen him – he had been waiting in the back seat.

'Look, I know who sent you,' he said, his voice tremulous.

At least I think I do ... Warwick had a lot of disgruntled clients and colleagues. He'd imagined that something like this might happen one day. Someone might be sent to fix him up. He'd been sent on such jobs himself.

'I have a lot of money,' he pleaded, trying to placate his unseen foe. 'In *cash*. Unmarked bills just waiting for you, yeah? They're hidden in a shed. I can give it all to you. I can pay you well.'

Warwick knew he could scream as loudly as he wanted to and no one would hear him, not here. No one would come to his rescue. He had to talk his way out of this.

The man in the back seat of his car said nothing.

Warwick strained his neck to look behind him and turned his cheek right into the cold barrel of a pistol. It had a long, cylindrical silencer on the end of it. This man meant business. You didn't come with a silencer if you didn't plan on firing.

Fuck, fuck, fuck!

'No, man, no! I — I can pay you! I'll do whatever you want!' he pleaded.

'Yes, you will.'

Warwick got a chill. *Fuck!* This guy was serious, and he had a pistol with a goddamned silencer at his face. *Fuck!*

'Anything! I've got money. I'll give it all to you and I can leave town, man. I'll leave! You won't ever see me again!' Warwick rambled, tears forming in his eyes. He was not ashamed to beg for his life. If he were this man, he would take the money. If it were enough money, he might even let himself live. 'I don't know what they're paying you, man, but I got lots in that shed. *Thousands*. Tens of thousands in cash!'

'Get out. Slowly,' was the only reply.

That voice. It was so deep and unfeeling. He thought he might have heard it somewhere before.

Warwick did as he was told. He slid out of the car with his hands up, still trying to placate the man. 'I'll do whatever you say, man, it's cool. Whatever you want ...'

The man now got out, gun still pointed at him. When he stood, his torso just kept rising and rising until he was head and shoulders above Warwick. He was a huge man. Tall *and* broad.

Oh Christ ...

But there was something familiar about him – it wasn't just the voice now. Even in the low light, he thought he recognised the man. 'Hey .. . hey, is that you?'

There was a smile in the dark – white teeth, but a strange smile. Something was wrong with it. Warwick's eyes were still adjusting, and when he looked at the man he saw that his skin looked funny.

Luther?

'Is that you, Luther, mate?'

There was a slow nod.

'Geez, man, you had me scared there for a sec! How the hell are you?' He hadn't seen Luther in, what – ten years maybe?

'Nothing personal,' Luther said.

Warwick had been so busy looking down the barrel of the gun that he had failed to notice the object in Luther's other hand. It was a tyre iron. It flew towards him at lightning speed, and with one crushing blow made contact squarely with Warwick's head. He cried out.

Now Warwick thought he was going to die.

'No, man, no!'

The tyre iron struck again, this time against Warwick's jaw. He nearly lost consciousness from that one blow.

'Stop, please! Stop!'

Luther Hand kicked him to the ground, and continued kicking him. He had steel-toed boots, and every blow brought incredible pain to Warwick's body. Warwick lost track of time as he was beaten into near unconsciousness. He no longer begged or pleaded. He could barely speak, and barely move.

Finally the beating stopped.

'Get in the trunk.'

'What?' Warwick tried to mumble through his swelling face. The word came out in a grunt.

'*GET–IN–THE–TRUNK.*'

Warwick tried to lift his body but failed. He wanted to do whatever Luther said. Luther was beating him, so he'd begun to hope that he wasn't going to kill him. He wasn't using his gun. This was about teaching him a lesson: Warwick would leave the Cavanaghs alone. The Cavanaghs or whomever else he had pissed off. He would leave them all alone so that no one would send Luther Hand to him again. He would skip town. He'd send a postcard to Madeline and she would join him one day. Maybe he'd go to Darwin. Or Perth. He would move far from Sydney and he would never come back.

Warwick dragged his body along the gritty

pavement of the parking lot, towards the rear of his car, while Luther watched in silence.

Luther had already opened the trunk.

There was no way Warwick could lift himself to get in. He was pretty sure his leg was broken. And one of his arms.

Luther bent down and hauled his victim up, pain soaring through Warwick's bruised and broken limbs. He couldn't help but cry out, blood mixed with tears and mucus oozing down his face.

He was shoved inside the trunk of his car. Warwick managed to open his swelling eyes just enough to see Luther's form above him, the light of a distant streetlamp giving the giant man a faint halo.

'I ...' Warwick began, but found he couldn't speak.

Luther slammed the trunk shut, leaving him in darkness. Warwick was relieved.

It's over. Thank God, it's over.

When he got out, he would leave Sydney and never come back.

After a few minutes his shaking began to ease. The full impact of his wounds sank in: he had been beaten to within an inch of his life. He didn't want to bleed to death; he hoped someone found him before that happened. He would need a good surgeon – someone to make his face look normal again. His nose was broken, his eyes swollen shut.

Then Warwick thought he smelled petrol

again, as he had when he'd first got into the car. The smell was stronger this time. Something dripped on his face and stung. He was confused.

The realisation hit him only as he felt the searing heat. Smoke poured into the trunk. He kicked against the lid of the trunk, screaming, shouting, coughing, struggling, but it was no use and he knew it.

This wasn't a lesson.

It was an execution.

CHAPTER 40

'I'VE GOT THE room set up. Come in and make yourself comfortable.'

'Okay,' Mak said and walked into the bedroom. Thankfully Loulou was busy with her boyfriend, and Donkey was comatose in front of the television, so there would be no more embarrassing talk. Mak wondered if Loulou had any idea how awkward she felt.

The modest guestroom had been temporarily transformed into a relaxing retreat; a couple of candles lit, the floor space cleared and a yoga mat stretched out for her to lie on, next to some towels. Her suitcase was pushed into a corner.

Mak took a deep breath.

'So you used to do this professionally?' Mak asked.

'Yes, one of my many and varied careers,' Bogey said, and laughed softly. 'I did remedial massage for about two years.' He gestured to the spot he'd set up. 'Are you okay to lie on the mat?'

'Sure.' She got on her knees at first, trying to

decide what to do about her clothing. 'Did you enjoy it? When you were doing massage?'

'Yes. It's nice to make people feel good. I still like to give massages once in a while.'

'I don't think I've ever met someone who used to be a musician, masseur and coffin-maker,' Mak commented.

'I guess I am still looking for something I'm good at.'

There was an uncomfortable silence while Mak pulled her jumper over her head and stretched out on her stomach on the mat. She realised she had only text messaged Andy to see that he had arrived safely in Virginia. She hadn't called. That was a little insensitive of her. Then again, neither had he contacted her once he'd touched down.

Andy, don't be gone too long.

'This is very kind of you. You don't have to just because Loulou suggested it,' Mak said then.

'No, it's my pleasure. As long as you are comfortable with it?'

'Absolutely,' she lied. She wanted the massage, but that didn't mean she was entirely comfortable about it.

Bogey asked her how hard she would like the pressure.

'Um, I like it hard. Ummm, deep tissue.'

I like it hard? Jesus, Mak . . .

She was blushing wildly by now, but she hoped he couldn't tell with her face pushed into the pillow.

'I'll take my T-shirt off, if that's okay,' she said. It was useless to try to have a massage fully clothed. She pushed herself up on her elbows and strained to pull her top over her head. It was a thrill to disrobe, even to this degree. Perhaps too much of a thrill. Was all this really harmless? *Of course it is. It's just a massage.* She hardly knew this guy, but he had been cool about her strange adventure at Thunderball, and he was a friend of Loulou's latest boyfriend. That sort of made him trustworthy, didn't it?

'Are you okay if I undo your –'

'Yes, yes, that's fine,' Mak said to him, and she reached behind her back to undo her bra. The elasticised straps sprung apart and hung from her sides.

She took another deep breath.

Now her back was entirely vulnerable and exposed. She felt the cold air of the room over her skin. Her face was continuing to flame, so she kept her head firmly on the pillow.

'Just close your eyes and relax,' Bogey told her.

She heard him rub his hands together briskly for a few seconds and when he placed them on her back they were hot. Her skin responded gratefully, and Mak felt her heart jump. His touch was electric.

'Take a deep breath for me,' he said.

She inhaled through her nose, filling her chest with oxygen, and letting it out slowly.

'Good. And another.'

She repeated the deep breathing, feeling her head sway slightly from the experience. With the red wine, she was feeling it even more.

Bogey gently pushed against her back with his palms, rocking her spine softly. She listened for the sound of a bottle as he filled his hands with oil and slicked her back with it in slow-moving rhythmic circles and strokes. The feeling of release was immediate and beautiful. He caressed her back with an almost loving grace, and as the minutes progressed and she lost herself in his touch, Mak allowed herself to imagine this interaction as a slow and sensual foreplay to lovemaking.

'That is beautiful,' she muttered guiltily, enjoying his touch.

'Just allow yourself to relax completely and enjoy it. Let everything go.'

She was beginning to feel warm between her legs. Being touched by another man, this young and fascinating Australian, was getting to her. She had sensed the danger of it. What if she rolled over and pulled him into her? What would he do?

She could feel her body respond as if for sex; as if this man, this near stranger, was worshipping every inch of her skin, section by section, before entering her and bringing her to orgasm, which she already felt tantalisingly close to reaching.

Stop it, Mak. Think about something else.

But she couldn't.

Perhaps the way she felt was just because of the change of scenery, or perhaps it was because of the way Andy had left and his proposed move to Canberra when he got back, never having discussed any of it with her, never talking about how she might fit into that picture. Mak felt tempted to take advantage of this moment.

She was alone with this man, and she might never be alone with him again.

* * *

Mak was relieved when Bogey was gone.

He had massaged her for nearly ninety minutes before gently running his fingertips in lines down her skin, and asking if she felt good.

Did she feel good?

She felt transported.

Now she was preparing for bed, feeling guilty at the pleasure she'd experienced. The temptation to step over the line had nearly overwhelmed her. Imagine if she had given in to it ... What would she do then? Tell Andy? Move back to Canada? Keep a naughty secret like that?

What was getting into her? Andy had left only yesterday and she was already acting like they had been apart for years.

Mak brushed her teeth in Drayson's bathroom and crept back to the guestroom in a long T-shirt and a pair of Andy's boxer shorts. The lights were off in the apartment, with only a soft glow coming from under the door of the main bedroom. She could hear Loulou giggling, the mattress squeaking. They would be having sex.

Oh God.

Mak fumbled for her doorway, wanting to cry. Her body was exploding with desire. She should have been relaxed, but she'd let her mind get away. The entire ninety minutes had been like an agonising foreplay. In reality it had just been a massage. A nice guy offering a massage – something he used to do professionally, something he likes to do for his friends. He was a friend, that was all; he was not courting her. Those strong hands had touched her body in friendship. He could not even know how she had desired him.

She felt the sharp edge of her loneliness, away from everyone she knew, away from her lover, her life displaced.

Mak reached for her mobile phone and started a text message.

MISSING YOU. LOVE YOU.

Mak pressed send and lay back against the sofa bed.

Dammit.

Frowning, she crawled between the sheets Loulou had prepared, feeling the lumps in the old mattress press against her body. Mak looked at the spot where the yoga mat had been, and her body tingled at the memory of Bogey's touch. Mak crossed her arms and stared at the ceiling, trying to concentrate on the way the shadows fell in the corners of the room, the form of the warm glow from the floor lamp. She wanted to cry.

Mak lay back under the sheet and let her fingers caress her thighs, fighting back the feelings of desire and guilt as she imagined being held, being touched, being made love to. She saw Andy's face, but it became Bogey's, with his touch burning into her, his strong hands caressing her back, sliding across to massage the sides of her breasts, turning her over gently and kissing her hard.

Her fingers found her moist centre, her pleasure point jumping under the light pressure. She did not take long to explode, shuddering with guilty ecstasy, a sigh escaping her lips.

Mak rolled onto her side, curling into a ball, conflict raging in her head. She wished Bogey had not gone home – and yet she was relieved that he had. Who was this young guy with the easygoing nature and the strong hands? She wanted to know so much more about him. What did her feelings mean? Or did they mean nothing at all?

CHAPTER 41

'WE HAVE A problem,' The American said. He did not want to alarm his client, but he had to give him the news. It was early on Monday morning, and they had met in Jack Cavanagh's office for an emergency debriefing, doors closed.

Jack Cavanagh wore his usual uniform of khaki pants and pressed shirt. He ran an unsteady hand across his face in response. 'What is it? Tell me.'

'I have confirmation that the video footage of Damien does exist and, though it is a little grainy, he is potentially identifiable.'

Jack closed his eyes. 'I don't want to see it.'

The American nodded. His costly NSA contact had traced all of the electronic communications of Meaghan Wallace in the lead-up to her death. The video SMS had been sent from Meaghan's mobile phone to her friend Amy Camilleri at the time of the party, before the phone had supposedly been 'destroyed' and then lost by Simon Aston. Miss Camilleri was in possession of the video, and she was now a target.

Who knew how many people she might have shown it to? He would now need to monitor all of her communications, and he would have to think up a way to remove the threat she posed without causing too much suspicion.

'The initial threats have been taken care of.'

Jack looked solemn. 'Good,' he said.

'But this is new. I will see to it that it's dealt with.'

'Use discretion,' Jack said. 'As you always do,' he added.

'I will,' The American replied.

With that confirmation of intent from his client, The American would now contact Mr Hand and issue him with his new set of instructions.

'I need access to your private jet.'

Jack Cavanagh nodded. 'I can have it ready for you in under an hour.'

Mr Hand would need to do this next job interstate.

CHAPTER 42

HOW ARE YOU FEELING TODAY?

Mak was scrounging around in the pantry of Drayson's apartment at eight-thirty on Monday morning when her mobile phone beeped. She lifted it into view.

At the sight of the number, her heart hurried a touch: it was Bogey. Mak closed her eyes and shook her head. She'd been hoping she'd be able to forget the feelings she'd had the night before. At least she had not acted on them. With him, anyway.

Makedde leaned against the kitchen counter and replied in a flash, her fingers working the keypad nimbly.

MY BACK IS MUCH BETTER THANKS. HEADING OFF TODAY. THANKS AGAIN.

She went back to searching the kitchen for some form of food, but her phone beeped again a minute later.

BREAKFAST?

Hmmm. Funny he should mention that.

For the past five minutes Mak had been looking

fruitlessly through the kitchen cupboards for anything remotely edible. She'd found a tiny bit of cereal at the bottom of a crinkled box, but no milk to eat it with. Nor were there any eggs or fruit or yoghurt – or even bread. Nothing that might help tide her hunger over. Her only option seemed to be Vegemite and vodka. *Mmmm.*

There was no sign of stirring from Drayson and Loulou's room, or Maroon's. Mak wasn't even sure if Maroon was home.

Um . . .

SURE she texted back, her chest feeling tight. She wanted to see him, but she could also see that her motivation might not be altogether pure. *It's fine*, she told herself. *You need more friends.* It was normal. He knew that she was in a relationship – after all, she'd said that the first night. And just because they'd watched a woman strip naked in front of them – just because he'd had his hands on her the night before, giving her a massage that had spurred her on to her own sensual release – didn't mean anything. It wasn't as if she'd made *him* give her that kind of release. He hadn't even been there. That was a private moment. He was just one of Loulou's new friends. No big deal. No one was cheating here, or anything even close.

BE THERE IN THIRTY MINS

Mak read his message and her heart began pounding immediately. She jumped in the

390

shower, freshened up and got dressed in black pants and a crisp white shirt. After an appraisal in the mirror, she changed her mind and slipped into her oldest ripped jeans, T-shirt and black boots. Casual.

Damn.

★ ★ ★

Mak leaned against the doorway at the entrance to Loulou's building, holding her coat close around her neck. It seemed unseasonably cold. She didn't want to wake Drayson and Loulou, so she had walked downstairs to make her calls and wait for Bogey.

A sour feeling about Andy had settled in her stomach.

She felt unbalanced by her psychological infidelity. She was living with him, and she had thought about another man when she made herself orgasm. No big deal, perhaps, but she was also about to share breakfast with that very same man. Even if it was innocent and normal, she had certainly started to feel guilty.

'Flynn,' he answered.

'Hi. How are you?'

'Good.'

'I wanted to catch you before I started my day.' She squinted in the wind. 'I tried calling you last night.' She felt the burden of her guilt over Bogey, even though her little betrayal had only been in her overactive imagination – unless that hour and a half of pleasure at Bogey's hands could be considered sexual, which some would argue it could. She certainly wouldn't be telling Andy about the massage. And that was enough of an indication of how she'd really felt.

'Did you? I got your text message.'

'Oh, that's right.' Mak shook her head. *Idiot.* 'How was your flight?'

'Fine.'

He never was very good on the phone.

'Great,' she answered. 'I hope everything goes really well,' she told him. 'Hey, I had this exciting breakthrough with the investigation yesterday. A lot of people seem to think he is innocent.'

'The druggie?'

'Yeah.' When Andy said it like that, it sounded silly for anyone to consider they had the wrong person for the murder.

'He's a junkie, Mak,' Andy declared. 'Junkies do horrible things to people they love. It happens all the time, and their loved ones are always in denial about it. No one wants to think their sweet little son is a killer.'

'His mother is dead, actually.'

'Yeah, well,' he replied. 'Look, Mak ... I've been thinking. I need to talk to you about something.'

His voice sounded strange.

'What?'

'You know, I feel badly that you will be all by

392

yourself there for three months. I mean, I could be even longer.'

'Yeah?'

'I just want you to know that it's okay if you don't want to wait for me.'

What?

The words took a while to sink in. Mak held the collar of her coat to her neck. *What is he saying?* She wished she could see his face, see the look in his eye. The phone was so impersonal.

She felt her heart sink. 'You want to take a break again?' she said, the words tasting bitter on her tongue. He'd done this before when she was in Canada.

'No. Unless that is what you want?' he said, further frustrating her.

Mak wanted him to fight for her, beg her to stay, beg her to wait for him – not this ...

'Do you think it would be best if I went back to Canada?' she asked, tears forming. But she kept her voice as strong as she could. She couldn't believe he was doing this over the phone. How could he do this by *phone*?

'No, no,' he hastily replied. 'It's up to you, of course.'

Mak clenched her jaw, tears rolling down her cheeks. 'Okay, well, I'll think about that, then,' she said.

'Oh, no – that came out all wrong. I don't want you to take it the wrong way. I only meant ...'

You only meant that you don't care if I wait for you.

'That's fine. I think I understand,' she told him.

'I want to be with you.'

Do you?

'It's just that I'll understand if –'

'If what?' she said. 'Oh Christ . . .'

Bogey's beautifully restored Mustang emerged, cruising down the street in her direction. It was the worst timing.

'I'm sorry, Andy, but I have to go. Can I call you later today?'

'Yes, of course. I've said the wrong thing, haven't I? I didn't mean to upset you.'

'I'm fine. I gotta go.'

Mak hung up and wiped her eyes.

Bloody hell. Did Andy want to break up – was that it? Or did he want her to stay? She couldn't figure him out.

'Hey . . .'

Humphrey Mortimer pulled up beside her in his cool car, with his cool hair, and his stereo playing some cool band Mak could not identify. The sight of him made Mak smile despite herself. The car was big and blue with gleaming cream leather interiors, and somehow it made Bogey's jet-black hair and glasses look right at home. He had the top down, obviously acclimatised to the Melbourne weather, and the car looked even more impressive than it had when she'd first seen it at night. Come to think of it, he did too.

Bogey leaned across and opened the door for

her, ever gallant, and Mak crawled into the large leather bucket seat on the passenger side. He was wearing black jeans and boots again, and a faded white Sex Pistols T-shirt with the sleeves rolled further up his biceps. He sure didn't seem to be feeling any chill.

'I was just getting desperate for food when your message came through,' she told him.

His alluring cupid's bow curved into a playful smirk. 'I figured as much. Vegemite and vodka, right? That's all he ever has in his fridge.' Obviously Bogey knew his friend very well. 'What time is your flight?' he asked.

'Oh, not till this afternoon.'

She heard the distinctive beep of her phone in her handbag. A text message. She ignored it; she didn't want to hear from Andy right now. She had just managed to compose herself, and some confusing message from him was not what she needed to see.

'I can give you a lift to the airport later, if you'd like,' Bogey offered.

'Well, don't go out of your way,' she said, smiling like an idiot to hide her sadness. 'I have a rental car I need to drop back. Maybe they will let me leave it at the airport?'

'Just let me know if I can be of help,' he kindly offered again.

'Don't you have that job you need to finish?' she reminded him. 'The staining?'

'I finished the staining last night. I have some

more work to do on it this afternoon once it dries, but I can make time. It's no trouble.'

Mak watched the road. The wind pushed her hair back, and she began to feel a touch better. This was just what she needed: good company and a full stomach. She'd feel so much better with a bit of food and some light conversation. 'I'd like to see your shop,' she said.

'Okay.' He turned a corner. 'Say, are you okay? You sound like you are coming down with a bit of a cold.'

Her eyes were probably a bit puffy and her sinuses clogged up. She had not quite let all the tears out. She'd held back, thank goodness. It would have been ridiculous for Bogey to pull up and see her crying on the side of the road.

That would have been pathetic.

'Too many late nights, I guess,' she said.

Mak was struck by how comfortable she felt with Bogey. She sensed that even if she had been crying, he would be okay with it. He wouldn't judge her.

'I know a great breakfast place a few blocks away.'

Mak nodded. 'Sounds good.' Actually, it sounded better than good. Her stomach was rumbling at the mere mention of breakfast. It was never wise to keep a Vanderwall from a meal.

'You're not on a diet or anything, are you?' he quipped.

Mak darkened a little. 'Just because I'm a

model doesn't mean I'm anorexic or that I sit around all day contemplating my body fat, or the rise and fall of the supermodel ...' she ranted, a little too used to being belittled by people she'd just met.

'I thought you were a psychologist ... and a PI?' Bogey said.

Oh my God, I am an idiot.

Mak felt sheepish. She was still a touch emotional. 'I am. I guess I'm used to copping flak about my model past. Donkey was giving me a hard time about it.'

'Don't mind him. You are beautiful, anyone can see that. But you are also very smart. It would be a waste for you not to use it.'

'Thanks,' she said, flattered, but more pleased that he had no hang-ups about her model past than she was by the compliment itself. The number of times someone had walked up to her and said, 'So yer a model, huh? *And* you went to uni? What was it – Phys Ed?'

'I only asked because this place I'm taking us to has great pancakes.'

'Pancakes? Yum,' Mak said. 'With real maple syrup?'

'Yes,' he said, and smiled. 'Canadian Maple syrup.'

She was pleased.

Bogey continued driving, his focus pulled to a car veering off to the left in front of them and signalling the wrong way. Those were the kind of people who literally drove Mak nuts when she was on her motorbike. But rather than road raging, as Andy might have, Bogey continued on course, his big car floating along the unfamiliar streets of Melbourne like a dream.

Mak relaxed into her seat and allowed herself to enjoy his company.

She had little reason not to.

CHAPTER 43

THE BUZZER ON the intercom went as Amy Camilleri was walking past it to the kitchen.

Huh?

Amy wasn't in the habit of answering Larry's door. She didn't want anyone knowing where she was, and if someone had a package for Larry they would just have to wait until he got home from work. But the intercom had buzzed, and now the small screen lit up, and she could clearly see that someone outside the gate was holding a basket with a big bow on it. The basket was right in front of the camera lens, obscuring everything else, and it didn't take Amy long to see that it was more than just some gift basket. There was a puppy sitting in it – a real, live puppy was in the basket with a big red bow around its neck. A card on the wicker handle of the basket said 'AMY', with a heart drawn around her name.

Oh my God! She melted instantly.

'Oh, Larry!' she cried.

Barely taking the time to breathe, Amy ran out the front door and down the drive. She pressed the button for the front gate to unlock, and ran out to grab the basket from the deliveryman's hand. She put the basket on the pavement and lifted the puppy up to her shoulder. It was a tiny poodle pup, no more than eight weeks old, with curly black fur and huge wet eyes. It felt warm on her chest as she held it. It licked her neck with its moist little tongue. It was adorable.

What a surprise! Larry was so sweet to send her a gift while he was away at work all day, leaving her alone.

'Oh my God … you are *sooo* cute, aren't you?' she told the puppy in a baby voice, while it wriggled in her arms and made little noises.

The delivery van was only a few feet away; WITHLUV FLOWERS AND GIFTS was displayed on its side. 'He is a cute puppy,' a man said in a deep voice. He was wearing a cap and a collared uniform shirt, leaning by the door of the van with a clipboard. He had a strange face, his skin pulled back. She looked away quickly.

'Uh, yeah. Thanks,' she said awkwardly. The puppy licked her wrist. 'Oh, he is such a little cutie!'

In a flash the deliveryman was next to her with his clipboard. 'This needs to be signed for. Do you have a purse with some ID?'

She had come out empty-handed. 'Hang on, I'll just get it.'

Amy remembered that her handbag was on a

table at the base of the stairs. She ran back to get it, and quickly returned to the front gate, not letting go of her new little companion for one moment.

'Oh, Larry is just too sweet,' she said, more to the dog than to the deliveryman, as she reached into her purse for her driver's licence. 'I can't believe he –'

Her words were cut off by a sharp, needle-like pain in her buttock.

'Whaaaaa ...' she babbled as her body rapidly grew weak.

Amy Camilleri's knees gave way, and when they did, Luther Hand caught her. He carried her to the van, looking over his shoulder to be sure there were no witnesses.

CHAPTER 44

'THIS IS IT,' said Bogey. 'My humble shop.'

After a breakfast of pancakes and syrup, he and Makedde had bought frozen yoghurts and walked with them from Acland Street, St Kilda, to Bogey's groovy custom furniture shop a couple of blocks away.

Mak felt like she was on holiday. She put her conversation with Andy in the back of her mind for the moment.

'This is cool. I like it,' she said.

Bogey's shop was narrow and deep, with one glass ceiling-to-floor front window, where he had an immaculate handmade table and chair displayed, both in minimalist, modern form, with no right angles. The corners were rounded and smoothed, tapering seamlessly into the legs.

'That is constructed from just one piece of timber,' Bogey commented when he noticed her staring at the table.

'Wow. What is it made out of?'

'Pine.'

She laughed.

'I guess I'm used to working with the stuff,' he joked.

The display area of the shop was clean and uncluttered, but not very large. He walked Mak through a doorway into the back.

'Are you ready for this? It's quite a mess.'

'I think I can handle it,' she replied.

He pulled a chain that hung from the ceiling and a bare lightbulb flickered on. She could see that it was Bogey's working space. There were industrial-looking floor lamps pointed this way and that, so that he could adjust them to get adequate light when he was working on the finer details of shaping or sanding. In one corner a broad work table was overflowing with sketches of design ideas and various photos of inspiring pieces of furniture or architecture. Beside the cluttered desk was a tall bookshelf stacked with thick art books.

'Wow, you have amazing books,' Mak said, and moved towards them. She ran her fingertips along the spines, reading the titles: *Modern Art, Classic Architecture* . . .

'Thanks,' Bogey said proudly. 'I collect books on art and architecture.'

Mak picked one up. *Australian Artists*.

'My favourite is Jeffrey Smart. He makes the most desolate urban settings compelling. Would you like me to show you?'

He opened the book to one of the middle pages and showed Makedde a series of stunning, deserted city streetscapes, painted to angular perfection. He stood close to her, and when she looked up at him there was a bolt of chemistry. They both pulled back immediately, awkward with each other.

'Um, I enjoy architecture, too,' Mak said, wanting to keep the conversation going. 'My favourite is Antonio Gaudi. La Sagrada Familia and Parco Guell in Barcelona.'

Mak regarded Gaudi as the Salvador Dali of architecture, with his melting shapes and bright designs. The Sagrada Familia church Gaudi had designed, but not finished before his death in 1926 – when he was hit by a tram – looked as if it was made of melting wax.

'Have you been?' he asked her.

She nodded.

'I'm jealous,' he said.

'How much does something like this go for, if it's not too rude to ask?' Mak said, pointing to the sixties-style armchair Bogey had only finished staining the night before.

'Well, it's custom-made and handmade. It's pretty expensive because it takes so many hours to create. It's not Ikea or anything.'

'I can see the craftsmanship,' Mak said, admiring the piece. 'You are very precise.'

'Thank you. I am giving this one a flat red leather seat,' he said, his open hands touching the air just inches from the drying wood, indicating the position of the leather.

'I like it. And I like your coffins, too,' she added.

Along the back wall Bogey had mounted a full-sized casket inlaid with strips of polished oak. It was very impressive. Next to it were a few smaller ones, of the type that the Coffin Cheaters might have commissioned him to make as coffee tables or Eskies. Mak had not seen anything like it before. Even in the average funeral home one was likely to see only one coffin at a time. And she'd never been coffin shopping before.

'There's a place here called Dracula's that commissioned a couple of those. It's a vampire-themed restaurant.'

Mak raised an eyebrow.

'The tall one is the only real casket,' Bogey explained.

'A casket, not a coffin?'

'Exactly. It's a heavier weight, more detailed. The caskets cost the big bucks.' He stopped. 'I'm sorry. This is all probably way too morbid for you.'

Makedde smiled. 'Not at all.'

Bogey walked to his latest piece and gently touched the surface. 'Still a bit tacky. I'll just go wash my hands. I'll be back in a second. Take a look around if you like.'

Mak instead took the opportunity to reach into her purse and check her phone message, which she had thankfully managed to almost

405

forget about in Bogey's fascinating company. It was probably a text from Andy, and likely one that she didn't want to read.

But it wasn't from Andy.

The text message was from a mobile phone number that she didn't recognise. Mak opened it and it took a while to load up. It was large file.

A photo of a white and brown blur – what? No, wait . . .

It wasn't a photo at all. It was a video. Mak's eyes narrowed. She pressed OK and it began to play.

The white and brown blur shifted and moved, the poor-quality recording gradually focusing on what looked like a room. She brought the phone closer to her ear and she could hear static and faint voices. The white was a light in the centre of a ceiling, and as the moving image became sharper Mak could make out two men talking, apparently unaware that they were being observed. One man was Caucasian and tall, the other Asian and shorter. The Caucasian one was without a shirt. With the poor quality of the recording there was no way Mak could make out what was being said between them, but their body language gave the impression of an argument, one of the men clearly angry or distraught, the other trying to placate him. The footage panned down to what the men were standing over – no doubt the source of the taller man's anguish: a young woman lying on a bed, partially clothed.

Mak felt her stomach tighten.

No, it wasn't a woman – it was a girl of perhaps eleven or twelve years of age. She wasn't moving. Her eyes were staring as if she was dead. The footage zoomed in close enough to make the face reasonably clear before panning up again and focussing for a few frames on the men's faces. Then there was a noise, and the image jumped and blurred again, cutting off. It was the end. The entire video was perhaps eight seconds in length.

'Oh my God,' Mak said under her breath just as Bogey was returning.

'What is it? What happened?'

Mak was speechless.

What is this?

'Mak, what is it?' he repeated. 'Are you okay?'

She gripped her phone. 'Nothing. Excuse me for a minute.' She got up, shaken, and walked out to the street. Bogey watched her through the glass window of his shop, clearly concerned.

Heart pounding, Mak stood on the street and returned a call to the sender of the strange and horrible video. She gripped the phone nervously as it rang and rang. Finally there was a beep. No voice message. No name.

Amy? Was that from you?

'Shit.'

Is that Damien Cavanagh? With a dead girl?

If Damien Cavanagh was knowingly using trafficked, underage girls for sex – as Amy had

407

suggested and this video appeared to show – it would be a very serious, damning and embarrassing fact to uncover publicly. Not to mention a criminal offence. His whole family would be tarred by the sins of the son.

Mak tried the number again. *I know it's you . . . come on, pick up.* But there was no answer.

Disappointed, Mak walked back inside. She knew she could hand the video over to the police and they would be able to do something. They might be able to identify the people in the video, and they could run a check on the mobile number to find out who it belonged to.

'Are you okay?'

'Yeah, I'm fine,' Mak lied.

'Is it about your investigation?' Bogey asked.

She nodded. 'I am going to show you something, and I want you to tell me what you see. Tell me if you recognise anyone or anything, okay?'

'Okay,' Bogey replied.

She hesitated. Should she show him?

'And you are sworn to secrecy about this. I need to trust you,' she said.

She took a deep breath and played him the video. Bogey watched, his brow pinched. When it was over, he looked at Mak with alarm.

'Where did you get this?'

'Never mind that. Tell me what you saw.'

'Well, um,' he began, struggling. 'I saw a pretty girl without many clothes on lying on a bed passed out, and a couple of men talking. There was something a bit familiar about one of them. I think I've seen him somewhere before. I saw a bed, a girl, two men and a Whiteley.'

'A what?'

'A Whiteley painting on the wall,' Bogey said.

'A Whiteley? Show me.'

She replayed the video.

'There, behind them,' said Bogey. 'It's a Brett Whiteley. Not one of his best-known works, but definitely done by him. I remember this one because the woman is pictured rubbing red lipstick on herself. I think it's from the eighties.'

Mak raised an eyebrow. 'You can see all that?'

'I think so, yes,' he told her.

She dug around in her purse and pulled out the crinkled news article that Amy had left on the table at Leo's Spaghetti Bar. 'What about this? Could this be the man in that video?' She pointed at Damien, just as Amy had done.

'Damien Cavanagh, the heir? Let me see again.'

They watched the video once more. Mak was mesmerised. She could hardly think straight. What on earth would make a young man like Damien Cavanagh, with everything going for him, risk so much? It brought to mind the story of the heir to the Max Factor fortune, the young and attractive Andrew Luster, who, despite his wealth and status, chose to drug at least three different women with GHB, a so-called date rape drug, and videotape himself raping them while they were unconscious. He was currently serving a 124-year sentence in the US for his crimes.

A jail sentence was probably not something Damien Cavanagh would want to live with. So why would a high flier like him get involved in all of that mess? Why would he choose the services of illegal and unregulated sex workers, when legal sex workers – Asian, Caucasian or any ethnicity he liked – were readily available? Was the experience with these women different? Did they allow unprotected sex – extreme sex?

What is his motivation? Would he risk all that just for a feeling of power?

The video finished playing.

Bogey shook his head. 'Yeah, I think that could be him. Or someone who looks like him. But that is definitely a Whiteley.'

Wow.

The Cavanagh family had status indeed, and like most in their position they would do anything in their power to avoid going from the top of the status food chain to the bottom – social A-list to common criminal.

If that video had come from Amy, then Mak had to get hold of her, and fast.

CHAPTER 45

LUTHER HAND KNELT down and examined the girl on the floor of the delivery van.

Amy Camilleri was attractive.

Luther wasn't often close to attractive women. Even the ones who were paid to keep men company baulked at the sight of his face and imposing build. Only the roughest, most desperate prostitutes in Mumbai had ever willingly agreed to visit him in all his years living there, especially since the cosmetic surgery to correct the scarring of his face had failed. He struck fear into women, and he could see it in their faces. Luther looked scary; he knew it. This girl had thought so, too. He'd noticed the fear in her eyes when she had seen him, and had quickly looked away.

She felt no fear now.

The target, Miss Camilleri, was on the floor of the rented van, mouth slack, eyes wide open and moving rhythmically from side to side, an involuntary response to the drugs he had administered to her. Beside her, the confused pup nuzzled against her hand, wanting to be patted. She was unresponsive. He could hear her deep, slow breaths. Luther had jabbed her with an intramuscular dose of the anaesthetic drug ketamine, enough to knock her out for about thirty minutes, relatively unharmed. He could leave her there for a while if he had to. She wasn't going anywhere.

Luther reached down and closed the target's softly painted eyelids, his calloused hands seeming oversized next to her smooth features.

Now she looked peaceful.

He returned to the driver's seat and drove the van several blocks away to an inconspicuous lane lined by high fencing and garbage bins, behind a series of residences; a spot he had chosen for its privacy during his planning. Within minutes he had taken off his cap and changed out of his delivery shirt and into a black T-shirt. He put a baseball cap on his head, and dark sunglasses, and went to the side of the van to take off the adhesive signage, looking both ways as he did so. The signage came off easily with a bit of muscle, and he balled it up and put it in a garbage bin in the lane. He returned to the target and closed the double doors of the van behind him. She still looked like she was sleeping, though beneath her closed eyelids her eyeballs continued to move rapidly, twitching. The pup had wandered back to its basket, where it sat with its head on its paws, staring at the girl.

Luther took a moment to observe her as she lay unconscious on the black rubber sheeting he'd spread out across the floor of the truck. She was wearing small denim shorts and a singlet that said HUSTLER on it. His eyes followed her form, the shape of her slim, bare legs; the tiny, straight scar on her left kneecap; the mole on her chest; her breasts that rose and fell with her heavy, drug-induced breathing. Her bleached hair spread out luxuriously from a messy ponytail. One knee lay open at an angle. Between her legs a glimpse of white panties showed under her brief shorts.

Back to work, Luther told himself.

He took his eyes away from the target to check through her purse. If the contents he needed were inside, he would be able to avoid returning to Mr Moon's house and disabling the elaborate surveillance equipment to get inside. Luther was adept at electronic surveillance – both enabling and disabling it – but with most systems he would run some small risk of setting off an undetected internal alarm. Furthermore, the pretext of the absence of Mr Moon's girlfriend would evaporate if it seemed that a professional was involved. It had been better to get her out of the house willingly – that was why Luther had risked letting the target back inside to get her purse. His client wanted that mobile phone, and Luther would much rather the target get it for him than have to go in and get it himself.

He had learned that the hard way on an early job on the Gold Coast that had seen him surprised by a returning spouse while he rummaged hopelessly through the house in search of the item he needed – an item, in hindsight, that he could have talked the target into retrieving for him at an earlier stage. It was best to avoid such unnecessary risks.

Luther had been watching carefully. He knew full well that the target, Miss Camilleri, was alone in Mr Moon's house. If she had gone back inside and not come out again, he would have gone in and got her.

Good.

The target's mobile phone was in her purse, as was her wallet, some make-up and a set of keys. The phone was all he had been briefed to collect and bring back. The mission had been a success. He only had one more instruction left to carry out before returning to Sydney.

Luther drove the truck into position in the narrow laneway behind Amy Camilleri's one-level Richmond home. He parked it just behind her back door, and returned to the van to check on her. The target looked cold, her lips slightly bluish and her skin paler than it had been on the street thirty minutes before. The rubber sheeting was not warm; there was no heating in the truck. She still breathed slowly, eyes darting back and forth beneath the lids.

Luther slipped on a pair of latex gloves with a

loud snap that inadvertently turned Amy's head in his direction.

The target is coming awake.

Her eyes looked in his direction, unfocused, eyelids heavy. She was slowly becoming conscious, but she would not be able to move quickly for a while. The target would most likely remain quiet. He was confident that he had no need to restrain or gag her. But he did not want her lucid as she was being transferred, or there might be some suspicious struggle.

'Here, this will keep you warm,' Luther told her, avoiding her eyes. He picked up a thick blanket from the back and unfolded it. He placed it over her body and she clung to it weakly, still not in full control of her motor functions.

'Who are you?' she managed.

Luther didn't answer. He prepared the syringe and took a rubber band from his case, then knelt beside her. She was shivering.

'It's okay,' he told her, pulling the blanket higher until it rested just under her soft chin. He pulled her left arm out and inspected the veins under her pale flesh. She didn't flinch or struggle at his prodding. The target was still very sleepy, her body malleable. She would be feeling very numb.

'Relax,' he said in her ear, and tied the rubber band tight around her arm, just above the elbow. Luther wasn't good with words. He didn't often need conversation, but he did his best to calm her. The girl was still shivering, despite the blanket.

The vein in the crook of her elbow was beginning to rise, bluish and plump. Once it became visible he wasted no time. In one jab he forced the tip of the needle in, causing her to shift at the feel of the pinprick. She barely flinched. Luther squeezed the end of the syringe until it was dry, the pure heroin flowing into her bloodstream in a lethal, irreversible dose.

'Ahhhhhooo . . .' she moaned, twisting her head. She would be feeling no pain, just a surge of pleasure and adrenaline.

Luther watched her face, gently placing her arm back under the blanket again. Almost immediately her breathing became shallow and harsh; her forehead broke out in a clammy sweat. He stroked her brow and hairline with his gloved hand, gently caressing the skin.

'It's okay,' he said, stroking, stroking. His latex fingertips pushed the light sweat back. 'It's okay . . .'

The target gasped and her leg jumped. Her body was beginning to cramp. Her breathing got worse. The whole time Luther knelt at her side, whispering softly to her and gently caressing her brow, stealing occasional looks at the second hand of his watch.

Thirty seconds . . . sixty . . . ninety . . .

It was over in less than three minutes. When her breathing stopped he checked her pulse with two fingers.

416

Dead.

The target, Miss Amy Camilleri, twenty-one years of age, had died from a massive heroin overdose. It was a tragedy when drug users, particularly those who were depressed and anxious after the loss of a loved one – a friend, for instance – came across a pure form of heroin and, in their careless state, underestimated its potency. It was dangerous to experiment with a cocktail of drugs, like the anaesthetic ketamine, for instance, which could be acquired on the street by confused young women who wanted to forget the loss of their dear murdered friend for a while. It was particularly sad, and potentially lethal, to inject alone at home with no witnesses. There could be no one to help when they ran into trouble. Even someone's protective new boyfriend was unlikely to break down the door and find them. It could be days before the neighbours complained about the objectionable and suspicious smell.

When it came time for the autopsy, the cause of death would be straightforward. Under the circumstances, it was unlikely that there would be much of an inquiry.

Luther wrapped the target's still body in the rubber sheeting, lifted her up over his shoulder and carried her inside her house through the back door, which he unlocked with the keys from her purse. Her home was small; it did not take him long to find the right spot. He placed her body on the square cream linoleum tiles of her kitchen floor with the syringe in her hand, careful to make a good imprint of her fingertip on it, as per his instructions. He kept the mobile phone but left her keys, the purse and its contents on the kitchen table, laid out casually next to the opened gift card.

AMY, I LOVE YOU MORE THAN ANYONE ELSE CAN XOX said the card.

Luther left the gift basket by the front door and let the puppy roam the kitchen.

He then called The American to give his update.

'Melbourne has been a success,' he said, looking down at the target's body. The puppy had circled the kitchen and now sat near Amy's face, its head cocked to one side. It whimpered.

'You have what we need?' The American asked.

'Yes,' Luther assured him. 'I have it.'

'Very good.'

Luther left, locking the back door behind him and pulling off his latex gloves as he reached the van. He would be back in Sydney by nightfall to deliver the target's phone to his client.

And to be briefed on his next assignment.

CHAPTER 46

'AND I'VE BEEN on the plan for two years, and...'

Makedde Vanderwall spent the entire flight back from Melbourne to Sydney ruminating over every word Amy Camilleri had said. The girl still was not answering her phone, but Mak was sure the video message had come from her.

Is that video how she knows that Damien Cavanagh is involved in Meaghan's death? Or was there more? What is the link? Who is the girl in the video?

The video had effectively taken Mak's mind off her conversation with Andy. *There is nothing you can do right now.* Mak wished she'd been able to think more clearly, but she had a talker sitting next to her.

'It actually reverses ageing,' the man went on, incessant in his desire to talk Mak's ear off. He'd already given her a business card she didn't want for his health clinic. 'Reverses it,' he repeated.

That's it.

Mak put down *The Age* newspaper that she had been pretending to read. 'Ageing can not be

419

reversed,' she said, irritated. 'It is age. It is time passing. Therefore, by its very nature, it cannot be reversed. You can't reverse or stop time from passing, only prevent premature physical signs of age. Which is not the same as reversing actual age.' She took a breath. 'I am pleased you have found a health program that works for you. Good for you.'

She brought her paper up again, feeling his eyes on her through the newsprint.

'How old are you?' he asked her, undeterred.

Mak rolled her eyes behind the pages. 'I'm forty-eight – why?' she lied, and gave him a look.

His eyes got big. 'Really? That's amazing.' He looked a little perplexed.

'Good genes, I guess,' she said.

The flight arrived right on time, and Mak was pleased to leave her talkative new friend. She switched her mobile phone back on as she disembarked and put it in her jacket pocket. Hopefully there would be some kind of message waiting for her, anything at all to explain the video and its origins.

Mak planned on taking a taxi straight to police headquarters to speak with Detective Sergeant Hunt, and to show him the video she had been sent; and while she was at it, she hoped they would run a CCR check on the phone number and be able to confirm whether or not Amy Camilleri had sent the message.

Mak strode past the gates towards the airport arrivals exit, head down. She stepped out into the fresh air through the exit doors and saw that the taxi rank had a long line-up.

Damn. This will take a while.

To her surprise, she was shoved sideways. She stumbled on the footpath, nearly losing her balance.

'Hey!' she called out, shocked.

It took her only a moment to realise that her handbag had been lifted from her shoulder.

'Hey! Stop! Police!' she yelled, registering what had happened.

She took off down the sidewalk after the man. He looked young and thin, wearing board shorts, a T-shirt and running shoes. And boy, he could run. Mak struggled along after him, hauling the weight of her overnight bag on her shoulder as he dodged the incoming traffic to cross the street and flee into the massive parking centre.

Shit!

'Someone stop him!' Mak yelled.

People stood around stupidly as Mak streaked past, fuming. She could still run when she had to, she was discovering, but no matter how fast her legs moved, the young man seemed to be able to move faster. He was getting ever more distant ahead, and she could see him bob and weave between parked cars.

'Dammit! That's my handbag!' she yelled, knowing it was useless. She stopped in the middle of the parking lot and caught her breath.

Great.

Mak's phone beeped and she pulled it out of her pocket to answer it.

'Hello?'

'Hey, Mak, how are you?' It was the familiar voice of her friend Detective Karen Mahoney. 'You sound out of breath!'

'I am,' Mak replied. 'Karen, I want you to meet me at the airport. It's kinda important and it would be a huge favour. Can you do it?'

'Well, sure,' Karen replied.

'I'll be in the airport police office, making a report.'

* * *

'Brown hair, short around the ears,' Mak explained. 'He was wearing a baseball cap, light blue, and board shorts. Five foot nine, mid-twenties.'

Frowning and irritated, Mak sat in the office of the airport police; it was a sparse headquarters for the many cops who worked the place. She had some standard forms to fill out to report the theft of her handbag, while she waited for Karen Mahoney to arrive. Sadly, she didn't really expect to get it back, but she had to report the guy.

A young, prematurely bald airport police officer with meaty lips and a pleasant demeanour took notes as she spoke. 'Anything else?' he said, impressed with her detailed description.

'The board shorts were kind of bright. Mambo, I think,' she added.

He smiled. 'You ever thought of becoming a cop?'

Mak smiled back.

'Hi, Mak.'

She turned. Detective Karen Mahoney had arrived.

'Karen, this is Officer Milgrom,' Mak said, standing and making the introduction.

'Hello, Officer Milgrom,' Karen replied. She was wearing her Irish curls in a tight ponytail, but the ends still bounced as she spoke.

Mak gave the officer an expectant look. 'Are we done here?' she finally asked.

'Oh, um, yeah. I'm sorry, ma'am.'

'Thanks. I hope you catch him.'

On the way to the terrace Makedde explained everything that had happened – at least, everything except her conversation with Andy, the lap dance with Charlotte and Bogey, and the massage. That would be for another night, when she had more distance from it all, and when the conversation could involve drinking.

'I've had a terrible day, Karen, I can't tell you. I need you to help me up onto the balcony,' Mak said. 'My house keys were in my handbag.'

'Oh, I see,' Karen said.

'And then I am going to send you something on your mobile phone that I need you take in to police headquarters. Do you have your phone with you?'

Karen nodded. 'Yeah.'

The sooner Mak got that video into police hands the better, she figured.

Maybe it isn't a coincidence that someone tried to steal your handbag? Maybe they wanted your phone?

How many people knew that Mak had the video? The sender. Bogey. Anyone else?

'Good. You're going to want to take it straight to Hunt. I think he'll want to call me when he sees it.'

'Oh.'

'Yeah, it's a doozey,' Mak said.

CHAPTER 47

IT HAD BEEN quite a scramble to break into the terrace through the first-floor balcony, but Makedde managed it. She reminded herself that she needed to have a look at securing that window and, now that someone had the key, it might not be a half-bad idea to change the locks, either. She could never be too careful, especially in her new line of work.

She was about to call Marian and tell her what had happened when she got a call from Brenda Bale.

Oh, Brenda.

Hopefully Brenda had decided to move on to a clinical psychologist more appropriate for her problems and she was calling to cancel their Friday appointment. Mak thought fleetingly of ignoring the call, but she answered.

'Makedde Vanderwall speaking.'

'Hi, Mak, it's Brenda.'

'How are you feeling about our last appointment?' Mak asked, ready to drop the hint about her moving on.

'Good, thanks. I was actually calling because there is someone I think you should speak to.'

Mak blinked. 'There is?'

'About your case ... I hope you don't mind, but Loulou mentioned it to me.'

Loulou, I am going to kill you.

How could Loulou do that? She knew that Mak's cases were confidential.

'I think this person might prove useful to your case. I took the liberty of setting up a meeting, and she can see you tonight ...'

★ ★ ★

'You are niiiicee. I wannnnna ...'

Mak looked over at the grey-haired man who struggled to stand as he called to her, full of bourbon and compliments, his eyes rolling in their sockets and his clothes reeking. She kept walking.

'You niiiiiice ...'

'Go home to your wife,' she said and shook her head as she passed him at the kerb. He swayed in place, mouth open and one arm extended, as if trying to think of a response, though his mind was mush.

Damned winos.

Mak didn't have the patience for him, not with the day she was having. She had walked the few metres from where she had parked her motorbike on Victoria Street reasonably unmolested, and was now nearing the address she sought. This was a place where the famous and the infamous came together to have a good time, and although it was already well into the evening, the day would just be starting for the vampires, whores and voyeurs who brought Kings Cross to life. With its notorious reputation for strip bars, sex shops and brothels, it was really no wonder that someone – perhaps a real estate agent – had encouraged the addresses on the other end of the very same street to be the suburb of 'Potts Point' and not Kings Cross. They were kidding themselves.

So it was a very short stroll from the famous Coca-Cola sign at the heart of the Cross to the more-civilised-sounding address in Potts Point where Mak had organised to have a word with the supposedly infamous Mistress Serenity, whom she hadn't heard of before Brenda filled her in. The two-level terrace house was so unassuming that Mak walked right past the door and had to double back. A faded red door with a small plaque confirmed that she had reached her destination.

THE TOWER

BY APPOINTMENT ONLY

She buzzed the intercom and identified herself. Before long a young woman swathed in shiny PVC opened the entrance and let her in, before again sealing the private realm of the bondage parlour known as The Tower from the outside world with two bolt locks.

Whoa, someone here likes red.

Mak stood in an entry hall of sorts, taken aback by the overwhelming womblike hue of the walls, the ceiling, the furniture. The Tower was not a tower at all, but simply a narrow house painted blood-red within, containing numerous 'tower rooms' within which clients could have their fantasies of bondage, dominance and submission fulfilled. The floors were concrete, painted a slick black, and Mak wondered if they were as slippery as they looked. She trod carefully as her host led her deeper inside the parlour.

'I am Electra.'

Of course you are. Electra had bone-straight hair the colour of cola, and an outfit of red and black PVC that exaggerated her compact, athletic build and pale skin. She must have been quite short, because even with her platform shoes she was barely up to Mak's chest. Mak could picture her as an aerobatic circus performer, breezing through the air in her PVC, mastering the flying trapeze before deciding on a more intimate life of theatre behind the closed doors of The Tower.

'You have an appointment?' Electra asked before they got any further.

'I have an appointment with Mistress Serenity. My name is Makedde Vanderwall.' Mak dutifully produced a business card for Marian Wendell's agency. 'I am an investigator.'

428

'Thank you. She is expecting you. If you wouldn't mind being discreet while you're here, please. Having a private investigator here might send the wrong message. Plus, we don't get a lot of female clients.'

'No problem.' *What, does she think I'm going to start flicking a whip around and cut her lunch or something?*

'The Mistress will be with you shortly, if you would like to come this way and take a seat, please.'

Mak followed. She was led into a cosy waiting room of yet more red and invited to sit on a black leather couch. Everything here, it seemed, was either black or that ever-dominating hue of red: red roses in a vase, black leather couch, red walls, black floors, red sidetable, black iron human-sized birdcage. Mak did a double take. *Yes, human-sized birdcage.*

Left alone in the room by Electra, Mak cocked her head to one side and considered what strange uses there might be for a human-sized birdcage. It was some time before she noticed that she was not, in fact, alone. A single, still customer was perched on the end of a couch opposite her in the waiting room. All she could see of him was his crossed legs in suit pants and a gleaming bald spot. He'd been so small and unmoving that she hadn't even noticed him. He appeared reasonably normal from what she could see – except he kept his head buried in *Skin II* fetish magazine. No backless chaps or leather harness. *Yet.* Mak felt apologetic for her intrusion on this man's evening. He probably only saw scarlet-lipsticked women in corsets with whips when he came for his sessions here. Or maybe her motorbike look was exactly what he was hoping to find.

Mak was distracted from her feeling of dis-ease when a striking figure began to descend a narrow red staircase into the waiting room. The figure appeared slowly, toes first, dominating the attention of those in the waiting room. The woman descended to their level in a kind of a fetish version of a Mae West entrance. Her shoes were blood-red patent platform heels with toe cut-outs, laced up to the calf; her legs were encased in fishnet stockings more refined and sexy than those chunky ones Loulou had such a penchant for. A tight and shiny latex skirt began mid-thigh and went up to meet a blood-red corset made of stiff rubber, laced hard against her ribs. A heaving bosom spilled from the top, held in only by a black netting of mesh that covered her chest and arms, and hooked around her thumbs. It was not difficult to guess that this was Mistress Serenity. She was perhaps fifty years old and wore surprisingly little make-up, apart from a dramatic winged liner on her eyes and the requisite blood-red lips. Her hair was swept into a stylish chignon.

Yes, a fetish Mae West, Mak decided. *One of the most feared, revered and infamous bondage mistresses in Australia. Wow.*

'Come this way,' the woman said haughtily, and Mak found herself obeying as if the headmistress had spoken. The bald man reading *Skin II* stayed perched in his place but looked noticeably disappointed that he was not being called – he pouted.

'You are a *bad boy*, and bad boys need to wait their turn. I will deal with you accordingly,' the Mistress instructed sternly, admonishing him and giving Mak quite a fright in the process. But rather than the man scurrying away, his pout vapourised and there was a delighted glint in his eye, though he dared not smile.

Mak followed Mistress Serenity up the staircase of The Tower to the hallway of the first floor. She heard the cracking of whips and a stifled moan, and it gave her a shiver and a sick sensation of curiosity.

She swallowed.

Mistress Serenity welcomed her to a back room where there was a small office space. She closed the door behind them and sat at a plain desk, clearly at home. She invited Mak to sit opposite.

Mistress Serenity pulled out Mak's business card, which Electra had obviously given her. She turned it over and looked at both sides, silent.

'Brenda said you might have some information for me,' Mak started. 'I appreciate you taking the time.'

'Brenda? You mean Mistress Scarlet.'

'Sorry, yes – Mistress Scarlet.'

'Yes. It is slow on Mondays. Mistress Scarlet asked me to speak to you.'

Mak nodded. *What is this all about?*

'Understand that my business revolves around discretion. You aren't recording this in any way, are you?'

'No,' Mak assured her.

'I don't want to testify in court or anything. It would ruin my business.'

'I'm working for my client, not the police.'

Mistress Serenity squinted for a moment, thinking. 'Understand that I protect my clients' privacy at all costs. That is an important part of my business. The only reason I don't mind offering you this information is because ... I think it is more important than my usual rules.'

Mak nodded, hoping that Mistress Serenity would have something useful to tell her.

'I wouldn't be telling you this if you were a cop.'

'I understand. I am not a police officer, just an investigator.'

'But your boyfriend is a cop,' Mistress said.

'Uh, yes. He keeps out of my affairs and I keep out of his. This is a private investigation ... a private matter.'

Mak had never had anyone use Andy against her before, but she guessed that she might need to get used to that. Some people were suspicious of the police. And Mistress Serenity certainly had her information on Mak.

'Also understand that whatever I tell you is in confidence. Mistress Scarlet let me know that you are someone to be trusted.'

Mak nodded. 'I can be trusted. I don't ever reveal my sources. That would be bad for *my* business.'

Mistress Scarlet seemed to like that comment. 'I don't know if you understand what we do here, exactly, but we provide extremely professional services for people with special needs. Some girls come here looking for work with the idea that they can just strut around in a fetish costume with a whip and make big cash without having to do anything. But the work is involved. It's an art. It requires not just acting but training in proper techniques, and medical knowledge. We don't allow full intercourse here at The Tower, but we promise clients a "happy ending" if they wish. Some girls can't handle the intimate nature of some of our services.'

Mak nodded, her mind stumbling to try to grasp the actual activities that would take place in a session. What did people come here for that required medical knowledge?

'Your friend Mistress Scarlet was a good worker. It was a blow for me when she left,' Mistress Serenity continued. 'I liked her and that's why I agreed to talk with you.'

Mistress Scarlet was not so much a friend of Mak's as an unofficial client, but fine – anything to help her get closer to good information for her client, whatever or whoever the source.

'We aren't like other places you might have heard of. We don't thrive on getting new girls every week like the brothels down the street. We have experienced women with special talents and I need to hang onto them when I find them. Our clients come here for reliable service, not fluffy bar girls with big tits.'

Mak suspected that she was being sold a line, but she didn't know why. Was this a rationalisation about Mistress Serenity's business? And she wasn't so sure she totally believed Mistress Serenity's vows of allegiance to Brenda/Mistress Scarlet even after she jumped ship. This was clearly a sharp, shrewd woman. It could be that there was something else in it for her, apart from a code of friendship among whip-wielding mistresses.

'Most of our clients are very loyal.'

Mak took that on board, wondering when the Mistress would get to the point, and exactly why she had been called here.

'But the client of ours that you are interested in ... I can tell you that he is not what we like here.'

Mak's ears perked up. *Client?*

'Simon Aston tried to poach a couple of my girls outside of the house. He wanted them to entertain his friends.'

Ah, Simon Aston.

'How did you find out?'

And how the hell did you find out I am interested in Simon? Loulou had looser lips than Mak thought – not that she'd done the wrong thing in getting Mak to this odd meeting. She would have to have a word to her, though …

'I know everything that happens in my house.' Mistress Serenity said the words forcefully, and Mak sat back in her chair, getting a taste of her dominating skills. 'Simon is not a true fetishist. Not even close,' she said with disdain. 'He's a thrill-seeker, nothing more. He could not handle any of the real work we do here.'

'Do you get a lot of clients like that – thrill-seekers?' Mak asked.

'Yes and no. We don't discourage those who are curious, but nor do we cater to every drunk sailor who comes in off the street looking for a freak show. Thrill-seekers like Simon come and go quickly, and we avoid them. We are discreet. It's word of mouth that brings people here, not advertising. We have a good, loyal clientele and we cater to their needs. That's why we are appointment only. Some of our services need days of preparation.'

Days of preparation? Mak's mind wandered off into possible scenarios.

'Simon Aston is what I call try-sexual. We see his type from time to time, but they never last long. His needs were purely superficial. After a couple of sessions when he more or less perved on my girls without getting down to any serious activities, he began trying to poach my girls to perform for him at his parties for nothing. He wanted to show off to his friends.'

Mak nodded. *Try-sexual*. She knew a few people like that.

'He took particular interest in my youngest girl – she was nineteen, you understand. That's not so unusual. But after he poached her for parties and discarded her, the word is he got hooked up with Lee Lin Tan, who runs a Surry Hills brothel with illegal sex workers. Sex slaves, basically, though some would argue they are just immigrant sex workers. They get paid squat, their conditions are shocking and they don't get to lay down their own rules of contact. It seems Simon and his buddies got what they wanted: a new thrill – underage girls who don't complain.'

Mak felt her stomach turn.

'I see,' Mak said, and wrote down Lee's name. Someone trying to poach her girls would put Mistress Serenity's nose seriously out of joint, but this was something worse. Getting the word out anonymously through Mak might mean the police would hear, which was perhaps why she was interested in the fact that Mak's boyfriend was a cop. Mak's guess is she would want the illegal business stopped – she wouldn't want that kind of competition. 'What happened to the girl he poached?'

'I don't know – I wouldn't have her back. It's a matter of loyalty.'

Mak nodded. 'I don't suppose there is any way I could contact her and have a word with her?'

The Mistress shook her head. End of story.

She wasn't about to give out the name of a previous employee. Mak had suspected as much.

Shame.

'What do you know about Simon Aston?'

'Simon,' the Mistress said, pretending to spit, 'is the worst breed there is – a leech. He uses his association with his rich friends to get what he wants. Especially his friendship with Damien Cavanagh. He managed to poach my girl that way, luring her with false promises. Word is that now he and his rich mate break in the new girls when they come from Asia.'

'How young are we talking, do you know?'

'Sixteen years old. Perhaps fourteen.'

Mak shook her head, feeling ill at the thought.

'I was also wondering if you know anything about a girl named Meaghan Wallace.'

'Meaghan?' Mistress Serenity squinted, looking off. 'I don't think so. The name doesn't ring a bell with me. She work in bondage?'

'No, I don't think so.' But anything is possible. 'Um, this Lee Lin Tan, do you know where he keeps his brothel? Do you have an address?'

'No. But everyone knows it. I think if you ask your cop friend he should be able to tell you.'

Right. 'And you know his girls are here illegally?'

'Yes. That's what I said, isn't it?'

Clearly Mistress Serenity did not like being questioned. But if the police knew about an illegal brothel like that, wouldn't it just be shut down? Particularly if some of the girls were underage? Weren't there serious repercussions for that type of crime?

'Okay. Thanks so much for your time. I appreciate you telling me all of this. I understand you must be very busy.'

'Yes, I am a busy woman. I have clients to attend to,' Mistress Serenity said coolly and stood. She made for the door in a whirl of latex and fishnets and led Mak out.

'I really do appreciate your time. Thank you,' Mak said to her back as they reached the top of the staircase. 'I have just one last question, if it's not too much trouble.'

Mistress Serenity turned, one hand on the banister. Her features were stern. She was back into her role-playing, and she'd clearly had quite enough of Twenty Questions.

'Why did you choose the name "Mistress Serenity"?' Mak asked.

The Mistress brightened a touch. 'It is my special word,' she replied calmly. 'My clients use it when they can't take the pain any more. They say "serenity", and I stop.'

Mistress Serenity disappeared down the staircase, leaving Mak dazzled. Electra then led her out.

Serenity, Mak thought. *If only that special word worked for real life.*

CHAPTER 48

ON TUESDAY, MAKEDDE slept in late. Between Thunderball strip club and The Tower, she'd had a lot of strange, late nights recently and she had sleep to catch up on. When she woke and poured herself some cereal, the house was strange without Andy. It wasn't that she was unfamiliar with his frequent absences, but it felt different knowing that he would not be home soon.

Three months.

Mak spent the remainder of her morning researching Damien Cavanagh and his family on her laptop; there was a wealth of information about them on the internet. Simon Aston's name came up a few times as well, though much less frequently, and always in relation to Damien. The good-looking Simon was only ever pictured near Damien, in the background, never sharing the limelight.

At midday she deemed the hour late enough for Loulou to be awake.

'Sweetie, how are you!'

'I'm good. How are you?' Mak asked. 'How are things with Drayson?'

'Oh, he is such a doll! A doll! When are you coming back to visit?'

'Not for a while, Loulou. I have this investigation to finish first, and I doubt I can justify another trip to Melbourne.' *Unless I hear back from Amy.* Amy had not called her again, and Mak had no verification that the video had been sent by her, although in her guts she knew. 'Loulou, I have to ask you something serious.'

Loulou paused. 'Okay, sweetie. Anything.'

'Who have you told about my case? Did you tell someone that I am looking into Simon Aston?' Mak asked gently.

'Oh, sweetie! I'm sorry. I just thought … you know, I thought Brenda might know about him, and she did. I was only trying to help. I hope you're not mad at me!'

It was hard to be mad at Loulou especially when the result had been a fruitful, albeit bizarre, meeting with Mistress Serenity. Still …

'Loulou, I just need confidentiality. That is a big part of investigation work. I could have got in a lot of trouble.'

'Oh, darling!'

Mak rolled her eyes. 'I know you meant well, and it was helpful to speak to Mistress Serenity, but I just need you to ask next time, okay? I need you to ask me first if it is okay to tell anyone.'

'Okay,' came Loulou's voice, sounding uncharacteristically serious. 'I promise.'

'Good.'

'So you're not mad at me?'

'No. Just don't do it again.'

When the phone rang at two, Mak expected it to be Sergent Hunt calling about the video. It had been nearly twenty-four hours since she'd sent Karen to him with it. Why the delay?

But it wasn't Hunt.

'Look, something's happened. Can you meet me at the office right away?'

The blood drained from Mak's face at the tone of Marian Wendell's voice. Her employer was not the type to sound concerned – she was always so cool about everything, so knowing.

'What's happened?'

Her reply did nothing to ease Mak's alarm. 'We shouldn't discuss it over the phone. Can you get here fast?'

Mak could.

She suited up and rode over to Marian's office as fast as she safely could, parked her black bike right outside and ran in without even stopping to take her helmet off. She found Marian standing outside her office doorway looking somewhat less composed than usual. Her hair had not been blow-dried into submission, and her usually confident demeanour had a touch of uncertainty about it.

Marian was not alone, either.

'Oh, hi, Pete,' Mak said, surprised to find Pete Don in Marian's office.

Mak had first become aware of Pete's work when he had been a guest lecturer at her Certificate III course on investigation, and Marian had mentioned him once or twice in the year Mak had been working for her, but he seemed out of context in this office. As a fellow investigator with his own outfit, he was, after all, one of Marian's competitors.

What's going on? What's he doing here?

Pete was a man in his forties with meaty arms like a gorilla and jet-black hair that he wore in a ponytail. He was a man of good humour with a disarming smile, but his physical attributes would certainly lend him a threatening appearance in other circumstances. As legend went, he was once one of the best undercover Drug Squad officers the New South Wales Police had. He even had bikie tattoos – more visible than Bogey's – dreadlocks and both the voice and look of a hard smoker and drinker. A smart and brave man, Pete Don had infiltrated all levels of the biggest organised criminal group in the state, helping the authorities collect evidence that eventually brought down a lot of the major players in the drug ring.

But after years of successful undercover work, his career came unstuck – and he nearly lost his life – when a routine covert driving exercise with other Drug Squad officers at a local racetrack was seen by an outsider. As the officers practised high-speed pursuits and spinouts on the track, a man asked one of the staff who the drivers were. His response? 'Ah, that's the undercover Drug Squad.' The man then took long-lens photographs of the undercover cops and circulated them amongst his gang friends. The stupidity of that staff member resulted in the men being confronted and searched for wires when they returned to their jobs. Two of them were beaten to death when discovered, and despite being attacked with a crowbar, Pete somehow escaped with his life. But his cover was blown and he could never return to his work. He was forced to choose between paper-pushing, or a new career under a new name. He chose to go into the private sector.

One obvious remnant of his altercation with the mob was the fact that he no longer had any cartilage whatsoever in his nose. He was not vain enough to have it reconstructed and, in fact, he seemed to like making a spectacle of it – in certain company, at least. He'd made Mak touch it on the second day of his class. 'There, have a feel,' he'd insisted. 'Take a good look, have a feel and then it won't distract you.' It had felt like a blob of putty on the end of his face.

Pete was wandering through the waiting room, brandishing what Mak recognised as a common hand-held debugging device. It was switched on, and a sequence of small red lights flashed up and down the face of it as it scanned the room for frequencies transmitted by any bugging devices.

'Is it clear?' Marian asked.

Pete nodded.

'Someone has been through the office,' Marian told Mak solemnly.

Mak wasn't sure exactly what she meant. 'What do you mean, "been through"? Was there a burglary?'

'Someone's ransacked it.'

The office didn't look ransacked to Mak. 'What's missing? Do you know?'

'I am not sure yet – I'm still taking inventory. This was well organised. They went through the filing cabinets. That's the reason I called you in – your file on Robert Groobelaar's assignment is missing. You didn't take it home for any reason, did you?'

Mak's blood ran cold. 'No.' Thankfully her laptop held copies of the work she had compiled so far, but having the information in that file stolen could potentially threaten the confidentiality of the client.

'And you had your handbag stolen.' Marian narrowed her eyes. 'That's bad luck.'

'Yeah,' Mak said. 'There's a lot of bad luck going around at the moment, isn't there? Does Groobelaar know about this?' She gestured to the office.

'He's been informed. He didn't seem as upset as I feared he would be. He knows his confidentiality is still protected, so he's fine.' Marian never kept client names or billing details with case files. All the information was encrypted in her system. If someone had stolen the file it would not have shown any direct link to the client, but it would still have a load of information on the people who were being investigated.

And now I'm probably out of a gig. After all that.

'Did he cancel the job?' Mak asked, dreading losing out on all the income for the assignment.

'No. It's still yours, unless you want to quit.'

Mak had never quit anything in her life, let alone when it got interesting.

'I'm no quitter,' she said. 'If there was an intruder here, you must have got them on tape?'

Marian was tight with security, and she had a surveillance system installed. There was a keyhole camera hidden in the front door, one in the waiting room and a third in her office.

'No, the cameras didn't get anything. They disabled them. The system calls Pete when someone disables any of the cameras. By the time he got here, they were gone.'

Pete specialised in the surveillance and security side of investigations. His previous work as an undercover police officer gave him a good background for it. It was the first time Mak had twigged that Pete had actually installed Marian's surveillance system. Was that such a good idea if he was a competitor?

'I have to say, nothing looks disturbed,' Mak commented. 'Why are you checking for bugs?'

'We found one under the desk,' Pete said.

Shit. 'Really?'

'This was professional, not a random burglary, there is no doubt about that,' he continued. 'There are a few files missing, including your current case, so I would recommend you be careful. It could be that someone doesn't want you poking around.'

Mak thought about that possibility. There were four known people central to her assignment thus far. The first was the client, who, as far as Mak could see, had no reason at all to steal the information he was already paying to have provided to him. The second was the victim, who was dead before Mak even got involved. The third, Tobias Murphy, was in jail. The fourth key person was Simon Aston.

Simon Bloody Try-Sexual Aston ... Or even Damien Cavanagh himself?

'Tell me something: are the other stolen files for current cases?' Mak asked.

'No. Not that we've found so far. Only yours. Which makes me think that the other files were taken to make it look less obvious.'

'That's interesting,' Mak said.

'Yes, it is.'

'Mak, I hate to ask you this but I need to know something. I need you to answer this truthfully.'

'Okay.'

'Have you said anything about the specifics on this case to your boyfriend or any other cop?'

Mak paused, trying to think of the implications. 'Yes,' she admitted. 'Well, I passed on that video, like I told you.' She'd worded Marian up on her arrival back in Sydney. 'I thought the police needed to have it. It might show a girl's death. But as it didn't show Meaghan Wallace, it probably isn't related to our investigation work anyway.'

Or is it?

'I've confidentially spoken about some aspects of the case to a police officer friend who I trust,' Mak continued, 'but not the client's details or anything sensitive – just my feelings on the murder and the kid they have as a suspect. I have some niggling doubt that the boy is guilty.' She and Karen had spoken about a lot of things on the way from the airport, but nothing that Mak felt compromised her investigation – to the contrary.

Marian nodded thoughtfully. 'So you haven't mentioned Groobelaar to anyone?'

'I would never do that.'

'Good girl,' she said. 'I knew you wouldn't. I am sorry I had to ask.'

'That's okay.' Marian would no doubt be feeling violated and suspicious, knowing that someone had penetrated her security. 'Wait a second ...' Mak clicked to her meaning. 'Are you saying that you think the cops might have done this?'

'All I know is, this was very professional,' Marian said. 'If all this was done to find out about your assignment, then you really need to be careful. Don't do anything that might compromise your position, or lose you your licence.'

Mak nodded. She was partial to bending the rules, but she rarely flat-out broke them. However, in light of what had just happened, Mak had some ideas that didn't quite fit into the *Private Investigators Act* of 1999.

'And you must have seen the article in the paper. I thought you'd be unhappy about it, bringing up that whole trial again.'

'What article? What paper?' Mak felt her big toe start to itch, exactly where the microsurgeon had sewn it back on. 'Why would there be an article about that? The trial was over two years ago. More. It was nearly three years ago, wasn't it?'

'I dunno, Mak. But your face is in the paper today. There's a copy in the waiting room. It says you are working for me as a private investigator. It kinda makes it sound like you can't get a job as a shrink. I think someone planted it. Someone is out for you, Mak.'

Mak felt her face flush. She ran out to the waiting room and grabbed the paper, Marian and Pete following close behind. She had to flip through several pages before she found it.

STILETTO MURDER VICTIM'S
SECRET LIFE IN SYDNEY

> Surviving Stiletto Murder victim, Canadian
> model Makede Van der Wall, has secretly
> returned to live with her detective boyfriend in
> Sydney, despite the horrors of her brutal rape
> and abduction here five years ago. The Stiletto
> Killer — the most prolific and violent killer in
> Australian history ...

Mak didn't think she could read on, but she
did. She found the part Marian was talking about:

> ... despite being a trained psychologist, Van der
> Wall had not been able to find work. She has
> been secretly working for Marian Wendell
> Private Investigations, where perhaps her past
> is less likely to be questioned.

Secret life? What secret? Mak stared at the article
disbelievingly, a quiet rage building in her. They
made her sound like some kind of freak.

'How can they write that? They even spelled
my name wrong. Who writes this shit?'

How can a few days turn so bad?

'It's bile, Mak. Don't pay it any attention,'
Marian said calmly.

Why now? Why me?

'Don't take it too harshly. No one believes
those rags anyway.'

'Well, you bought a copy, didn't you?' Mak countered. And so did hundreds of thousands of other people who read it daily.

Marian shrugged.

'I think you might be right. Someone is trying to discredit me,' Mak said as calmly as she could. *And I think I might know who that someone is.* She turned to Pete. 'Is your mate Sergei working at the moment?' Mak asked him.

Pete smiled. 'Looking to do some shopping, are you?'

Mak grinned back, but her lips were sealed. The only thing to do when she was angry was to get to work.

★   ★   ★

Mak arrived at the terrace and parked her black bike next to Andy's little red Honda. She was going to have to borrow it again – not that he'd care. She needed a car for what she was planning to do.

She put a call in to Pete's contact Sergei. 'Hi, I'm sorry to bother you. I know you're probably closing soon.'

'Yep.'

'I have something urgent. I just need a couple of items. How's your stock at the moment?'

'Pretty good,' he responded.

'Can I swing past?'

There was not much of a pause. Sergei's cash register was always willing to accept payment.

When Mak pulled up at the daggy little doorway on Parramatta Road with the shop sign that said SPY WORLD – complete with a cartoon symbol of big eyes doing a suspicious sideways glance – Sergei was just opening the door for her.

'So what can I help you with this afternoon, Miss Vanderwall?'

Sergei never called anyone by his or her first name. He was a lanky Russian immigrant with a heavy accent, a number-one buzz cut and a remarkable talent for being able to turn just about any basic household item – photo albums, cans of soup, desk clocks, light switches, thermostats – into surveillance devices. He could probably implant a tiny camera into your dentures if you wanted it.

'Ah, I am just looking for the usual, Sergei. Throwaways. Nothing too fancy.'

Mak followed him through the doorway and up a staircase to the first floor. Inside his shop were glass display cases filled with every type of surveillance equipment Mak could hope for, and then some.

'So what do you need?'

'A couple of taps.' Phone tappers.

Sergei disappeared into the back room to get them for her while she perused some of his keyhole camera handiwork longingly. One day she wanted to be on a job where she needed one of his infamous button cameras. The camera was a tiny keyhole lens positioned in the centre hole of a regular jacket button. The video images it could capture were as clear as day, and it fed all of the footage into a receiver Mak could carry in a small purse. It was a brilliant piece of craftsmanship. It even came with extra matching buttons so the jacket would look uniform. It would take a highly trained – and suspicious – eye to spot the miniature lens. There was a similar set-up available in the head of a screw, which could be fitted to any wall or device. It too came with extra screws to match the doorway or wall the lens was fitted to. It was a tight surveillance unit with high quality reception, and it was *very* expensive. Mak couldn't afford it unless a client was picking up the tab, and in this case there was no way to warrant filming anyone's activities. Not yet, anyway. Nonetheless, she drooled over the items in the glass cases as if they were rare and precious jewels.

Sergei returned with the phone tappers, which were basically small double clamps to be attached to a phone line and fed back via transmitter. The recording device only kicked in when the line became active, so it recorded only conversation, never dead air.

He also appeared to be holding something behind his back. Mak was alarmed.

'Sergei, what are you –'

'I thought you might want to have a look at these,' he said, and triumphantly passed her a pair of dark sunglasses.

'You didn't!' she squealed, noticing that the glasses were a large Jackie O–style shape.

Sergei smiled, clearly pleased with himself.

She tried the glasses on. 'These are brilliant. Utterly brilliant!' She pulled her hair back and examined the range on them. 'Wow.'

With carefully applied airbrushed mirror paint, Sergei had turned a pair of designer sunglasses into spyglasses. On the outside the glasses looked completely normal, but on the inside of the lens the outer corner was mirrored so that the wearer could actually see behind themselves. Mak was very impressed with the work.

'I can't believe you did this.'

'Well, you said they would be nice if they were designer shape.'

Sergei carried some cheap ready-made ones that were somewhat lacking in style. Obviously he had taken her comments about them to heart.

'Well, obviously I will have to take those beauties.' She placed them on the counter with the tappers.

Sergei was practically glowing with pride. 'How is the phone going?'

'Brilliant, thanks. Works a charm. I got to use it in an insurance sting last month.'

The phone he had sold her was a fake mobile fitted with a small lens in the top, where infrared usually went. Mak could place it on a table pointed in the direction she wanted to film, or hold it in her hand and pretend to be checking messages, all the while clearly recording everything her subject was doing. The resolution was incredible.

She'd only used the phone once so far, but the insurance company had been very impressed with her work. She had filmed one of their suspicious worker's compensation beneficiaries bowling at the local alley, even though his claim stated that his back injury prevented him from lifting anything. Yeah, right.

Mak paused, thinking of what else she might need. Sergei had a lot of tempting equipment that she couldn't afford.

'Oh, yeah, I nearly forgot – do you have a double adapter in stock at the moment?'

★   ★   ★

Marian had told Mak many times that there were no coincidences. Perhaps she was right. Mak's handbag had been stolen, Marian's office bugged, and the police had not even called her about the video. But Mak still resisted the idea that the cops might have actually stolen files from Marian's office without a warrant and bugged the place. The implications would be unnecessarily ugly.

Nonetheless, things were getting weird.

If there were no coincidences, then someone knew about Mak's investigation and didn't like it one bit. She was planning on staying a little quieter about the rest of her investigation now. Especially this next part. Having Marian's office broken into was exactly the sort of thing a guilty person did to find out what others knew about their activities. But who was it? Robert Groobelaar had no reason at all to steal his file, Tobias was in jail, and on Mak's radar that only left Simon Aston and his rich buddy. That was where Mak planned to concentrate her efforts until she got some answers.

CHAPTER 49

'WE HAVE A cop outside the house.'

The American frowned. There shouldn't be any police bothering the Cavanaghs. Not now. Not ever. It was his job to see that they didn't.

'It's a red Honda,' his security man Stone continued. 'He drove past slowly, twice, with his lights off. Now he is down the block with the engine running. I'm not sure if he is planning to come in or what.'

This could be troublesome.

'Name?' he asked.

'I ran the plates. Car is registered to an Andrew Flynn. A homicide detective.'

'I see. And is the front gate closed?'

'Yes.'

The walls protecting the Cavanagh home were tall and could not easily be scaled, and the front gate too was large and impenetrable. This police officer could not enter without a search warrant; The American would see to it that they didn't get one. If the cop rang the doorbell, The American would advise that they not answer.

456

'Okay. The client is at home,' The American said. 'Keep an eye on that car. I will let him know –'

'Wait,' Stone said, interrupting him. 'The car is moving again. He's driving off. No … not he, a *she*. There is a blonde woman driving.'

'Not the detective?' he said, puzzled.

'Not unless he is crouched down in the vehicle next to her. It is a woman and it looks like she is alone.'

'What is she doing now?' The American asked.

'She's at the end of the street now. I think she's leaving.'

'Follow her.'

CHAPTER 50

MAK SAT LOW in the passenger seat of Andy's red Honda.

From the information she could glean, Damien Cavanagh still lived with his parents in their luxurious Darling Point home, even though he was almost thirty years old. He could probably stay there indefinitely, never needing to think about getting a job. In contrast, Mak had moved out at fifteen to head overseas and start working as a model. Would she have been his type, at fifteen? Would she have been naive enough to go to a party like the ones he threw?

As Mak had discovered, the Cavanagh house was flanked by impenetrable stone walls. She could not even see the house itself from the street, and she would not have been able to scale the walls. Perhaps she could see more from the water side? Mak didn't own a boat, but she could rent one.

There is nothing you can do tonight. And remember, he's not even on your client's list.

But Simon Aston was on the list.

She was going to observe Simon's house and, once the coast was clear, she wanted to get inside and plant a bug. But it could be a long wait before she found her moment. In the meantime she sat in Andy's car with the lights and engine off, and in the passenger seat, as if the driver was about to return. Few people took much notice of a woman waiting on the passenger side of a car. Mak sat low so that the car would look empty to a casual passer-by.

She watched and waited. This was when people fell asleep on surveillance, Pete Don had warned her. And she could see how it could happen – it was like watching grass grow.

Finally the living room light went off, and a few seconds later an outside light flickered on, illuminating the driveway. A man was exiting the house.

It was Simon.

Mak perked up. *There you are.*

It was certainly him, although his hair was slightly longer than in the photos she'd seen. He was good-looking and fit, with handsome features, although there appeared to be something along his chin – stitches and a cut.

He was alone. The house was dark inside; it should be empty. She watched as he locked his front door, looked both ways and walked to his van. *Only people who are scared or guilty look both ways when leaving their house.*

Simon started up his van and drove away.

Where are you going at eight o'clock on this fine evening? she wondered.

When he was around the corner, Mak jumped into the driver's side of the Honda and followed him, cautiously dogging him a block behind. She followed him all the way into Bondi, to the main strip of restaurants on Campbell Parade. Was he meeting with someone? Was it relevant to the case?

Simon parked.

Mak coasted past the roundabout and watched as he made an order at a pizza place, alone.

He's getting takeaway.

This was Mak's opportunity. She drove back to the Tamarama house as fast as she could, knowing she had only perhaps fifteen minutes to get safely inside and plant the bug.

God, I hope this works.

Mak parked in the same spot as before, pulled on a pair of leather gloves and scurried across the street. She didn't want to end up like Ferris Hetherington, with her driver's licence stuck in the door, so she had a set of lock picks – a rake and a piece of spring steel – to manipulate pin tumbler locks of the type found on most back doors of residential homes. She had done some rehearsals of picking locks, but not much practice in the field.

This was her moment to give it a try.

She hoped Simon hadn't employed any deadlocks, or her plan would be shot. And she hoped those tumbler locks had only a few pins.

She had worked with up to five pins in a security lock. The more pins to line up properly with the lock pick tools, the trickier it was to pick.

You can do it.

Once inside, the radio frequency bug disguised as a double adapter would work well in his home office, if he had one, or even in his bedroom. If he was already using a double adaptor in one of those areas, as many people did, she would simply switch it over and he would never know. The only way to even tell the difference was that the bugged adaptor had a slightly heavier weight. In every other way it was identical to the adaptors most people had scattered through their homes. She would not have to retrieve it when she was done, as it was unlikely to be found and could not be traced back to her. A day or two of sitting in the car a block away, tuned into the right radio frequency, and Mak would know everything Simon was cooking up. And she might even be able to confirm whether he had set up the handbag-snatching or the break-in at Marian's office. Not that she could prove it in a court of law, of course. Because everything she was about to do was quite illegal.

Four minutes later she was still struggling with the lock on Simon's back door.

Fucking thing!

Mak counted not five but seven pins in the tumbler lock. And she was running out of time. She had perhaps five minutes left to get inside and

461

plant the device before Simon was due back with his pizza. She could attach the phone taps later, if it was safe, but that was even trickier work.

Dammit!

All of the windows and doors had been locked shut – she had checked first. His back door seemed the best option. It was shielded from the road and the neighbours' windows. But here she was, with a flashlight in her mouth, working the pins of the lock with her tools, and it was slow going. It had taken her four full minutes already and she wanted to shake her hands out, it was such fiddly work. Her fingers were going numb. An expert would have got through a seven-pin lock in sixty seconds.

Note to self: practise, practise, practise.

To Mak's surprise, there was the sound of a loud car horn on the street right out front. It startled her, making her drop her tools.

Dammit! Now I have to start all over again.

The horn went again.

What the . . . ?

Staying low, Mak crept around to the corner of the house and peered out onto the street.

'Oh my God,' she whispered under her breath.

The cops.

A police cruiser was parked just behind the red Honda. One uniformed officer sat in the cruiser, and the other leaned against the door of Andy's car. She'd left the window down to get fresh air while she'd waited, and he had obviously reached into the car and honked the horn. She felt herself panic. As she wasn't a locksmith, just being in possession of lock pick tools like this could be considered a criminal offence. Not to mention the phone taps.

'Miss Vanderwall?' came a voice.

Shit. They know I'm here. Have they been watching me the whole time?

Mak stashed her tools under a row of shrubs at the back of the house, brushed some dirt off her hands, straightened her clothes and walked out onto the street.

'Good evening, officers, how are you?'

'Can I see your licence, please?'

'Um, sure.'

She opened the car door, found her wallet and produced her driver's licence.

The officer looked it over while his partner stayed in the car behind, watching.

'Not using your motorbike this evening, Miss Vanderwall?'

'No. I just thought I'd sit and watch the waves for a while. It's a beautiful view here, don't you think?' she commented, and smiled. She leaned her hip against the side of the car and flicked her hair behind one shoulder.

He didn't give her even the slightest smile in return.

'And your private investigator's licence.'

Oh, this is bullshit.

'Certainly,' she said.

Mak dug around in her wallet and produced the licence. She would never offer it up without being asked, but these guys knew everything about her already, it seemed. Someone had given them a word-up. She handed it to him and the officer peered down his nose at it.

'Is there some problem, officer?'

'What were you doing on that property?'

'Which one?'

'Pardon?' he said.

'I just saw a wombat, I think, and I went to find it. I'm not sure which property it went onto. Over there somewhere ...' She pointed across the street.

'You said you were doing what?'

'I thought I saw a wombat run into the hedges and I went to check it out.'

'And why would you go looking for a wombat?' he asked her incredulously.

'I'm from Canada, you see, and we don't have wombats there. They are interesting little creatures, aren't they? It's still legal to enjoy the splendour and wildlife of this city, isn't it?'

'Uh-huh,' he mumbled. 'Well, Miss Vander-wall, I suggest that you do your nature loving somewhere else.'

'Absolutely, sir.' He held the door open for her and she stepped into her car. 'You have a good night, officers.'

'We'll tell your boyfriend at Quantico that you say hi.'

'Oh, yes. Thanks. Do that.'

Fuck!

She drove home with her tail between her legs.

CHAPTER 51

ON WEDNESDAY MAK sat curled by the bedroom window, deep in contemplation. It was too soon after her run-in with the cops to pay another visit to Simon's house, and Karen swore she had passed on the video to Sergeant Hunt but he had not called. Amy wasn't calling either.

Waiting, waiting . . .

Mak wasn't sure how to move forwards yet, but she wasn't about to give up. Something was going on, and she was determined to figure out what.

A near-empty jar of crunchy peanut butter sat between her bare feet, the lid tossed aside. Her shoulder rested against the cool glass of the window, her skin soaking up the fading rays of golden light as the sun began to set. Absent-mindedly she licked a dollop of peanut butter off the end of a dessertspoon, her blue-green eyes lazily scanning the street, her mind wrestling with her concerns. The embarrassing incident the night before had really made her feel like a fool. What would have happened if she'd been caught breaking in? They must have known she was there. Was she being watched?

Of course you are being watched.

But by whom exactly?

On top of Mak's concerns about the case, she had considerable worries about her own life. She was feeling increasingly out of place in this terrace of Andy's. She had been so put out by his call that she hadn't called him back. Should she just call it quits and take that Justice Department job back in Canada? Was that what he wanted? And what if she waited for him and they moved to Canberra together when he got back? Would she leave her work for Marian and never be an investigator again? The thought made her sad.

And what about my friends? What about Bogey?

Movement directed Makedde's attention to the first-storey windowsill directly across the street. It was the neighbour's tabby cat curling up in the last of the day's sunlight, much like Mak.

What do you think, kitty?

Impatient, she dialled Marian again.

'Marian, um, I was wondering if you've heard back from the client about the boat expense?' She didn't have the money to rent a boat to spy on the Cavanaghs herself. She had to clear it.

'He said no. He's not interested in the Cavanaghs, he said. Stick to Simon Aston.'

Mak nodded. 'I thought so.'

When she hung up, disappointed but not surprised, her mobile phone rang in her hand.

I could rent a kayak and use a long lens . . .

'Makedde speaking,' Mak answered.

'Um, Mak? This is Larry Moon.'

'Hi, Larry. How are you?' she said, sitting upright.

'Amy's missing.'

'What do you mean by "missing"?' Mak jumped up and scrambled for a piece of paper. She had been afraid something might have happened to Amy. 'When did you last see her?'

'It's been a couple of days.'

She nodded to herself. 'She's not at her house?'

'No. She isn't answering her door. I tell you, she wouldn't leave here without saying something to me. She never left my house alone – she was too scared. And now she's gone – with the front gate wide open and not a word from her. No, it doesn't seem right to me.'

'Have you reported this to the police?'

'I have quite a few cop buddies who come to my club. They knew she was staying with me. I told them what happened. They said they'd do what they can, but she won't be listed as missing for a while yet.'

'Of course.' He wasn't a spouse; she wasn't officially living with him. There was little the cops could do if she went walkabout. Perhaps Amy had left him for someone else? It was possible. They certainly didn't seem like a match to last. But still, in light of the video, Mak thought the worst.

'She left things here,' Larry went on. 'All of her clothes.'

That was odd. Even if she had left him it was unlikely that she would leave without packing her things, unless she was in a big hurry – or unless something altogether different had happened. Perhaps Larry was not being totally honest about the circumstances of her departure? Perhaps they'd had a fight and she had stormed out? Or was it something sinister? Amy had seemed paranoid when they met up at Leo's. Maybe she had been correct to be afraid?

'Her favourite jacket is right here at the front door,' he said. 'Why would she leave it?' Mak could hear by the slight tremor in his voice that he was genuinely concerned. She found his reaction somehow more emotional than she would have expected. It was almost touching. 'She'd never leave without her jacket,' he repeated, distressed.

'She didn't leave a note or anything? No messages?'

'No, but someone delivered a puppy to her and she left.'

'What? A puppy?'

'I have security footage.'

The surveillance cameras. Of course.

'Have you showed the police the tapes?'

'Yes, but it's useless. You can't see anything.

No faces, no licence plate numbers in view, nothing identifiable. Just a basket and then her leaving. That's it.'

That did seem odd, unless Amy was expecting something from another lover – perhaps someone was trying to win her back?

'I'm glad you called, Larry. There may not be much I can do at this end but I'll keep my ear to the ground and I'll let you know if I hear anything, okay? I'm sure she's fine. She'll turn up soon.'

But Mak wasn't so sure she believed that herself. It could be that whatever Amy had been running from had finally caught up with her.

'One more thing, Larry – I got a message that I think was from Amy.'

'Yeah? When?'

'The day after I saw you guys at Leo's. I need to know something – hang on …' She scrolled through her mobile phone address book. 'Is her number zero four zero one …' She read out the mysterious number that she had got the SMS video from.

There was a pause.

'Yes,' Larry said. 'That's her number.'

Oh God. It was *her.*

★　★　★

After a day of researching the Cavanaghs and her client, Robert Groobelaar – who, as it turned out, was in bed with Jack Cavanagh's real estate ventures – it was time for dinner.

470

Amy sent me the video, and now she is missing. Someone stole my handbag, possibly to try to get my phone . . .

She wished she could ask Andy to help out, but she was well and truly on her own.

Mak pulled open the hall cupboard, unbuttoned her jeans and stepped out of them. She stood in her T-shirt and panties, feeling the cool airconditioning on her skin, and folded her jeans neatly over a clothes hanger suspended by a hook inside the closet.

The cops aren't acting fast enough ... or, at least, no one is telling me anything.

Inside the closet, placed with considerably less care, were her motorcycling clothes, crammed into a pile of heavy black leather in a cardboard box beside her helmet and boots. She had soon discovered that her leathers bent hangers out of shape, so she never bothered dragging them all upstairs to her clothes closet. She hauled the bundle out and stepped into the sturdy pants first. She'd bought them over a year before, and the stiffness of the leather was gradually easing; in the first week she had barely been able to throw her leg over her motorbike. Mak zipped the pants up and buttoned the clasp high on her stomach, the cut designed to protect the skin on her torso in a crash. Safety was important – the leathers were also fitted with titanium-plated knees and elbows – but that high cut also made them uncomfortable to bend in. Mak struggled to do up her boots as she finished dressing, her mind absent.

She had now left two messages for Detective Hunt, and Karen had given him the video. He had not got back to her.

What is he waiting for?

Mak grasped the zipper of her fitted jacket and pulled upwards, feeling the snug leather and protective armour squeeze her frame securely, the jacket's back protector giving her a slight turtle-backed bulge.

Nothing is making sense.

She pulled her thick, fair hair into an elastic band and tucked it into her jacket collar for the windy journey, snapped the stiff collar closed and grabbed her helmet.

★ ★ ★

'Delivery,' Mak cried in a singsong voice, the words muffled by her bike helmet.

She stood at Detective Karen Mahoney's door, bearing dinner in takeaway bags.

Her friend Karen opened the door and responded with a quick embrace. 'Oh my God, you feel like you are made of steel in that suit. It's like Lara Croft has just arrived at my door.'

Mak handed Karen the bags of takeaway and stepped inside. She took her helmet off and put it on the floor. 'I have had such a crap week, I can't even tell you,' she lamented.

'Really, what happened?'

'No seriously, I can't tell you.'

'*Shut up!*' Karen said, in a tone that suggested she meant the opposite.

Karen's apartment was cramped but homey. The young detective had adorned her walls with a couple of movie posters, and furnished the space with garage-sale bookshelves, and a table and chairs. Her bed was from Ikea. It made Mak think of Bogey's comment.

They set up the coffee table in front of the television, where a DVD menu for the movie *Mulholland Drive* was on the screen.

'I waited for you to get here before I started it,' Karen said.

'Thanks.'

'You know, I've seen it before. Maybe this time I will figure out what it is really about.'

'Just watch for the red lamp,' Mak told her.

'What?'

'It's a clue,' she said.

'Something about the red lamp ...'

'Exactly,' Mak confirmed. 'I'll dish up.'

When they'd eaten and the movie was over, they settled into the inevitable raging debate about the plot of *Mulholland Drive*.

'I saw the lamp. That was confusing, but what about the blue box? What's the blue box?'

Mak cocked her head to one side. 'I think it's about the colour ... think of the key. But it isn't so much about the box but what it reveals, right?

473

It's the box of truth, and once he pans inside it, we see things as they really are.'

'I'm totally confused,' Karen admitted.

Mak sat back on the couch, smiling. She had been struck by how much the director character, Adam Kesher, had looked like Bogey. Maybe it was his hair. Or maybe it was that Mak was thinking about Bogey too much. She had more important issues to ponder for the moment.

'Well, real life is a bit confusing at the moment, too,' Mak declared. 'You saw the video? You know, Hunt hasn't called me back.'

Karen sat up and looked at her. 'Really?'

'Really.'

'I gave it to him on Monday.'

'Two days ago, and he's not returning my messages.'

Karen frowned. 'That's weird.'

'And what did you think of the video when you saw it? It looks like a murder, right?'

She sighed, and twisted one long red curl in her fingertips while Mak sat next to her on the arm of the sofa, tense.

'I think the girl in the video could be a Jane Doe from another case.'

Mak nodded. 'The Dumpster Girl.'

'Yes.'

Andy had referred to the victim that way. It was convenience not disrespect that made cops use nicknames for cases.

'And what about the other people in the video?' Mak continued.

'Well, the Caucasian one bears some resemblance to Damien Cavanagh.'

Mak sat up. '*Some* resemblance? You don't think it's him?'

'I'm not sure, honestly.' Karen seemed conflicted. 'It could be. I wouldn't be surprised either way.'

'And what does Hunt think?'

'Hunt is a knob.'

Makedde laughed, letting off tension.

'He became a knob the day he became sergeant,' Karen snarled. 'There was a real beauty the other day – this guy's prints were found in Meaghan Wallace's apartment, and he came up as having a record. Interesting lead, I would have thought. Who is this guy to the victim? What are his prints doing there? Well, Hunt practically ignored it, like it was nothing.'

That *was* interesting. Hunt seemed to be ignoring a lot of things.

'Are you even allowed to tell me this stuff?' Makedde asked.

Karen rolled onto her side and looked at her friend. 'What? I don't know what you are talking about, ma'am.'

Mak laughed again. 'Right.'

'This is all off the record, of course, but let's face it – you're working for the same aims, basically. I don't see any conflict of interest.'

That was true.

'But if Hunt found out I was talking about him, my head would be on a platter.'

'My lips are sealed.'

'You think the kid's innocent, don't you?' Karen said.

'Tobias? I don't know. He was a junkie looking for his next hit, right?' *Maybe.* 'Look, I haven't even met him, so what would I know? Let me just say that I haven't had so much bad luck on a case before ... there are purse snatchers and unco-operative cops everywhere I turn, not including you obviously. And that article in the paper. It could all be coincidence, but I doubt it. Someone doesn't want me snooping around. It could be that Tobias didn't act alone, or it could be that he was framed. If he went to her apartment every fortnight for money, like clockwork, someone could have known he was coming and set him up.'

'She was giving him money?' Karen said, surprised.

'Yes. Each fortnight out of her pay cheque from the real estate job. Every second Thursday. She was helping him out.'

Karen frowned. Mak could see that she had given the constable food for thought. 'Well, someone murdered that poor woman. To see Meaghan Wallace there on her floor all cut up and bled out made me feel sick.'

'Yes, it was a terrible crime.'

And all the worse if the wrong person is locked away for it.

CHAPTER 52

MAK FOUND HERSELF procrastinating over her arrival home. Whether it was nerves or the thought of spending another lonely night in the terrace – one of many to come – Mak had put off coming home until she was tired enough to go straight to sleep. She chose a circuitous route along the clear back roads, tucked into her solid K1200R, enjoying the feeling of the ride.

She pulled up in front of the terrace, revving the engine lower as she drove up onto the kerb and found a spot on the sidewalk alongside where she'd parked Andy's car. Mak popped the motorbike into neutral, the little green 'N' light momentarily illuminating the dark before she switched off the ignition and gently let the heavy bike settle on its kickstand. She swung her leg over and hopped off, removing her helmet and shaking her hair out of her ponytail.

The street was dark, and the humid air brought wafts of barbecue smell. A block or two away she heard a house party, probably with open windows or a balcony, with guests chatting away, their voices carried along in the warm gusts of wind. Someone was making the best of the balmy night. The city was still enjoying the hot days and nights of the Australian summer. Twenty-eight degrees. Thirty. Warm for a Canadian, especially one in leather.

Makedde squinted to find the keyhole, and turned the lock. She was barely two steps inside the front door when she sensed that something was wrong.

The front door was locked. The lights are off. It's fine, Mak.

But it wasn't, and she knew it.

Mak switched the lights on and looked around the hallway, her senses on edge.

Nothing was noticeably out of place. The doormat was slightly askew, but then she might have done that walking out.

This whole convoluted investigation is making you paranoid.

Makedde took her heavy backpack off, popped it down and removed her mobile phone from her top pocket, placing it on the hall table.

Wait.

What was that noise? A creak?

The house is just settling.

She felt hot in her leathers now that she was standing still. Mak would have liked to unzip her jacket, but for now she didn't make a sound. She just stood at the entry hall, listening.

You are imagining things.

Luther Hand had seen Makedde pull up. He'd been waiting, and had watched through the first-floor window as the woman dismounted and shook her blonde hair out like a lion shakes off water.

It was the new mark.

Makedde Vanderwall.

So here she was, so many years later. It was funny how things in life came full circle. Five years ago he'd lost the tip of his ear in this woman's backyard. His attacker – a small, swift man, probably staked out to protect her – had taught Luther the value of skill with knives. In a roundabout way, this woman, Makedde, had not only caused him to lose part of his ear but had also helped lead to him regrouping, relearning and emerging with a new international career. If he hadn't been injured like that, he might not have fled to Queensland, and he might not have come to the attention of Madame Q.

Yes. Full circle.

So this familiar mark was arriving home. He'd been expecting her.

Luther had to make it look like Miss Vanderwall had happened across a burglary in progress. He would knife her, check that the house was staged right, take the few jewels he'd found, and maybe the television set and laptop, and go. The last time he'd seen her, he'd had thoughts ... unprofessional thoughts. These thoughts occurred to him again as he set eyes on her once more, but he squashed them as soon as they came up. There had been a lot of lessons learned since he'd last seen this woman. Luther was a professional now. A total professional.

Follow the instructions.

Now he was flush against the wall of the kitchen on the ground floor, Makedde in the hallway. She had put something down on the floor. He'd heard the tinkle of keys. But now she was quiet.

He could just hear her breathe.

★ ★ ★

Makedde stood perfectly still in the hallway of the terrace, helmet in hand, her ears straining for a breath, a sigh, the creak of floorboards, anything.

Something . . .

She squinted into the dark spaces of the rooms beyond the lit hallway. She hesitated.

A glint of light caught her eye. She turned just as there was a whirl of movement close by, a large figure in dark clothes that she registered a second too late, its body weight hitting her dully on her head and shoulder, pushing down on her and nearly sending her sprawling backwards.

Oh God!

There was an intruder! She'd known. She'd sensed it.

Mak's motorcycle helmet was her only weapon, and she reacted quickly with it. Crouching, and taking the weight on her heels, she swung upwards, the straps curled into her tight fist. The helmet made contact with something. She'd been aiming for her attacker's head, but he moved and she slammed the hard helmet in his shoulder.

Her attacker was a man. A big man. When he stood upright he was easily half a foot taller than her.

Jesus, he's huge . . .

Mak couldn't see his face because he was wearing a black balaclava. He was all in black: black gloves, black long-sleeved top and pants. A burglar. Standing in the shadows, she might not have seen him. He'd been there watching her, she knew. There was another glint of light reflecting off metal — it was a blade, a sharp blade like the one in her nightmare . . .

The man stabbed at her, and Makedde screamed. But to her relief the knife did not penetrate her. Her leather jacket was still on, still zipped up. The knife merely glanced off the leather, too tough to penetrate. For a beat the man seemed confused by this. But she wasn't. It gave Mak time to react, and she kicked out with her heavy boots as hard as she could, striking his right kneecap to break it. He winced but did not fall, and she swung her helmet again with all her might, yelling angrily and as aggressively as she could, 'Get the fuck out of my house, motherfucker!'

This time her helmet made contact with the

man's head with a loud *crack*, and she heard an exhalation of breath from under that mask. Blood poured out from the breathing hole. She had broken his nose.

That won't hold him for long . . .

Mak spun around and made for the front door, flinging it open, grabbing the keys in her hand as she ran past. She sprinted for her motorbike, shoving the helmet on her head as she crossed the grass, strands of hair falling across her eyes and the leathers cumbersome for her sprint. She reached the bike and practically threw herself on it, stealing a glance at the open front door, which so far stood empty.

The engine will still be warm. Please start! Please!

Mak turned the key and revved the engine. The bike started, and it sounded right, the engine strong. She flicked up the kickstand and pulled back on the accelerator. When she let out the clutch the bike peeled onto the pavement and flew off the kerb, nearly throwing her off.

Oh fuck! Steady!

The burglar was making chase, running after her, and falling only metres short as she sped off down the road. She would ride straight to the police station, where she would be safe. It was her best option.

Her adrenaline soaring, it took Mak a few blocks to realise that her pursuer had not let her be. He was still after her.

By car.

Mak heard him before she even saw him. A car sped quickly around the corner after her, tyres squealing, and Mak watched with horror in her side mirrors as a jet-black sedan rocketed along the road behind her, gaining ground. Mak felt sick at the sight.

Oh my God, he's not letting up!

Mak pulled on the throttle and watched as the speedometer topped eighty, riding dangerously fast for the dark and winding residential streets, hoping that no one pulled out of a driveway or opened a door of a parked car as she sped past at lightning speed.

Steady . . . steady . . .

The car kept in hot pursuit. She could see him behind the wheel, still wearing his mask.

Who are you?

She knew he was no burglar. A burglar did not pursue their victims like this.

Makedde knew the roads well, and she raced down them, taking tight corners and laying her knee right to the ground, her wheels gripping the tarmac. She hoped to lose him but, confident on his four wheels, he cornered hard and stayed right with her, tyres squealing, the bonnet of the car coming up dangerously close to her back wheel.

If that car bumped her wheel, she would be lost.

I need traffic. I can lose him in traffic.

Mak made for the main streets of Bondi Junction, where the trains and buses connected, and hordes of people would be driving to and from the city.

Come on . . . come on . . .

She emerged from the rows of houses onto a straight stretch of main road and pulled the throttle back. She geared up to third, to fourth, to fifth. She was doing 140 kilometres an hour, the wind pounding against her. The vibration of the bike was frightening at that speed, the heat of it. If she hit anything, any stone or bump, she would lose control and die on impact. But still she had the steadiness to go faster. And she had to. In the side mirrors she could see that he was right behind her. She sped up to 150. She'd never clocked 150 before on her bike. Never. She'd never wanted to get booked for speeding, but now she hoped for it. She wanted sirens. She wanted help. Anyone. Anything. *Please.*

The lights of Bondi Junction were rapidly approaching, the tall buildings and shopping centre coming into view. She was nearly there. Traffic is backed up at any time of day there, and he would get stuck. He had to get stuck, and she could weave through where he couldn't and speed past to safety. Surely this man wouldn't try anything too rash. She had to get him in public. Then he would have to back off.

He was wearing a goddamned mask for goodness' sake. He has to back off. Someone would surely see him and call the cops.

Please won't someone call the cops?

Mak raced through the intersection and into Bondi Junction, past the giant complex of department stores and into the traffic.

And then she saw it.

The truck.

The sick taste of metal rose in her throat as a giant eighteen-wheeler pulled out right in front of her. She braked hard, tyres slipping, losing speed – but not fast enough. She felt her back wheel wobble, wobble again, and she was skidding – still fast, far too fast – and she saw herself sailing straight towards her death as if in slow motion. She was going to die on impact.

Oh God, help me . . .

Mak lay the bike sideways and felt her body hit the pavement. There was terrible vibration, heat and noise . . .

And then nothing.

CHAPTER 53

MAKEDDE VANDERWALL COULD not feel anything.

She could hear noise – voices – but she could not speak. She wanted so badly to get up and get off the road, away from the traffic, but her body was slow to respond. Her eyes flickered open, and she saw the tops of the streetlamps. She was face up, her body straight and arms folded as if she was ready for the luge. Strangely, she did not feel any pain. She could not feel anything except the heat of friction, and her body's odd, stubborn refusal to get up.

Get up!

Mak sat up and her head swam. How much time had passed? Where was the man who had broken into the house? The man with the knife?

She looked around, vision blurry.

Just get up!

With great effort she rose to her feet and took a step. Her body crumpled beneath her, and she went to her knees.

'Hey! Don't move! An ambulance is on its way!'

Mak had no idea where the voice was coming from. She saw that people were around her, people with shocked faces. Everyone was standing back, afraid to touch her. She could see the massive truck she had slid underneath. It sat inert in the roadway, the cab door open and traffic backed up behind it. The driver would have thought he'd killed her.

Get the police, Mak wanted to say. Her mouth still wouldn't work.

'Hey, just relax. Just relax. Take it easy. Don't move ...'

Mak ignored the words and got to her feet again. She swayed but stayed upright, and looked frantically for signs of the black car that had chased her from the house. *Where is he?* She wanted to see more clearly.

She needed to get somewhere safe.

Mak moved herself forwards, the feeling coming back too slowly as adrenaline dissipated a bit. She was okay. She would get through this. She had already been through worse. She was strong. There was no siren yet. Not much time would have passed, then. He could be somewhere nearby. She should hide.

Mak made for the protection of the doorway to a massive bank building, everyone still staring but standing back, afraid to get near. She pushed her back into the corner, looking around for the car.

Oh.

Mak spotted her motorcycle and her heart sank. There was no way she would be riding it out of this mess. It was wrapped around a telephone pole on one side of the far intersection, still running, the engine screeching. Smoke rose up from the exhaust. She must have still been doing at least sixty when she went into the slide and her beloved BMW had continued on its course right into the pole.

Despite the fact that she clearly had more important issues to worry about, she couldn't help but feel pained at the sight of the mangled machine. She wanted to tell someone to get to the kill switch but it hardly mattered now. Her voice wouldn't come. The feeling in her body was too distant to be real. But she was okay. She was alive.

Bang.

Her motorbike shut itself off with a thump, going silent.

Stunned, Mak looked at herself and noticed the shredded surface of her clothing, examining her leathers with renewed admiration. Those leathers had saved her skin − literally. There were grey patches of worn suede left at the contact points from her slide, as if someone had gone at the dyed leather with a cheese grater. That could have been her flesh.

Yes!

Makedde could hear sirens. She was not even sure of the direction; the sound came up out of nowhere and filled her ears with its shrill but welcome cry, and she felt safe again. Her body sank back into the pavement in the doorway, still numb. Mak curled up on the ground.

She closed her eyes.

CHAPTER 54

DETECTIVE JIMMY CASSIMATIS strode down the corridors, his heart in his throat.

Andy is going to shit himself . . .

When he reached the room, Makedde was sitting up in her hospital bed with a pen and a pad of paper, scribbling something. She looked up. 'Hey, Jimmy,' she said casually while he gaped at her. He felt a flood of relief. She looked like she might actually be all right. She was in one piece.

'*Skata!* Thank Christ!' he exclaimed. 'Are you okay?'

'I'm fine, Jimmy. I'm fine,' she assured him.

Her face was pale, her eyes bloodshot, and there was a light, clammy sweat on her brow, but she appeared to have all her limbs. He'd expected much worse.

'Did you break anything? Any gravel rash?'

'No breaks. I don't feel so hot but ...'

Jimmy thought he'd seen everything, but this he couldn't believe. 'You slid under an eighteen-wheel Mac truck. Ironic,' he said. '*Mak* goes under a *Mac*.'

'You have no idea how lucky I am, Jimmy. There was someone at the house. He tried to stab me, and then he chased me down. Those leathers saved me twice tonight,' Mak said.

'I've seen some of those guys come in here,' Jimmy warned her. 'The ambulance looks clean but their insides look like a milkshake.'

Mak raised an eyebrow.

Can't you ever say the right thing, he berated himself.

To his relief, she smiled. 'No milkshakes here. I think . . .'

'You'll be fine, you'll be fine,' he tried to reassure her after his gaffe.

Andy is going to completely go out of his head.

She put her pad of paper down. 'Jimmy, have you seen that video I handed in to Hunt?'

'What video?'

Her face went even paler. 'What video! The one of the murdered girl. I gave it to Karen and she passed it on to Hunt.'

'Are you sure?'

'Yes, I'm sure,' she protested. 'Why would she lie to me?'

No one had told Jimmy about a video.

'You were with Andy at the autopsy, weren't you? The Dumpster Girl? Well, I think the video shows her death.'

Ah.

Since Hunt had taken on the case, and Andy had left to pursue his career break, Jimmy had been feeling out of the loop. It was as if Hunt didn't even want him around.

'Jimmy, I don't think I'm nuts, but I believe this is all related. Someone stole my handbag. Someone went through my employer's office and now there's someone at the house,' Mak told him. 'It is about this case. I know it. All that can't be coincidence. Maybe this guy who came after me is the same guy who killed Meaghan?'

From everything Jimmy knew, the case against Tobias Murphy was a strong one. Andy had told him about Mak's theory, but he was doubtful that her feelings about his innocence were warranted. He didn't want to encourage her thinking, but perhaps now was not the time to talk about all that, or how everyone knew that she'd been pulled up snooping around some guy's house in Tamarama.

He held his tongue.

'They sent a unit over to check for signs of forced entry.'

'He was wearing gloves,' she said, her eyes faraway. 'Damn. They probably won't get prints.'

'It's okay, they'll get him. Tell me what happened,' he prompted her.

'I've been writing down a description of the car and the man, and everything else I remember, so that I don't forget anything. I didn't get a full licence plate but it was a black sedan with plate FST something.'

'Okay,' he said, and jotted the information in

his notebook. He was proud of her. Not many would remember important details like that after an accident. She was all right, for a girl.

'I came home late after dinner with Karen –'

'Mahoney?'

'Yeah. And when I arrived at the terrace I just felt that something was wrong,' she explained. 'This guy was in the house. He sprang at me. He was huge. He must have been several inches taller than me. Six foot six maybe?'

'So you saw him?'

'Oh yeah,' she said with a flicker in her eye. 'I saw him, but the bastard had a mask on. I didn't see his face. I think I gave him a broken nose, though.'

Amazing, she is. Andy doesn't know what he has in this girl.

'He came at me with a knife and it nicked my leathers but didn't penetrate. Like I said, they saved me twice tonight. I took off ... I just got right back on my bike and rode off, thinking he would stay in the house and get what he wanted, and would probably be gone by the time the cavalry arrived. But the bastard followed. *He followed.* He not only followed me but he practically tried to run me off the road. I'm sure that was what he was trying to do.'

Jimmy was perplexed. Why would a burglar follow their victim? Why, if everything he wanted to steal was in the house?

'I was speeding. He was going to bump me off

493

my bike. I don't remember much else except that a truck came up and I couldn't stop in time. I braked and started sliding. That was it.'

'Well, let's get a doctor in here to see if you are okay.'

'They are waiting on X-rays, I think.'

She reached a hand out and he approached her, awkwardly. They had never been on the best terms, he knew.

Mak squeezed his hand. She looked at him with bloodshot eyes. 'Jimmy, I need your help.'

CHAPTER 55

'OH MY GOD. I'm so glad she's okay,' Detective Karen Mahoney marvelled.

Karen had thought the worst when she was told what had happened. When she'd seen Mak leave for home, she had no idea she'd see her again so soon, and in such terrible circumstances.

'Yeah, she doesn't look bad for someone who went under a truck,' Jimmy quipped with his usual blokey sensitivity.

'She'll be feeling it tomorrow, I'm sure.'

They had left Mak to rest for a while, and Karen took the elevator with Jimmy down from Mak's floor to the hospital cafeteria on the ground floor. It was a sterile and unwelcoming place, most of the tables empty. They got two Styrofoam cups of drip coffee, and she watched in awe as Jimmy drowned his in milk and sugar.

They took a seat in the corner with their backs to the wall.

Jimmy wasn't his usual affable self. He was probably shaken by what had happened to Mak, too.

'Tell me about this video,' he said. 'No one told me nothin' 'bout it.'

Karen was shocked. 'Really?'

'Yeah. What is it?'

He really doesn't know.

Karen explained the video, what was on it, who it appeared to show and how Mak had handed it over. They'd done a CCR check and confirmed that it was from the mobile phone of Amy Camilleri, just as Mak had suspected. That was two days ago, and now the word from Melbourne was that Amy Camilleri was nowhere to be found.

'She's missing?'

Karen nodded solemnly.

'Hunt hasn't brought Mak in for questioning about it?'

Karen nodded again.

'*Skata,*' he swore in his native Greek.

'Exactly.'

'Look, I'm no good at this political bullshit. I don't pay no attention, but I gotta say that since Andy left for the US, things have gone weird, don't you think?' he said.

Weird was one way of putting it. 'How do you mean, exactly?'

'I say someone's trying to discredit his girlfriend, you know, with the kinda work she does, the modelling, her history . . .'

'What? What do you mean, her *history?*' Karen asked, offended at the idea.

Did he mean the newspaper article, or was there more?

'You know …' Jimmy seemed uncomfortable with what he had to say. 'Her tendency to always be on the radar of some psycho.'

Karen felt her anger boil. 'I'm not going to defend my friend when she hasn't done anything wrong. She handed in that video because it was the right thing to do. Fuck Hunt if he hasn't seen fit to follow it up properly. I don't know what his problem is. And it's not a crime to be a victim of crime. It took a lot of courage for her to get on the stand and convict Ed Brown. Her testimony was half the case.'

Without her, the Stiletto Murderer might never have been brought to trial.

'I know, I know. Don't go lookin' at me,' Jimmy shrugged. 'I'm not sayin' I agree or nothin'. I just gotta tell you some stuff I been hearing. I told ya, since Andy left it ain't the same in there.'

He looked really uncomfortable − downright sheepish. Karen wondered what the hell was going on.

'You know she got busted tryin' to break into the house of some guy named Simon Aston?'

'What?' Karen was shocked.

'I know. Apparently she was trying to break in. They just let her off.'

'Who let her off?'

'A couple of connies in the area.'

Oh, really? …

CHAPTER 56

'THE ITEM HAS been leaked,' The American said.

Luther gripped the phone and gritted his teeth with displeasure.

This was not the news he wanted. The video his client had asked him to obtain was in the hands of the police. He felt his rage bubbling up – self-directed rage.

He had failed.

'She made it?' He had to know.

'Yes.'

So Makedde Vanderwall survived the motorcycle crash. Dying in a crash would have been perfect for his client, but somehow he felt strangely relieved that she'd survived. Perhaps because that meant he could get up close and personal with her one more time. He had another chance to do it right.

'We have to be cautious now,' the American voice said. 'I'm doing what I can with the police, but the focus has shifted our way.'

Luther nodded. He understood that they were now under suspicion. It had become riskier.

'She is the girlfriend of a cop, you understand. We need to be very careful.'

Luther listened.

'Top priority, we need her silenced, but carefully. It can't look deliberate. This one is tricky. We can't screw this up.'

'Okay,' Luther said.

He would get started right away on a new plan.

CHAPTER 57

MAK FOUND HERSELF drifting in and out of sleep for the next few days. She needed a lot of rest, more than she had expected. The nurses had warned her that this would be the case. She might have all her limbs, but her body had some recovering to do. She dreamed of the horrible, shadowy creature who had begun to haunt her again, except now he was shadowy because he wore a black mask, and the blood that filled everything came from his nose.

On Saturday afternoon the doorbell disturbed her.

Mak rolled over, feeling heavy on the sheets. She was in Andy's terrace, in their bedroom. A thin trail of her own drool was cool on the pillow. Oddly, she felt as if she'd been tied to a Tilt-A-Whirl for hours, and needed stillness, but she urged herself up. She wiped her mouth, embarrassed, crawled into a robe and went to answer the door.

No more sleeping ... there are things to do ... things to solve ...

The terrace smelled of flowers. The bed was flanked by bouquets of red and white roses, one of which she remembered receiving, and one she didn't. Andy had called every day to check on her, and every day his roses arrived, she knew that much. She wondered how long he would keep it up. He had not yet mentioned their odd conversation on Monday. There had been a lot of other odd things since then.

Mak was walking, though stiffly. Her body felt heavy, but it was working. She was already at the bottom of the stairs when she remembered she was not alone.

'How are you feeling?'

It was Constable Sykes.

'Oh, Anne. Sorry, I forgot you were here for a moment,' Mak said. 'I must look like Frankenstein's bride or something.'

With evidence of the break-in into their home, and the suspicious circumstances, Andy had insisted on installing Sykes at the terrace. Mak had for once not protested about the added security. Not this time.

'Some more flowers arrived for you.' Mak saw another of Andy's red and white bouquets waiting in the hall. 'I didn't want to wake you. Oh, and these arrived for you yesterday afternoon.'

'Yesterday?' Obviously she had slept and slept. A huge bouquet of flowers sat on the coffee table in the living room. They weren't roses.

'I hope you don't mind, but I put them in water for you. You seemed so tired, I didn't want to disturb you.'

'Who are they from? Did they come with a card?' Makedde asked. She went straight to them and inspected the flowers.

Who?

'There was a card. It's just there.'

Mak saw it propped up against some books, still in its sealed envelope. 'Thanks,' she said, and pocketed it with a fleeting sensation of guilt, hoping it might be from Bogey.

'Your girlfriend Loulou is at the door again. You want me to let her in?'

'She was here before?' Mak said.

'An hour ago. You were asleep. Shall I let her in?'

'I don't know if I have the energy,' Mak joked. She tended to want to make light of things when she was in pain. Sykes only smiled.

Sykes opened the door and let Loulou inside. The policewoman looked both ways and then locked the door again. Mak noticed that the curtains were drawn, but it was still a bright afternoon outside.

'Sweetheart!' Loulou lunged for a hug and Mak recoiled.

'Not too rough, please!' Mak cried.

Loulou had kept her wild black and purple hair, and she wore a crazy striped sailor dress with fishnet stockings and platform boots. She looked worried. 'How are you feeling, darling?' she said, concern pushing out her brightly painted lower lip.

'I was really lucky. I've been so tired, though. I feel like I haven't been able to lift my head for days, except to eat. It's Saturday, isn't it?'

'Yes, it's Saturday! Oh gawd, girl, I had to come and see you. I was so worried.'

'Come in, come in,' Mak said.

Sykes was in the living room, so Mak took Loulou upstairs for privacy. It was only one flight of stairs but Mak felt her muscles burn on every step. When they reached the bedroom, Loulou marvelled at the bouquets of roses.

'Andy's been sending them every day,' said Mak. 'There is another one downstairs.'

Loulou gaped. 'Wow. Big damn roses! That boy must be fretting that he isn't here.'

I don't know.

'I'll just go freshen up for a sec,' Mak said, and disappeared into the en-suite bathroom.

Mak brushed her teeth eagerly and splashed water on her face. Her hairline appeared to be a touch greasy, the back of her hair in knots. She looked terrible. Her bright eyes seemed even greener than usual, surrounded by burst capillaries. Her face was pale. With a sense of trepidation, she grasped the left side of her robe and slowly lifted it up. A large, deep bruise coloured her outer thigh and hip with blue and purple. The centre was yellowish. She'd come down hard on her side when she'd slid.

Yick.

Mak felt the card crinkle in her pocket. She let go of the robe and opened the envelope. The card inside said *Thinking of you. Get well soon. Bogey.*

Mak closed it again, grinning to herself. *Bogey.* And then she saw the front of the card: it was a picture of the Sagrada Familia in Barcelona.

Damn, he's good.

She'd pocketed it and read it upstairs because she didn't want Constable Sykes to see who it was from. Anything Sykes knew, Andy would find out. Bogey's message was certainly brief. He was clearly sensitive to and respectful of Mak's living arrangements.

When Mak came back out, Loulou was sitting on the bed. She'd opened the curtains and the room was filled with light. It was a huge improvement, so much less dark and depressing. 'This whole thing has been so wild.'

Mak nodded. 'You bet it has. When did you get back?'

'We drove up Thursday, after I heard.'

We. 'You guys drove? Wow.'

'Ah, it's only ten hours. Eight, the way Bogey drives.'

'Oh ... Bogey is here too?' Mak tried to sound casual. 'You came with Bogey?'

'Yeah, he said he had some clients to visit. ECC are thinking about putting some of his stuff in their showroom. He's making a weekend of it, I think.'

Mak restrained herself from asking more about him, specifically where he was and if he had said anything about her.

'Mak, sweetheart, I've got to tell you,' Loulou said, breaking Mak's train of thought. 'There is this fetish photographer I know, Rico ... Actually, he is a friend of Julio's. Julio is Mistress Scarlet's slave ... um, Brenda's boy, you know. Has she introduced you?'

'No,' Mak said. *No, Brenda has not introduced me to her slave, strange as that may seem.*

'Anyway, Julio's friend Rico has seen your picture, and he is dying to do a shoot with you. He is a part-time snapper, you know, to pay the bills, and he said something interesting. He's in town for the social event of the year, apparently: Damien Cavanagh's thirtieth birthday party.'

Mak was instantly alert.

Of course.

Mak had heard about it, but with everything else going on, she'd forgotten.

'I hope you don't mind. I know that Simon Aston guy will be there. I thought I should tell you about it.'

Mak was very interested that the Cavanaghs were putting on a party. Not only was Simon Aston going to be there, but Mak was keen to find out more about Damien Cavanagh, too. Amy, who was now missing, seemed convinced that Damien was the man standing over the girl in the video. Mak had to know.

'Is it a very big party, do you know?' she asked.

'*Is it?*' Loulou responded with her usual drama. 'Mak, sweetheart, it's only the *biggest* party of the year, or maybe even the decade. Are you kidding?' She seemed not to comprehend her friend's social ignorance. 'It's been the biggest story in the gossip pages for months.

'It's going to be huge, darling,' Loulou said. 'And it's tonight.'

★   ★   ★

Luther Hand sat in a car across the street from the terrace.

He watched Mak and the mohawked girl through the upstairs window. If he had clearance to, he could get a good sniper shot at Mak, and in seconds it would be over. But he couldn't do that, and nor did he particularly want to.

He had to get her out of the house, and away from that cop.

And when he killed her, he had to make it look like an accident.

There will be no more mistakes.

506

CHAPTER 58

AN EXPLOSION RIPPED through the sky.

Another.

The crowd of party guests looked up as one, riveted by the colourful drama unfolding above them. Mouths held open and eyes wide, they took in the impressive sight of a surprise fireworks display as it screeched and flashed red sparks, filling the humid night with a sunset of smoke. Glasses were raised, and a round of cheers momentarily drowned out the crashing sounds of the fireworks as the guests toasted their extravagant host.

It was midnight at the Cavanagh house on Sydney Harbour, and the party was just starting to get into full swing. Though it was several weeks after the real Chinese New Year, 350 glamorous A-listers, socialites and VIPs had gathered at this place on the shore, dressed in the theme of the night. The women wore updated versions of the traditional Chinese cheongsam neck-to-knee dress, many reworked into abbreviated minis, or slit to the waist to better flaunt the women's tanned assets. One infamous men's magazine model had arrived with her 'dress' created using body paint on her generous curves. The men wore silk brocade or kung-fu-style suits, and still others arrived shirtless, Bruce Lee-style, to reveal their dedicated personal trainers' work. Waiters wore high-necked black ensembles, balancing trays of drinks or circulating with bottles of Moët to top up champagne glasses. A steady flow of Asian canapés tempted guests, though few of the carefully dressed women dared touch them for fear of smearing their silk outfits with a stray spring roll or dribble of hoi sin sauce.

The Darling Point residence where the esteemed guests had gathered was impressive by even the most privileged standards. It boasted fifteen bedrooms, luxurious living areas – the largest of which had been cleared of furniture for the night and currently housed a DJ and his sound equipment – a sprawling kitchen of marble and stainless steel, a home theatrette and a gym, maid's quarters and a tennis court. Tonight, torches and red lanterns lit the manicured pathways at the back of the house, coaxing guests down to the outdoor pool area, where they sipped cocktails and admired an unobstructed view of the continuing fireworks. With panoramic views over Sydney Harbour, palatial gardens, and its own private waterfront and small pier, the Cavanagh property was one of the most costly slices of land in the country, owned by one of Australia's richest families.

And didn't the guests know it.

The most coveted hairdressers from the upmarket suburb of Double Bay had been booked out for days beforehand, grooming ageing socialites and hot young It girls for the exclusive event. The parade of gleaming Maseratis, Rolls-Royce limos, Ferraris and Porsches that appeared at the front door had been waxed and polished, some having been surreptitiously rented by guests in anticipation of their brief but important first impression on the valet outside. Unable to pass the security guards to gain entry to the private grounds, paparazzi huddled at the kerb to snap what they could of the rich and the famous as they arrived. For weeks, gossip writers had filled their Sunday columns with speculation over who would make the guest list and who would not. And the chosen crowd did not disappoint: visiting movie stars, heiresses, Olympians and a handful of minor royals mingled with the movers and shakers of big business and politics. Anyone who was anyone was there, and those who had not been invited knew too well that they would be overlooked on the invite lists of the Sydney social scene for the rest of the year.

Makedde Vanderwall was not concerned about invite lists or the social circuit.

Nor was she vying for the opportunity to shake hands with Australia's A-list, or flirt with one of the country's most eligible bachelors.

The budding private investigator had other ideas.

She had chosen her moment of arrival carefully. It was after eleven and most of the guests were already inside; security were getting bored in their duties. As she neared the house, she noticed the still-hopeful paparazzi leaning against the stone outer walls of the property, not permitted to enter the party. They smoked cigarettes and chatted like soldiers on a break before the next battle. This was probably quite a different crew to the photographers who had rushed her on the steps of the Supreme Court during the Stiletto Murder trial, Mak reminded herself. These were full-time celebrity snappers, here for the movie stars, heiresses and royalty. Even if some of the photographers were the same, she thought it unlikely that anyone from the courthouse steps would recognise her here, in these circumstances, as that scared witness.

Mak took a deep breath.

You can do it. This will be easy.

Her driver turned the car into the driveway, the photographers now watching with great interest as the polished Lamborghini Murcielago slunk past, low to the ground, gleaming in the light of the streetlamps. A couple of quick flashes went off at Mak in the passenger seat, startling her. The mood changed quite suddenly. A handful of men threw their cigarettes to the ground and ran up the drive towards the entrance, hauling their cameras up to their faces. Security moved forwards and kept the growing throng of overtired photographers back on the other side of the car so that Mak could get out near the steps.

This is it.

Mak had decided that this charade was her best hope of getting inside. If she blew it, she had scant hope of scaling those stone walls or getting past security.

Come on.

Brenda Bale's alarmingly thin slave, Julio – a wealthy luxury car dealer with a fetishist's nocturnal life who looked to Mak like Riff Raff from *The Rocky Horror Picture Show* – was dressed in a smart black rented uniform and driver's cap. He stopped his car and came around to Mak's side while she sat with her hands in her lap, heart pounding. The door clicked, unlocking. Julio pulled it open and Mak swung one foot out onto the drive, then the other. The photographers slunk around the sides of the car, shoving against one another to jostle for position and pushing the boundaries of the security guards, who held them back firmly with open palms.

'Hey. Stay back. Stay back!' someone said.

Mak exited Julio's luxury vehicle and stood; like a star shower, the night was illuminated by flashes. Photos were taken in such rapid succession that Mak found it dizzying, the flashes nearly blinding in the dark. Yellow blobs floated before her eyes when she closed them. She stepped forwards as casually as she could and flipped her hair back, letting it fall again over her shoulders and one side of her face, both intentionally glamorous and cleverly obscuring her identity. She sauntered towards the front door alone, head up with an air of importance, putting on the act of her life.

Owww.

Her bruises throbbed. Thankfully the party was black tie, and she'd worn a long dress with a slit up the right side. She had to concentrate on walking elegantly. Her body didn't like the movement, the high heels. She would take them off as soon as she could.

Mak could see two security guards swathed in black flanking the entrance.

Please don't stop me . . . please don't stop me . . .

The security guards watched her approach, coolly. One of them had a clipboard with what was obviously the guest list on it – the list that she was most certainly *not* on. Mak didn't want to have to give them a name. Stopping to give them a name – any name – would be social death. She had to be able to sail right through, too important to pause for security and their petty lists. That was the only way to do this. Unwittingly playing into her hands, the photographers continued to snap excitedly, and she used them. Mak turned and gave them a quick wave, egging them on and pausing for a few seconds to give a cheeky smile over one shoulder, a pose she'd seen starlets do on the Oscars red carpet. The photographers snapped away, and before they were done getting their shot she'd sauntered straight into the doorway past security, still minxing like a supermodel.

And she kept going.

Behind her she overheard Brenda's friend Julio say loudly enough for the security to hear, 'Where shall I park Ms Schiffer's car?'

Mak coughed. *Schiffer?* She was no Claudia Schiffer! She restrained herself from looking back to see the fuss outside. Now that she was past security they did not have her face for comparison. Who knows – they might even believe that she was indeed Claudia. The photographers, though, would not be so easily fooled, especially when they reviewed the images on their digital camera screens. Still, Julio's request would be enough to keep security occupied while she slipped away into the crowd at the party.

She was in.

CHAPTER 59

SIMON CHECKED HIS watch. It was time.

It was nearly two hours after the last of the main guests had arrived, and it was the moment for the grand arrival of the birthday boy himself.

Simon prompted the DJ to put on the theme to the James Bond film *Live and Let Die*, played so loud that no one could miss it. The crowd, enchanted by the fireworks, stopped what they were doing and turned towards the harbour, anticipating whatever was about to happen. As the bursts of fireworks halted above, a spotlight from the shore fixed itself on an old Chinese junk approaching just beyond the pier. A grinning Damien Cavanagh stood on the deck, bathed in the spotlight. He wore a blue silk smoking jacket emblazoned with gold dragons, and held a cigar between his lips. Reminiscent of a self-conscious young Hugh Hefner, or a wannabe Bond, he was surrounded by a bevy of scantily clad Chinese beauties who helped him down the ladder on the side of the small vessel to board the jet ski that came to fetch him. A round of cheers rose up from his mates in the waiting crowd, as others clapped politely.

Damien would be delighted with his entrance, Simon knew. Though many would find this flashy arrival unbearably gauche, the truth was, they would never say so. And one man who wouldn't be commenting was Damien's father, Jack Cavanagh. He and Bev had greeted a number of the guests and made a low-key departure shortly before eleven, to be driven to their sprawling Palm Beach abode, leaving Damien for the remainder of the weekend to enjoy his extravagant thirtieth birthday party with the younger crowd. Nor was Damien's boring fiancée around to ruin things. Carolyn had spent Friday night out with Damien at a swanky restaurant, and had afterwards flown to Paris to shop, with Simon's encouragement – '*It will just be a boring party. Corporate types sucking up to Jack ...*' The last thing Simon wanted was either Carolyn or Jack hanging around complicating things after everything that had gone on.

Now that Damien had arrived, the party would really get into full swing. The chosen guests, fuelled by rounds of free-flowing Moët and vodka Red Bull cocktails, cheered their young host's birthday as if it was the most important night of their life.

And, for some, it would be.

CHAPTER 60

WOW.

Mak had rarely seen a private home of this size.

Walking through the Cavanagh home with a glass of champagne in her hand, moving past the smattering of guests not already outside watching the spectacle on the shore, Mak found the size of the sprawling urban residence almost obscene. How many people actually lived here, in these fifteen bedrooms? Maybe three, including the son? Within every room could be found another space decorated flawlessly with expensive furnishings and art. If one measured success purely in material wealth, Mak imagined that the owner of this home must be deeply unhappy by now, as there could be little left to purchase.

She made her way into a living room where empty cocktail glasses sat on a sleek coffee table. A handbag sat on a settee; a jacket was thrown over a chair. Their owners were pressed up against the balcony railing, their backs to her, oblivious to her presence. Mak moved through the room and spotted a doorway at the back that had been deliberately and uninvitingly closed to the partygoers. She tried the handle – it wasn't locked. She took advantage of the distraction of the celebrations outside to go quietly through it into the hallway beyond, shutting it behind her carefully, even though the noise outside meant that she was unlikely to be heard.

Mak put her glass down for a moment and slipped her stilettos off. She bent over painfully and picked up her shoes, holding them in one hand, the straps slipping through her fingers. She grabbed her cool champagne glass again – a prop to help her blend in if she was seen.

Mak took a small sip and stretched her sore legs, circling her stiff ankles.

Ahhhh. That's better.

Okay. To the bedrooms.

This side of the house was quiet and dark. It seemed that everyone, including the Cavanagh family, was outside watching the fireworks. But there was a possibility that security would patrol these areas of the house, particularly if she was right in her suspicions and the Cavanaghs were worried about covering their tracks.

Please, God, let me be right about this, or I don't know if I'll ever live it down.

The long, dark hallway was lit only with a couple of large glowing candelabras. She admired statues and paintings in gilded frames as she made her way past them barefoot. The paintings were impressive: original Jeffrey Smarts and Arthur

517

Boyds, but no Brett Whiteley that she could see. Yet. She reached a staircase that extended both upwards and down, and decided to start at the top, where she felt the bedrooms were most likely to be.

She began her ascent.

Only three stairs up, Mak heard a noise from above and froze in place. It sounded like a door closing, and footsteps. A guest using a toilet back here? A family member? Was it Jack Cavanagh himself? Or one of his security crew?

Damn.

Whoever it was, Mak couldn't afford to be seen. She retreated back down the stairs, weighed her options and decided to continue down to the ground floor to wait. Fortunately the stairway carpet made for a near-silent descent. Quickly and quietly she descended the stairs, legs burning again, until she stood at the bottom of the staircase, holding the banister and listening ...

Makedde had hoped to find an 'at home' piece in some stylish magazine in the library archives that might have helped her to find her way around the Cavanagh house; or even a photo spread that pictured the Cavanagh family with the Whiteley itself in the background – but there had been nothing. Despite the notorious beauty and size of the place, and the press surrounding the Cavanaghs' major business deals, the family seemed to be very private. They did not invite the press into their homes. Mak was left to roam the impressive residence with little information to go on except the grainy, disturbing images of a mysteriously sent video.

Footsteps.

The slam of a door.

Mak gripped the railing in the dark and hoped that whoever was upstairs would not come her way.

CHAPTER 61

'ARE YOU *SURE*?' Simon Aston demanded. 'But how?'

'I'm telling you, I saw her. She walked right past me.'

'Vanderwall, the investigator?' he asked again, disbelieving. This girl had been caught poking around his house, and now this. The American had warned Simon about her in case she approached him.

'Yes. Only she looks more like Elle Macpherson than a PI, and what she's wearing doesn't leave much to the imagination. She has legs like a gazelle. I've seen her picture in the papers ...'

'Are you absolutely sure?' Simon stood out on the lawn, out of earshot of Damien, listening with horror to what his friend Jason was saying over the phone. He shook his head. 'Well, why the fuck is she here? This is just what I bloody need, some nosy bitch snooping around.'

'She was wearing some black dress slit up the wazoo. I wouldn't kick her out of bed, I tell ya.'

'Thanks, Jason, I'll be sure to fuck her before I ask her why she is trying to ruin my life,' he spat. 'Keep an eye out and find her for me. If you see her again, corner her and call me straightaway. I'll be looking.'

Simon ended the call and gripped his mobile tensely. *What the fuck? How can that investigator be here at the party?* An investigator snooping around the house could be a major disaster. He hoped to God that Jason was wrong. Surely it was some other blonde who had walked in?

Simon looked over to Damien, who was oblivious to the conversation. After his grand entrance, the birthday boy was standing near the garden steps only a few feet away, still in his robes, having the ashes of his cigar tapped by some young Asian babe the model agency had organised. Simon had to admit that she was a good-looking chick, even if she wasn't his type.

You've got no idea, my friend, no idea the things I do for you . . .

Damien looked over and gave Simon the thumbs up. Simon smiled in return and returned the sign. He pretended to answer another call, then laughed and signalled to Damien to say he would take the call elsewhere. Damien didn't seem to notice that his friend was heading inside. He just took another drag of his Cuban and told lame jokes to the hired women who hung on his every word, while Simon disappeared to look through the crowd for a meddlesome blonde investigator named Makedde Vanderwall.

If the girl was here, he'd take care of her.

CHAPTER 62

MAK OPENED A door on the lower floor and was hit with a cold rush of air.

There'll be no Whiteleys in here.

It wasn't a bedroom, but a garage. And what a garage it was, containing not one or two but half-a-dozen magnificent luxury vehicles. Mak spotted a Jag, a four-wheel-drive BMW and even a low-slung red Ferrari among the cars. This was where models like the Enzo Ferrari ended up, apparently. Two millions dollars' worth of car, and it could not even be driven on the streets. These were boys' toys – *very rich* boys' toys. Mak stopped gawking and closed the door again quickly, not wanting to be identified in case there was a video surveillance system or alarm protecting the glinting cars.

The rest of the ground floor of the Cavanagh house contained bedrooms and sitting rooms, each dark and unoccupied. One by one Mak investigated the rooms, listening first for noise, trying the doorknob, flicking on the light and taking a quick tour. She was mindful of the time.

She had been away from the party for twenty minutes so far and counting. She had to assume that her entry had worked – no one seemed on the lookout for a limping girl with big hair in a black dress who had pretended to be Claudia Schiffer. She'd made it. But Mak also assumed that the security staff might do a round of the house every thirty minutes or so.

As with many homes of people of great wealth, the rooms in the grand Cavanagh home were stylish and yet somehow devoid of personality or individualism, decorated as they were in the impossibly perfect style of an upmarket showroom. Everything was in its place – just that little bit too perfect – each key item no doubt worth more than Mak's entire annual income. Room after room was the same, be it a lounge or spare bedroom; not one thing out of place, and not one single item of bad taste or curious beauty to be found. She could not find any personal artefacts tucked away in a corner room, not even here on the ground floor. It left Mak with the impression that one could not glean a single piece of relevant information about the owners from the décor, except perhaps that they had an unlimited budget for a good decorator.

After taking a quick look through half-a-dozen rooms, Mak cupped her hand around the doorknob of the last doorway in the hall and listened for movement. There was no sound or vibration. Confident that the room was unoccupied, she turned the knob and flicked on the light.

Her heart skipped.

Across the room was a painting of pale flesh against white, depicting a sitting woman with generous, exaggerated curves, painting her lower abdomen with red lipstick.

The Whiteley. Bogey was right!

Momentarily forgetting herself, Mak raced towards it and read the signature on the lower left-hand corner. *Whiteley. Yes.* Three feet by two-and-a-half feet. An original. There was no question that this was the exact painting Bogey had showed her in his book. Unless there had been an imitation or print in the video, this was the very painting that had hung over the scene of the young girl's death.

It was here in the Cavanagh house. I was right.

Mak stood, squinting at the painting, puzzled. The remaining conundrum was that this room was not a bedroom.

She found herself in a lounge decorated with two small cream sofas, a coffee table and an entertainment unit. A huge flat-screen TV took up half of one wall and closed curtains took up another. It was different than the other rooms, less put together. While the furniture was nice, it didn't quite match so perfectly.

Mak could not afford to become sloppy and get discovered now. She sprinted back to the doorway, temporarily forgetting her soreness, and looked down the hall both ways. The corridor appeared empty. Heart beating a little too quickly, she shut the door, dropped her shoes and put her champagne glass down, then brought out her digital camera. Was this the scene of the death in that video? It had to be, didn't it? With the reputation of people like the Cavanaghs at stake, if she was wrong, her career would be well and truly over practically before it had begun.

She had to be certain.

Mak took a deep breath and walked 'the grid' across the carpet in a straight pattern, careful not to disturb anything. *Think, Mak. Think.* She switched on the date and time code bar on her camera to imprint the photos with their proper sequence, and began taking photos at every possible angle, scanning every minute detail of the room as she did. Yes, this was the painting Bogey had shown her, there was no doubt about that. But was this the same room? There was a window directly across the room on the other side. Mak pulled the curtains back a fraction to see a courtyard that would most probably throw sunlight into the room during the day. She moved across the room and cautiously lifted one corner of the painting. The wall was a slightly different hue underneath, the paint protected from sunlight.

Yes.

The painting had hung in that position for a

long time. So unless there was a copy somewhere, this lounge room had to have been a bedroom recently. Perhaps that was why the room seemed different. No interior decorator had put his or her touch on this.

This was a rush job, to cover up a crime.

CHAPTER 63

HUFFING AND IRRITATED, Simon Aston
flicked on the light in the garage.

*That investigator better not be anywhere near
this party . . .*

He made straight for the four-wheel drive he
always borrowed, leaned inside and opened the
glove box.

He feasted his eyes on a brand-new .22 pistol.

Look at that.

His heart pounded uneasily in his chest at the
sight of it, something like exhilaration and fear
filling him, offsetting the mellow cocktails in his
bloodstream. He'd had a few drinks, blowing off
steam. Simon picked the weapon up, the feel of
the cold metal in his hands giving him pause, but
only momentarily. He didn't have experience
with guns.

*That fucking bitch had better not be here, or she'll
regret it.*

Simon had never shot a handgun before, but
he certainly wasn't afraid to, especially feeling
like he was. If this investigator bitch didn't know

what was good for her, he would give her a fright. He'd give her a really good fright.

Behind the gun was a box filled with ammunition. Jason had shown him how to load the magazine, and now Simon impatiently stuffed it with rounds.

One ... two ... three ... four.

That will do.

Armed and with the gun half-cocked, Simon blundered out of the Cavanagh garage and set off to search for the uninvited guest.

CHAPTER 64

MAK WAS ON her hands and knees in the hastily renovated former spare bedroom of the Cavanagh house, her face to the plush carpet, sweeping her eyes across the grain, when she thought she heard a noise.

Oh shit.

She limped to her feet and shut the light off, body throbbing. In the dark she listened.

Mak had already found two slightly flattened areas of carpet, each smaller than a fist and about six feet apart. *Bed legs.* Someone had taken a bed out of here and moved the furniture around to make it into a lounge, but the indents from the bed legs remained. The other two indents would be under one of those sofas near the wall.

My God, I am standing in a crime scene.

With the painting and the indents of the bed legs, Mak was convinced she had proof that this was the room in the video. She only had to call it in now, before she was discovered and all hell broke loose.

Mak kept her ear to the door. The hall seemed

quiet, and slowly her heart returned to its normal pace. It had probably been a noise from another floor, she thought, or perhaps it had even been her imagination. She was so wound up that she might imagine anything. Satisfied that it was safe, she got out her mobile phone. It was time to get a crime-scene investigation team in to find any evidence that hadn't been cleaned over. She only hoped that they would believe her, and act fast.

'Cassimatis,' Jimmy answered on the second ring.

'Jimmy, it's Mak,' she said softly, her hand over the mouthpiece.

'Mak? Is that you? *Skata*, I can't barely hear you.'

'Sorry. I can't talk too loud right now,' she whispered. 'I'm in the Cavanagh house.'

'What!' He went off in a flurry of Greek expletives, and she held the phone away as he continued to rant. 'Hunt is gonna shit a brick!'

Once he stopped yelling she brought the phone back. 'Just calm down. As part of my investigation work I happened across the crime scene from your murdered Jane Doe, the Dumpster Girl in that video. You've got to get Crime Scene on this right away before there's no trace evidence left. The man in that video is definitely Damien Cavanagh. I am standing in the room right now. That's why I have to be quiet.'

'What? Hold on. Hold on ... What are you saying?' Jimmy was clearly distressed, unsure of what to do. 'You *happened across* a crime scene at the house of the Cavanagh family? Christ!'

She didn't want to explain the whole thing over the phone, and she didn't have the time to, either. She might be discovered at any moment. 'Jimmy, I know everyone thinks the Tobias Murphy case is open and shut,' she said, 'but there is more to it. And now I have the proof. Meaghan Wallace filmed that video of the Dumpster Girl and sent it to her friend, and then she was killed. And now her friend is missing. Just trust me – this is it. Get a team over here right now. Hunt seems to have the brakes on, but that doesn't matter now. You can go around him. The Cavanagh son was involved in the death of your Jane Doe, and that girl died right here in the Cavanagh house. Just send police here now to cordon it off. *Please*, Jimmy. Just trust me.'

His protests became weaker. '*Skata*, Mak. This could be my job. Are you ... sure?'

'Yes.'

There was a long pause. 'Okay. What's the address and the location of the room?'

Mak explained the location. 'Send the nearest patrols. And you'll want a good crime-scene investigation team in here. Someone has cleaned up the room and moved things around, but if your team is good enough they'll probably still find plenty of trace evidence.'

'Mak –'

'I'll be waiting here,' she said firmly and hung up.

Mak closed her eyes and leaned against the wall by the door. Jimmy was a good guy, for all his faults. She could trust him to act on what she'd said. She hoped.

Wait.

A sound.

Dammit. Someone might have heard me.

Mak stood in the dark with her back to the wall, listening for movement outside the door. Someone was definitely in the hall. And approaching. Mak hurled herself behind the nearest leather couch, misjudging the distance and hitting her leg against the arm, right where her bruise was. She stifled her yelp with one hand.

Oh fucking hell, that hurt . . .

The door opened.

The light came on.

From her position pressed up against the wall behind the couch, Mak could see a man through a gap between the cushions. It was a tall, good-looking man in a dinner suit and trendy T-shirt. He looked familiar.

Oh my God.

Simon Aston.

Standing out starkly against his matinee-idol looks was a row of stitches that ran across his chin and down his neck. They appeared fresh. She'd caught a glimpse of them when he'd

533

come out of his house in Tamarama, but they looked worse up close, the edges of the cut an angry pink.

Maybe that poor girl did it to him, before he and his mate killed her.

Mak realised her mobile phone was on. She hoped to God that Jimmy didn't call her back. Even taking the battery off the back of it might make enough noise at that distance to alert Simon to her presence. She wasn't going to move one centimetre. Stifling her breath with one hand, she sat motionless, curled up awkwardly, one leg aching and the other starting to go to sleep.

Mak kept her eyes on him through the thin view between the cushions as he walked over to the coffee table and picked up her half-empty glass of champagne.

Dammit.

It had a smudge of her lipstick on the rim. And just near his feet were her discarded stilettos.

Oh no . . .

He hadn't seen them yet, but it was only a matter of time.

And then Mak saw something terrible. She got a cold feeling in her belly at the sight of it.

He retreated to the doorway, brandishing a gun he'd removed from his suit jacket.

Things were out of control. She shouldn't have risked all this. It was just an investigation, right? Not enough to risk her life over.

'Where are you? I know you're in here!' His voice gave Mak a chill.

Mak had no weapons with her. She could use a pistol well – probably better than this guy could, by the looks of the way he was handling the .22. But Mak didn't like guns. Guns were terrible things, and she'd had to use them before. She knew what they could do.

Mak was unarmed but she had her mobile phone still in her hand. She took a leaf out of poor Meaghan Wallace's book and pressed record on the phone's humble video camera.

The video probably wouldn't be very clear, but she could give it a try.

CHAPTER 65

'HEY, YOU …'

Luther Hand turned.

It was a quarter to midnight, and Luther was on the walkway to the front door of the Cavanagh house, where he had been informed that his priority target, Makedde Vanderwall, had made an entrance. She had not left through the front door of her terrace, where he'd been waiting. It had not even occurred to him that she might leave by any other way. He'd expected to have to lose the cop to get to Mak, but he hadn't expected to lose Mak herself.

We've all underestimated her.

'Hey, you!' the security guard repeated. 'Name, please,' he said, holding up his clipboard.

Luther had no time for bullshit. He tried to walk on but the man unwisely stopped him.

'I'm talking to you, pal. No one gets in who's not on the list.' He put a hand on Luther's broad chest. No one had done anything like that in a long time.

In a flash Luther moved next to the guard, put an arm around his shoulder and grasped his neck. He did it so fast that for a split second the guard's eyes got as wide as a satellite dish. Luther squeezed, and the guard – who was big in his own right – simply fell backwards, unconscious. Luther caught him and dragged him behind one of the huge stone sculptures at the front door. He propped him up, seated, against the house. The guard would look like he'd taken a break and fallen asleep. His security buddy – and Luther had been informed there were two guards – was probably on a pee break.

Luther continued on his course through the front door, unmolested.

There were crowds of people inside the house, all of them dressed up. Following his instructions from The American, he found a doorway that would take him to the staircase. He moved down the stairs rapidly, ready for anything. When Luther reached the downstairs hallway, he was just in time to see Simon Aston as he backed out of one of the rooms, waving some kind of gun.

That idiot is going to ruin everything.

Luther pounced, grabbing Simon from behind, and pulling the gun from his hand. In seconds he had Simon up against the wall of the hallway by his neck. Simon's face was rapidly turning violet as Luther applied pressure to his throat.

'I can get rid of you, fast,' Luther whispered gruffly into his ear. 'And I have permission to do so. So don't fuck with me.'

Bright red veins popped up in the wide whites of Simon's bulging eyes. His jaw was slack, mouth quivering. Luther could see that Simon was hearing him.

'I'll take another souvenir this time if I feel like it. Perhaps an appendage you value.' He thrust his fist into Simon's groin, not quite enough to castrate him, but enough to make his point clear. 'Your life means nothing.'

Simon cried out in pain, the sound coming out in an animal gurgle, until Luther squeezed his windpipe tighter. He soon went quiet and still. Luther let him drop to the hallway floor with a discreet thud. He didn't want to kill him in the house. Besides, he was unlikely to be paid anything extra, as he wasn't on the list. He wasn't worth it.

'She's been here. It's her. There's her glass ...' Simon spluttered, holding his neck with one hand and pointing with the other. There was a champagne glass inside the room. It had the stain of a woman's lipstick on it.

Thump.

They both spun in the direction of the noise. Someone was in the room.

The window.

Luther just caught a glimpse of a slender foot as someone hauled their body out of the ground-floor window, disappearing behind the heavy curtains.

Shit.

Luther lumbered to the window, pulled the curtains back to get a clear shot and held his finger on the trigger of his gun. It was a young woman, the elusive one he had been looking for; the one who had unexpectedly bashed him with her motorcycle helmet and broken his nose; the one who had crashed her motorbike. The one on his list.

He lined up his shot.

CHAPTER 66

OH GOD . . . RUN . . .

Makedde found herself in the garden at the front of the Cavanagh house, her knees scraped and covered in dirt, the circular driveway only metres ahead. She could see that the front gate was still open for visitors.

Thank God.

She could never have scaled those stone walls. Mak had to get out of that gate or to Julio's car.

Barefoot and covered in leaves and dirt, Mak emerged from the bushes in her gown and ran full tilt as best she could out the front gate, barely registering her terrible pain, or that a handful of remaining photographers, still loitering and smoking cigarettes, had spotted her, their flashes lighting up the darkness. She had to get onto the street.

The police should arrive soon, she hoped.

That was where that poor girl in the video died. I was right. I can't believe I was right . . .

CHAPTER 67

MAKEDDE VANDERWALL SAT in the interrogation room of police headquarters with her arms crossed. She looked tired, but still frustratingly hot, Jimmy thought. Andy was one lucky bastard. Her hair was wilder than usual, giving her the appearance of a warrior lion.

She must have known that he was watching through the two-way mirror, because she flashed a wry smile in his direction and waved.

'Just answer my question, Miss Vanderwall,' Detective Matthew Parker pressed.

'Come on, give me a break,' she replied and rolled her eyes.

'Sorry, Mak. You know I –'

'Yeah, yeah, you have to do this, Matt, I know.'

Mak was sitting in the very room in which Andy had first interviewed her, back when she was a witness and all that was between them was Mak's rage over the murder of her friend Catherine Gerber and what she saw as the ineptitude of the police in solving it. Back then,

Jimmy and Andy had both wished that she'd mind her own business. Now they knew better. If there was anything that the last five years had taught Jimmy, it was that it was pointless to try to get Mak to butt out, and maybe that was a good thing. She had managed to get herself right into that case and she had ended up providing the evidence that no one else had had the foresight or the balls to provide.

Jimmy continued to watch Mak through the large two-way mirror while Detective Parker tried to talk Mak through what had happened at the Cavanagh house, and exactly how she had found herself at the crime scene of the Jane Doe.

Parker had no hope of matching her.

The door opened. Detective Karen Mahoney entered the dark back room behind the glass and sidled up to Jimmy.

'How's he doing?'

'You mean, how's Mak doing?' Jimmy replied.

'No, I mean him. How is Matt holding up?'

Jimmy chuckled.

'Here,' Karen said and passed him a cup of coffee. 'She's pretty good, huh?'

He nodded. 'Yeah, I guess she is. She never wanted to be a cop, you think?'

'I don't know,' Karen replied. 'I don't know that she could take orders from guys like Hunt.'

Detective Parker was still struggling in the interview room. 'So tell me once more what you were doing at the Cavanagh house.'

Through the glass they watched as Mak sighed, clearly bored with the game. 'I was invited to a social gathering at the home,' she answered into the microphone mounted to the table, as if making a scripted speech. 'It was only when I happened across the lounge room with the Brett Whiteley painting on the wall that I realised that it might actually be the same painting and the same room as the one in the video that I was anonymously sent. As with the video, I contacted the police immediately about my concerns and made sure that the authorities had all that potentially important evidence.'

Parker ran a hand through his hair, obviously not buying it. But he said nothing.

Mak blinked in response to whatever look he gave her, her expression deadpan. That was her story and she was sticking to it. *Smart girl*, Jimmy thought.

'Hunt is going to come in here and ask me all the same questions, isn't he?' Mak asked.

'Um ... probably.'

Detective Sergeant Hunt, they'd been told, was busy working on Simon Aston.

* * *

'Do you admit that the GHB found in the four-wheel drive BMW was yours?' Detective Sergeant Hunt pressed.

Hunt had been interviewing Simon Aston for

nearly an hour. He wanted to interview him alone, without the assistance or prying eyes of Detectives Mahoney or Parker.

Simon was spineless. It had taken him little time to confess.

Simon's story was that his friend Damien Cavanagh had developed a preference for petite Asian girls – young ones – and for nearly a year Simon had procured girls for his friend's pleasures. Since Operation Paper Tiger in the nineties, Hunt himself had known about the racket that brought girls like the Dumpster Girl into Australia. These girls were in enough demand that they were constantly being trafficked from poorer countries like Thailand and the Philippines, where they would either be coerced into sexual slavery or would happily accept the prospect of prostitution in order to make the money they and their families desperately needed. Some of them were even sold by their own parents, such was the desperation in their villages.

As Simon told it, this particular girl was given champagne and cocaine at the party; after sex, when Damien had got up to shower, Simon believed she had drunk from a plain water bottle which contained not water but the colourless and odourless psychoactive substance GHB, or gamma-hydroxybutyrate, otherwise known as Grievous Bodily Harm, the latest drug Simon had introduced Damien to.

When Damien returned and found the girl

unconscious and with no perceptible heartbeat, he called for Simon.

'The GHB in the vehicle was yours?' Hunt repeated impatiently.

'Um, yeah. But it was for Damien. He had tried Fantasy and liked it,' Simon said. Fantasy. GHB. GBH. 'He'd been having a fling with it for a couple of months, but I warned him that you can't mix it with other stuff. No alcohol or anything. He was careful. But this girl must have drunk nearly the whole bottle of the stuff. When I came downstairs she was already out cold.' Simon scratched his head, agitated. 'I got her a shot of speed. It's supposed to reverse it.'

'But it didn't, did it?'

'No,' Simon admitted. He looked ashamed.

'That's manslaughter, you know,' Hunt told him.

Hunt was disgusted. A lot of drug dealers were under the false perception that speed could counteract the effects of GHB. In fact, it only sped up the process of death. The girl's only hope of living would have been a hospital. If they had got to her in time, they could have saved her life and had her walking around again the next day, almost as if nothing had happened.

This guy was a total idiot. He'd put a lot of people in danger, and he'd embarrassed some very important members of society.

'She had no pulse. Damien was freaking out. I called Lee ... the guy who brings the girls.'

Lee Lin Tan. He and his wife had recently become the unfortunate victims of yet another Vietnamese gang slaying. They'd been killed with hatchets, the trademark of the gangs.

'I stepped away for two minutes and when I came back this bloody chick is in the hallway watching them. Watching them and the dead girl! She had her phone in her hand and I was afraid she was recording it, so I got the phone off her and drove her home.'

'That was it? You just took her phone away and drove her home?'

'Yeah,' Simon said, but Hunt knew he was lying.

'I gave her a little something to help her relax,' Simon admitted.

'You gave her the GHB.'

'Yeah. Just a little something to help her sleep.'

'And then what?' Hunt asked.

'That should have been it. But then she couldn't forget it. She started making waves.'

'That is when you hired Warwick O'Connor to kill the girl.'

Simon nodded sheepishly. 'It wasn't all my idea or anything.'

'I understand,' Hunt lied. 'Thank you for your cooperation, Mr Aston.' Hunt stood up. 'We will have further questions for you. In the meantime, you are free to go. Just don't leave the state.'

'Really? I'm free to go?' He seemed surprised.

Simon Aston failed to notice that the red light of the video recorder had not been on. His statements did not exist, and Sergeant Hunt had made sure no one else heard what he had to say about Damien Cavanagh's involvement.

As far as he was concerned, Simon had killed the girl and covered it up. And he had acted alone.

CHAPTER 68

SIMON ASTON DROVE home to the Tamarama house in a state of numb shock. His senses were overwhelmed, his life turned upside down.

He had cooperated with Detective Hunt. Simon had told him everything he knew, and he had hardly believed his good fortune when he was allowed to go. He would cooperate all the way, and they would see that it wasn't his fault. He'd had to do the things that he did. He was not the guilty one.

Anyone else would have done the same.

Simon expected that he might not hear from Damien again for a little while. Damien had told Simon that he was being sent away to join his fiancée in Paris for an indefinite amount of time, and that his father had cut him off from his allowance and personal accounts. No money to party with. No money for his vices. Jack Cavanagh would control Damien's spending and activities, and had threatened to make him work to earn every dollar. For a time, at least.

Simon hoped that Damien's punishment didn't last long. Perhaps he would get a call – maybe in two weeks, maybe in two months – and then things would return to normal. Simon didn't know how long he could survive without Damien in his life – without those important connections and his money, he had nothing.

When the heat is off, Damien will call me. We'll be friends again ...

Simon rubbed his eyes; he was tired. He hadn't slept a wink since the big party, and barely a few hours since he'd hired Warwick and everything had gone wrong. It had been such a stressful time. So stressful. He walked up the staircase and drifted into his kitchen. He looked through the pantry. *Kahlua.* He cracked the bottle open and had a drink, straight up. It would take the edge off. He desperately needed it.

I need to sleep now.

He took another drink, this time bigger. A rush of alcohol went to his brain. He desperately needed to relax.

What?

There was a noise from the other room. A thump, and the tinkle of crystal. Puzzled, Simon put down the Kahlua and walked out of the kitchen.

He didn't see it coming.

★ ★ ★

Luther Hand was quick and quiet.

He had looped the rope around the crystal chandelier, and now in a flash he slipped the noose around the neck of Simon Aston and pulled the knot tight.

'What?' Simon choked in bewilderment just before he was wrenched straight off his feet by Luther's mighty strength.

Simon was pulled violently forwards, and as the rope went slack for a moment, he fell to his knees at the top of the stairs, spluttering and gasping for air. Luther moved forwards and looped the rope around the banister for better leverage. The next pull dragged Simon off the edge of the carpet and out over the two-storey staircase. He struggled in the air, thrashing this way and that, his hands grasping feebly at his neck to loosen the noose. Luther tied the rope off on the banister railing at just the right length, and waited.

Thump.

Thump.

Simon's legs kicked out at the walls, desperately searching for a foothold.

He didn't struggle for long.

Soon, his head slumped forwards, his tongue protruding.

This hit gave Luther Hand a certain bittersweet satisfaction. He had killed a large number of people in his career, many of whom he had no opinion about whatsoever, and some of whom he had even liked. But this man was a parasite. An irritation. Luther had been very pleased to get the call from his American-accented client to say that Simon Aston was now on the list. He'd been hoping that would happen.

Luther cocked his head to one side and watched Simon swing from the rope on the chandelier.

Good.

Luther liked him much better dead.

The witnesses were taken care of now. Simon Aston would not be telling any more tales about the Cavanagh son now that he hung from his noose, a perfect guilty suicide. The video was in police hands but nothing would be done about it. It would not be seen by any court. Simon Aston would get the blame. Dead men don't talk.

Makedde Vanderwall was no longer on the list. She was considered too well connected to the police, and too high-profile a target to do anything about. For the moment, anyway. The Sunday papers had been covered in photos of her spectacularly fleeing the Cavanagh house, running down the driveway in her gown, barefoot. Simon Aston – the out-of-control con man who had duped the innocent Cavanaghs, and had now ended his own life, suffocated by guilt – had threatened her at the party with an illegally purchased gun.

The loose ends were neatly tied up.

The assignment is complete.

EPILOGUE

'COME ON, ANDY, this is a joke!'

'Mak . . .'

'Why is Damien Cavanagh not under arrest? Why has he been allowed to leave the country? There is video evidence of him standing over that dead girl, and her hairs were found in that bedroom in their house. I saw it with my own eyes! Anyone else in that position would be arrested by now.'

'Mak, calm down,' Andy said, his voice sounding distant on the phone. 'Sometimes these things aren't so simple. It takes time,' he said.

It's not right. It's just not right.

Simon Aston looked responsible for killing the Dumpster Girl at the Cavanagh house, possibly by accident, and later hiring a hit man to kill Meaghan Wallace for having witnessed it. Simon was being blamed for everything, and now that he had committed suicide, no one would hear his side of the story.

Amy had been so certain that Damien had been involved and now, sadly, she had turned up dead herself. Another suicide. She had been found with an overdose of drugs in her system, lying on her kitchen floor, decomposing; a puppy sat whimpering next to her, evidently a gift from a lover. And Simon had got drunk and hanged himself from a chandelier.

Now no one was alive to point the finger at the Cavanaghs. It was all very convenient. And the higher powers in the police force certainly did not seem keen to pursue any potential link between Damien Cavanagh, the overdose of the Thai girl, and the Meaghan Wallace hit. The hairs found at the Cavanagh house had perfectly matched those of the Dumpster Girl. How was that not enough to warrant further inquiry?

Through their very highly paid lawyer, the Cavanagh family had expressed 'great concern and regret that anything untoward might have taken place in their home' without their knowledge. The late Simon Aston had been a friend, but not a close friend. Certainly no one had known the extent of his activities until it was too late. The Cavanagh son, Damien, did not know of his friend's illegal activities, their lawyer claimed. Questioning anyone who may have been present at the party that night would no doubt be a long process, and probably a fruitless one. The case was dead in the water.

It's not right.

It was little wonder that Mak's client, Robert Groobelaar, had been so paranoid about his confidentiality. If the Cavanaghs found out he had started an investigation of his own, who knows what they might have done to him or his business to shut him down?

Makedde shook her head with disgust and frustration.

The one upside was that young Tobias Murphy had been cleared of the murder, thanks to Simon Aston's apparent confession to Detective Hunt that he had hired a thug named Warwick O'Connor to do the hit. O'Connor had not yet been tracked down. Tobias had been in the wrong place at the wrong time, coming to his cousin for money on that Thursday night, as he did every fortnight. Though he had been through a terrible loss and no one could replace his sympathetic cousin, his being arrested had quite possibly saved his life. He was now in a rehabilitation program, finally getting the help he needed, and just as importantly, he was back in communication with his biological father, Kevin, and was going to live with him and his new family.

'Just think of what could have happened,' Mak said, watching the quiet street outside the terrace, the phone cradled between her ear and shoulder. 'That poor kid was going to go to jail for a murder he didn't commit.'

Clearly, for reasons she could not come to terms with, Sergeant Hunt and the police were not going at Damien Cavanagh with both barrels.

They'd never done more than pussyfoot around.

'Don't be so quick to blame the police, Mak,' Andy told her, defending his colleagues from afar. 'It's not always so simple, you know. No one has been able to prove that it's Damien in that video.'

Mak shook her head. *Bullshit*.

'Are you sure you don't want me to fly back? Just for a few days?' he asked.

'No, I insist. I have plenty here to keep me busy. In fact, I've never been so busy in my life.'

Robert Groobelaar had been more than satisfied with the amount of information she had uncovered; in particular, that Meaghan Wallace had not been having an affair with Simon Aston. That seemed to have put his mind at ease. Another happy customer. And there was something else: several new cases had come in for her since the nasty article about her had been in the paper. The phone was practically ringing off the hook for her services.

Oh, the irony.

Mak was sure that the Cavanaghs, or whoever had planted that article, had done so to discredit her investigation work and maybe lose her the case. Few could have anticipated it having the opposite effect. Apparently her particular brand of infamy and experience could be an asset in the profession.

Mak sat up when she saw Bogey's gleaming blue convertible pull up outside the house. The top was down. She watched Loulou with her exploding hairdo bound out of the passenger seat and run up towards the house. Bogey slowly opened the driver's side door and stood up. He wore slim black jeans and a faded blue T-shirt. She watched him with interest, her heart speeding up a touch.

'It looks like I may be back in four months or so,' Andy said.

'So they have extended your stay? That's good, isn't it?' Mak suspected that now he was at Quantico, Andy was seeing new opportunities for his career. He would probably be there for much longer than he first thought. Perhaps he was trying to break it to her gently.

'Yes,' Andy admitted. 'Hopefully not for too long . . .'

'No, no, it's good,' Mak insisted. 'I'm proud of you, Andy. You need to do this. It will be great for your career.'

'You're not mad at me because of what I said before?' Andy said.

'That conversation seems like another lifetime. Don't worry, I'm not mad at you, Andy. What will be will be.'

There was a long pause.

It had not yet been a fortnight since his departure, but Mak realised that it felt like much longer. 'I'll call you later,' she said. 'Loulou and Bogey are at the door. Don't worry about me, Andy. Just take care of yourself, okay? I'm proud of you.'

Whatever happened, she *was* proud of him. And maybe of herself, too. Mak wasn't sure where things would lead, but for the moment at least, she would happily take the ride and find out. Things had a way of working themselves out.

She hung up the phone and made her way to the door. When she opened it, she was smothered by Loulou's hugs.

'We've got Gatorade, cold presses, chicken soup, and enough DVDs for a movie marathon! Karen said she'll stop by after her shift, too. We won't have to leave the house for days.'

Mak laughed. *So much for recovering in private.*

She was glad of it, though.

Humphrey Mortimer closed the trunk and walked up to the house, smiling gently and holding bags of groceries.

'Loulou, you are the best,' Mak told her, and held the door open for them both.

★ ★ ★

Cathy Davis emerged from her Redfern flat. She held her purse in one hand and an empty cloth shopping bag in the other, ready to run her errands for the day. A slew of carefully clipped grocery coupons bulged from the hip pocket of her long apricot cardigan, the elbows of which she had recently mended with wool a touch too orange to match the rest. She carefully locked her door, shut the torn flyscreen and made her way across the small porch.

I need milk, a packet of gravy, three eggs, one potato, one carrot and one onion, she thought, counting up the items she planned to buy with her coupons and coins to sustain her for another few days.

She stopped.

There was a package on her doorstep.

How odd.

She could not remember the last time anyone had sent her a package of any kind. All she ever received were bills and the humble government cheques that kept her going. Slowly, she stooped to pick up the parcel, thinking it was surely for one of her neighbours. But it was not. A card taped to the top said, TO: CATHY DAVIS.

Cathy carried it to the bench on her porch and took a seat, moving aside some filthy newspapers that had floated down and lodged in the corners of the wooden boards.

With some effort, she slid a fingernail through the tape that held the box closed. She pulled the lid back and peered inside.

The box was filled with money.

Lots of it.

It looked like Monopoly money to Cathy Davis, who was fifty-nine and had not been employed since she was in her forties. Even back when the cheques that came were bigger than what the Government saw fit to pay her now, she had never seen money like this. Ever. The bills were wrapped together in elastic bands. She looked at them quizzically, not sure if they were real.

There must have been hundreds of dollars in the box – no, thousands.

Mrs Davis looked around, bewildered. Who would do such a thing?

★ ★ ★

Overhead, a 747 jetted through the clear sky and Cathy's son, Luther, settled into his trip to Mumbai. He hoped to return to Australia one day when the time was right. He had unfinished business in Sydney. Business with his mother – and with a woman named Makedde Vanderwall.

ACKNOWLEDGMENTS

EVERY NOVEL IS a new adventure and a fresh research challenge, and I have been blessed to be able to spend time as a 'forensic tourist' amongst specialists and wonderful real-life characters who have been generous with their time and assistance. A special thank you must go to former police officer, forensic polygraph examiner and great mate Steve Van Aperen of Australian Polygraph Services International; poisons expert, award-winning author and pharmacist Gail Bell; pharmacist John Fregon; psychopathy expert Dr Robert Hare; barristers at law Jason Pennell and Sarah Fregon; forensic psychologists Tim Watson-Munro and Carla Lechner; security specialist and private investigator Carl Donadio and Once Blue; Tony Zalewski of the Australian Institute of Public Safety; the Quantico FBI Academy; Sergeant Glenn 'Standing By' Hayward; Spy Quip World; Mistress Serenity; The Castle; the larger-than-life Maxine Fensom; Alison Arnot-Bradshaw; Abracadabra Films for *Trafficked*; and Ray and the ladies of Goldfingers

– with a special mention to Charlotte for my first private dance. Also, thank you to John Austin for the coffins; Drayson at O'Connell's for the name; my anonymous Mistress friends for the peek into your world; and to the two-wheeled fiends at the Victorian branch of Women's International Motorcycling Association and Netrider.

Thank you so much to my literary agent and fairy godmother Selwa Anthony for the faith and support. You made my childhood dream of being a published writer come true. I am grateful to the whole gang at HarperCollins Australia for believing in me when I was an unpublished gamble. Special thanks go to Shona Martyn, Linda Funnell, Mel Cain, Louisa Dear and Angelo Loukakis. Also thanks to National Geographic Channel; Craig Schneider of Pinnacle PR; the lovely Di Rolle; Martin Walsh at Chadwick; Saxtons; Bolinda Audio; and everyone at Sisters In Crime.

Lots of love to the Moss, Carlson, Bosch, Hooft, Fregon and Pennell clans, particularly my wonderful sister, Jackie; my father, Bob; lovely Lou; Auntie Ellie and Herman; Oma and our beloved Opa (we miss you); Heather; John; Nell (the life of the party, we miss you); Louise; Sarah; Jason and little Ella; and all my great friends, especially Captain Millimum; 'the gang': Irving, Hugh, Deb, Ava and Oscar; Gloria; Mark; Jac and Mitchell; brilliant artist and friend Nafisa Naomi; Russell; Mindy; John and Flynn;

fabulous Amelia; Desi and Robert; Linda (Miss J forever!); Bob and Margot Atkins; Xanthe; Laidley and the McLaughlin family; the Myman clan (when are you moving?); Misty; Pete and Anne; Tracey and Charles Millard and Charlie (thank you for the Brisbane *Covet* launch!).

Love to my buddies Bo, Gomez, Thing and the pond dwellers for the furry and scaly writer's companionship on countless dark nights burning the midnight oil.

Mum, I never forget you.